The King's Mother

Author applause for *The King's Mother*:

'A gripping and vivid powerhouse of a novel. It thrums with the passion and resolve of the women it brings to life'

JOANNE BURN, author of
The Hemlock Cure **and** *The Bone Hunters*

'Annie's much-anticipated second novel lives up to all expectations. It is propulsive, moving and vital . . . Brillant!'

KATE SAWYER, author of
The Stranding **and** *This Family*

'This is history at its most powerful: intimate and personal, visceral and devastating, brought to life through Garthwaite's sparkling prose'

JENNIFER SAINT, author of *Ariadne*

'Elegant and propulsive . . . I had to fight myself to put it down'

A. K. BLAKEMORE, author of
The Manningtree Witches **and** *Glutton*

'A momentous achievement! Utterly compelling storytelling in crisp prose that is by turns witty, lyrical, moving and brutal'

VICTORIA MACKENZIE, author of
For Thy Great Pain Have Mercy on My Little Pain

'*The King's Mother* is so assured in its vision, and Cecily rises triumphant from Garthwaite's world. It's utterly gripping, beautifully judged and deeply feminist'

ELIZABETH BUCHAN, author of
Two Women in Rome

The King's Mother

ANNIE GARTHWAITE

PENGUIN BOOKS

PENGUIN BOOKS

UK | USA | Canada | Ireland | Australia
India | New Zealand | South Africa

Penguin Books is part of the Penguin Random House group of companies
whose addresses can be found at global.penguinrandomhouse.com.

Penguin Random House UK,
One Embassy Gardens, 8 Viaduct Gardens, London SW11 7BW

penguin.co.uk

First published by Viking 2024
Published in Penguin Books 2025
001

Typeset by Six Red Marbles UK, Thetford, Norfolk
Printed and bound in Great Britain by Clays Ltd, Elcograf S.p.A.

The authorized representative in the EEA is Penguin Random House Ireland,
Morrison Chambers, 32 Nassau Street, Dublin D02 YH68

A CIP catalogue record for this book is available from the British Library

ISBN: 978-0-241-99868-7

Penguin Random House is committed to a sustainable future
for our business, our readers and our planet. This book is made from
Forest Stewardship Council® certified paper.

For Lisa, wise beyond words.
And for Mike, the man who gave up glaciers for love.

Cast of Characters

In 1461, as the novel opens, the main characters stand in relation to each other as follows:

House of York

Cecily Neville, the King's Mother, widow of Richard, Duke of York
Edward IV, her eldest son
George and Richard, her younger sons (later Dukes of Clarence and Gloucester respectively)
Anne, Duchess of Exeter, Cecily's oldest daughter and estranged wife of Henry Holland, Duke of Exeter
Elizabeth, Duchess of Suffolk, Cecily's second daughter
Meg (Margaret), Cecily's youngest daughter (later Duchess of Burgundy)

House of Lancaster

Henry VI (mad Henry), former king of England
Marguerite of Anjou, his French-born queen
Edouard, their son (possibly Marguerite's illegitimate son)

House of Neville

Richard Neville, Earl of Warwick, Cecily's nephew
Anne Beauchamp, his wife

Isabel Neville, their elder daughter

Anne Neville, their younger daughter

John Neville, Warwick's brother (later Earl of Northumberland then Marquess of Montagu)

George Neville, Warwick's brother, Bishop of Exeter and Chancellor of England (later Archbishop of York)

Thomas Neville, Warwick's brother

House of Beaufort

Henry Beaufort, 3rd Duke of Somerset

Edmund Beaufort, his brother

John Beaufort, their brother

Margaret Beaufort, Henry and Edmund's cousin, widow of Edmund Tudor and mother of Henry Tudor, now married to Sir Henry Stafford, Cecily's nephew (later married to Thomas Stanley)

Henry Tudor, son of Margaret Beaufort and Edmund Tudor

House of Woodville

Jacquetta Woodville, Dowager Duchess of Bedford

Sir Richard Woodville, her husband (later Earl Rivers)

Elizabeth Woodville, their eldest daughter, widow of Sir John Grey (later Edward IV's queen)

Anthony Woodville, Elizabeth's oldest brother

Katherine Woodville, Elizabeth's sister

Lionel, Edward, Richard and John, Elizabeth's younger brothers

Thomas Grey, Elizabeth's elder son by Sir John Grey

Richard Grey, Elizabeth's younger son by Sir John Grey

Others

Anne, Dowager Duchess of Buckingham, Cecily's sister
Sir Henry Stafford, her son
Henry Stafford, Duke of Buckingham, her grandson (by a deceased elder son, Humphrey)
Katherine, Dowager Duchess of Norfolk, Cecily's sister
John Mowbray, Duke of Norfolk, her grandson
Thomas Neville, the Bastard of Fauconberg, Cecily's illegitimate nephew
Jasper Tudor, brother-in-law of Margaret Beaufort, half-brother to Henry VI
Eleanor Talbot, a Lancastrian widow
Robert Stillington, priest (later Bishop of Bath and Wells)

Readers who wish to study in greater detail the family relationships that fuel the dynastic allegiances and political rivalries described in this novel will find genealogies at the back of the book. These include an illustration of rival claims to the throne in the final years of the Wars of the Roses.

Prologue

Easter, 1461

A new dynasty is born in blood. Eighteen-year-old Edward Plantagenet cuts a swathe through his enemies to make England's crown his own. And his mother, matriarch of the House of York, takes for herself a new title, one no woman in England has ever borne.

Cecily, the King's Mother.

It acknowledges her body, which brought this young king forth, and the courage with which she cleared his path to the throne. It signals the guiding hand she will lay on his kingship: mother, confidant, counsellor and guide. It is hers by right and by earning. In the getting of it, she has lost a son and her husband, York's royal duke.

But, in the progress of Edward's tumultuous reign, there will be other women who, driven by ambition, necessity or dread, will seek the throne for other sons. They will be no less fierce nor resolute. They will have no less cause.

Cecily. Marguerite. Elizabeth. Margaret. King's Mother. There can be only one.

I.

Westminster

Tenebrae, vigil for the crucified Christ, and in the darkness before dawn a single candle is passed, hand to hand. Cecily is cold. She has not slept, nor broken her fast since the Passion began. But when the flame comes at last to her, she wraps a hand about it and arcs her face to its bright heat. She curls her fingers close, then closer still, till they begin to burn and her eyes to smart. She won't shrink from it. Instead, she lowers her lids, lets the light play upon them, and smiles, tight against the pain. This is God's promise, she tells herself. Edward, her son, still lives. So far from her, yet still her flesh feels the fire in him.

It's three weeks since he rode to war against Lancaster, a king proclaimed but not yet crowned. 'Let me earn it first,' he told the cheering crowd. 'The usurper Henry still lives. His bitch queen Marguerite and her bastard son. When I've put them down, then I'll take up my kingdom.' They cheered him all the more for that, just as Cecily said they would when she told him to say it.

She stood beside him, relishing the weight of his army at her back; the bladed ranks of archers, pikemen and foot, the lumbering artillery with its pent-up violence of powder and shot. His men called out for him as he mounted then quieted at their captains' barking, till there was only the impatient creak of harness, the chink and shear of steel and, high above her head, the snapping of royal pennants; the lions of England rampant, and his own devices bright and new; the sun in splendour, the white

3

gilded rose. She watched him stand in the saddle for one last look behind, a brisk nod to his captains, then a settling, a shift in his focus, a widening of the space between them before even a step was taken. She laid her hand on his horse's shoulder and felt the slide of muscle over bone. He reined in, and leaned down so only she would see his grin. 'Keep my kingdom, Captain Mother. Till I come back for it.' Then he grasped her hand and kissed it, his mouth against her fingers warm as a bed.

There's been precious little warmth since.

A terrible time for fighting, with the country still snow-swept and spring slow to come. Worse in the north where he's gone. Where father and brother went before him and now lie dead. Their severed heads have been staring out at winter from York's walls since the year turned. The bitch queen Marguerite put them there, Cecily knows. Now Edward has gone to fight her and the whole country is up. From every corner of England men are marching. Many for York, more for Lancaster. Somewhere, they'll meet. It's madness to believe he can win. But then, Cecily tells herself, he's Edward, isn't he? Doesn't the very sun rise for him?

The house is waking as they leave the chapel. Grey river-light ghosting narrow windows, servants stepping soft-shoed about their business, whispering in deference to the mournful season. In the great hall her men of business wait sharp-quilled for her orders and her nephew George Neville, England's Chancellor, is ready to shepherd councillors and city men and Europe's ambassadors, who hover daily at her door for news, knowing it will come first to her.

'Nothing?' she asks, as he steps to her side, but before he can shake his head, there's a commotion at the door and a messenger pushing through it, mud-splattered and sodden, his boots ringing. 'Lady,' he says, 'a great battle outside York. On Palm Sunday. Six days past.' He comes to his knee before her, raises his face, tired but shining. 'And your son, our king, its victor.' The paper in his hand bears her son's seal and, when she breaks it, there's his name at the foot of the page, in his own bold hand: Edward.

His words are brief and scrawling. 'I've kept my oath to you,' he writes. 'The heads of our enemies are piked on Micklegate Bar, in place of my father's and my brother's. Those precious relics I've taken down and decently buried.'

My husband's head, thinks Cecily, her grip tightening. My son's.

'Mother, I think every man in England was in the field. We'll be days counting the dead. I can't say for sure yet who's among them but take heart; those we love who fought with us are not.'

'Your brother Warwick lives,' she whispers to George Neville, pointing to the page where Edward has written . . .

'. . . for who could kill my cousin, that bold beloved bastard?'

She reads on. 'No surprise, but mad Henry didn't come to the fight. Marguerite kept him in her skirts at York Minster. If they spent the day praying, it was wasted, for God was with me at Towton. Now she's dragged Henry north again, to Scotland. So, we make haste after.

'As for me, bruised to buggery, but well enough. Chin up, Captain Mother. Didn't I tell you I would win?'

The relief is dizzying. She'd like to sit down, here, on the floor and weep for it. She feels a sob pushing against her throat, the air in her lungs thinned and painful, her pulse hammering in every vein. But there are men crowding her, maws gaping, hungry for news.

She slows her breath, schools her face to calmness, lays a hand on the messenger's shoulder and takes time to look about her, drawing every eye.

'Give this man a cup of wine, someone.' She looks down her arm to him, her smile a benediction. 'And feed him, will you? For no man was ever so welcome or brought us better news.'

She squeezes, lets go: a dismissal. 'Gentlemen.' Her voice carries the length of the hall. She takes a moment to smooth her sleeves. To raise her chin. 'The mad man you once called the sixth King Henry was a usurper, who ruled over you without divine right or God's blessing. All of England has suffered for it. You have suffered, and so have I. Extortion, rape, murder, the shedding of innocent blood. Every injustice has been commonplace and unpunished. It has damaged our trade, shamed our people, and made England weak in the world.

'Now God has sent us a new king. Edward. Of my body and his father's royal blood. A man of strong mind, true heart and right claim. And God has given him this victory.' She holds the letter, aloft. 'At Towton, in the north country, through God's grace, he has cast down your enemies. And by that same grace, he will remake England.'

All around her, cheering, men laughing and slapping each other's backs. She holds up her hands to quell the sound. 'I go now to thank God on my knees. I urge you to do likewise. Come to me this afternoon and let the work begin; the rebuilding of England and the crowning of her king.'

She turns and is walking away, skirts flying, her daughters scurrying after and George Neville hurrying to her side. 'That was . . . stirring,' he tells her.

'Good,' she says, sharp. 'Don't imagine it was unrehearsed.'

2.

June 1461

London

Summer coming in, and while Edward drains the dregs of war in the north, Cecily sees to business and sets the world to rights; his world, and hers. She signs every letter and edict in the new authority she has created for herself; not Cecily York's Duchess, but Cecily the King's Mother, a title no woman in England has assumed before.

'Did I not bring this great king forth from my body?' she demands when the men of the council raise their eyebrows at it. 'Did he not bid me keep his kingdom? Do he and I not speak with one voice?'

The ambassadors of Europe write their princes that Edward is now master of England, and that the people adore him, as if he were their god. 'But, if we want to do business there,' they write, 'we must do it with his mother.'

'Let me tell you how this new world works,' Cecily tells the lords of England. 'It works just as the old one did before mad Henry corrupted it. You depend upon the King, he upon you, all upon God. Keep the King's peace, uphold his justice, pay your dues and he'll leave you to it. Do otherwise and, well . . . I think you know, by now.'

Widows whose men died fighting for Lancaster petition for the restoration of their jointures, protection for their children. Those who are yet wives beg pardon for husbands and sons.

'Are they conformable to the house of York?' she asks them. 'Are you?'

She practises mercy where she can. She isn't vengeful.

Jacquetta is among those that come. She reminds Cecily that her golden Woodville husband served Cecily's own well in France.

'That was a long time ago,' says Cecily. 'More recently he has fought for Marguerite in England, who last winter put my husband's head on a pike and cut my son Edmund's throat.'

Jacquetta weeps a little at that. She has a practised use of tears. It tries Cecily's patience, but she's known Jacquetta since they were sixteen, and has observed that she has always had the sense to leave a ship that's sinking.

'For old friendship's sake, I will urge my son to mercy,' Cecily tells her. 'Advise your husband to look contrite when he comes before him.'

'And my son, Anthony?'

A shrug. 'He's my godson, after all.'

'And my Elizabeth, my firstborn? Her lord dead in the fight and her lands lost. Her two boys have nothing . . .'

'Jacquetta, do you never know when to stop?'

Edward isn't the first of her sons to come home. Isabella, her old friend and Burgundy's duchess, has kept faith and sheltered Cecily's youngest, George and Dickon, across the sea. She sent them there for sanctuary when her husband was killed and all seemed lost. The parting almost broke her. Half mad with grief and panic she pulled them from bed to dockside at dead of night and tumbled them from ice-rimed steps into a boat's belly. In the last instant Dickon's hand grasped for hers, but the oarsman's pull had already carried him beyond her reach. She'd had no time to kiss them, and now her mouth craves the taste of their skin.

They're back in England by early June. Much fêted by the look of things, tricked out in Flemish finery and with jewelled daggers at their belts. They're brought to Baynard's, Cecily's town house on the Thames, in the early evening and it's all she can do not to run the length of its great hall and pull them to her. But she checks herself, smiles and lets them come. They are well-schooled enough to make neat bows and to kiss her hand when she gives it. George has grown taller in the four months since she saw him last. Not quite twelve, he looks likely, almost, to equal Edward for height. There's the promise of breadth at his shoulder and his fair hair darkening to the copper of coin. Dickon, four years his junior, looks paler and his hand, while she speaks, travels to his breast where, she knows, a bull's blood ruby ring hangs on a cord beneath his shirt, gifted to him by his father on the day of their final parting. Her husband Richard always made a great favourite of this youngest boy, their last child. Perhaps he saw himself in him, for Dickon's dark hair falls across his brow just as his own did and the boy's testing fingers have all the gentle length of his. It should be a comfort, feels like a blow.

'You're welcome home, my young lords,' she tells them, letting her hand fall, just once and for a moment, on Dickon's head. 'Now. We rest here tonight. Then tomorrow to Sheen. Your brother Edward is coming, and we'll meet him there.'

Dickon almost smiles at that, eyes dark in a tired face. George nods and says, 'No doubt my brother will be glad to see me. For now he's king and Edmund dead, I'm his heir.'

She has struck even before she knows it; the slap of her hand against his cheek a shock to them both. He stares at her, petulant and angry, and the men who had been smiling at their reunion turn shamefaced away. She clasps her stinging fingers. She has schooled herself to hear the words 'Edmund' and 'dead' from other men's lips without weeping. But hearing his brother speak them, and of their advantage to him, opens a rich vein of grief and pain.

'Well,' she says, and her voice is cold, 'did you think that out for yourself, George? Or did someone have to explain it to you?'

There are tears standing on George's lashes, a red weal rising below his eye, and though his chin is raised in defiance, his lips tremble.

'You will remember, George, that you are first and foremost the King your brother's subject, and when he comes you will be honoured to swear your loyalty to him on your knees. You both will.'

Dickon has turned his face from her, but nods, and the nurse, Annette, who alone in all the world Cecily trusted to take her boys into exile, has laid a hand on the shoulder of each, which George shrugs off but Dickon bears.

Cecily sighs. She will make a peace. She has three living sons and thanks Heaven for them, daily. God knows, she's lost enough. 'George,' she says. 'Dickon. I'm glad to have you home. But I've business to tend to and it grows late. I'll come to you tonight, and we'll talk of all that's happened while you were in Burgundy.'

But by the time the last dispatches are gone, and her secretaries have sealed up their inkpots and bowed themselves from her company, the boys are long abed. So she questions Annette, instead, who is sewing by a fire when Cecily finds her, a shirt which, from the size of it, must be Dickon's.

'We were welcome enough once news came of Towton,' Annette tells her. 'Till then it was lean pickings and a hole in the corner miles from anywhere. Utrecht, I tell you, is a city I hope never to see again. It stinks of fish. Then suddenly their brother is king and they're royal princes and must go to the court and be shown to every man alive. And feasting every night, which made Dickon sick. And every man fawning on them. Not good for George, I can tell you, now so puffed up and made to think he's a marvel. Well, you've seen.'

'And Dickon?'

'He still weeps for his father.'

'Well,' says Cecily, folding her hands in her lap and looking into the flames, 'he's not alone in that.'

There have been nights when she has cried like a beaten dog for Richard. When she has curled cold on the floor because she couldn't bear a bed warmed by anything but his flesh.

Annette pauses mid-stitch. 'I'm sorry. I'm sure you . . .'

But Cecily holds up her hand, shakes her head. 'I will speak of anything but that.'

Annette sighs, turns the cloth in her hand, plies the needle again. 'Well, Isabella was kind. She visited and told them stories of when you were there with your lord husband. And reminded them they had a loving mother waiting for them at home.' She is bold enough to look Cecily in the eye as she says this.

'You think I should have gone with them. But I knew they'd be safe with you.'

'Did you?' says Annette, frowning.

'I had to stay. You know why.'

Annette smooths out a stitch. 'Well, yes,' grudging. 'For Edward. You were right about him at least. He is, I suppose, the saviour of us all.'

'Yes.'

'And yet Marguerite still lives. Her husband. And her son.'

'For a woman who abhors politics, Annette, you have a firm grasp of their salient points.'

Near thirty thousand dead at Towton. More in the rout that followed. They say the snow lay blooded twelve miles from there to York, and that men crossed rivers on bridges of bodies to flee the battlefield. More dead than could be buried in a month. More than in any battle ever known or written of, so that men, on hearing of it, even seasoned veterans who bear their limps and scars tight-lipped, turn pale and cross themselves. So many. Yet those she most needs dead are not among them: the mad King Henry, his bitch queen Marguerite who would have put her bastard on the throne. Cecily would have gone to Hell herself to throw its doors open for them. Instead, they've run clamouring to Scotland and found refuge beyond the borders of Edward's kingdom. And so Annette is right. England's new king isn't secure while the old one and his heir still live and breathe.

But really, who, on seeing Edward, could want any other? After three days of sullen cloud, he brings the sun with him to Sheen, riding in through the gatehouse bare-headed and in shirt sleeves, his horse lathered beneath him and William Hastings laughing at his side.

'We raced the last mile or so, Mother,' he shouts as he throws his reins to a groom and strides towards her.

'Ten miles by the look of that horse,' she shouts back at him, 'or did you gallop it all the way from York?'

Her whole body is a heartbeat and the time it takes him to cross the courtyard is an age, pushing hair from his face, shaking sweat from his fingertips.

'Well, Mother, I was so very keen to see you, I dare say I hurried.'

He's standing before her at last and, tall as she is, she must stretch her neck to see his white-toothed smile in a face branded by summer. For a moment she can't speak, only raise a hand and lay it against his breast, where his strong heart beats beneath the damp threads of his shirt. She catches herself and smiles up at him as he clasps her fingers and kisses them.

'Now,' he says. 'Let me greet my brothers.'

Waiting at her side, both boys drop to their knees, but Edward only laughs and pulls them up into bear hugs. 'George and Dickon, Will,' he tells William Hastings, who stands smiling behind him, 'the boldest boys in Christendom.' He pulls away at last, leaving a hand about George's shoulder. 'Duke of Clarence for this one,' he says over his shoulder. 'Lieutenant of Ireland perhaps, since he was born there. George, the dragon slayer.'

'Let him prove worthy of it,' says Cecily, before the boy can speak.

But now Edward's turned to Dickon and thrown him on to his shoulders, and the boy is laughing with delight and clasping his brother's hair to keep from falling as he's spun about the court-yard in leaps and turns. 'And what for you, young lord? What will we do for York's youngest?'

'We will put him down and be sensible for a moment,' says Cecily. 'He's not a child.'

And Edward lowers him to the ground, crouches before him, puts a hand on each cheek and says, 'No, indeed he's not,' and kisses his forehead before leaning to his ear. 'Do you wear it still?' she hears him whisper. 'Our father's ruby?' The boy nods, earnest. 'Good lad.' And he ruffles his hair before bracing his knees to stand. 'Well, Mother, let's inside, I'm famished.'

3.

Monday, 29 June 1461

Westminster

Now her son comes to the world's table, and is himself the feast laid upon it. Two days Edward has sat enthroned in Westminster Abbey. Yesterday, England's nobility came on their knees, to kiss his hand and swear allegiance. Today the common people are welcomed in to gawp. It pleases her to see it. If she had her way she'd drag in every man from the street, every labourer from the fields, shake them by the collar and say, 'Look at the king I've given you. This sun I have put in your sky.'

To make the message of him plain, she's had it painted out on gilded boards that line the abbey's aisles, so people must file past them as they wait. On the largest, at the entrance to the choir, the tangled lineages of York and Lancaster grow upward through a rose-briar, each Lancastrian head a cankered flower, each Yorkist bloom engorged and strong. At the head of the plant, a golden Edward sits cushioned on roses while, beneath him, mad Henry, dizzied, empty-handed and uncrowned, flails among thorns. It is the world as Cecily sees it and officers of the Crown are briefed and ready to explain its meaning to all: that Edward is king by right, by conquest, and by God's order. That he has put down the usurper and set their world to rights. That England will flourish under his hand; that their purses and bellies will be full.

For the nobles, yesterday, her message was simpler: the house of York is here to stay. Get used to it.

At last night's coronation feast, she watched them finding their feet in this world remade. Those who had fought with Edward laughed loud and drank deep. Those grateful to be pardoned for fighting against him ate frugally and kept their mouths shut, unless to praise the King or ask for salt. That is, until, as custom demands, the King's champion clattered his warhorse into Westminster Hall and offered to prove his sword against any who opposed Cecily's son. Then they cheered the loudest, knowing her eyes to be upon them.

All but one. That chit of a girl, Margaret Beaufort, didn't cheer. With eyes as sharp as her chin she watched horse and rider career about the hall as if their offer of violence concerned her not at all. She only laid her hand on her husband's wrist and then, noticing Cecily's gaze, raised a cup to her and drank.

There will always be reminders, she supposes, that her sister Anne's family fought for Lancaster. This Beaufort girl is married to Anne's son, Henry. But he's not her first husband. She was married before him to the mad King's half-brother, Edmund Tudor, and, while still a child herself, bore him a son. Who still lives. Well, Cecily sighs, that's one more thing I must deal with.

That's where she should be today, she thinks. Taking care of such business instead of indulging herself in the brightness of the abbey and the sight of her son.

But for now, surely, she's done enough. Let today be a feast that she savours. She's been so hungry for so long and yesterday, at Edward's crowning, had gorged on joy till she thought she would die of it. When he had turned from his anointing and raised his crowned head, and Archbishop Bourchier had called out to ask if England would have Edward as king, her whole body – viscera, bones and flesh – had cried out 'yes!', though her mouth could form not a single word, gulping instead on light-spangled air. And the roar that filled the abbey threatened to burst her heart, as every voice cried out for her son, and the bells rang and rang. Even now, the memory of it sets her head reeling. She shakes herself, comes back to the present. One can't live long in such moments, she thinks, so close to the sun, without burning.

When she looks up, she's surprised to see that the endless line has dwindled and the light at the windows grown dim. No more time to be idle. She stands as the last man, a clerk by the looks of him, some inky scrivener, comes before the throne. Edward looks down at him, then breaking all protocol gets to his feet, takes the man's hand and says, 'Thank you for your patience, friend,' claps him on the arm and laughs. 'And now I must to supper!'

Guards step forward to lead the man away, who nearly trips for looking wide-eyed over his shoulder at the young god who just touched him. Cecily can't help but smile. Edward's been doing this all day. He was meant to sit still and look magnificent. But, if he spotted a man he recognized – a soldier who wore his badge, a merchant he owes money to, a pretty girl on her father's arm – he'd come down smiling from his high seat to speak a word, shake a hand or clap a shoulder. To flirt. Cecily has nodded her head at it. It's a gift, she thinks, this power to touch hearts. They'll go home and say, 'Young Edward of York now, he's the king for us.'

He has handed off the crown to Archbishop Bourchier and stands, shaking the weight of it from his shoulders and limbs. 'Captain Mother.' He raises his chin as she approaches. 'Duty done, thank God. It's hard work sitting on your arse all day.'

'At least you've been sitting,' mutters George. Edward's brothers have stood behind him through the long hours, flanking his throne, left and right. A trial for one so young as Dickon, Cecily thinks, but no reason why George shouldn't be up to it.

'It's your honour to stand at your brother's side, George.'

'Let go, Mother, it's been a long day.' Edward beams at her and puts his hands on his brothers' shoulders. 'George and Richard, you dine with me tonight.'

'Richard?' says Cecily, the name a shock that tumbles her stomach.

Edward shrugs. 'It's time, isn't it? You gave him his father's name, let him have it.'

The boy's pale face looks up into hers, his eyes wide and

waiting. He must be dead on his feet, she thinks. There are dark smudges beneath his eyes and his skin is as white as vellum. She never knew her husband at this age. That Richard was twelve when first he came to her, but he looked a little like this when he was brought out of the snow into her father's hall; sleep-starved and hungry, a little knocked about by the world but still looking at it squarely enough. She wonders how much it will hurt her to speak her husband's name and have his son answer. But she concedes the right of it. So she stoops down to look into his face. 'Richard, then,' she says. And there's that smile, as wide and open as his father's, and just as rarely seen.

4.

Edward had wanted Cecily to dine with him tonight too and join the celebrations. But she told him no. Marguerite may be beyond her reach, but Margaret Beaufort she can deal with. Margaret Beaufort and her boy.

She's sent for her sister and told her to bring Margaret with her to Baynard's, but when Anne comes, she comes alone.

'Now, don't give me that look, Cecily. Margaret will be here soon enough.'

The air indoors is stale and the sky outside not fully dark, so Cecily, who has been breathing incense all day, leads her sister into the garden, where evening teases the scent from gillyflowers and water pours from a fountain to a rill. They sit within sound of it on a cushioned bench and Cecily takes a moment to smooth her sleeves. 'Now, what keeps young Margaret? I'd have thought myself worth her whistle.'

Anne holds up a palm. 'I asked her to delay. I wanted to speak to you first.'

'Are you afraid I might bite her?'

'For his opposition to your husband, you've every reason to hate John Beaufort's daughter.'

Cecily shrugs. 'He rode roughshod over everything my lord and I achieved in France and I've hated him heartily for it. But it was years ago and he's long dead. I never hate without cause and Margaret can't help her birth, I suppose.'

'Nor even knew her father.'

'No, indeed. But how well does she know her cousin Henry Beaufort, who is still so very much alive? He led an army against me in Ludlow and another that killed my husband at Wakefield.

Then gave his body to Marguerite and, I'm told, laughed when she had the head severed from it. He runs with her still and wrongs me by breathing.'

Anne looks away. 'She barely knows him.'

'And what of her son's uncle, Jasper Tudor? Who even now leads a resistance against us in Wales.'

'Cecily, you're asking if Margaret is amenable to York, and I tell you she is. She's of my house now, not Beaufort's or Tudor's. She follows my loyalties.'

'But your loyalties are so newly made, Anne.'

Cecily watches, as her sister's hands flutter in her lap, knuckled and swollen, while her face, cushioned in jowls, draws down into a frown. She's past fifty now and has aged badly since her husband died last summer; leading an army against Edward, falling in the first attack.

Cecily sighs and stills her sister's hands with her own. 'Tell me then. What does young Margaret want?'

'Can't you guess, Cecily? She wants her son.'

Well, of course she does. 'Little Henry Tudor. How old is he now? Three? Four?'

'Four, Cecily. And he's in Wales with his uncle Jasper, who your son has sent an army against and will pursue until he's dead.'

It's true. Edward has sent an army with orders to besiege Jasper Tudor in his castle of Pembroke; to raze every stone and break every timber to bring his base-born neck to the blade.

'What? Does she think we'll kill the boy?' Cecily's on her feet now, anger not so far away. 'Jasper Tudor is our clear enemy and I'll thank God for news of his death. But we don't kill children.'

Anne rises, placatory. 'No, Cecily, she doesn't think that. She only thinks her son is in danger and wants him out of it. She wants him with her.'

'Does she now? She was happy enough to leave him with Jasper when she married your Henry. He can't have been more than a year old then.'

'Jasper made it a condition of the marriage.'

'I can see that he would. Mad Henry's half-brother keeping this slip of Lancaster in his pocket.'

Anne looks away, as if at a loss till Cecily takes pity. 'Come,' she says, 'let's walk, I've been still too long.' It gives them something else to focus on; slow steps on a dusty path, the first stars lighting.

'What would your son think of his wife bringing another man's son home?'

Anne shrugs and says nothing, so Cecily presses.

'He's yet to get a boy of his own on her, after all.'

Anne's hands are clasped tight before her and her eyes are on her feet. 'It isn't likely that he will.'

'Oh?'

Anne sighs. 'Cecily, I think Margaret can't . . .' she falters.

Cecily stops, quirks an eyebrow. 'What?'

Anne inhales a breath, shakes her head and lets it go. 'She was twelve years old, Cecily, when Jasper's brother married her.'

'Mmm. And he not willing to wait.'

Anne tuts, then, under her breath, 'From altar to bed before the candles were snuffed. Barely thirteen when she had her son.'

'That's bad.'

'You've seen the size of her. It nearly . . .' They pace on. 'She's ruined . . .' she unclenches a hand to signal '. . . down there. And no surprise to anyone if she no longer cares for bed sport.'

'Few men would give her the choice.'

'Well,' Anne fidgets. 'My son isn't much of a man for women.'

Cecily's heard the rumours. 'What a pair they make.'

'They rub along together, well enough.'

'I'm sure. She brought a very good dower.'

'And the marriage bound us close to King Henry and his kin.'

Cecily raises an eyebrow.

'Don't pretend to be shocked,' her sister tells her. 'It mattered then.'

'Of course. A good marriage when you made it. She's not much use to you now though. I'm surprised you fight for her.'

Anne stops pacing at that and, when Cecily turns to face her, lifts her chin to look at her straight. 'I pity her, Cecily.'

Cecily concedes with a nod. 'Yes, it is pitiable. But do you think I should put her son into a household so lately conformed to York?'

It seems Anne has no answer, but they are disturbed, anyway, by sounds of arrival. They look back to the house to see Cecily's steward signalling the way towards them and there, dark against the light that spills from the doorway, stands the slight, stiff figure of Margaret Beaufort and the ruin beneath her skirts.

They've come inside to Cecily's chamber, where candles have been lit and windows left open to the cool night air. She has bidden Margaret to be comfortable and studies her now as she sits across the table with her hands folded in her lap, not drinking the wine that has been poured for her, but not quailing, either, under Cecily's stare. Which is admirable enough, she supposes.

She's surprised by just how young Margaret looks. She passed eighteen at May's end, but seems a girl still, skinny and flat-chested. She wears a dress of murrey velvet, the livery colour of York, which Cecily thinks is a little obvious. But at least she's made the effort. There's nothing to hate here. Just a young woman worried for her son, and brave enough to face her for him.

'Do you play chess, Margaret?'

The girl looks surprised but recovers quickly. 'Yes. Yes, I do. Though I've been told you're formidable.'

Cecily laughs, a little. 'Oh, well . . .'

There's a board beside them and Cecily signals Margaret to draw it forward and set up her side. There's no sound for a time but the gentle click of the pieces as they're set down. Anne has tutted and gone with her wine to sit by the window, resigned to a long wait.

The game is even, for a time; Margaret's moves practised and considered, bold but well defended. As the game goes on they talk, or rather, Cecily questions. About Margaret's present life, her home in the Lincolnshire Fens, the old castle at Bourne that had been her father's. It seems she's lived there content enough in the three years of her new marriage.

'And I suppose you must know Lincoln well?' Cecily leans back from the board, taking a pawn that Margaret risked too far.

'Yes.'

'My mother is buried in its cathedral.'

'I know. I've lit candles for her there.'

Cecily is surprised, a little, and Margaret looks up at her from the board. 'She was a Beaufort before her marriage, just as I am. We are cousins, of a kind, you and I.'

'You would claim kinship with me?'

Margaret cocks her head, moves a knight forward, sets it softly down and says more softly still, 'More than with my son's father.'

My, thinks Cecily, you play a bold game. She begins to like her. 'Ah.' She slides a pawn of her own. 'I think you mean to speak to me of your son.'

'I would like him with me.'

'So my sister says. Yet few women are lucky enough to keep their sons with them. My own Edward left my household at seven years.' Margaret lowers her head. 'And you want his inheritance secured, I suppose. The earldom of Richmond?'

'He has committed no crime that it should be forfeit.'

'He's been on the losing side.'

Margaret shrugs. 'Yet I've seen the King be merciful. To my good mother here,' she nods to Anne. 'And to others of his kin.'

'You claim much for kinship. Your husband's been pardoned and you've been granted your own lands, is that not generosity enough?'

It's time to bring this game to an end, Cecily decides. She is exposed in the board's centre. So she leans forward and, with deft fingers, switches king and rook.

Now it's Margaret's turn to look surprised. Her hand hovers over a board suddenly re-shaped. She had thought herself winning and is unsure what Cecily has done.

'It's a new move,' Cecily tells her. 'Do you not know it? If no other pieces lie between, it is allowed to move both rook and king. Church and state.' She smiles at her own joke. 'It's made my king, as you can see, unassailable.' She lays a possessive finger on the crowned piece.

Margaret swallows, nods. 'Yes. I see. But I didn't expect . . .'

'I imagine not. Play on.'

From there Margaret's game unravels. She stumbles, is checked, then mated. Cecily watches her survey the wreckage of the board.

'It's true. You are formidable.' Margaret manages a wry smile as she looks up.

'Yet you play well, Margaret. You must only practise the new rules until they come naturally to you. Now, let's clear the board and I'll tell you what I'll do for your son.'

And, as Margaret slowly collects the pieces and returns them, one by one, to their box, Cecily does.

'My son's men will break the siege at Pembroke. Jasper's fate is inescapable. But your son's safety, I will assure.'

Leaning back in her chair, she watches Margaret's hand become still and hover as her face lifts with hope.

'But he won't be returned to you.'

The young woman's head dips again as her fingers curl on air.

Cecily leans forward, her elbows on the arms of her chair and her fingers joined at their tips. 'I'll do better for him than that, Margaret. Listen. I'll give his wardship to a man whose loyalty is absolute and unshakeable. Your son's mind is young and malleable, it will be shaped by York. He will forget Tudor and Beaufort and mad King Henry, and all the old allegiances you've lived by. It will be the saving of him.' She sits back, shakes out a sleeve. 'He will learn to love my house and serve it. And when that's done, and he's of age, my son may very well grant him his earldom. And call him king's man.'

The pieces are boxed now, and Margaret's hands lie empty in her lap. There is a small sound. A sob? Or just a sigh?

'Who?' Margaret asks.

'William Herbert.'

Margaret's face pales. 'Isn't he the man who leads an army now against Jasper Tudor?'

'Yes. At my son's bidding. But he's a fair man, Margaret. An old friend. And his wife is good-hearted. They've a bevy of children young Henry will grow among. And, this way, your boy need not leave Wales.'

'Then am I never to see him?'

'Oh, I don't know. Wales isn't so very far. Learn the new rules, Margaret. Live by them. Then there'll be no reason to disallow the occasional visit; a summer foray, a convivial Christmas.'

Margaret nods. 'Yes.'

'Now.' Cecily moves to stand. 'It's time for my sister to take you home.'

She walks with them to the chamber door, lifts her hand for Margaret's kiss. She was right, the lashes of those fine dark eyes are wet. There's no need to say more, but, for kindness sake, 'I've given less than you hoped for, Margaret. But more, surely, than you could expect. I know what it is to have sons. You have only this one, and I can see that he is dear. One day, I hope you'll thank me. I've given him a world in which he can flourish.'

Margaret's courtesy is deep and Cecily's hand, when she raises her, gentle.

5.

Eltham

By Christmas, the game has played out much as Cecily said it would. Well, almost. Jasper Tudor is a slippery bastard and, when William Herbert took Pembroke Castle and pushed his way through every bolted door, he found him gone, leaving little Henry Tudor behind with no better defence than his nurse's skirts. Cecily hears Jasper's made his way to Marguerite in Scotland. Well, he'll be on short rations there.

If Margaret Beaufort mourns the rout of Lancastrian resistance from Wales, she shows no sign of it. There she sits, down the table, her hand backing her son's tow-coloured head, wiping goose grease from his face with a napkin while her mother-in-law fusses and her husband leans back to allow a salver of plump baked plovers to be set before him.

Cecily finds she can smile at the sight. She's had the little Tudor brought here to Eltham and reunited with his mother for the season; a Christmas gift all unexpected that brought Margaret to her knees this morning, pressing her forehead against Cecily's clasped hands and kissing her fingers in thanks.

'This is a very great kindness,' Cecily's sister Anne had said, as Margaret sought to wrap the boy, who clearly didn't recognize or remember her, in her arms.

'I know,' Cecily whispered as the boy began to whimper and they stepped away from the scene. 'Sometimes I surprise myself.'

Her own younger sons sit at table with her now, dipping greedily into shared plates. If she only leaned a little forward, she could push her fingers among George's copper curls or smooth the cowlick on Richard's brow. She'll do no such thing. George, at least, wouldn't thank her for it. Her married daughters, Elizabeth and Anne, are at court, but her youngest, her own Margaret, her faithful Meg, sits by her now, drawing every eye. Her fifteen-year-old beauty, no paltry thing, is much enhanced by kinship to a king; the length of her neck made more graceful by the collar of diamond-dewed roses that encircles it. I must think of her marriage, Cecily reminds herself. She leans to whisper in the girl's ear, 'There's not a man in all England worthy of your beauty, Meg. We'll find a prince of Europe for you.'

The eyes Meg turns on her are as softly grey as a rabbit's back and the light in them bright as new-minted silver. 'A year ago, you'd have struggled to find a pot boy willing to marry me for my beauty, Mother. The princes of Europe will take me for their advantage, not my looks.'

'Be that as it may, we will make you a very great lady.'

'Well enough. But don't hurry on my account. Besides, shouldn't you get Edward married first?' And here at last her lips turn up a little. 'If Edward gets himself an heir George might be a little less insufferable.' George's affronted expression widens her smile. 'And it might do Edward good to have one woman's bed that it's actually his duty to go to. I think the biggest decision he faces each day is who will have the pleasure of him at the end of it.'

Cecily raps her knife on the table. 'Do you think this talk becoming?' She nods her head towards young Richard, who, as ever, is listening attentively as he chews. 'Edward is a young man, and a king. It should be no surprise that he takes willing women to his bed.'

No surprise at all. But sure, he goes to it with an appetite. He and Will Hastings, who is his chamberlain now and closer than flesh to bone, share them as they would a trencher of meat or a flagon of wine. They lick their lips, pick their teeth and compare notes the morning after. Well, no matter. As long as he's not a fool for them, men will admire him for it.

The latest, though, has proved more than a single night's distraction: Elizabeth Lucy, widow of some fool boy who got himself killed for Lancaster at Towton. She petitioned Edward when he was on progress this summer, pleading for her jointure. She must have done so winsomely. She got all she asked for, along with a fine set of grass stains on her skirts. She walks the corridors of Windsor now, where Edward keeps his Christmas court, cradling a curved belly in her hand and smiling like a cat. Not for much longer though. Edward's already asked Cecily to find a husband for her. That's easy enough. There's no shortage of men ready to curry favour by raising the King's by-blow as their own. But it isn't work Cecily likes.

'I'll not be your pander, Edward,' she told him.

'God's blood, Mother, I don't need you to find women for me. I trip over them in corridors.'

'Just get rid of them when you're done?'

He'd grinned at that, and she'd slapped his shoulder before grinning with him.

So, Edward's is a young man's court and, for these days of Christ's nativity at least, she chooses to be away from it. While he keeps a riotous season at Windsor, she sits in quiet state at Eltham. The food is as good and the music better, but the feasting is punctuated by the offices of prayer. In this way she and Edward present to the world the twin faces of York: its potency and its piety, its dominion on earth and favour in Heaven. They've divided their guest list accordingly. If she's drawn a quieter crowd it doesn't matter. It's enough that she can hawk in the mornings and, in the evenings, watch her daughters dance. She should welcome this time for reflection, she supposes. A pause to catch her breath.

Once crowned in June she'd sent Edward off to show himself to the country. While his cousin Warwick quelled rebels in the north and William Herbert ousted Tudor from Wales, Edward rode the south and west of England, dispensing justice, accepting largesse. And all the while, she kept the wheels of government turning in London, a hub for news of progress on every front. In October, he returned to her at Greenwich. A month of preparation, then together to Westminster for his first Parliament, where the changes of the year were at last enshrined in law: the defeat of Lancaster, the supremacy of York, set down with ink on vellum. She was with him every hour and everywhere, except when the door closed on the Painted Chamber, where only men can go. But no word said there was beyond her consideration, no decision taken to which she didn't agree.

So, time to rest now. To reflect. To give thanks, her confessor says. But in truth, she'll be glad when the twelve days are over and the wheels of business turn again. Most especially, she wishes the sixth day done.

On that day she waits for Edward on the steps of St Paul's with only Archbishop Bourchier for company. He has the good sense not to speak and, in that blessing, she can imagine herself alone. Her children and family are already inside, pooled in the light of a thousand candles, a bright lure to draw the dead.

'The whole world would come to honour them, you know,' Edward had told her when they made their plans for this year's mind, this anniversary of death.

'So they should,' she answered. 'But I'll have no one there who doesn't share blood with us – and none who fought against us even if they do, however penitent or reconciled.'

It's a year since her husband's blood stained the snow at Wakefield; since her son Edmund's blue-veined throat burst open on a blade. If the veil between worlds is to be thinned today, if God will grant their souls to come close, she wants no presence here that will trouble them. No heart that will not welcome them with love.

It's snowing again now; goose-down softness from a dull steel sky. Though shielded by a canopy that bears the arms of York and England quartered, errant flakes still settle on the dark hem of her gown and a cold wind from the river lifts the veil that frames her face. She narrows her eyes and turns into it. She has already taken off her gloves. She welcomes the cold, fancies it will bring her closer to them. Graves, too, are bitter. Her fingers, clasped before her, are thin and bloodless, as if already dead. She examines them, notes the looseness of her rings, the thickening of her knuckles, and wonders if the flesh has fallen yet from her husband's bones, if the shield wall of Edmund's ribs has collapsed about his heart. She rubs the smooth tips of her fingers against her thumb, then raises them to the jewel at her breast, a golden lily set with pearls that once belonged to the King of France. Her husband had pinned it to her breast the night of his first victory against the French at Pontoise; the night, she is sure, that Edward was conceived. Dear God, she remembers, as, beneath her cloak, she wraps thin arms about a lean frame, she was warm enough then.

At last, the snow-muffled clop of many hooves tells her he is come, and her pulse, which has been slow and stumbling, picks up. Edward leaves his guard at the foot of the steps and climbs to her alone. He won't let her bow to him, but takes her hands in both of his and kisses them, before wrapping her arm within his own and leading her into the dim heart of the cathedral and on, towards the pale upturned faces in their pool of golden light.

There is no thinning of the veil. Through the long service she waits and watches and quiets her heart and yet feels nothing but the coldness of the cathedral's stone floor rising from knee to thigh. Sees nothing but the frost of her breath disappearing like unanswered prayer. At the close of the solemn mass, she looks about her and sees Edward's face, tight-lipped, awash with tears. Richard's small fingers are clasped in his broad fist and a weight of hand rests on George's shoulder. Her daughter Elizabeth sobs quietly against her husband's velvet chest, while her eldest, Anne, rubs her back in slow circles. Meg's fingers rest atop her own. She can feel a shiver through them.

At last, the archbishop gives his final blessing and relinquishes her dead to the abode of spirits; to life without end, to riches that will not pass away and cannot be stolen from them. Where they need not fight, but only rest. 'Amen,' he says. And she finds she cannot answer. What will her husband do there, she wonders? He who fought all his life and died so bloodily, with so much left undone?

She has come to Baynard's tonight. She's tired and worn and will return to Eltham in the morning. She farewelled Edward at the cathedral door and watched him vanish into the company of his guard. They will carry him to Westminster and, tomorrow, to the river and against its swollen flow to Windsor. She has told her children she wants no company and they've taken themselves away. They'll be in bed by now, she supposes. Safe enough. And she should be away to her own, but that it's empty, and Richard, her husband, sleeping far away and quiet in his grave. The fire has burned low and the candles are on their ends. But there's a noise on the stair and a page enters and says, 'Lady,' then the door is pushed wider, and there is Edward. She wonders if he's been drinking, but he stands sober enough.

'I'm no good for other company tonight,' he says. So she draws him to the fire, which the page hurries to add wood to, puts wine in his hand and pours for herself.

'You've eaten?'

He shrugs. 'All I want.'

She hasn't eaten at all, but her body doesn't burn up food as his does.

'I miss Edmund,' he says.

'Well. Of course.' She's not seen him maudlin before. It's a new thing.

'And you must miss my father?'

I'm only half myself without him, she wants to say. As lonely as an anchorite though standing in a crowd. But if she speaks her grief she will drown in it, so she only nods and allows herself a single word, 'Yes.'

He leans across the fire to take her hand, his eyes earnest. 'I'll bring them home, Mother. I swear it. I'll bring them back to Fotheringhay and bury them with honour.'

The church at Fotheringhay is the mausoleum of Cecily's house. There lie all her children lost in the cradle: Henry and John, William and Thomas, last-born Ursula, given to God. Long ago she promised Richard she and he would take their own long sleep there, side by side for all eternity. The thought of it has been, through all their struggles while he lived, her deepest comfort, her last redoubt. Now he and Edmund lie in a hasty grave in Pontefract. A place she's never been to and will never go.

She imagines the keeping of Edward's promise. The long cortège and the honour guard riding beside it, swords unsheathed and heads bare; the masses sung at every stop or crossroad, the overnight vigils in abbeys and cathedrals. She imagines the crowds that will line the roads for a glimpse of the hearse, word of it passing from mouth to mouth, like coppers from market-day purses, a currency of gossip that will remind all who hear it of York's bitterest defeat, its darkest day. She imagines it all and knows it can't happen.

She squeezes Edward's warm and living hand, then lets it go, reaches for the jug and pours for him again. 'It's the sixth night of Christmas, Edward. Tonight we honour God's labour of creation.' She brings her cup to his, a gentle chink. 'It will take you and I a little longer, I think, to shape the world to our purpose.'

'What's more to do? I'm king.'

She sits back in her chair, with a sigh. 'Still young enough to be fooled by our own rhetoric, Edward?' she chides. 'It's there to dazzle others, not you. Our work is far from done. Marguerite and her bastard still live. She'll come against us again. Likely soon. She won't give up. And she'll train her pup to fight. We must destroy her, and him, utterly. And that fool husband of hers.' She folds her hands, one within the other. 'Only then can we bring your father and your brother home.'

He wipes a hand across his eyes and cannot look at her. She leans to him again, lifts her fingers to his blazing hair, lays them against his cheek. 'But until that day men must see only York victorious. We must show them York living, Edward. Not remind them of York dead.'

6.

April to October 1462

London

There's a new king in France and Marguerite, Cecily learns, is gone to meet him, slipping out of Scotland in the first calm weather, in the last hungry days of Lent.

'She looks for resurrection,' Cecily writes to Edward, who rides after stag at Windsor and thinks himself done with war for now.

'Let her try,' he writes back. 'Even King Louis can't raise Lancaster's hopes from the dead.'

But it's hard to know yet what Louis can do. They know him for a hard-faced bastard, that's all, who made war against his father, lost, then kept out of France for sixteen years. The old King begged for his son when dying, mumbling his name past the infection that devoured his jaw. Louis wouldn't come. Just took himself to Reims where French kings are made, and sat himself down to wait. When the news came, he was off to the cathedral and a crown on his head before the messenger had brushed the sweat from his horse's flanks. He'll want to prove himself now, Cecily guesses. What better way for a new French king to court his people's love than to muscle up against old enemy England? And what better excuse for it than his French kinswoman's honour? They're cousins, Louis and Marguerite, though they've seen nothing of each other in the seventeen years since Marguerite was dispatched from France like a parcel, a fifteen-year-old bride for England's woeful king. He'll make something of it, Cecily imagines, though for policy's sake, not family feeling.

She's right. Come spring, the fighting season, there's talk of a French army, Henry bloody Beaufort at its head, coming to put Marguerite's mad husband back on his throne. Edward takes to the road again, keeps Easter in Lichfield, then on to Leicester at a clip. Best for a king to be in the centre of England when rumour of invasion runs like a hare; ready to turn on it wherever it breaks cover and take out its throat with a snap.

Edward isn't the only man on the move. His cousin Warwick rides the Scottish borders like a vengeance, raiding and harrying and giving Scottish Queen Marie no rest. Serves her right for harbouring royal fugitives.

'Warwick fights like a devil,' Edward writes. 'And gives more in my service than any man alive.'

'So he should,' Cecily replies. 'He's got a lot to fight for, thanks to you. Anyway, you've made him Lord of the North, which makes Scotland his business.' She has nothing against her nephew Warwick but knows him to be a canny man who serves his own best interests first.

She imagines Edward's shrug as he reads her words. His cousin has shared exile, hardship and battle at Edward's side. And grief, for he lost his own father when Edward lost his. He's been well rewarded for it; his dead father's titles added to his own, and every honour asked for granted by Edward with an open hand and a loving kiss. Now no one but Edward wields more power in England than Warwick, or does so with more swagger.

Well, whatever she thinks of it, it's working. Harassed and harried, and with Marguerite out of sight and mind, Queen Marie sues for peace and Warwick brokers a three-month truce. A breathing space.

'There,' says Edward. 'Didn't I tell you he can do anything?'

'Scotland's a distraction,' says Cecily. 'The real threat sits with Marguerite, and Louis.'

There, too, Warwick's in the frame. Remembering the days of exile when they pirated the Channel together, Edward has made

Warwick High Admiral, charged him with the fleet that patrols England's coast; men spidering ships' rigging, a thousand eyes straining for the first sight of French sails, blinking and tearing at the empty brightness of sunlight on calm water.

But as summer comes to a close and autumn blows in, there's nothing to report, except that the waters of the Channel grow restless again and still, no sails in sight. It becomes possible to imagine that Louis has lost interest.

'If they come now at all it will be to East Anglia,' writes Warwick. 'Or the southern coast. The shorter crossings.'

So Edward edges southward and by September is in London, and Cecily can hardly believe she's seeing him again with no blood spilled. And Edward, who has fought all his battles in winter, paces like a lion until Cecily says, 'Take yourself where you think it will come then,' and he heads off to East Anglia, to Fotheringhay, where he can hold court and gather men within striking distance of the coast. And, because she relishes being beside him, and because she wants to see for herself the lie of the land, she rides with him, through blustery days and good hawking weather.

If she allows herself to forget Marguerite and Louis for a moment, it feels almost like a holiday. Edward has gifted her a new horse: a forward grey mare that steps high and challenges the strength of her shoulders to hold it; strong, like the horses her husband used to choose for her when they were young and would race one another across the flat meadowland that banked the Nene, with the walls of Fotheringhay's castle rising before them.

She'll not stay there with Edward. If her husband can't come home to Fotheringhay, it would be beyond bearing to go there herself.

'Where then?' Edward asks.

'Stamford first,' she tells him.

He huffs. 'Cold comfort there, Mother.'

She's long been Stamford's lady, Yorkist heartland not ten miles from Fotheringhay. No wonder, then, that the town suffered badly when Marguerite brought her looting mob south. Almost two years ago now and the town's streets are still scarred by fire; its small castle, already shabby, now beyond repair.

'They'll be after you for reparation.'

She nods, slowly, thinking of the lives Stamford and a hundred towns like it have given to her cause over long years. 'Likely I'll give it.'

'Hm. And where will you lodge? Not the castle, I hope?'

She smiles, sly. 'Are you concerned for my welfare, Edward? Do you fancy yourself the man over me now?'

'I wouldn't dare. I'm only the King. You're the King's Mother.'

'Quite right. Don't worry, I'll do well enough.'

'Yes, but where, Mother?'

'I'm to stay with the nuns.' And at the look of consternation on his face, she looses her reins and lets her mare stretch its muscles into a thrumming canter.

It's restful sometimes, she has found, to pray only with women; with women whose duty isn't tied to hers and who have no interest in her affairs. She can set business aside a while, and let softer voices than her own carry her prayers to God. She's spent the day with her bailiff, suffering his tedious litany of excuses for tenants being laggard with their rents; relieving him with news that they are waived until next Lady's Day.

'But that's it, mind,' she tells him. 'No more.'

By the time she rides back along the slow-moving Welland, the sun is starting to dip and the wind off the river turning cold. Among its bluster and flying leaves, she hears the bell calling the sisters to vespers. She sighs, sorry to miss it.

When she arrives at the gate of the priory's guesthouse, she finds the youngest of the novices waiting for her, chapped hands fluttering, leading her inside and speaking over her shoulder to explain that, 'The prioress ordered I absent myself from prayers to wait for you, Lady. To tell you,' she turns the latch on Cecily's chamber door and pushes it open, 'you have a visitor.'

And there, all unexpected by a fresh-lit fire, stands her sister, Katherine.

It's been years since these two met. Not since Marguerite was brought to church after birthing that bastard son of hers. Eight years ago, is it? Nine? Before the world turned, anyway. Katherine has eighteen years on Cecily but looks older still. Well, thinks Cecily, I dare say grief has aged us all.

'I'm sorry for your son,' Cecily tells her when wine has been poured and wafers brought, and the hovering novice has built up the fire and left them. Katherine's boy John, who was Norfolk's duke, died last winter.

'I'm sorry, also, for yours,' Katherine says. 'For Edmund, I mean. And for your husband. I've not written but . . .'

It has rankled, the lack of any word.

'Are you? Sorry, I mean,' Cecily asks, searching Katherine's hooded eyes for a lie. 'We're such a divided family, after all.'

Katherine's third husband lost his life fighting for mad Henry against Edward. Against me, Cecily thinks.

'Do you assume, Cecily, that every woman holds her husband's loyalties as her own?'

'I suppose not,' Cecily concedes. 'Do you miss him?'

Katherine sniffs. 'Not much.'

Cecily barks a laugh.

'Might we bury our differences alongside him?' Katherine ventures.

Cecily sighs and, at last, looks fondly at her sister. 'I suppose that would be entirely reasonable.' She pulls herself from her chair, takes up the bell to call a servant. 'I assume you'll stay for supper?'

'What do you think? I'm here for the night. It's a long road from Framlingham. I'm too old for such a distance without a rest-up.'

Over supper then, Cecily finds the moment to ask. 'So, why have you taken the long road from Framlingham to see me?'

'Well, yes. Of course, you're wondering.' Katherine sets down her knife, wipes her crotched fingers on her napkin, and folds them before her. 'I'm here on women's business, so a place of women seems appropriate. Away from the court's wagging tongues.'

'Women's business?'

Now Katherine's eyes are intent on her face, as if she, now, were looking for a lie. 'I'm here on behalf of one you know well enough. Eleanor Talbot. Old Talbot's daughter.'

'Eleanor? Eleanor has sent you to me?'

Katherine's eyes, now, are steely. 'I didn't say that. I said I came on her behalf. Does it surprise you?'

'Well, yes . . .'

'You remember my grandson is married to her sister?'

'I keep careful record of all my family connections, Katherine. One never knows when they'll be useful. But what business has Eleanor Talbot with me?'

'It's your son's business with her that should concern you. She believes herself married to him.'

The idea is so preposterous, so ludicrous, that Cecily can't contain the gasp of laughter that explodes from her throat. 'Married? Dear God, Katherine, they've barely met!' But she remembers suddenly that, when last she saw Eleanor, the night of Edward's crowning, she'd been struck by the high sheen of her brow, the fine bones of her throat. She was lovely, and a widow, and Edward had danced with her, leading her in slow turns. But then, he'd danced with everyone.

She shakes her head. 'Impossible. He wouldn't be such a fool.'

'Well, certainly he's had her.'

'When?'

'At Norwich first, as he travelled back to London after Towton. He stayed with my grandson there a few days,' she huffs. 'Making merry.'

Yes, Cecily thinks. Young men together after the heat of battle. They would be merry.

'And then at the crowning.'

Dear God.

'And she was at Westminster last Christmas. When you were at Eltham. She says that was when . . .'

'But he had Elizabeth Lucy on his arm then . . .'

'Not in his bed though, she was heavy with his child. Anyway, Eleanor's heard nothing from him since then, though he wrote frequently enough before. And she's in despair.'

'She can't think herself married? You can't think it?'

'I don't think this is the way a king goes about getting a wife.' Katherine picks up her napkin, folds it needlessly, for it was already neat. 'Well. I can see from your face you knew nothing of it.' She throws the linen to the table, washes her hands of it.

'And how long have you known?'

'Only this month. We've been talking to her of a new marriage, my grandson and I. We thought it was time. But she says she can't marry, because she believes herself bound to your Edward.'

'Because she was fool enough to open her legs for him?' Cecily is incredulous.

'Because promises were made,' Katherine corrects. 'And because there was a priest.'

7.

October 1462

Fotheringhay

She swore never to come here again. But even if her son is a fool, he is King of England and won't come like a dog to her whistle. So, she rides to Fotheringhay, after a night without sleep or even the sustenance of prayer. You can't come before God with murder in your heart, and this morning she's fit to kill anyone who so much as looks at her askance.

'Lord Hastings, it's always a pleasure to see you, but what I have to say to my son this morning isn't for your ears.'

Edward's servants have wasted no time bringing her to him, and here she stands, in the chamber that used to be her husband's. In those days it was neat and orderly. Today the bed's unmade and the litter of a half-eaten breakfast is still strewn across the table along with dice from last night's game. Edward's in his shirt sleeves and his face has yet to meet with either soap or blade. When Cecily juts her chin towards the door Will Hastings, no less dishevelled than his master, has at least the sense to bow his way out and ask no questions.

'And close the door behind you!' she barks without taking her eyes from her son's face.

'Good morning, Mother.' She watches him wipe a hand across his bristled chin, pull himself a little straighter in his chair and gaze about the table. 'There's small beer here,' he spots the jug and gestures towards it. 'I'd offer you a cup, but you look as if you might throw it in my face.' He has the nerve to grin.

'You'll be lucky if that's all I throw.'

She squares up the chair that Hastings has hurried from and sits herself opposite her son. She takes the time to straighten her sleeves, then folds her hands in her lap and pins him with her gaze. 'But let me start by throwing a name at you. A woman's name. Hmm? Eleanor. Eleanor Talbot.'

'Ah.' The grin still lingers, but he turns aside a little to hide it. 'Eleanor.' He shakes his head, puts his hands to his chair arms, makes to draw himself to standing.

Her voice, even to her own ears, is cold enough to freeze. 'Sit down. I'm talking to you.'

He lets himself fall back into the chair, huffs air from his lungs and spreads his hands. 'Eleanor . . .'

'Eleanor.'

He shrugs and at least has shame enough to blush, '. . . is an attractive woman . . .'

'She's the daughter of an earl, Edward. Of a man who served your father in France and who both he and I called friend, while he lived. But let's put that aside for the moment and talk about what you've made of her, shall we? Let me see . . .'

He's needled now. She feels his temper rising to meet her own. Before she can speak again he's on his feet, turning his back to her, shouldering towards the window. She's up and before him in a moment, her finger sharp against his chest. 'What have you made of her, Edward?'

He's taller by a measure and looks deliberately over her head, all scowls and shuffling belligerence. She hasn't seen him like this since he was eight years old. Her finger on his chest becomes a slap to his cheek, light, provoking, just enough to force his attention. Then his arms are up, stopping just short of pushing her away.

'Don't raise your hands to me, boy.'

Now he does look at her and his face is murderous. 'I'm your king, Mother. Not your boy.'

'Is that right? And what's Eleanor then? Your whore? Your leavings? Or is she your queen, perhaps?'

Now their faces are inches apart, his teeth bare, his morning breath stale in her nose.

'I fucked her. Why do you care?'

She looks aside, takes a deep breath of fresher air, turns to him again, and speaks. And while his voice has shivered with rage, her own is steady. 'I don't care who you fuck, Edward. I care about the promises you make. And how you belittle yourself by them. I care when you think with that,' a poke to his groin, 'instead of that,' a slap to his head. She points back to the table. 'Now. We will sit down. You will answer my questions. And I'll decide what's to be done.'

He throws himself wide-legged into the chair, folds his arms across his chest and stares at the table, at the floor, anywhere but at her. 'You abuse my good humour, Mother.'

'Oh, Edward,' she snarls. 'Grow up.'

She searches among the debris for two clean cups, pours ale, pushes one across the table to him then lowers herself to sit, her own cup set before her, wrinkling her nose with its sour smell.

'What I'd first like to know is, who was the priest?'

'Priest?' he spits, but his brow creases, as if genuinely puzzled. Idiot.

'The priest before whom you made marriage promises when Eleanor wouldn't otherwise go to your bed.'

His arms are still folded but now his knee is jigging. 'I wasn't serious.'

'I didn't ask if you were serious. I asked, who was the priest?'

'Why?'

'Because we're going to have to shut him up.'

'He's not much of a priest.' A shrug of the shoulder.

'Oh? I find I'm not completely sure what "not much of a priest" means. He's in holy orders, I assume?'

'Yes,' through clenched teeth.

'Then he's priest enough. In the eyes of God and the law you're married, Edward. So I'm asking again. Who was the priest?'

'Stillington.'

For the first time since last night she feels the tension in her shoulders ease. Robert Stillington of all men. Well, he's malleable enough. More lawyer than priest and lives for preferment. He was her husband's man, and her husband knew how to use him. Knew him as a man to do his bidding and not ask too many questions. Now he does the same for Edward. And is his whoring partner too, she must now suppose.

'All right,' she nods and folds her hands again in her lap. 'Now tell me how it happened.'

And out comes the sordid tale. It was at the Christmas court, twelfth night, when the Lord of Misrule held drunken sway.

'But in fact I'd already slept with her by then.'

'After your crowning. And even before that, in Norwich.'

'In Norwich, yes.' He raises his cup to her. 'You really do know everything.'

'You should always assume that.'

'Well. At Christmas, she was playing hard to get. She didn't like that I'd been with Elizabeth Lucy.'

'I imagine she wouldn't. And I imagine you didn't want to sleep with the Lucy girl while her belly was full, so . . .'

He shrugs. 'So she was all tears and tantrums. Said it was a sin and to do it again would compound that sin and . . .'

'And I suppose she said you could save her from sin by marrying her.'

'Something like that.' He empties his cup in a wet mouthful, pours another. 'And Stillington was to hand, so . . .'

'And what exactly did you say before Stillington?'

'I was very far from sober.'

'I'm not entirely sure that makes a difference.'

'Oh, I don't know. That I'd marry her, I suppose. That I'd make it good. Stillington was hardly less drunk than I was.' He huffs, waves a hand in the air, careering up, down, left, right. 'He could barely sign the cross.'

He looks from her towards the window. 'She shouldn't have taken it seriously.'

'I dare say she wasn't as drunk as you.'

Again, he shrugs.

'Was anyone else there?'

'No. We were in my chamber.'

'You're sure?'

'Yes.'

'No servants hovering, no,' her voice grinds disdain like salt in a mill, 'gentlemen of your bed chamber?'

'No.'

'Well, that's two things to be thankful for. That it was Stillington. And no one else.'

'Except Eleanor herself, of course.'

'Well, I suppose I'll have to deal with Eleanor.'

At last, he looks up at her. A hint of contrition. 'Is she going to make trouble?'

'Well, Edward, I don't know. Certainly you've put it in her power to do so.'

She shakes out her sleeves and prepares to rise. At last, he looks up at her.

'I suppose if I have to be married to her, it wouldn't be the end of the world. I have to marry someone. And she's pretty enough . . .'

'Don't compound your crassness with idiocy, Edward. Your marriage is a thing of policy, not a drunken tumble. Your marriage can buy us an alliance with France, or peace with Scotland. If nothing else it can bring us a rich dowry, which your treasury badly needs. It's not a thing to be thrown away on Eleanor Talbot. Pretty though she may be.'

8.

October 1462

Easthall

In truth, Eleanor Talbot isn't pretty. She's beautiful. Her skin white as milk in a pail, her eyes dark almonds under a high-plucked brow. Her gown today is simple, a bruise-blue velvet, un-patterned, her only jewel a deep collar of sapphires that spans a smooth plane of flesh between shoulders framed in miniver. Sitting across the fire from her, watching the play of shadows on her cheek, Cecily can see why Edward wanted her, and why now he's done. Her look is a light a man might find his way by at midnight, a silver coin he'd reach for and pocket. But Eleanor, like the moon, is a cool body, too tranquil to share an arc of sky with the sun.

Eleanor greeted Cecily on the steps of Easthall, just as the brightness of the autumn day began to deepen into gold. Her obeisance was low, gracious enough, but her look when Cecily bade her rise was direct, shameless even. Until a shaft of low sun crossing the crenellated walls of the gatehouse caused her to raise a hand, to shield her eyes and turn towards the house. 'Come inside,' she said, and led Cecily through a shadowed entrance into a narrow-windowed hall, where candles were already lit and, suddenly, it was evening.

Wine has been brought and the boy who poured it sent away. Eleanor has asked her about the length of her ride, been re-assured that she will trouble her for only one night; that tomorrow she will ride on to Norwich, where she has business.

'I'm often there myself,' Eleanor tells her. 'I'm a benefactress of the Carmelite house. And, of course, my sister's husband has much to do in the city, and so, we go together.' She smiles a little. 'This,' she raises a hand, indicates the room with a turn of her wrist, 'is my sister's house. Oh, I don't mean that she lives here, of course. I mean that she owns it, but that she lets me make my home here.'

'Your late husband's lands were in the west country, I believe?'

'Yes. But there's less to bind me there than here,' her lashes cast a shadow on her cheek. 'No family, I mean.'

Then she shakes her shoulders, raises her head. 'Oh dear, you and I don't know each other very well, but I recall your appetite for small talk is slight. So, please forgive me. I believe you're here because you've spoken with your own sister.'

Cecily hadn't expected such directness, but finds herself thankful for it. 'I suppose I am.'

'I'm sorry. I asked her not to speak of my business to you, but she was determined.'

'Is it not a subject I should take an interest in?'

'No more so than your son does. And that's very little.'

'Well. I've heard it from my sister's side and my son's. I'd rather like to hear it from yours.'

'I don't think it would differ very much. I told your sister all that happened and I'm sure she'll have relayed it faithfully. And Edward is capable of many things, but not, I think, of lying to you.'

'And yet, I'm afraid that, with yourself, he's dealt most dishonestly.'

She watches the young woman's lips thin, the slow incline of head that concedes the point. 'Ah, well. Perhaps.'

'You can't think his promises were honest?'

'Oddly I did.'

'And now?'

'He spoke most convincingly of love then. I've known so little of that commodity that I quite failed to recognize that what he really felt was something else entirely. Something quite as urgent, I suppose, but less, what shall we say? Enduring?' She sighs. 'I'm not a fool, Lady. These months of silence have made it very clear to me that I've been set aside.'

Fool enough to open your legs on so slight a pretext as love, thinks Cecily. But then, she herself has never known love's lack. She recalls the old days in France with the Talbots, when their children toddled together in Rouen's English enclave. She saw old Talbot pet his dogs more often than this daughter. He'd look at her sometimes, when she was called to his attention, as if he barely recognized her, or remembered why she was there. And then, when she was of an age, he picked a husband for her as like himself as his reflection in a glass. Against all sense, she finds herself moved to pity.

'My advice to you, Eleanor, is that when a man speaks to you of bedding or wedding, you'd do better to quiz him about the size of your jointure than the extent of his love. It has a more certain future and you can have papers signed that will make it yours forever.'

The laugh Eleanor gives her is a painful thing to hear. 'I'm sure you're very wise on such matters.'

But now pity must be set aside. She leans forward, touches the back of the young woman's hand to draw her eyes to hers. 'But let me make it very clear, Eleanor. There's nothing binding between Edward and you. He'll say he promised you nothing . . .'

'There was a priest . . .'

'Who will deny he was ever there. He'll swear it on his soul, and on God's holy word.'

Eleanor rises, the fire is dying and the sky outside is now full dark. She picks up another log from its pile, leans in to place it, her hand stretching to the stone lintel for support. Once done she wipes her palms, one against the other, to rid them of dust. She watches to see that the flames are catching, thoughtful a moment, and then, 'God forbid that either Edward or Robert Stillington should be made to imperil their souls by lying.' She returns to her seat, rests her elbows on her knees, the heels of her hands against her eyes, and speaks from behind the shelter of her arms. 'Lady Cecily, I will speak plain. You needn't fear that I'll try to press my case. It would be pointless, I know. He doesn't want it. And you would never allow it.'

'I would not.'

She watches the girl draw her hands from her eyes, sit back in her chair, turn her face away. 'Then it's resolved.'

Cecily dares to relax a little, lets her shoulders fall. For a while, it's easy just to watch the fire, listen to its quiet breaks and falls. But the young woman's silence calls to her and, when she looks across, she sees a face paler than ever, eyes wide and fixed on nothing. She will give her some good advice if she can. 'Then I suggest you submit to your family's good intentions, let them make a new marriage for you . . .'

'No, no, no.' She shakes her head and, for the first time, there is vehemence. 'Though it would suit you to have me married. Experience has not endeared me to that state. I will return to my first love. I'll take vows.'

'You're for a nunnery?'

Again, that painful laugh, low in her throat. Her gaze turns entirely on Cecily, and there is steel in it. 'Ah, no. How can I be a bride of Christ, when I'm married to your son?' A long slow blink and the focus of her eye has not changed. 'He may deny it all he likes. So may you. As I've said, I'll not contest.' A single finger raised. 'But God is not mocked.'

'What then?'

'I'll attach myself to the Carmelites in Norwich, but as a lay-woman, not a nun. I'll swear obedience. And chastity, of course. And to abide always within the call of the order's house.' That turn of the wrist again, that takes in all of this shadowed room, the wide, empty fenland beyond it. 'I'll swear not to stir from this place without the permission of Father Peter there. He'll keep me on a straight path, away from such temptations as your son might present or my family would offer.'

'It seems a narrow life, Eleanor. No family. No children.'

'These things are barred from me now. Since I sinned with your son.'

'Do you think God so merciless? Do you imagine he can't forgive this single error?'

'Oh, Lady,' she reaches out a hand, and Cecily feels the cool dryness of it come to rest upon her own. 'I never thought to teach you theology. My sin is most certainly forgiven; confessed, absolved, washed clean as if it never was.' She looks again towards the fire and Cecily follows her gaze into its blistering heart. 'But the consequence of sin, the bitter fruits of it, are not so easily wiped away. If I deny what was done that night, then I bind the sin to myself, to the very great peril of my soul.'

'You could say the same for my son.'

'I can. I do.'

Cecily leans forward, imperative, takes Eleanor's pale face between her hands and looks into her eyes. 'Eleanor, there was no marriage made that night. There was nothing at all. Just a foolish young man mumbling words he didn't mean and a foolish young woman love-struck enough to listen to them. I won't believe your souls imperilled for it. His or yours.'

'What you believe doesn't alter what is.'

'And will you give up all your life, all your future for it?'

She shrugs her narrow shoulders. 'I give up very little, really. I shall live freely here, subject only to God. And, when I die, I will go to Him unencumbered.'

Cecily takes her hands away, brings them back to herself. 'Then, there's nothing I can do for you.'

'No.' Then a thought, a knuckle to her lip. 'Well, perhaps one thing.'

Cecily looks the question.

'Convince your sister, and my sister and her lord, to let me do as I please. Like you, they think me obstinate.'

Cecily shakes her head; it saddens her, all of this, though it shouldn't. She should be glad. Eleanor must be the only woman in England to bed a king and not wish herself a queen.

'Oh come now,' Eleanor coaxes, 'surely this is everything you came here wishing for. The game is yours. I remove myself from the board. I'm sure you arrived here with that end in mind; what it might cost to achieve it, and here I am offering it to you free gratis. Can't you at least help me to secure a future that satisfies us both? And drink a toast to it?'

Eleanor pours, and they drink. The wine is rich, sweeter than Cecily likes, and later, lying abed in this quiet house, she feels the taste of it still coating her tongue, and the start of a headache behind her eyes. She thinks of Eleanor sleeping alone, now and always. And of Edward, and all the bodies he will bring to his bed, to be consumed in the heat of him that he cannot help. God made him so, she reasons, let Him account for it. You can't put a sun in the sky and damn it for burning.

9.

October 1462 to January 1463

Westminster

Trust Warwick to be wrong again. Marguerite, with Henry Beaufort as her general, her husband among her skirts and a French army in tow, lands not in East Anglia, but Northumberland, braving late October gales and a fierce northern sea. And the fickle families of the north return to her and to their old loyalties. 'Like dogs to their vomit,' says Cecily. 'Let them choke on it.'

But she's as like to choke herself. For though the bones of Towton's dead have a year or more of rot on them, in her waking dreams they stir and shift, and lift up grim-edged swords to fight again. They are driven to defy death by the power of Marguerite's desperate resolve, which Cecily knows and fears, for it finds its equal in her own.

So as the fortresses of Alnwick, Dunstanburgh and Bamburgh open their gates to welcome King Henry home, King Edward is riding up-country again, face-first into winter, with an army at his back and his mother's admonishment bludgeoning his ears. 'We need an end to this, Edward. Marguerite at our feet and Henry's head on a spike.'

'Both Henrys, I assume?' he'd asked, flexing a metalled hand. 'Beaufort's and the old King's?'

'Both. Yes.'

'Trust me for it, Captain Mother.' And off he went, all strut and muscle, spoiling for a fight.

She herself is left to pace the halls of Westminster, to manage a kingdom that's holding its breath, to steady a world that might just turn again and bring her to the dust.

And Jacquetta comes a-fluttering. 'To keep you company in these dark days,' she says. But in fact to remind Cecily that her dearest husband, her golden Woodville, and her firstborn son, yes, her darling Anthony, ride in Edward's train, pledging their lives to his service. 'For no one loves your Edward as we do, who remember him so well as a child.'

'You, Jacquetta, are testament to the fickleness of love. Let's not forget your husband and son fought against my Edward at Towton.' But when Jacquetta's face pales she shows mercy. 'Don't mind me. We're on the same side now, I suppose. I'm grateful.'

Jacquetta is emboldened. 'But then, my poor daughter,' she says, 'my poor Elizabeth, robbed of her sons' inheritance, cheated of her lands . . .'

'And you think I've time for that now?' Cecily snaps. Always one step too far with Jacquetta.

A week into December, better news. Cecily snatches the letter from the courier's hand and scans it, fast. The approach of Edward's fearsome army, with forty lords and their affinity in its train, was more than Marguerite had stomach for.

'She mistrusted her French mercenaries,' the hasty script tells her. 'They were too few and, besides, Louis hadn't paid them. And the Scottish army she hoped for didn't come. We must, at least, thank Warwick for that. His truce holds.'

She'd been so hungry for news she hadn't looked to see who it came from, so now scans seal and signature. It's from Hastings, who writes, he says, on Edward's behalf and at his bidding. There's little love between Hastings and Warwick, she knows, both jealous of Edward's favour, of each preferment given to the other. It must irk him to praise his rival.

'So Marguerite took to her ships again,' Hastings writes. 'And sailed into a wrecking storm.' Now, here's a choice morsel to roll about the mouth and chew on. Most of Marguerite's men, it seems, foundered with their ships. The rag-tag remainder were thrown from the bosom of the sea on to the shores of Holy Lindisfarne, in full sight of its priory. 'They must have thought their prayers answered when they saw the monks running across the fields to help them. But Warwick's coastguards ran faster and cut their shipwrecked throats as they staggered up the beach.'

Bless Hastings. He always gives good news.

But it's a morsel, not a meal. Though Marguerite's own ship went down, she and mad Henry were pulled from the waves like herring, flashing silver in trade for safe passage to Scotland. They're in Edinburgh now. Damn it. Could the bitch not just drown?

Cecily turns the page, but there's no more news. Just, 'Edward sends his honour and says he will write himself, soon.'

She throws the paper on to her table and slumps to a chair. Why not now? Why must I have news secondhand and from lesser men?

Two days later she learns why. Another letter, this time from Stillington. Written at Durham as the other had been; not at Edward's urging, but his physician's 'Edward is grievous sick,' he writes. 'And his life feared for. You must pray, Lady. Pray and prepare.'

It was already dusk when the messenger came. It is deep dark now and, in the sanctuary of her chamber, nothing but a lick of candle flame to draw her mind towards God. Her knees burn, her eyes ache, and before her face a painted virgin, her haloed face blank with acceptance, holds up the Christ child for a blessing. Did Mary know then, Cecily wonders, how her own son would die? Did the angel, who told her she would bear the world's salvation, confess that the price of it would be wrung from her own heart? She imagines this is not how the Mother looked when she wept in the mud at Golgotha, tortured by soldiers with the breaking of her son's bones.

I'd have taken up the hammer and driven the nails into their own hands, she thinks. I'd have torn down the cross and buried them beneath it. She'd fight the devil himself for Edward. She'd fight anyone. And so, though she kneels at His altar, Cecily doesn't so much pray to God as stare him down. Don't you dare, she says in her heart, though her lips, pinched and dry, say nothing.

From beside her comes the steady intonation of Annette's prayers. Cecily's children no longer need a nurse, but Cecily still needs Annette to speak to God on her behalf when she herself is dumb with fear or mute with rage. Annette has the pliant voice for it after all, and a head ready to bow in submission.

Besides, she herself must hearken to Stillington's second admonition. She must prepare. Tomorrow she will have her younger sons brought to her, she will keep them close. If Edward dies, George is his heir, barely thirteen and petulant as a child. And the great lords of England, who would be called upon to uphold his right, are far in the north, laying siege to castles where her enemies, with Henry bloody Beaufort, still hold out for Marguerite and her whelp. She swallows and pushes her hand against her mouth to hold down what is rising in her gullet; closes her eyes against its watering sting.

'Pray on,' she tells Annette and rises to her feet. She must write to Stillington. He must keep Edward's secrets again. 'No one must know who doesn't already,' she instructs him. 'And they mustn't speak. Word must be sent only to me. If you must say anything to his captains, say he rallies,' she writes. 'Tell them to fight on.'

She seals the letter, orders a messenger pulled from his bed, leans from the window to watch him mount, taking up the reins and swinging his satchel on to his back. When he's gone, she imagines the long journey north, the changes of horse, the passing of the packet from hand to hand, to Stillington. By the time it arrives, Edward will be recovered, she tells herself, and will laugh at my fears. Or he'll be stiff and dead. He may be so already. The wind is bitter. She latches the window and turns back to the room, the papers on her table, the ash of the fire. She sits before it and takes up Stillington's letter again.

The weather had turned foul as they went north, she reads. Not snow, yet, but merciless rain that turned the roads to mud and soaked horse and rider to the bone. They thought he'd caught a cold at first, and no surprise, but by the time they reached Durham he had to be pulled from his horse. They put him to bed. 'A chill,' he said. 'I'll fight it off in a day.' When, after two days, he hadn't, he sent his army on ahead, Warwick leading them. News of Marguerite's soaking cheered him and it was thought he'd rally well enough, but that night his fever peaked and his flesh grew livid. Not plague, said the physician, measles, thank God. He'll survive that. But now his chest has taken the infection. He struggles for breath and knows no one.

'I've not given extreme unction yet,' Stillington writes. 'I wait and hope. I'm at his side as I write and will not leave it. It grieves me to send such news. I pray he'll wake well this morning or next and, when I tell him I've written you, he'll break my head for it and curse me for a fool. I'll bear it gladly. Your servant, Robert Stillington, Keeper of the Privy Seal.'

Ten days, and every day a letter. In the first, his fever rages still. In the second, he wanders in delirium and fights Towton again in his sleep. Then, he no longer shivers, but his breath rattles in his chest. His priests stand, ever ready, for the deliverance of his soul.

Among her children, only Meg knows, and she says nothing. But she comes to Cecily's threshold at the end of every day, distracts her with talk of George and Richard, with whom she spends much time.

'George suspects,' Meg tells her one evening as their quills stroke over vellum: lists of favours they'll give on Christ's birthday, gifts for those whose goodwill is worth buying.

Cecily nods. She knows it already. At dinner, each evening, she watches him court the attention of men much older than he, who nod and smile at his words, not because what he says is clever or interesting, but because he's the King's heir and, well, you never know. Just tonight, as she moved her food around without eating it, she'd heard the tail end of a joke from him, felt a buffet of laughter, and turned her head in time to see men slapping his shoulder, filling his cup. He beamed and looked up the table to make sure she'd noticed it, his pale eyes hungry for something not on his plate. When he had her attention he lifted his chin. See, his look told her, I'm no less fine than my brother. No less loved.

'What news of my brother the King?' he asked, stepping to her side when the meal was done.

'He's well, George. Triumphing at every turn.'

He fell silent then, his head drooping a little, and she noticed how his fingers fidgeted at his sleeve. She laid a hand on his shoulder. 'Come,' she said. 'Sit with your sister and me and tell us how your swordplay goes.'

But he'd shrugged free and said he was for a card game, that his friends were waiting. Waiting to take your money, she thought, sadly. Why are you such a fool?

In the last week of advent, Stillington's daily bulletins bring better news: 'Edward's fever is broken.' 'He woke this morning and knew himself.' Then, 'He's well enough today to take a little broth.' 'His physicians no longer fear for him.' 'He's in health enough, now, to shout at his servants. And at me.'

At last, as the twelfth night's broken meats are doled out to the morning's poor, comes the best news yet. He was out of his bed today to meet with Henry Beaufort, who surrendered to War-wick at Christmas. The war is over and victory won.

Cecily sits an hour with the paper in her hand, watching the river flow past her window, sluggish with ice. My new year's gift is coming, she promises herself. A little late, but no less welcome. Henry Beaufort, who mocked my husband's severed head, will have his own set on a spike.

IO.

24 February 1463

Westminster

The water brings Edward home to her at last. On a February morning when pale sunlight barely breaks the frost on Westminster's
lawns and ice crackles at the river's edges. He stands in the prow of
the barge bare-headed, his cloak thrown back, waving double-
handed at the cheering flotilla of boats that have braved the river
tide to guide him home. He looks thin, she thinks, as she stands on
the dockside, wrapped in furs. And where's his hat, his gloves?

Beside him, Warwick.

If you had to guess which man has spent the winter on his arse
in the mud and which in the soft billows of his bed, you'd say the
other way around. Warwick's face is all ruddy health, while
Edward's, but for the flag of colour the cold has brought to his
cheeks, is pale. But her son's smile, when he turns it on her, is as
brilliant as ever and she feels her own heart leap with life.

'God greet you, Captain Mother!' he shouts across the water,
and she feels the cold air against her teeth as she grins.

As the barge docks, there's a tussle as both men make to step
ashore at the same time, until Warwick, remembering his place,
stands back, bows an apology to his king. But Edward only
throws his arm around his cousin's shoulder and draws him close,
so that they step on to dry land together, William Hastings just
behind, and Stillington. All four are laughing as they come, their
breath misting the air.

He comes to a stop before her. 'Captain Mother,' he says, and
makes to kiss her hand. But she reaches up, cups his head to draw

it down and presses her lips to his brow. His skin is chill beneath the kiss, but his whole body thrums with life. He only wants feeding up, she thinks. He's well, and will be better.

'Aunt.'

Now here's Warwick, all charm and swagger, drawing himself to her attention. This time she must give it without reserve, for, while Edward sickened, all the castles of the north have fallen to him. And Henry Beaufort, with all of Marguerite's captains, has forsworn his old allegiance and surrendered to her house. For that, she lets him kiss her hand and when that's done, bends a knee and calls him, 'My dear brother's son, my Lord of Warwick, our strength and stay.'

'I live to serve your son, Aunt. And all your house.'

Oh, yes? she thinks. So long as it suits you.

'And my Lord Hastings is always glad to see you, Mother.' Edward draws forward Will, who kisses her hand and winks wryly as he rises. She can't help but smile at him. There are few she'd allow such familiarity, but he's one. 'You're always welcome, my Lord.'

Then, 'Robert.' A nod to Stillington, who sketches a hasty blessing and nods back, no words needed.

'And now, Mother, there's another in my company you must give welcome to.' And suddenly no one's smiling and Hastings can't look her in the eye and, as men move to one side among a general shuffling of feet, she looks up and there he stands, Henry Beaufort, his long chin jutting, his mouth a rigid line, his hands unbound, his head not severed.

She looks at Edward, raises a brow. He says nothing, but nods in Beaufort's direction. She turns her gaze back, unhurried.

'My Lord of Somerset.'

She doesn't offer her hand and his bow is formal. The other men take a step back, develop a sudden interest in their boots.

She feigns a thought. 'Oh, but are you still that? Lord of Somerset, I mean? Lord of anything?' She looks to Edward. 'What is he now? What should I call him?'

Beside her, Edward turns a little, so that only she can see his face, the quirk of his lips and the creasing of his eyes. He's enjoying this.

'What I am is at your son's service, Lady,' says Beaufort, drawing her attention back to him.

'Ah. Shall I call you his servant then? His dog?'

He doesn't answer, but the skin across his cheekbones grows white.

She studies his face; his eyes that saw her husband dead, his mouth that mocked it. She looks down at her sleeves, takes time to smooth them, keeps him waiting, looks up and cocks her head to one side.

'Now. What should you call me?'

She watches the slide of his throat as he swallows.

'Mother,' says Edward beneath his breath. She holds up a hand but keeps her eyes on Beaufort. Steps a little closer.

'Let me help you.' Her voice is a shear of steel. 'When last we met, at Ludlow. When you led an army to my door, looted my town and killed my people, you called me York's bitch.'

The silence is absolute. She lets it hang a moment, then, 'But you may call me the King's Mother now.'

She turns on her heel, shows Beaufort her back and holds out her arm to her son. 'Edward.'

As they walk at stately pace towards the palace, she listens to the murmur of men falling into place behind her as Beaufort, with not a word to say, is roughly shuffled to the back of the pack.

'I wanted him in chains at my feet. I wanted his head on a spike.'

Edward shrugs. 'He surrendered so . . .'

'Well, I've heard that. I've been waiting for news that his head was off.'

'. . . so I pardoned him.'

She has followed him to his rooms, sent his servants scattering and slammed the door at their backs. She prowls as he pulls off his cloak, throws it across a chair, leans back against a table and folds his arms before him, ready. She circles, comes close.

'Have I raised a fool?'

'I don't kill men who surrender, Mother. It discourages others, don't you see? Makes them think there's no point in it. Surrendering, I mean.'

'He's our enemy.'

He carries on, as if she hadn't spoken. 'I like it when men surrender. Saves time and effort. I shouldn't have to teach you that. You understand strategy.'

'Don't dare patronize me.'

He pushes up from the table, looks about for the jug of wine that must surely be waiting for him. She follows him when he spies it, seethes while he pours.

'Mother, Warwick was manning four sieges. In winter. Our soldiers were in no better state than the men they were starving out. And all the time expecting a Scottish army to descend.' He lifts the cup, drinks as if he needs it, turns at last to face her. 'Which it did. Eventually.' He hides a grin in his cup. 'A bit late for Beaufort though. He'd already given up hope of it and brought his men over to us.'

'How galling for him,' she mocks.

'They came in force, Mother, the Scots. Well-armed and not hungry. Frenchmen with them. And Beaufort, who today you disdain,' he uncurls a finger from his cup and points it at her, 'stood shoulder to shoulder with Warwick ready to fight them.'

'Oh, really? I've heard that with one look from the god-like Warwick, the Scots turned tail and fled.'

'Perhaps from the sight of the god-like Warwick with their former general at his side.'

She nods, all right, and turns away. It's a good point, she'll concede it. But still. 'Henry Beaufort led the field against your father at Wakefield. He fought you at Towton.'

'Yes, yes.' He pours and drinks again. 'And so did a thousand others who today you smile at. We've made peace with all of them. Why not him?'

It's true, of course. Even her own kin. She's made peace with others who wronged her a thousand times. But those others didn't stand by while her husband's broken head was severed from his corpse. They didn't fashion with their fingers a paper mockery of a crown, or wield the hammer that nailed it to his skull. These things are beyond pardon. Beyond policy or strategy or reason. She returns to Edward, lays a hand against each cheek, and looks deep into his eyes. 'I'll say this very slowly, so your simple mind might understand. He is my sworn enemy.'

'Oh, Mother.' He takes her hands, pulls them from his face but holds them still, firm. 'You don't have sworn enemies. You treat people as you must, you do what must be done. At least, that's what you've always taught me.'

'And you think you must pardon Henry Beaufort?' she goads.

'I must nothing, Mother. I think it sensible. I think it wise. I think it to our advantage. He was the best of Marguerite's generals and now he fights for me.' He wraps her hands more firmly in his, leans in a little, coaxing. 'Only think how Marguerite will spit, to know that her favourite now walks arm in arm with Edward of England. And bends the knee to his mother. Don't you like that?'

She leans too, as if to whisper treason in his ear. 'She'd piss herself to know him dead with his bollocks burned before his eyes. I'd like that better.'

'Yes, I'm sure you would. But then every other man who stands with her now would say, well, there's nothing for it, we'll have to stick with Marguerite. This way they see a way out. They'll say, if Henry Beaufort can find a new home with Edward, so can I.'

'He killed your father.'

'Yes. As good as.' He's thoughtful a moment, then shrugs. 'And my father as good as killed his. We can go on like that forever. Or we can stop now.'

She circles him again, sneers over her shoulder, 'What? Forgive and forget?'

'Make a peace. It's not the same.'

'Make peace with your father's killer if it suits you,' she snarls. 'I'd kill him with my own hands. Then follow him to Hell and watch him burn.'

She turns from him. Tears threaten her eyes and she'll not let him have them.

He reaches a hand, 'Mother . . .'

She shrugs away, but he reaches again and takes her arm. He coaxes her into a chair, then crouches before her, taking her hands, which are fists, between his.

'Mother, the best way to beat Marguerite is to isolate her. To win men from her with mercy. France won't support her if no English will fight on her side. She'll just be a woman alone . . .'

'And a woman alone can do nothing, you think?'

'Marguerite alone can do nothing,' he corrects himself, then raises his brows, fake solemn. 'I'd never be fool enough to say that of you.'

'You've no more idea than your father had about what Marguerite can do. See what that cost him.'

'I'll not make my father's mistakes.'

'No. You'll make your own and likely worse.'

II.

March 1463 to May 1464

London

Henry Beaufort learns fast even if Edward doesn't. An easy lesson: that, for him at least, the light of Edward's love isn't bright enough to live by. Not when every other man alive waits only for a patch of shadow to hide the knife they'll put in his back. Edward, though, ignores the snarling envy and throws the royal arm of friendship about Beaufort's neck. There's love enough to go around, after all, and every man his brother. Let's ride to hounds. Let's drink till we're blind. Lend me your whore. We're men of the new world, aren't we? Brothers in chivalry.

As the weeks pass, Cecily watches Beaufort's looks turn cautious, while Hastings scowls and Warwick spits in the rushes.

'Why do you do it, Edward?' she asks at the dog end of an April evening. They sit together before her hearth at Baynard's watching the fire, hands nesting cups in their laps. These late-night visits have become a habit. The river brings him just when she's thinking of her bed. He comes alone, to talk politics and drink her good wine. She'd offer a chess game, but he never has the patience for it. So she speaks of policy, watches him nod, and is pleased to know that her ideas will be his in the morning.

He claims to come only for an hour's peace, away from the court and the rubbing demands of every man's attention. It seems a poor pretext to her. She's always observed that men's attention nourishes rather than drains him. He always seems taller in company, or perhaps it's only that other men seem small.

This time, though, she wants an answer and he gives none, so she taps his foot with hers. 'Why?'

'Why what?'

'Why do you provoke me and all men by flaunting your friendship with Beaufort?'

'Is that what I do?'

'You eat with him. You hunt with him. He rides at your stirrup and drinks from your cup. Sleeps in your chambers, so I'm told.'

He scoffs. 'Don't believe everything you hear. Anyway, I don't do it to provoke you.'

'Why then?'

He stretches his feet further to the fire, smiles at her over the brim of his cup. 'To provoke Marguerite.'

'Who is in France with her head still on her shoulders. I doubt she even hears of it.'

'Oh,' he says, relishing another pull of wine. 'She hears.'

'Warwick doesn't like it. Hastings likes it less.'

A shrug. 'Should I care for their liking?'

'You've made them powerful men.'

'Warwick tells me he was that already.'

'I suppose he was – Earl of Warwick and his father's heir. Between times though, a stateless exile. A pirate.'

'Ah, well. He became those things for my sake. We were those things together.' The way he smiles then, the light of the fire glinting on his teeth, you'd think he'd have those dangerous days back again and gladly. Then the smile is gone. 'But,' he says, 'he should remember that whatever he is today I made him.'

'Does he need reminding, do you think?'

'It does him no harm to see he's not the only man who can rise by my favour.'

'Ah, so that's what you're about.'

She thinks a while, balancing the two men in her mind. She knows Beaufort's puling love for her son is born of self-interest, while Warwick pledged himself to her house long ago and has stuck with it, though it cost him dear. Not for love though, she reminds herself, for all he's her brother's son. He stayed out of the fight with Marguerite until directly threatened, then backed Cecily's husband and hoped he'd win for him, and though her husband didn't, her son did. Still, Warwick gambled everything, and a man who's done that expects a great prize.

'You've rewarded him well,' she says, coming to herself again. 'Warwick, I mean.'

'And yet, however much I give, the debt remains.' His mouth turns sulky, then he points a wagging hand at her, petulant and goading. 'Here he comes with his tally stick, reminding me of everything I owe.' He shrugs. 'It can be exhausting, being grateful.'

She leans forward, places a hand on his, curled around a cup in need of filling. She'll pour again, in a moment. 'You must endure being grateful to Warwick a little longer. Marguerite still threatens us. And Louis's playing dangerous games. There's more fighting to be done, and Warwick can raise more men than anyone in England. Not just because he has money to pay them. Because they love him.' It's what you have in common, she thinks, the power to draw men to you and bind their hearts.

'I know. He is loved. I love him too,' he admits. 'More than any man alive.'

'Then don't push him too far by flaunting Beaufort in his face.'

'Hmm.'

'What about Will Hastings?'

A low nod then, a last slow draw that drains his cup. 'Will knows my heart, well enough.'

Hastings, of course, was nothing before Edward made him. Chamberlain now and a rich man. However much he's goaded by Beaufort he, at least, can't look back at any time before and think, well, maybe I was better off then.

Relations between states are no less tetchy than those between friends. In spring, French King Louis sends ambassadors to

England's capital to talk peace, and soldiers to her northern borders to make war.

'Two-faced French diplomacy, Edward. Get used to it,' Cecily tells her son when he rants.

In the heat of his temper, Edward sends Warwick north to fight again. In its cooling, he feeds the French ambassadors on peacock and swan, and promises that a return envoy will fly the Channel by summer.

'I crave nothing more than peace with my cousin of France,' he tells them and smiles his charming smile.

'Will you send the Lord Warwick to us?' they ask. 'Our king so longs to meet this great man.'

'Likely,' says Edward. 'Though he must deal with some little trouble in the north first. Of course it's nothing. A flea bite.'

Sometimes that charming smile can seem wolfish.

'Whoever we send will speak with the King of England's voice,' Cecily reassures.

'Ah, but the Earl of Warwick,' they say. 'He has not only the King's voice but his ear, *n'est-ce pas*? His heart?'

The trouble in the north is more than a flea bite. French troops and Scots, all backing Marguerite. When Warwick writes for help, Edward stirs himself and follows, Hastings on his right side, Beaufort on his left, all jostling harness and horse sweat in the heat of July.

Days later, Hastings writes Cecily from Northampton. 'No one knows,' he tells her, 'who stirred up the mob that threatened to put a spit up Henry Beaufort's arse and roast him; who demanded with such violence that the King cast him off.'

Who, indeed, would dare? But Cecily, as she reads, recalls that Hastings is, among many other things, Constable of Northampton Castle, so in that town, his voice has more power to move men than most.

Edward's own letter, when it comes, is blistering. 'Who dares tell me who I can keep company with!' he storms.

The angry mob had broken into the royal lodging and the scene looked set to turn bloody but, 'Thank God Hastings got the Sheriff's men out fast enough to quell the bastards.'

They ended the night placated, quaffing wine in the town square supplied by the quick-thinking Constable. She smiles at that. She knows Will Hastings well, his boldness, his way with words to sway a crowd. She's seen him do it often enough. His letter closes with the news that Edward, with deep regret, has sent Beaufort away and into Wales. 'For his safety, of course.'

A laugh escapes her throat. How safe can Beaufort be outside of Edward's company? She folds both letters, sets them aside and smooths her sleeves. Clever William Hastings, to have his rival banished and earn his king's thanks for it. Next Edward writes there's no need to go further north, for, together, his Neville cousins have driven Marguerite overseas to France.

'Could they not just kill her?' Cecily complains to Annette. 'Must she always slip away like an eel from a basket?'

'Perhaps you should pick up a sword and go kill her yourself,' suggests Annette, stitching while Cecily paces.

'Perhaps I should. Since it seems no man alive can do it for me.'

'The old bitch'll get short shrift from Louis this time,' Warwick crows.

Warwick and Louis have been writing to each other, it seems. Little *billets-doux* wafting across the Channel. Nothing wrong in that, of course, he has Edward's licence for diplomacy. But there have been gifts, too. A pair of fine French hunting dogs with noses as sniffy and high as the French king's, so Warwick's wife tells her.

'And the jewels about their collars as fine as anything I have to wear,' she confides.

They must be very fine indeed, for Warwick stints nothing in the keeping of his wife.

The *billets-doux*, Cecily knows, speak of marriage. A French marriage for Edward to seal a treaty. God knows it would be good to have one, and a marriage might make it stick. Warwick had angled first for Louis's own daughter, but she's three years old and Edward shouldn't wait so long for sons. Now Louis dangles his own queen's sister. Fourteen this summer and ripe. Edward has said yes to it, though with little enough enthusiasm.

'A wedding's cheaper than a war, Edward,' Cecily tells him. 'Much as you'd like to, we can't afford to fight France.'

So, in summer Edward sends envoys to talk peace and love to Louis. Come autumn they return with a truce.

As Advent candles are lit, better news still. Scotland's queen, regent for her twelve-year-old son, dies and the boy's new protectors decide they can't afford a war either. So Warwick has another truce to boast of, having been on the spot to negotiate it. And here comes a happy Christmas, a chance to catch their breath.

But then comes news so amazing it rivals a virgin birth. While Marguerite's hopes are at their lowest ebb, Henry Beaufort slips from Wales to the cold fastness of Bamburgh Castle, throws himself at mad Henry's feet and gives, again, his heart to Lancaster.

New year and the country's up. Pockets of trouble stirred up by Beaufort, the Scots straining at the leash, and across the Channel Marguerite's in talks with France and Brittany about an invasion of England.

'They'll be ready to listen now she has a captain fit to fight for her again,' says Cecily, who spends more nights pacing than sleeping.

But hope lives on and diplomacy keeps it breathing. In spring the French envoys return, prating about perpetual peace between their nations.

'Talking out of both sides of their mouths,' complains Edward.

'Keeping their options open,' says Cecily. 'It's how diplomacy works.'

Edward smiles at them but lets Warwick do the talking. And sends Warwick's brother, John, north to talk likewise to the Scots.

As John rides north, Henry Beaufort offers battle. Never one to say no to a fight, John accepts.

It's been more than a year since Cecily asked for Henry Beaufort's head on a spike. Now here it is. Sent down to London in a battered leather satchel after John Neville parted it from its trunk in Hexham marketplace. He'd dragged the living man there from the battlefield, beaten and bloody and begging for mercy.

'On London Bridge,' Edward instructed. 'Put it up. Let the world see. Treacherous bastard.'

He'd sounded hurt. Foolish boy.

She comes out to see it herself, standing in her barge in the centre of the Thames looking up while her oarsmen stretch muscle to steady the boat against the river's pull. There's not much to see from this distance, just a blank silhouette against a clear sky. It seems awkwardly done, as if the point it's mounted upon went badly in. His face is to the heavens, so that his chin juts, prideful, as it did in life. She might not have known him otherwise, among the other heads speared there, thirty or more; all the leaders of Lancaster's northern resistance, lopped on John Neville's order after battle was done.

But among the gory throng her guard has pointed Beaufort out, so she has no doubt, and she has in her hand a copy of the indictment that hangs on a board from the spear he's spiked upon: 'Henry Beaufort, twice traitor to the King.'

She'd thought to relish the moment and is surprised to feel nothing much. The joy had come at news of his killing, of his head severed. Though not as her husband's was. Better. For Henry Beaufort had been alive to see the axe, to hear its whistling fall and feel its terror. The thought of it had opened a light space in her chest and drawn a gasping laugh from her. She tries now to rekindle the feeling, but the ashes are cold. Alive, Henry Beaufort had been her enemy. Dead he's just a fresh addition to the river's stink, a ball of meat set up to baste in summer's heat.

It will hurt Marguerite, she consoles herself. And there is some pleasure in that. I'll have my joy again when she is dead.

'Turn the boat about,' she tells the oarsmen. She sits, closes her eyes and lets herself think of Edward. He'll be home soon. Chastened, she hopes. A little wiser. He must learn to manage it better, the gift of his love.

12.

Tuesday, 13 September 1464

Reading

In the end, she goes to him. Summer has brought the plague to London and, fired by August's heat, it consumes two hundred souls a day. So the Great Council that was planned for Westminster is removed to Reading's calm and cloistered abbey. Cecily has been settled now a day or two in the abbot's house, her children with her; George because at fourteen he now sits on King's council, Richard because she thinks he should observe his brother at work, her daughters because she wants them safe from contagion.

The council meets tomorrow to talk money. It sometimes seems to Cecily it's all they ever talk of: the lack of it, the getting of it, the thousand ways it's spent. Edward inherited an impoverished treasury, and three wrangling years have done nothing to enrich it. War's expensive, and her son is a costly king.

So, now there's peace with France and Scotland, now Marguerite and her son are friendless exiles, mad Henry helpless and hiding somewhere in the north, Beaufort dead, there's time to do something about it. The council is to be presented with plans to renew England's coinage. Here's how it will work: the money men will bring their old coins to the mint and be given new ones. Less gold in them, that's true, less silver, more tin. But the face value's the same and they'll get more of them, shiny as ever.

'Good,' says Cecily. 'Things have the value we ascribe to them.'

Another windfall is expected, too. Warwick has secured the French king's agreement for the marriage of his sister-in-law.

Edward has only to ratify his choice and Bona of Savoy, richly dowered, will become England's queen. For that, Cecily will bear even the sight of Warwick, cock-sure and pleased with himself for being the maker of the match.

'I'd rather marry Burgundy than France,' says Edward when he arrives in the evening and his cousin embraces him with the news. He seems sulky and put out, though he has, as far as Cecily can see, no cause to be.

'Burgundy has no one for you to marry,' she tells him. 'Anyway, you've said almost-yes to France for long enough. Pity your poor cousin here.'

She spares Warwick an almost-smile as he strides forward, slaps a hand to Edward's shoulder and speaks, jocular and admonishing, as a father might to a son.

'Go to it, lad.'

Does Cecily imagine it, or does Edward's fist clench?

'Mother, you must come!' She hears George's feet pounding the tiled corridor to her rooms and his voice, high and gleeful, even before her door cracks back on its hinges. 'Edward says he's married!'

Cecily's daughters, seated about her, gasp.

'Married?' For a moment her mind casts about and then, of course . . . Eleanor. The name almost leaps from her mouth, but she checks and swallows it down with her shock. 'What nonsense are you talking now, George?'

His hand is still on the door latch, his body swinging into the room, his face lit less with outrage than relish. 'He says he won't have the French marriage. That he's married already. To Elizabeth Woodville.'

'Elizabeth . . . ?'

George shakes a hand at her, bouncing on his toes. 'You know. Old Jacquetta Bedford's daughter.' He's a dangerous inch away from laughter.

'Dear God, George. I know who Elizabeth Woodville is,' she hisses, already on her feet and passing him at the door.

'Edward!' As she crosses the broad square of grass before the open door of the council hall, she sees her son at the foot of the steps that lead to it. His head is down, bull-like, his hands on his hips, while Warwick, arms flailing, remonstrates and curses. The men of the council are clustered whey-faced about the thrown-open door.

She has almost reached him when she sees Edward's arm flex back, his fist balling for a strike.

'Edward!'

The fist hovers, then becomes a jabbing finger, no less vicious, no less an assault. And his words, as provoking as blows. 'You're my servant, not my master. And it's no business of yours who I marry.'

When Warwick opens his mouth to shout again, Cecily knows him for a fool. Edward's fingers close around his doublet's collar and pull him close, till teeth speak snarlingly to teeth. 'I'm your king. Understand? I do as I please. You can like it or you can go fuck yourself!'

Warwick throws up his hands to break the hold. Edward draws him tight again. 'Strike me and I'll kill you.'

Then he lets go, juts his chin as if daring the blow. John Neville, Earl of Northumberland since he lopped Beaufort's head, steps forward to put his body between the two men, one hand raised, placatory, to his king, the other against his brother's chest. 'Come away now, brother.' His voice is low but urgent. 'Be wise. Come away.' And Warwick, belligerent still but knowing he's done, allows himself to be led.

'My Lord Hastings.' Cecily's hand beckons Edward's chamberlain from the edge of the crowd. 'Clear this space. Adjourn the council.' And now, in a low voice, she asks the impossible. 'Keep this quiet, if you can.'

As Hastings moves into action and the crowd begins to disperse, she steps into Edward's line of sight. He's shaking with anger, burning with it. Well, he's not the only one. Her own voice is dagger-sharp. 'Edward.'

'Don't you start,' he snarls.

'What? Will you fight me now? Strike me? You're not your father's son if you do.'

His teeth still bared, he leans in, but it's Richard, Dickon, who steps forward, lays a hand on Edward's arm, all calmness, and says quietly, 'Brother.'

Well, he can hardly strike a child, can he? So he turns at his mother's signal and matches his stride to hers back to her chamber, while his family have the good sense to fall back and let them be.

She's walking fast. 'Mother . . .' he says.

'Not a word, Edward. Not a word till we're inside.'

13.

She has closed the door, directed him to a chair, pushed him down to sit, slopped small beer into a cup and thrust it at him. The anger has drained from his face and left it ashen. But it's in his body still, tense, like a blade in a ready hand. Well, hers too.

'So,' she says, sitting straight-backed in the seat opposite, 'Elizabeth Woodville.'

His eyes are lethal. 'Elizabeth. And there's nothing you can do about it. There was a priest. There were witnesses. And now,' his thrust-out arm re-imagines a crowd, 'the whole council knows. You can't fix it.' He leans forward, snarling. 'I don't want it fixed.'

She gives her attention to her sleeves, smoothing the lining of ivory silk under grey. 'A widow with no money or property, whose husband died fighting for Marguerite . . .'

'Yes.'

'. . . who was so much a no one I can't even recall his name.'

'John Grey.'

John Grey. That's it. The forgettable John Grey, who gave her two little Grey sons. 'Your,' she can't help but sneer, 'stepchildren now, I suppose.'

'She'll get more sons, from me.'

'Well, at least that's one good thing we can say about her; she's not barren.'

'And that she's the daughter of your good friend.'

'Jacquetta?' The very name is a clatter of irritation. 'Oh, yes. I first met Jacquetta in a French stable with the Duke of Bedford's hand up her cunt. By allowing such freedoms she made herself his wife. Has Elizabeth done likewise with you?'

He's up now, and pacing.

Her eyes follow him. 'Let me think,' she says. 'Bedford was dead within months. And then Jacquetta married that nobody Richard Woodville, who was . . . I don't know, nobody remembers what, in Bedford's service. I wonder who Elizabeth will marry when she's worn you out. Your stable boy, perhaps. Your wiper of the royal arse.'

'Elizabeth's father is Baron Rivers now and sits on my council, remember.'

'Yes. I saw him in the crowd there. Looking smug.'

'It was you asked me to pardon him after Towton. A favour to Jacquetta.'

'A favour?' She's incredulous. 'Edward, I suggested you pardon him because we were in the business, then, of binding as many of the old Lancastrian families to York as we could. Jacquetta's family is easily bound. They're natural prostitutes.'

His words are a threat of violence. 'You mustn't speak so, of my kin.'

'Your kin? Oh, Edward, how did I breed such a fool? You could have had the King of France for your kin. And Bona's dowry in your treasury. Now what do you have?'

He throws himself back into his chair, runs fingers through his hair. 'I have Elizabeth. I could get her no other way.'

She pushes herself to standing, looks down at him in disgust. 'For the love of God, Edward, will you marry any woman that won't bend her back for you?'

'She's virtuous.'

She throws up her hands. 'Edward, listen to yourself! She's a sly bitch, like her mother. And she's tricked you into a marriage that makes her a queen and you a laughing stock.'

He looks away, out of the window, anywhere but at her. His chest heaves and his fists clench and unclench about the chair arm as she circles him.

The waste of it makes her blood boil and her fingers itch to slap. But she needs information more than the satisfaction of blows. So she sits back down, taps his shin with her foot to draw his attention and demands, 'Tell me how it happened.'

'Why?' he snarls. 'So you can look for ways to unravel it? So you can make it disappear? I don't want you to.'

She pushes again at his shin, hard, hoping it will bruise. 'Think only that I'm a mother, robbed of a son's wedding. At least tell me what I missed.'

His view from the window must be captivating.

'Come on,' her foot kicks again. 'When and where?'

'Grafton. Two weeks ago.'

'Ah, in the bosom of her family then.' The manor at Grafton, not two days' ride from Fotheringhay, has long been Jacquetta's home. 'I dare say her mother stood witness?'

A nod. 'And others.'

'Oh yes, Jacquetta would see it properly done.' A clean-living priest. Witnesses with good names, solid reputations. She'd make sure of the consummation too. She's probably kept the sheets. No blood stain, Elizabeth's no virgin, but she'd revel enough in the stink of sex. 'Come on then, tell me how it was?'

And so it comes out, the whole sorry story. He'd seen Elizabeth at court, of course. Danced with her a time or two. Well, Jacquetta would have put her in his way. Then an invitation to Grafton in April and she dallying in the deer park as he rode through.

'She petitioned for the restoration of her sons' inheritance,' he says.

'Which you granted, I imagine. Bountiful as you are.'

He shrugs.

'Wasn't that enough to open her legs?'

Apparently not. So he returned in August for another go and, well, here we are.

'And did you imagine, when you arrived at Grafton a free man, you'd depart a husband?'

'Does it matter?' he spits.

No. Not now, she supposes as she watches his wide defiant face. She'll canvas the witnesses of course, interrogate the priest. But no, it will all be in order. Jacquetta's no fool. Likely her daughter isn't either.

'Pah!' she says, turning her head from him. 'This is Eleanor Talbot all over again. You'll tire of her in a month.'

'Mother.' He leans across the space between them, and his fingers close hard about her wrist, so that she must turn to him as the pain registers. 'Be very sure. I will never tire of Elizabeth.'

His eyes hold hers, and she sees in them a defiance never aimed at her before. It's a look reserved for his enemies, for those who cross his will.

'What,' she snarls, ignoring the smarting of her wrist. 'Love, is it?'

'I suppose it is.' His face is fixed, his grip on her wrist tightens.

'What nonsense. The King of France, and your cousin Warwick, will be much aggrieved.'

'It'll do the King of France good to know that the Earl of Warwick doesn't have the King of England in his pocket.' He shrugs. 'It'll do the Earl of Warwick no harm to know it either.'

'Oh, not love after all then. Policy.'

His grip tightens again, then he lets go as she pulls her hand away from him.

'It is my will,' he says. 'Warwick must submit to it and so must you. The King of France can go to Hell.'

Then he looks at her, a little shamefaced, nods to her burning wrist drawn back against her breast. 'Have I hurt you?'

She lets the hand fall, shakes it out, all disdain. 'Don't imagine yourself man enough.'

A shake of his head, a grudging smile. 'God, you must have been a match for my father.'

'We came to blows, from time to time.'

'Loving blows, I'd say.'

She shrugs, what would he know of it?

'Well, perhaps Elizabeth and I will come to such blows.'

'I hope she beats you black and blue. Though likely your cousin will first.'

'Ah, Warwick.' And now he looks away.

'You shouldn't have humiliated him so, in front of the council. Edward, you can't afford to make an enemy of him as well as the King of France.'

He nods. Lowers his head and sighs. 'I know. I'll make it up to him.'

14.

Reading

That night, while Edward wins back Warwick's friendship with drink and promises, Cecily sits alone and thinks. There isn't a nobleman in England who'll like this match. They'll look at Elizabeth Woodville and say to their wives, well, if Edward can marry that one, he could have married our daughter. We're as good as any Woodville. Better. There'll be anger, resentment, and from Warwick more than any.

She has some sympathy. She's been King's Mother three years now, the nearest thing England's had to a queen. And now she must bend the knee to Jacquetta's daughter? She allows her teeth to grind once at the thought, feels her nostrils flare as she exhales it into the room.

Well. She's done harder things. Not many.

On her table is a collection of coin. A test striking of Edward's new currency. She picks one up and turns it in her fingers. On one side St Michael smites the devil in a dragon's guise. On the other the ship of faith, Christ's cross its mast, Edward's arms its blazon. There's nothing much she won't do to keep that ship afloat. She grasps it tight – its bright gold, its base metal – sharp-edged against her palm. She'll even accept Elizabeth if she must – bright and base as she is. And she'll make sure the world accepts her, too. Every noble family. Every man of ambition. Every woman with a daughter unwed.

She unfolds her hand, holds the coin to the candle's light twixt finger and thumb and watches it shimmer. Polished bold and bright as any coin of the kingdom, for all it's more tin than gold. A thing has the value we ascribe to it. Gold's gold if we say it is. She will polish Elizabeth to a lustre. There must be an earldom for her father and good marriages for her sisters and brothers. Her mother has old Burgundian blood. It's nothing much, God knows, but she can work with it.

Two weeks later, the work begins. Elizabeth is brought to Cecily at Reading, her mother simpering at her side. 'What a day, Cecily!' Jacquetta says. 'I can hardly believe it.'

'I'm struggling myself.'

'And, of course, this marriage between our families makes you and I something very like sisters.'

'Nothing like, Jacquetta,' Cecily says, peeling the lady's hand from her sleeve. 'Will you wait outside while I speak with your daughter?'

When the door has closed on Jacquetta's back, Cecily's attention returns to Elizabeth, who falls into a deep courtesy. Cecily, who had steeled herself to greet her son's wife as her equal, is, for a moment, wrong-footed.

'Get up,' she says softly. But Elizabeth doesn't move.

'Let me give you this dignity today,' Elizabeth says. 'As queen, I'm told, I need never kneel to you again. Or to any woman. I do it now to show my respect.' Then she tilts her head, looks up at Cecily through silver lashes and lets her perfectly carmined lips curve upwards. If she looked so at Edward, Cecily thinks, it's no wonder we find ourselves where we are today.

'Then since I'm never to have this experience again, let me make the most of it,' Cecily tells her. And while Elizabeth remains kneeling, she circles about her, taking in every inch. When she's done, she holds out a hand to help her rise. 'That was a pretty way to put us each in our places,' she says as their faces draw level. 'Who taught you such clever compliments?'

'My mother said . . .'

'I advise you, take no more lessons from her. She's skilled in courtship, which I'm sure has been useful to you, but not in queenliness. It's one thing to turn a young king's head with a smile. Quite another to wear a crown and win the respect of his nobles.'

As Elizabeth's cheeks pale, Cecily lays a hand on her arm. 'You think me discourteous. I'm not. You're my son's wife, his queen, so your success is in every way essential to me. I will be a friend to you. And a better teacher than your mother.'

Elizabeth swallows, testing, no doubt, the steadiness of her voice. It barely trembles when she answers, 'I will welcome the lesson, madam.'

'Good. Now, we must take you in hand. You're well enough dressed to be Jacquetta's daughter, but not nearly well enough to be mine.'

An hour later, when Elizabeth stands ready to be presented to the lords of England as their queen, her gilt hair is caught up in a net of gold, diamonds glint at her throat, and her gown – a rich river of purple flowing from her shoulders – is edged with ermine at wrist and hem.

'No other woman in England can wear this but you or I,' Cecily tells her, checking the fall of velvet over a flawless shoulder. 'The law forbids this colour, this fur, to all but the King's close kin.' Then she looks hard into her face, its perfect cheekbones, its high-plucked brow. 'Until now it's been enough for you to be beautiful. Now you must be so much more. You must look, act and think – every waking moment, always – like a queen.'

The bowed lips part. Almost, they tremble, and her breath catches. 'You will help me?'

Cecily finds herself smiling. 'Yes.' Then leads her out into the sunlight, and to the royal guardsmen who will bring them to the abbey, where King and company await.

'First to kneel to you will be the Earl of Warwick,' she tells her as they walk. 'He is second in power only to Edward. After him my son George Duke of Clarence, who is Edward's heir, till you give him a son. Once they are seen to do homage, all will follow.'

As the abbey doors are thrown open, and as music and expectation meet them in a wave, Elizabeth reaches for Cecily's hand and whispers, 'I think the Earl of Warwick doesn't like me.' But Cecily has already stepped back into her new place behind the Queen, and Elizabeth's fingers close on air.

'Then charm him, Elizabeth,' she whispers. 'You know how to do that.'

But there's little charm within the abbey. Only Warwick's stiff obeisance, the slightest tip of Elizabeth's narrow chin, and her look turned on him, lustrous but unsmiling. Then, when every man has come, lowered his head and backed away, Edward, at last, steps forward, lifts her hand as if it is a sacred thing, then turns to the crowd and into the silence says, 'My wife. Your queen.'

And, in that moment, Elizabeth appears every inch royal; rich, unknowable, untouchable and in every way desired. And if her hand grasps Edward's a little too tightly, if her breast rises and falls with shallow breaths, Cecily can imagine she alone sees it.

15.

Sunday, 11 February 1466

Westminster

Elizabeth's been here before, of course. The two sons she birthed for her first husband, that dead, un-mourned nobody, will have taught her the way of it. So Cecily expects the Queen to go about today's work in business-like fashion, as is her way. Cecily has taken time, since Reading, to study her daughter-in-law's way of doing things. Elizabeth, she has observed, pays careful attention to detail. She is a stickler for protocol, and insists, though graciously and with lowered eyes, that every respect due to her high office is paid in full. Though not born to queenliness, she studies hard to achieve it. Joan Peasemarsh, the lady Cecily has loaned to school Elizabeth in the manners of a sophisticated court, reports that her new mistress asks many questions, and makes careful note of the answers. That she makes few mistakes and none twice.

'Stands very high on her dignity though,' says Joan.

Cecily shrugs.

'Nervy, if you ask me. Tight as a bowstring.'

She'll be better after today, Cecily thinks. Providing she gives Edward a son.

So, when a messenger comes at dawn to tell her that the Queen's pains have begun, and that her barge stands manned and muscled to take her to Westminster and the royal lying-in, Cecily decides also to be business-like. She is, after all, more interested in the outcome than the labour and it will be hours yet. She thanks the messenger and leaves the barge bobbing on the river.

She goes to mass and breaks her fast. She discusses land transactions with her steward, reads her letters and makes reply. She visits the mews to check the progress of her falcon's moult. It all needs doing, and it all takes time.

So, when the doors open to admit her to the Queen's chambers, the noon bell is already ringing. In place of the women who usually attend here, there are only men, who have taken it upon themselves to loiter in the outer rooms, playing at cards, paring their nails, leaning against walls and talking in low voices. One of the card players is her son George. He looks up when she enters and away when she catches his eye. Well yes, thinks Cecily. You're waiting to see if you'll be as important tomorrow as you are today. As she crosses the room, the men pull themselves up to give her courtesy.

'What are you all doing here?' she asks, irritated.

'We're ready to carry good news to the King,' one suggests. 'If . . .' he waves towards the inner sanctuary, its guarded door, '. . . when there is good news to carry.'

'It takes a dozen of you, does it?'

She passes into the warm fug of the birthing chamber, where curtains are drawn against the winter sun, and the fire casts a watchful light. Here are the women. Some of them are praying, jewelled rosaries flickering between white fingers. One is drawing slow chords from a lute. The mood is more cautious than expectant, and there's no talk but for that directed to God. Jacquetta looks to Cecily and nods. She alone is standing while Elizabeth walks, watching every step as if eager to take them herself.

'Coming close and steady now, the pains,' Jacquetta says before Cecily can ask. 'Just as they should be.' Then, a little prideful, 'She bears them bravely.'

The Queen's pacing brings her close. Cecily gives her the courtesy she's due. Elizabeth makes to return it, but her belly won't let her and it becomes a halting bob.

'No need for that now,' says Cecily. 'Focus on the task.'

She sees her advice isn't needed. Elizabeth has the look all women have at every birthing but their first; turned in on herself, preparing for the ordeal to come in full knowledge of its rigour. The Queen nods, once, and moves on, then on again, from door to bedpost to fireplace, to her altar with its reliquaries, to the great gilded crib canopied with England's arms. She touches it as she passes, as if her fingertips alone can make good the promise of a prince.

'Come sit, Mother. It will be a while yet.' It's her own daughter, Anne, calling to her from across the room and clearing linens from a chair. Since none of Elizabeth's sisters are mothers they can't come into this place of women, so Cecily's eldest is here in their stead. She calls it her duty, to wait upon her brother's wife. God knows, she's been tutored well enough in that.

Cecily has had cause to be thankful for Anne's duty. It meant that, last month, when Cecily asked her to give her own little daughter in marriage to Elizabeth's eldest son, Thomas Grey, she knew better than to ask, 'Do I have a choice?'

She only said, 'What? My only child to nobody-son-of-nobody?'

'He isn't nobody now, is he?' Cecily reminded her. 'He's the King your brother's stepson. And, when he marries your daughter he'll be rich enough to be worth anyone's notice.'

'Well, Mother. You've always known the value of a good marriage.'

Cecily smiled, pretending to believe her daughter had made a joke. That she wasn't remembering the misery of her own union with Henry Holland, made for her by Cecily for the sake of a dukedom. He runs with Marguerite now so, as far as that, she's free of him.

'Anne, give me no trouble for this. It's only one of many marriages I must make for Edward's foolishness. It's tiresome work.'

'I'm sure you'll forgive him for it.'

'A king doesn't ask forgiveness. Nor does a king's mother grant it. She only does what must be done.'

Anne did smile then, a little and drily, and turned from the window. 'All right. But let Edward explain it to my cousin Warwick.' Anne's daughter, with her rich inheritance, had long been promised to Warwick's nephew, John Neville's son. They'd only been waiting for the boy to gain a little in age. He has, at present, only five years to the girl's ten. 'John himself will take it quietly as he takes all things, but Warwick's nose will be out of joint.'

'I dare say.'

Nor would this be the only blow to Warwick's nose. And the second would sting more. For all his great good fortune, Warwick has no sons, so his daughters, only two of them and no more likely, must marry men noble enough to raise his family higher. And when you're Warwick, and no man stands higher than you but the King, that means King's kin. For his eldest, Isabel, he'd wanted Henry Stafford, Cecily's sister's grandson. He's a catch. Ten years old and already Duke of Buckingham, likely the richest boy in England. Now promises made in good faith have been broken and Warwick's Isabel, who at fifteen is old enough to feel the slight, must give way to the Queen's eight-year-old sister, Katherine.

Cecily let Edward break that news to Warwick too. They had a shouting match over it, then clasped arms and got drunk. But Warwick's duchess came to Cecily the next day and dared to say, 'My Lord fears that your son seeks to untie every bond of love between our families.'

It was last May, when the sun was hot. The day after Elizabeth's crowning at Westminster, marked by a joust in which Anthony Woodville, in fine Italian armour he couldn't have afforded a year earlier, won everything. They walked the cinder paths between beds of herbs and gillyflowers, while the sound of steel on steel was carried to them from the lists.

'We undo nothing,' Cecily told her, stepping evenly. 'These bonds between children are never firmly tied. Nor is there any falling off of love.' Then, placatory, 'But you see how we're placed. The Queen's family must be raised.'

'I see it, Cecily, well enough. But my Lord sees only other men, less worthy men, raised at his expense. First Henry Beaufort, now the Woodvilles, a family he's more used to facing across a battlefield than a tiltyard. A family that fought for Lancaster when his father was slain.'

'And my husband,' Cecily reminds her. 'And my son. If I can stomach it, he can.'

'It irks him to see Woodville children made duchesses and dukes by marriage, while he, who has given so much for York, remains an earl.'

Cecily has often been proud of her hold on her temper. Never more than at that moment. Her voice was as soft as her step.

'By Edward's gift, your lord is Captain of Calais, Admiral and Chamberlain of England and the King's Lieutenant in the north. He is Earl of Warwick and Salisbury, both. And let's look at his brothers now. John is made Earl of Northumberland. George is Edward's chancellor, and if power on earth isn't enough for him, I hear he's soon to be named Archbishop of York. Power in Heaven too. So, if preferments and high honours are proof of love, your lord – and all his kin, surely – hold the King's heart in their hands.'

'And yet,' said Warwick's wife. 'My lord asks, "To whom shall I marry my daughters, when there's a Woodville in every noble bed?"'

'There are young men, surely.'

Then it was as if her old friend had screwed up her courage and must speak or lose it. She held up a hand, which trembled only a little.

'He'll ask for the King's brothers, Cecily. Your George for Isabel. Your Richard for my Anne.'

Cecily almost laughed, certain it was a jest. But she saw the lady's face, pinched and determined, and said, 'You must counsel him, very firmly, against that.'

'I know.' She shook her head. 'I mean, I know he shouldn't ask now. I've told him so. Not while they're the King's heirs. But with Edward married, and when Elizabeth gives him a son, then surely, they'll be . . .'

Cecily's voice was cold. 'They'll still be the King's brothers. They'll still be my sons. We'll make marriages for them to strengthen England, not to slake your husband's ambition.'

'My husband might say that, all these years, he has been England's strength. That he fought harder than any to put your son on the throne. He would say,' she drew a breath, 'a bond of marriage between our families would make England invincible.'

Cecily held up a hand. 'It is too close. My final word. Tell your husband.'

At that moment a great cry went up from the tiltyard, a clash of metal and a breaking of lances. They stood to listen as the applause subsided, heard the distant heralds call the scores, then a waiting hush. If she had been watching from her seat in the stands she couldn't have felt it more keenly; the rising tension that comes when metalled fists draw horses, tight-reined and snorting, back to the lists. Then the reach for fresh weapons, the cupping of the lance, the bunching of sweat-slick haunches at the turn, the muscled push and spurring on, the headlong gallop. She held her breath until it came again, the crash and cry and roar. At the peak of the noise, in the heat of the day, with the sun on her back and the sky blazing, she felt her flesh chill at the thought of Warwick's ambition, his hunger for every proof of love.

There is no chill now. This room is stifling, and the maid is feeding another log to the fire that must burn always to ward the devil from the open door of the Queen's body. And still, Elizabeth walks. Three more times around, three touches to the crib, three prayers for a son, and then the midwife calls to her, draws her to the bed, parts her knees, looks and feels and says, 'Not yet.'

So Elizabeth walks again, her long gilt braid roping down her back, her bare fingers netted below her belly, her shift clinging.

And at every turn, Cecily remembers other marriages she's made for this moment; Elizabeth's sisters to the earldoms of Essex, Arundel, Kent and Pembroke. Cecily's own thrice-widowed sister, Katherine, seventy, if she lives another year, to Elizabeth's brother John, fresh-faced and twenty. Warwick called it diabolical. Katherine herself laughed and said, 'Why not?' Then, more seriously, 'As long as you don't expect me to bed him.'

'I think he'll be happy with the inheritance when you die,' Cecily assured her.

Marriages, land and titles, all poured into Woodville laps. The golden Woodville, Elizabeth's father, the man himself, is Earl Rivers now, Treasurer of England. And every Woodville boy knighted. Cecily can see why Warwick is resentful. She's resentful, too.

On the next turn, at the touch of the crib, there's a groan and Elizabeth sinks to her knees, falls forward to all fours and gives her first stuttering cry, 'Jesus, Mary!' Cecily feels the pull of it in her own dry womb. It's a lie, she thinks, that women forget the pain. The memory of it, the certainty of its coming again, is heavy on Elizabeth now. Her mother and the midwife are lifting her to her feet, bringing her to the bed. She doesn't want to go. 'No,' she says, 'here.'

She wants to be on her knees again, to writhe on the floor and push. Cecily understands that, the animal urge.

'A queen doesn't give birth like a dog on the ground,' her mother chides.

So Elizabeth rises and goes to the bed and doesn't contest or cry out again as she labours, until the midwife says at last, 'Push now. Bear down!' and the women flock about her on their knees with talismans and prayers, and Jacquetta, a veteran of fourteen childbeds, supports Elizabeth's body in her arms, pulls sweat-drenched hair from her face and whispers to her that she's brave and strong and a queen.

And Cecily, fixed in her seat, can only watch, her rosary bound tight among her fingers, as Elizabeth's muscles tighten and her bare teeth clench in effort.

'Give her a boy,' Cecily prays silently, as the beads pass between finger and thumb. 'For all I've done and had taken from me. Give her a son like my Edward. So that England can have an heir and my house be secure. And so I can give, if I have to, one of my own boys to Warwick for his wretched daughters to squabble over.'

'Once more!' says the midwife, and Elizabeth howls and pushes until a new cry joins hers, high and hungry. And Cecily is on her feet now, straining for a view over the other women's shoulders. At last, between the Queen's quivering thighs, she sees it: a body, slick and squirming, cupped in the midwife's broad hand, its mouth working, its tiny fists pummelling the air, the coiling cord that binds it to its mother gorged with royal blood and there, between its flailing legs, the thin cleft of a girl.

16.

May 1466

London

Warwick, of course, already has one of Cecily's sons in his keeping. Young Richard was sent to him after Elizabeth was crowned. A sop to Warwick's pride. 'A sign of trust and love,' Edward called it. 'The honour of training my brother in the arts of lordship and war.'

'I hope that's all he learns,' Cecily grumbled to Annette then. 'I hope he doesn't learn Warwick's swagger. I hope he doesn't come back in love with himself as Warwick is.' Now she only hopes his head isn't turned. That he doesn't learn to love the earl his cousin better than his brother the King.

She's comforted that he writes to her weekly. Diligent, and in his own neat hand. 'My Lady Mother,' he begins. And then an account of his days. Through him, she walks again the great strongholds of Barnard Castle, Sheriff Hutton, Middleham and Bolton. Castles she knew as a girl when her brother ruled the north from them, that now belong to Warwick, her brother's son. She rides beside him through a landscape where every man wears Warwick's livery. Where Warwick is the law and people love him. Where any poor man can come knocking at his kitchen door and leave with as much meat as he can carry on his dagger. With such charity, she knows, he buys men's hearts. Ask a North-man who rules him and he's as like to say Warwick as the King. And then add, 'God bless him.' It used not to worry her.

Richard writes of his lessons. He's reading Lull's *Order of Chivalry*, which urges faith, good sense and strength of arm in the making of a knight. He's learning the rules of disputation and the practice of diplomacy. He's training hard, he tells her. He's fitted for armour and learning to bear its weight. He prefers the axe to the sword. He spars with the wards and squires of Warwick's household, keeps careful count of the bouts, and reports all to her, even his losses, the causes of which he examines meticulously. 'To eradicate my errors,' he says.

In February he rode with Warwick and John Neville all through Wensleydale, taking the assizes from town to town.

'Justice was given in my name, as Duke of Gloucester,' he told her. 'Though my cousins decided what that should be. But, in every case, they asked my opinion and tested my knowledge of the law. Many times, they approved my judgements.' A touch of pride, there.

Then they took him to the great Abbey at Rievaulx, where the monks breed horses for the King. 'My uncle Warwick bought me a destrier colt,' he writes. 'And I'm to have the training of him.'

More recently he's been to York and lit candles in its great minster, for her and for all his family. For Edward and his queen. 'And for my father, whose city it was.'

She shows his letters to Edward.

'I don't need to read them,' he says. 'He writes to me, too.' It's evening and he's drinking by her fire at Baynard's. The days are warm, but there's an evening chill off the river. 'He's very earnest.'

'Yes. He is.'

'Was I, at his age?'

She looks at the length of his legs, crossed at the ankle, stretching into her hearth. 'No, Edward. You were always a feckless fool.' She says such things for the sheer pleasure of seeing him grin. 'Richard is like his father.'

'Aah, well. No bad thing.'

Edward's quiet a while, turning the wine cup in his hands. She knows it to be a prelude to a more serious conversation.

'You didn't come to hear me talk about Richard's adventures in the north, did you?'

'No,' he says, 'I didn't.'

'Then why?'

He sits forward, puts down the cup and spreads his hands. 'I've come to talk about a decision. A choice.'

'Must I make up your mind for you?'

'No. I've done that. But I want you to know my thinking. It's likely to cause . . . what can I say? Family problems.'

She puts down Richard's letter, gives her attention wholly to him. 'Well, Warwick returned from his embassy yesterday. So I assume it's to do with him.'

Edward's face clouds, the ghost of anger subdued but not forgotten.

In March, Edward sent Warwick to Burgundy to talk about a wedding.

Though Burgundy's Duchess Isabella and her husband Philip have long been friends to Cecily's house, their son, Charles, has always favoured Lancaster over York. But now Charles's father is on his deathbed and France is threatening him with war, so he needs an ally. So, he seeks a closer alliance with Edward's England and, since his wife is dead, offers to seal it with a marriage to Edward's sister, Meg. Warwick's job was simple enough: negotiate the terms. Edward wants greater access to Burgundian trade as well as a romance. On both counts, he tells Cecily now, Warwick has failed entirely.

'He was, perhaps, not your best choice of ambassador. You know very well he favours France.'

'Yes. So I sent Hastings with him as a steadying influence.'

'So what went wrong?'

'Warwick tells me Charles wouldn't offer enough on trade. But Hastings tells me the talks fell apart when Charles suggested that, if he was to make my sister Duchess of Burgundy, he'd like me to make his daughter Duchess of Clarence.'

'He wants George for his daughter?' Charles's dead wife left him a girl to remember her by. She's almost ten. High time she was wed.

'Reciprocal marriages. My sister for himself. My brother for his daughter.'

She considers a moment. 'No. George is your heir. If you die it would make her Queen of England.'

'I'm not planning to die. But Warwick didn't refuse the match for my sake.'

'Ah.' She looks sideways at him, testing what he knows. 'You'll have guessed by now that he wants George for his own Isabel.'

'Which I'll allow when hell freezes over.'

'So, Warwick left Burgundy empty-handed. What next?'

'He puts Hastings on a boat to England and saunters straight off to Louis in Paris.'

'And what gifts does he bring you from there?'

'An extension to our current truce with France, if I care to sign it.'

'Well, that's useful.'

'And Louis's agreement not to support Marguerite against us, if we don't support Burgundy against him.'

'Oh yes?' sniffs Cecily. 'For as long as that suits him.'

For a year or more mad Henry's been under lock and key in the Tower, taken when travelling between safe houses on the Scottish border. But that matters little while Marguerite's still on the loose, dragging her son around the courts of Europe. She knocks hard on the doors of France and Brittany, begging help to take England back, promising much in return when it's done. Louis may not be listening for now, but Cecily knows that could change.

Edward shrugs. 'Well, it suits him at the moment. Louis wants no war with me while he's planning one with Burgundy.'

'Then you're his friend. For now.'

'As I might be friends with a scorpion.'

'One who throws his arms wide in welcome then turns up his tail to sting?'

'Indeed.'

The tension that's been building in him as they talked now brings him to his feet. He prowls to the open window, leans out to catch the evening breeze, his arms spread wide to span the embrasure.

'Warwick brings back terms for much more than a truce with France. Louis offers a treaty of perpetual peace.'

She speaks to his back. 'Does he now? Well, since peace would be a welcome thing, I assume it's the terms you dislike?'

He turns to face her, raises his hands in mock applause. 'Oh, no, Mother, I stand to gain mightily! A French marriage for Meg instead of Burgundian one, which Louis will finance entirely, no dowry required, and a pension of forty thousand crowns a year for myself.'

'That's generous. He must want a great deal in return.'

He returns to his chair, sits again, leans towards her very close, his hands loose-clasped between his knees. 'Yes. That he and I join forces in a war that will utterly annihilate Burgundy.'

'Ah.'

'I'd rather, you know, fight against France than beside France.'

'I'm sure. And that's exactly what Louis fears you'll do one day. With Burgundy at your side, you might think yourself strong enough to do it.'

'With Burgundy at my side, perhaps I will be.'

She smiles.

'There's more.'

She waits.

'When Louis and I have defeated Burgundy it will be divided, and a share of it – Holland, Zeeland, Brabant – will come to England.' She raises an eyebrow, he lifts a finger for her attention. 'But not to me, Captain Mother. Oh, no. For his good services in uniting our great realms, Warwick is to be rewarded with the marriage of his daughter Isabel to my brother George. And the Burgundian lands are to be their marriage portion. Warwick tells me this was all Louis's idea.'

'Ah.' She sees now the game in play, the sly twists and turns of it. Her eyes narrow against the heat of the fire.

'Well?' He is waiting for her word.

'Louis,' she tells him, looking up, 'is very good at tempting vain men with the desires of their hearts. He knows you'll say no, and he'll use that no to drive a wedge between Warwick and yourself. It suits him to have the house of York at odds with itself.'

He folds his arms, spreads his feet. 'He's a tricky bastard.'

'You might say that,' she shrugs. 'Or you might say he's mastered one of the great skills of diplomacy: keep your enemies always divided, too occupied with suspicion and division to ever turn their hungry eyes your way. Surely you see what he's thinking? Fight with me against Burgundy. Or fight among yourselves.'

'Warwick would never fight me. He's the brother of my heart.'

'Let's hope you're right. Your challenge will be to find a way to say no to Louis that won't drive Warwick further into his arms. And be careful of your brother. See how he stands to gain by this. Warwick plays on George's vanity just as Louis plays on his.'

'George is just a boy,' says Edward, dismissive.

'He's nearly seventeen, Edward. With nothing to do all day except listen to people tell him how important he is. Put him to work. And keep him out of Warwick's way. And keep Warwick close. If you love him as you say you do, find a way to appease him.'

He considers, then speaks. 'I'm not worried about George, he'll do as he's told.' He stands again, belligerent. 'And I'll appease Warwick only so far. My choice is Burgundy and my choice stands.'

'All right,' she says carefully.

'My wife is half Burgundian, after all.'

'Surely not helpful to remind Warwick of that.'

'Meg will marry Charles. And Louis can go to hell. And if Warwick won't tell him so, I will.'

'Oh, Edward.' She shakes her head.

The fire has burned down so she rises, leans to put fresh wood on it. Straightening she feels a pain in her back and puts her hand to it. She's growing old, past fifty now, and has spent her life watching the barbed dance between England, Burgundy and France. Is she the only one who remembers the steps?

'Listen. Burgundy's your choice. Good. It's mine too. But not for your wife's sake or because I imagine Charles loves us. Burgundy needs us to fend off France. France needs us to threaten Burgundy. We're three countries spoiling for a fight, and none of us strong enough to win alone. So we keep each other guessing, we talk out of both sides of our mouths, we never declare our hands.'

She turns now to face him. 'Ally with Burgundy, Edward, yes. Make Meg its duchess. Good. She'll be England's ears there and keep Charles in line – or at least let us know when he's out of it. But sign Louis's truce too – you know you must. And on the subject of perpetual peace, keep talking, keep him dangling. Don't give him reason or opportunity to turn your cousin Warwick into a weapon to be used against us.'

17.

June 1466 to August 1467

So Edward ratifies Warwick's truce, and before all the council thanks him for his good service in France, kisses him on both cheeks, and calls him beloved cousin. Behind closed doors, he tells him he may talk to Louis all he wishes, that he should, for England's sake. 'But there'll be no war with Burgundy,' he tells him. 'Though, of course, you needn't tell Louis that.' He looks him in the eye then. 'And be very sure of this: though I love you, I have no other marriages in mind for my family than Meg's to Burgundy.'

Warwick complains of it to Cecily. He comes to the chambers she keeps in Westminster, blustering, belligerent, shouldering the air. When he finally stops shouting, she urges him to patience. 'You know how the political tides turn, Nephew. Burgundy today. Tomorrow, who knows? Edward relies on you to keep Louis guessing.'

'But this disregard for France! This favouritism for Burgundy.' His fist to his forehead, spit on his lip. 'That bitch the Queen breeds it in him. Her and her leeching Woodville kin.'

Cecily places a hand on his shoulder, comforting, consoling, as if a co-conspirator. 'Well, young men are often very foolish for love . . .'

'Ha!'

'. . . but, believe me, Edward understands very well the game we play with France. And trusts you as its most accomplished player.'

'I should think so.' He nods, grudging, mollified a little, before he shrugs his shoulder from beneath her hand. She feels the thrum of anger fading in him. 'But it's thankless work.'

Her hand to her heart. 'Then I thank you.' Her smile bears every sign of sincerity.

Next summer Edward welcomes Antoine, Charles of Burgundy's bastard brother, to London. He's come to talk of Meg's marriage, and to make a great show of love between England and Burgundy; to remind England what a great land its queen's ancestors hail from.

'We must do something to make people love her, I suppose,' Cecily says to Meg.

'Spit and polish,' says Meg. 'Shine her up.'

There's a great tournament at Smithfield; the best of Burgundy and the bravest of England turn the arts of war into a game. It's designed to show the world – and Louis, if his spies are watching – how good they are at playing it.

Elizabeth is flanked by her mothers as she comes into the lists; by Cecily, of course, and by Jacquetta, whose father, as she always reminds everyone, was a Burgundian prince. Well, a count, but let's not quibble. And, indeed, Elizabeth appears buffed and shining; swelling with another child, carrying high, her face beneath the steepled henin framed by cloth of silver. She's good at entrances, Cecily concedes. Chin up, eyes down. As she walks between the rows of bowing nobles she rests a hand on the roundness of her belly, a demure gesture that proclaims to all that their lusty king has got his wife with child again. Surely this time a prince?

When she comes to her place in the great stand, when Edward reaches out a hand to her and she raises her eyes to take it, the sight of them together is as potent as a spell. Across the field, men shift and women sigh as Edward turns her to face them, and into the breathless silence shouts, 'Your queen!' Then the crowd roars and Edward grins. And the Lord Antoine, Charles of Burgundy's beloved brother, falls to his knees at Elizabeth's feet.

It's said no man is Antoine's equal in the joust, so he's pitched against the Queen's brother Anthony, who says the same about himself. They both carry the Queen's favours into the contest, for each has pledged his honour to her beauty. They fight on horseback and on foot, with sword and axe and dagger. In every bout they come to a draw, equal in chivalry. And when all's done, pledge never to fight again. Burgundy and England, brothers in arms.

It's a spectacle that would turn Warwick's stomach were he there to witness it. But he's with Louis again in Rouen. Rumours fly the Channel that he is much fêted there, that Louis himself came to the mouth of the Seine to greet him, that they entered Rouen together, arm in arm. And that Marguerite was in King Louis's company.

'What the fuck's that all about?' Edward asks Cecily, enraged.

'Louis playing his divisive games,' says Cecily, cross. 'He's reminding Warwick that Marguerite's husband still lives – and has a son – which you still don't, I might add. And that that husband might rule England, if Warwick chose to put him back on the throne.'

'He overplays his hand there. Warwick'll tear the old bitch's head off!'

But when the rumour runs that Warwick and Marguerite found much to speak of, Edward's rattled enough to take a tilt at his old friend. He rides across London himself, demands the Great Seal from Warwick's brother George Neville, gives it to Robert Stillington, and the chancellorship of England changes hands, just like that.

'Edward,' demands Cecily, 'what do you think you're doing?'

'I'm reminding Warwick that his family's high offices depend on the English king, not the French one,' says Edward.

Then Warwick comes back with a French embassy in tow offering fresh concessions from Louis, and Edward sends them straight back over the Channel again, empty-handed. Humiliated and enraged, Warwick stomps off to his own lands and, when summoned to a council, says he'll come to no place where Edward surrounds himself with Woodville leeches who rob his family of the favour due to them, that lead his king into folly and his country towards ruin.

'This is a very great way to make peace with the brother of your heart,' she scolds. She's taken the trouble to come to Windsor. The river was stinking, the weather as hot as her temper. His servants made themselves scarce at the mere sight of her. 'Do you want a war?'

'If Warwick is talking with Marguerite, I have nothing to say to him,' says Edward, petulant.

'Oh, Edward!' Her voice is scathing, even to her own ears. 'Louis only put them in a room together. It's you that's driving them to talk.'

'I'm his king!'

'Yes, and a swaggering fool. Just as he is. And you're both playing into Louis's hands.'

When he turns from her she carries on talking to his back. 'Edward of England and the Earl of Warwick. A partnership Louis knows he can't beat. So, he finds cracks in your friendship and widens them to chasms. Marguerite's only the latest wedge he drives between you.'

'One day,' he bellows, beating fist against chest, 'I will lead an army into France.'

'And win another Agincourt?' she sneers. 'Oh yes, I dare say.'

'And Warwick can fight with me or against me. His choice.'

'That's your answer to everything, is it? Fists up, bloody noses all round? Grow up, Edward! You can't afford to fight France and you can't afford to make an enemy of Warwick. Nor will you, if you've any sense.'

He turns back to her, slumps into a chair. He'd been out shooting at the butts before she came, and has yet to change his shirt; it clings to him and his hair sticks damply to his forehead. He clasps his hands over his brow to push it back. 'I don't know.' And suddenly he just looks sad. 'When I was young I wanted nothing more than Warwick's love. To be like him.'

'Well, you've grown. So what now?'

'I'm my own man now. King. He must learn that.'

'Yes,' she tells him. 'He must. But you've made him too powerful to curb him too quickly. I'll give you a rule, Edward, one your father taught me, take it to heart. Only fight when you have to. Though always look ready, and as if you would win.'

She leans forward, curls his hand into a fist and holds it. There's nothing soft there; a handy fist to carry a punch, as nicked and scarred as any fighter's is. She opens the palm and runs fingers across sword calluses.

'Keep your sword sharp, Edward, likely you'll need it one day. But fight with your head first.'

18.

August 1467

Windsor

She goes from Edward to Elizabeth, who was churched from her second childbed two weeks ago. She keeps herself quiet, still. Edward says she's resting. Cecily thinks she's keeping her head down. Another girl isn't much to boast about. Mary, named for the virgin. A strong babe and thriving, with her mother's silver gilt hair lying soft on her brow.

When they visit the nursery together, and Cecily compliments Elizabeth on its fairness, the Queen looks at the child guzzling in the wet nurse's arms and shrugs. 'She's a babe. Likely it will darken,' then moves away to let Cecily gaze. But little Lizzie, eighteen months old now and toddling, pulls herself up by the nurse's skirts and stretches a chubby finger to stroke her sister's cheek. The nurse cups the girl's face and smiles, first at her, then at Cecily. 'She's besotted with her baby sister, dear thing.'

It's as well someone is, thinks Cecily. We'd all be, were she a boy

When Cecily looks up Elizabeth is already at the door. 'Come,' she says, beckoning. 'It's hot. We'll walk in the garden.'

They come outside, not to the close-kept garden, which holds the sun, but on to the terraces above the vineyard, where a breeze from the river brings fresher air. Looking down, Cecily can see her barge standing ready to take her home, the oarsmen loitering in the sun. She'd like to be gone but, for the first time, has a request to make of her queen. It's irksome to be a supplicant, so she asks plainly if Elizabeth can do nothing to help heal the breach between Edward and Warwick.

'My husband's affairs are his own,' Elizabeth answers. 'I treat the Lord Warwick – and his people – with respect. What more should I do?'

It sounds like more would need to be drawn from her with pincers.

'And yet, I've heard that, among your own people, and even to Edward himself, you speak disparagingly of him. And scathingly of his policy.'

'I think you yourself don't like his policy.'

Cecily concedes. 'No. Not always.'

'Yet you tolerate him. You entreat for him, to me.'

'For Edward's sake. Warwick is Edward's oldest friend. And a powerful ally . . .'

'And your nephew.'

'That hardly signifies.'

They've come to the end of the terrace. Elizabeth stops and looks out across the fall of ground where workmen are moving bolts of timber. 'We're extending the deer park. Edward says you're a great one for the hunt. You should come another day and ride with him.'

Now this becomes tiresome. 'I will. Thank you for not thinking me too old for it.' She smiles but won't be deflected. 'But while I'm still young enough I'd rather speak of Warwick. It harms Edward to be estranged from him.'

Elizabeth turns suddenly to face her. Cecily sees that her patience, too, is stretched, and that she's less skilled at hiding it.

'Then if we must speak of Warwick,' Elizabeth says, 'I'll speak plain. He resents my family. He calls my father an upstart and me a bitch. He says I won Edward's heart with witchcraft, that my mother and I are thick in it.'

Lord, Cecily thinks, Warwick is a blabbermouth. 'A queen would do well to rise above such things.'

'You think so?'

'A woman with a face like yours has no need of spells.'

When flattery doesn't work she turns to pragmatism. 'And besides, which of us hasn't been called witch when we've out-foxed men to get what we want? Do you imagine Warwick is the only man who wonders why Edward married you when he could have had any woman in Christendom?'

'Oh, madam, I could name you another.' Elizabeth's eyes are flashing now. 'The Earl of Warwick says these things in the company of your son, George. Who is Edward's heir. Still. And I'm told that George, yes, your son George, laughs at it.'

'I'd like to know who tells you these things.'

'It is the common talk.'

'Do you imagine there is common talk that I don't hear of?'

Elizabeth's face is pale with rage. 'Oh, I think you hear it. I think you give your family licence to disparage your queen!'

'My queen!'

It's laughable really. She's always thought of Elizabeth as Edward's queen, the Queen, England's. Never her own. Well, if the day demands it she'll concede the point. Elizabeth's chin is raised, defiant, her hands balled into fists. But the effort of it is obvious and there's fear in her eyes, and hurt.

In her heart conceding nothing, Cecily takes a breath and falls into a deep obeisance. 'You are,' she says, 'every inch my queen.'

She hears a sob and rises to find Elizabeth's face threatened by tears. Dear God.

'Shall we sit?' She draws Elizabeth to a stone bench against the wall, waits for her to grow calm, then speaks.

'Now I too will be plain. Elizabeth, you've made yourself queen . . .'

'No,' Elizabeth corrects, urgent. 'Edward made me queen. He raised me up.'

'Yes, well, that's a good enough story for the court. Edward and Elizabeth, the love that couldn't be denied. But between ourselves, I think, we'll own the truth. You made yourself queen. Not by witchcraft or tricks, but by your own power. Because you wanted it.'

Elizabeth gasps a little, puts her hand to her mouth. She is, Cecily sees, shocked to have her actions understood, laid bare. 'And if I did?' she asks, a whisper.

'Then hold your nerve.'

Really, it's like teaching a child. But she has Elizabeth's attention now.

'Listen. I didn't want your marriage. You know that. But I've done a very great deal to promote your queenship. Not for your sake, but for Edward's. And for England's. And I'll continue to do it. There. That's my promise. You can be sure I don't make it lightly.'

Elizabeth nods, looks down at her fingers twisted in her lap.

'But now,' says Cecily sitting back, 'I ask a promise in return.'

'What?'

'Don't stoke this discontent between Edward and Warwick. You can't gain from it and Edward could lose much. I'll tolerate no disparagement of you within my family, you have my word. But because you're queen, and because your husband holds you in such high esteem . . .'

'Loves me.'

'Yes, all right, if you prefer. Then you can afford to be gracious. To ignore such little slights as these.'

Elizabeth turns a face to her that's now more bitter than tearful. 'Do you think? With only daughters in my cradle?'

'Then keep at it. Get a son.'

19.

June 1468

London

If the honour of escorting Meg to her marriage with Burgundy is intended as a peace offering, it is ill-chosen and grudgingly accepted. 'I'll take her as far as the coast,' Warwick concedes when Edward asks him. 'I've no wish to cross to Burgundy.'

When Elizabeth then suggests that her brother Anthony should step in, and Edward agrees, Cecily wants to strangle her and slap him. It makes some sense though, she supposes. While Warwick has spent the year sulking, Anthony's been in Burgundy, finalizing the marriage arrangements, bartering the dowry. With his father now dead, Charles is Duke of Burgundy in fact, so his price has gone up. Edward has borrowed heavily to pay it, but still won't stint his sister's send-off. A Burgundian alliance sealed by a royal marriage, he says, is a thing the whole country should celebrate. And all the family too, of course. So when Warwick rides down from the north, he brings young Richard with him, whose horse barely comes to a halt before he's off it and on his knees to his brother the King, who sweeps him into a back-slapping embrace. He's fifteen now, but if Cecily was hoping for more height he's not achieved it. He barely reaches Edward's shoulder, and even George looks down on him. But he comes to her confidently and kisses her hand.

'Glad to be back?' she asks him.

He smiles his wry chess-playing smile. 'Very much. The weather in the north, you know . . .'

'The weather? Outdoors or in?'

He lets his eyes slide across the courtyard to where Warwick greets his king without an embrace.

'Both,' he says. 'Best to be out of it.'

On the five-day journey to the Kent coast, Cecily rides with her daughters. Meg in place of honour, of course. Side by side ahead of them ride Warwick and Anthony Woodville in place of equal dignity, and before them, Edward and his queen, flanked by his royal brothers. But as the road and the hours stretch out full of dust and sun, Edward can't be still. He's up and down the line to speak to this man or that, or challenging his brothers to a race. He draws back to ride with Cecily sometimes, or to tease his sister with tales of husbands and wedding nights. When he does, Anthony moves up to chatter with his sister and Warwick inserts himself between Cecily's younger sons.

They are fêted in every town they pass through and, in every village, people come from their houses to gawp at their king and farewell their princess. Meg accepts their attentions graciously, calm as she ever is, long-backed and fine, riding side-saddle in the new fashion. Cecily is so proud of her, and feels her heart divided between triumph and grief. Her daughter will be Duchess of Burgundy, a great lady of that polished court, which Cecily visited so long ago with her husband, her true Richard, not his son, who rides before her now stretching narrow shoulders in the sun. She wishes that first Richard were here to share the glory of it. He would chide her sorrow and remind her that she has achieved all she desired.

I suppose I have, she admits to him in her heart. But there's no rest in it, is there, it's only you who gets to sleep in peace.

She puts spur to flank and pushes forward to place herself between George and Warwick, who ride, she thinks, too close. She interrupts whatever occupies them with talk of trivial matters: the heat of the road, the breeding of their horses, last night's dinner. She pretends not to notice how they bridle and shift.

On the last night of the journey, they are guests of the Benedictines. They've ridden from that order's great abbey at Canterbury, then to this grange, their coastal outpost. They've dined within sound of the sea and now, from her casement, Cecily can hear the tide begin its fall. In the morning, when it rises again, it will take the last of her daughters from her, and because she can no longer imagine ever leaving England, she fears she'll never see her again. So, as the sun sets across the wheat fields, she goes to her. Arriving at Meg's chamber door she's surprised to hear voices from within, and more surprised when she knocks and Richard opens. He has cards in his hand. When she raises an eyebrow at them he only says, 'Mustn't let Meg see. She's a terrible cheat.'

From her seat by the open window Meg laughs. 'I must be terrible indeed, because he's winning. Again.'

He smiles, then shrugs and says he's sorry, though he doesn't look it. They've been playing Ronfle, their tricks are laid out beside their places either side of a table. The vacant place, Richard's, has more.

'Not chess?' Cecily asks, coming around to look at Meg's hand.

'No,' Meg tells her. 'I'm too jittery for that.'

Cecily nods, walks back to where Richard stands by his chair, and prises the cards an inch or so from his chest. 'She'll beat you this time,' she tells him. And Meg grins.

'Then I might as well say goodnight,' he decides, and bows to his mother. 'I expect, anyway, that you want to talk with Meg.'

Of course, she does. But, when he's gone, closing the door softly behind him, it's hard to speak. She only watches her daughter gathering the cards, picking up each trick, smoothing them into the pack.

'He's been telling me all he knows of Burgundy,' Meg explains. 'And of Charles. He met him there, of course.'

'Seven years ago, when he was still a child. I'm not sure what he could tell you.'

'Well, no, and those were dangerous days. But I trust him to give an honest account. When I ask Anthony Woodville about my husband he says he's a paragon of Christian virtue. When I ask cousin Warwick he tells me he's a monster, as like to kill me in my bed as pleasure me there.'

'Their opinions on any matter rarely match.'

Meg shrugs. 'I imagine the truth is somewhere in between.'

Cecily has always felt her own good fortune. She wasn't asked to wed a man she'd never known. She was married at eight, bedded at fifteen. She'd had time between to learn her husband's nature and find it a match for her own. Meg, she knows, can only guess at her husband's character, and at twenty-four her own is already set.

'Do you fear it?'

Meg pauses, places the cards in their felt bag, draws the cord around it. 'No.' She puts her head on one side. 'Richard warns me Charles has a temper. That he can be rash.' Then she smiles, sly. 'But, he confirms he's handsome, which is helpful, and that he listens to his mother, which is encouraging.' The cards are sealed. She puts them aside, clasps her hands. 'I dare say I'll manage well enough.'

'I'm sure of it. You'll be Duchess of Burgundy.' She feels the prick of tears behind her eyes. 'And every hour in my prayers.' She leans across, lays her hand on Meg's. 'I wish I could be there to see it.'

Suddenly Meg's fingers close on hers, urgent. 'Well, you could, of course, come to my wedding.'

She lets herself imagine it for just a moment, crossing the sea with Meg, to see with her the great palaces of Dijon and Bruges. To say, 'Here I danced with your father long before you were born.'

To see her dance there, young and beautiful as she herself was then. But she shakes her head. 'No,' she says. 'I can't.'

'Why?' Meg asks, then shakes away the question and the point-lessness of asking it. She softens her hold on Cecily's hand. 'No. I know. You're right. Not while things here are so . . .' she struggles for the word '. . . uncertain.'

'This trouble between Edward and Warwick . . .'

'Yes.' Meg looks away a moment, then back, and speaks in a troubled voice to their joined hands. 'And George, all caught up between them. Keep an eye on him when I'm gone.'

Cecily hasn't spoken of this to Meg, but isn't surprised she's guessed. She has a sense for trouble and where it comes from. 'Oh well.' She really doesn't want to speak of George tonight. 'He resents that Edward won't let him marry Warwick's daugh-ter. Myself, I lack patience for it. He can marry where he likes when Edward has a son.'

'Then poor George,' says Meg. 'If Elizabeth gives Edward an heir, he's dispossessed. If she doesn't, he'll never be free. It's not a happy position.'

'As Warwick reminds him daily, I'm sure.'

'Yes. And I'm sure George listens.'

Her daughter's face is all earnest now, looking up at her.

'And have you concluded, as I have, that this is a danger to us?' Cecily asks.

'I very much fear,' Meg answers, 'that it's a danger to George.'

'Only if he's foolish.'

'I think we both know he is.'

She nods. 'Well, yes.' Then her thoughts turn to Richard, play-ing at cards, winning tricks. 'So what of your other brother then? He's been in Warwick's household three years now. What does Warwick say to him? And does he listen?'

Meg leans back, lets go her mother's hand. 'Oh,' she sighs. 'You needn't worry about Richard.'

Cecily presses, 'Why?'

Meg thinks for a moment, then speaks. 'You'll have noticed that he wears Father's ring on his finger now?'

Cecily shakes her head. She hadn't. It's been on a cord about his neck, that old bull's blood ruby, ever since his father gave it to him, three weeks before he died.

'He's had it adjusted to fit. You should get him to show you what he's had engraved inside the band.'

So, next morning, when Meg's ship is nothing but a speck against blue sky and wide sea, and Cecily's heart is as hollow as a drum, she walks with Richard from the quayside and asks. He takes it off, and lays it easily in her hand; this soft rub of gold, so well-remembered. But it's changed. There are ten nubs about its band now, raised from its smooth surface. He points to them. 'My Aves,' he tells her, then to the ruby. 'My Pater Noster. It guides my prayers.' She tests them with her finger, then turns the ring and reads within: *loyalty binds me.*

She looks from it to him, where he stands, his hands behind his back, his face appraising.

'And to whom does it bind you?' she asks.

He brings a hand around to lift the ring from her palm, places it about his heart finger, pushes it firmly down, stretches his hand and examines it. 'To my brother the King, of course.' He lets his hand fall and walks thoughtful beside her a stride or two before he speaks again. 'Feel free to tell him so. I've told the Earl of Warwick myself.'

20.

June 1469

Port of Sandwich

The Earl of Warwick has built a ship. Its smell of fresh tar sears Cecily's nose and the caulking of its timbers shines glossy in the sun. She's arrived too late, the harbour master tells her, as sorry as he can be. 'It was finished and blessed for the sea two days ago by George Neville, the Archbishop of York himself.'

She walks the quayside beside him, looking up at the ship's gunwales painted red as sin, its forecastle broad and polished, white sails furled and waiting. 'That must have been quite a spectacle,' she ponders.

'Indeed! And the Earl himself striding the deck.'

'I can imagine.' In her mind, she sees that familiar swagger, the piratical roll of Warwick's shoulders.

'Oh, and of course,' he fumbles a moment, thinking, perhaps he should have mentioned this great man first, 'your own son, the fine young Duke of Clarence with him . . .'

Ah yes, George, she thinks. I thought you'd be here.

'. . . and their ladies, all so fine . . .'

George has a lady, does he?

She nods again to the ship. 'For the royal fleet, or Warwick's own?'

In answer he points her to the mast top, where a standard lifts light in a breeze from the river; the bear and staff, the symbol of the earldom of Warwick, for its lords are beasts in battle and fell giants with the trunks of trees. Or so it's said. So they say of themselves.

'For trade or war?'

'This ship,' he says, slapping the hull and as pleased as if he'd built it himself. 'This ship'll serve you in any turn.'

Will it now? she wonders.

She hears a noise beside her as the harbour master steps back and bends himself into a bow. She turns and here comes the bear himself, the Earl of Warwick, marching down the quayside from the town. And behind him a stride or two, George, her son. They're surprised to see her and pretending not to be. A little out of sorts, like children taken unawares stowing secrets in their pockets, walking fast away from things they don't want you to see.

'We had word the King's Mother had arrived,' calls Warwick as he approaches. 'We've come to see if it's true.' All grins, all bravado.

'I thought I'd surprise you,' she calls back.

She holds out a hand as he reaches her. He takes and kisses it, then steps back, so that son can greet mother.

'George,' she says. His lips against her fingers are dry and quick.

'Mother.'

'I hadn't expected to see you here. An extra pleasure. God must be pleased with me. I've been visiting His house in Canterbury and the abbot told me of the Earl's great enterprise, so I thought I'd come see it myself. I came by river, of course.' She signals to the barge that Canterbury's abbey loaned to bring her down the Stour. 'I hope you can put me up. I'm a small party.' At the mooring, four men in her livery stand waiting with bags and boxes.

'How are the young princesses?' Warwick's wife asks as they sit down to dine in the mullioned twilight of the Lord's lodging house at the heart of the town. There are three royal daughters in Elizabeth's nursery now. The last came at winter's end, bringing nothing but disappointment with her. For everyone except Edward of course, who is disappointed at nothing and deals with failure by pretending not to see it. 'Sons will come,' he said, smiling into this new one's face while little Lizzie tried to climb his legs and Mary, littler still, pulled herself to standing by his bootstraps. 'We're calling her Cecily, Mother. For you.'

She thanked him warmly enough, though she'd have rather a son and call him what you like.

'They're all well. And growing fast, I'm glad to tell you.' She nods to the basket of roses at the table's centre. 'The court poets have taken to calling them the flowers of England.' She leans to her hostess and laughs a little at the nonsense of it. 'Flowers, in my experience, are less noisome and smell better.'

She's feigning light-heartedness in a room that sparks with tension. When she walked up here from the quay and found not only Warwick's archbishop brother but also his wife and eldest daughter Isabel waiting she'd greeted them calmly enough, though they themselves were flustered and carried colour high in their cheeks. Warwick's lady seldom comes south other than to show herself at court, and her daughters are so rarely seen that their very existence is sometimes called into question. So why are they here? And why is George? He's taken a seat at the opposite end of the table from Isabel and is studiously ignoring her in a way that can't fail to call attention.

'There's nothing wrong with daughters,' Lady Warwick says, which sets George smirking into his cup. 'And the King? And his dear queen?' she asks as the wine is passed.

'On pilgrimage. To give thanks for a safe delivery. They go to Walsingham and to Bury. Though, in truth, Edward marries reverence with work. He's raising men to go north. You know, of course, of the trouble there.'

There have been uprisings in the northern counties since the spring. Led by Robin of Redesdale, some local militant who stirs up the people and hides behind a hero's name. He complains of high taxes and poor lordship.

'It is,' says Cecily, 'the eternal cry of the commons – that they have not enough of anything except rich men dipping into their pockets.'

'He's going himself then?' Warwick asks, and when she nods, adds blunt, 'Good. I told him he should.'

'Then I'm glad he listens to you.'

'Put the fear of God up them.'

'That's his intention. Though your own brother John has been doing staunch work for us there. But this Robin proves elusive. It is . . . perplexing.'

She expects, now, some urgent commendation of his brother's efforts. Or some excuse for why Northumberland, where that brother is earl, is so troubled. But Warwick has only a question, 'When does Edward leave for the north?'

The table is suddenly quiet. 'Not too soon.' She takes time to listen to the nature of the silence. 'He takes a leisurely route.'

A breath across the table. Lady Warwick is laying her knife across her empty plate. 'I'm sure he's right to do so. This trouble will boil up and die down soon enough.'

Cecily addresses herself to George. 'Your brother Richard goes north with the King. I wonder you don't.'

He shrugs, nonchalant. He's been hard at the wine all through dinner and it's loosened him. 'I've had no order from Edward.'

'And you've not offered your assistance, or any men?'

'Why, does he lack them?'

'George . . .' A whisper of warning down the table. It's the first time Isabel's spoken and it sets the men's eyes flickering, from their laps to the tabletop, the window, the door. Means of escape, should they be needed.

It's the archbishop who recovers first. 'My brother here, and I, thought to assist by sea. Take this new ship north. Scan the coast, keep it clear.'

'I'd not thought peasant rebels would have access to naval warfare,' Cecily points out.

'But who else might threaten while the King is occupied with them?' asks Warwick. 'We have, already, boats of the fleet posted, looking out for a strike from France or from Scotland . . .'

'With both of whom we have a peace,' says Cecily. 'Though I take your point. Peace treaties, often enough, aren't worth the scraping of the vellum. Especially not when Louis's signature is at their foot.'

There's a certain pleasure in watching Warwick bridle as he does now. Though she shouldn't indulge it. She turns, instead, her attention to his wife. 'And you, and your daughter, where will you go when your menfolk venture forth?'

Lady Warwick looks up, a moment's hesitation, an indrawn breath. The expression of one who has realized, of a sudden, that they need a convenient lie, and haven't thought to have one to hand.

'They'll sail with us,' says Warwick. 'We'll drop them at Newcastle and, from there, home to Middleham.'

'To Middleham, yes,' recovers his wife. 'Exactly so.'

'A voyage. How adventurous!' Cecily clasps her hands, feigning relish. 'Then I wish you fine weather.' She makes to rise; a servant steps forward to draw back her chair. All charm, she turns again to the company.

'It's been a long day. I'd like to say compline and then to my bed. I've no chaplain with me. Archbishop, I wonder if you would like . . .'

He can't really say no.

21.

They pray together in the chamber appointed for her, before the triptych altar that travels with her everywhere she goes. On its miniature panels Christ suffers, while Heaven's angels weep crystal tears. The Virgin, dry-eyed and certain of her son's destiny as no earthly mother can be, observes his anguish from the foot of the cross, while his blood, carmine-tinted gold, pools at her feet.

Reminded of God's sacrifice, they pray to be made deserving, to be kept from the snares of the enemy, for the light of Heaven to vanquish dark deeds. They ask that, despite the changes and chances of this fleeting world, they might repose in peace tonight, lapped in God's unchanging love.

At the last Amen, Cecily asks a blessing, but notes that her nephew's thumb, where it marks the cross upon her brow, has a tremble in it, as if uncertain of its path.

'Thank you,' she whispers, as she takes his hand and turns it to kiss the cold stone of his bishop's ring. 'I feel the need of a blessing to anchor me tonight. I fear our world stands on the brink of change. As if ground we thought steady begins to shift beneath our feet.'

As she raises her head, she catches his eyes with her own. There's nothing of rest in them. They are not the eyes of a man certain of his prayers, or his worthiness to say them.

She sighs. 'Perhaps you feel it too?'

He looks down again. 'Perhaps.'

'Hmm. I'm sure it grieves you still, the loss of the chancellorship.'

It's been two years, but she knows the smart was deep. It will help to acknowledge it, it will soften him.

He looks aside, his smile wry. 'The wind blows very cold when a king's love is turned from you.'

'Is that what you think has happened?' They are still on their knees and she makes no effort to rise. She wants him to understand that this conversation, no less than their prayers, is heard by God. 'You know, you couldn't be more wrong.'

'My brother Warwick feels it most intently. As do I.'

'And with least cause. There are no men alive that Edward loves more than his Neville cousins. Warwick most especially. But you know how it is. In foolish anger, we often strike hardest at those we love most.'

He sighs. 'I wish we could . . .' His hand signals a wish for reversal.

'Turn back time?'

'Hmm. Yes. I suppose.'

'To the dawn of Edward's reign?'

'Yes. To that precise moment.'

She nods. To a time before the Woodville marriage. Before Henry Beaufort's pardon. When no counsellor spoke more closely in Edward's ear than Warwick. When Warwick and Edward would have shed their own blood, each for the other. She remembers a story Edward told her once, of a skirmish at Ferry Bridge, just before the battle at Towton, where the enemy held the river crossing against them. They were outnumbered, and their men looked set to run until Warwick leapt from his horse, drew his sword across its neck before them all and, while the poor creature staggered and choked on its blood, cried out, 'Stand with me, for by no means will I flee this fight.'

So like Warwick, she'd thought, the grand gesture. She'd smiled, commended the act, and was about to remind Edward that, for certain, Warwick had other horses standing by. But when she looked, tears stood in his eyes and she didn't have the heart. So she only nodded and agreed when he ended, 'I think there's no man braver, or more my friend.'

Yes. That would be the moment to go back to.

'I don't think it's too late,' she says.

The archbishop's shoulders are slumped. No man, she thinks, has ever looked more miserable.

'Oh, I don't mean we can change what's happened,' she admits. 'Even I can't make Elizabeth disappear. But we can make a peace with it, can't we? With a little humility on either side?'

He looks very much as if he wishes it.

She touches his hand, where the bishop's ring girds his finger. 'I don't know why you're all here in Sandwich, or what you plan to do. But I suspect it's something that could set much change in motion.'

He looks away from her. To the altar and its angels in their grief.

'I'll leave here in the morning,' she tells him. 'I urge you to go to your brother tonight and give him your counsel as a man of God, not as a man of war. Tell him there's always forgiveness. Reconcilement and repose. Sail north, as you say you will, and stand with your good friend, the King.'

He nods. He says they will. That this was ever all their intent. She half believes him. Not that it was, but that it might be now. So, as he stands and makes to leave, she gives one more spur to his resolve. 'There is a point, you know, a step that, once taken, can never be retraced. I fear you're on the brink of it, your brother and you. And if you were to take it, I think the wind would blow both bitter and ceaseless.' She goes to him, to the threshold where he pauses. 'And if you take my son George on that road with you, I promise, that wind will carry knives.'

Next morning, when she's ready to leave, they walk her to the quayside, to the barge that will carry her back to Canterbury. From there she'll ride to London. She feels a need to be within the city's walls, where she can judge the turn of events with the tools of office ready to her hand.

There are smiles as she goes and the mood is lightened, as if they'd all gone to bed early and slept well with clear conscience. They admire the ship again.

'I named it *The Trinity* to honour the three sons of York,' Warwick says, expansive. 'Did I tell you?'

Cecily laughs. 'I think that might be a blasphemy. But if it is, it's a cheering one.' Then she asks, because she must, 'When do you expect to arrive in the north?'

'Oh, I don't know. Two weeks or so, perhaps three. There's a bit more provisioning to be done before she can sail. She's blessed by God, you know, but the carpentry isn't finished!'

It looks finished.

'Well, there's always more to do,' she says. 'I'll write Edward and tell him to look for you then.' And there's a warning in that.

She asks George to take her the last walk along the quay. Before she steps into her barge she feels compelled to kiss him, as she hasn't done in years, to feel his deep copper hair between her fingers. She remembers a time when all she had to do to curb his foolishness was grasp his hand in hers and say 'Don't!' But that was nigh on twenty years ago, and he's no longer a child.

So she only offers him her hand and, when he has put reluctant lips to it, says, 'I'm sorry you can't marry Isabel.'

'I don't see why I can't,' folding his arms about himself, grinding a peevish heel against the cobbles.

'Your brother the King has forbidden it.'

'He married to please himself. No one forbade him.'

She smiles, coaxing. 'No one had the chance. I would have.'

His mouth turns down.

'Come now. Isabel's got nothing much to say for herself, after all.'

He looks at her askance.

'All right,' she admits. 'I know it's not about the conversation.' It is, she knows, about the money. It's about Isabel's rich inheritance and the idea that, with it, he can be as liberal and as loved as her father. 'We'll find you a wife soon. A rich one. I promise.'

'One Edward won't say no to?'

'Well, there must be someone, don't you think?'

She steps into the barge but turns, for one last word. 'Son. Don't go with Warwick. Either north to Edward, or anywhere else he'd have you go. I say it for your own good, so mind me.'

She watches him nod as her men help her settle. She's done all she can for now. As the barge sets its nose into the river's flow she looks back and sees that, already, George has turned from her. He looks across the quayside towards the ship, to *The Trinity* and its false naming, where Warwick and his family are waiting.

22.

18 July 1469

Westminster

'Guard yourself against Warwick,' Cecily wrote to Edward when she returned to London. 'If he doesn't come to you by mid-July, look for him coming against you soon after. And find out who this bloody Robin is. And whether his other name is Neville.'

She'd not expected, then, to see Warwick first herself. But here he is, before the gates of London with an army at his back; men of the Calais garrison, men of Kent, bladed and ready. And flanking him on either side, his brother the archbishop and her own fool of a son, George.

'Let us in,' Warwick says. 'We've come for the good of the country. We've come to set England to rights.'

Have you now, thinks Cecily.

London's mayor, at a loss, sends word. 'He's your nephew. He's the King's cousin. What are we to do?'

She must buy time. 'Ask him what he wants,' she says. 'And keep the gates closed till he tells us.'

She already knows what he wants, for she knows what he intends. News of it arrived three days ago, a proclamation sent from Calais for every man in possession of a sword. It must be on every church door in England by now. It calls for a muster to ride to the King's aid; to relieve him from rebellion and free him from evil counsellors. Robin of Redesdale's grievances are just, it says. All England groans under Edward's rule. But the King's not to blame. Oh no, not at all. The fault lies with those who influence him for ill; the Queen's kin, corrupt, avaricious and vile. We will remove them, writes Warwick. We will quell rebellion by rooting out its cause.

So he'll be asking for men, for money and arms. Asking for the Queen herself, she supposes. Well, she's not here, thank God. She's in Norwich, her daughters with her. Cecily hopes her frantic letter will have reached them. Stay where you are, it says. Take sanctuary of the church, if you must. The Queen's father and two of her brothers are with Edward. To the rest, she's sent word, and to their mother, Jacquetta, at home at Grafton. And to Edward himself, of course, somewhere on the road north, God knows when it'll reach him, or if. She hopes he's heeded her earlier warning, that he's already mustering men to stand against his cousin's assault. That he's not stupid enough still to be saying to himself, Warwick would never betray me and my brother George is a good enough lad.

She knows and has told him that George and Warwick are handfast in betrayal now. For when they sailed *The Trinity* out of Sandwich, they took her to Calais, where Isabel and George were married.

The mayor returns with Warwick's expected answer. Money, he wants. Men and arms. The next he can barely bring himself to say. 'And the surrender of the Queen, and her children.' He hangs his head. 'For their safety.'

'And what do you imagine he will do with them?' she asks. 'Drag them north in his baggage train?'

'No,' says the mayor, twisting his hat in his hands. 'He says your son George, the Duke of Clarence, will hold authority in London in the King's name. The Queen will be in his keeping . . .' He hesitates. '. . . and you, yourself.'

'George my gaoler?' The thought ignites a furious rage, but when the mayor, from whom she must demand much, quails, she relents and begs him to sit, to be still, to bethink himself.

She sits opposite him. Clasps her hands until the metal of her widow's ring grinds on bone. She uses the pain to steady her mind, clear her thoughts. 'We've been here before, sir,' she says.

He sighs. 'Aye.'

'Last time an army sat down at London's gate and begged entry, mad Henry's wife Marguerite led it.'

'She did.'

'And I begged you to keep the city's gates locked, and promised my son would come to save us.'

'I've not forgotten.'

'And I was right. Wasn't I? He did.'

'You were right.'

'Then trust me to be right again. Don't give the city to Warwick.'

'He's a hard one to gainsay. The most powerful man in England, save the King.'

'Yes. Save the King.'

'And he says he intends no harm . . .'

'Sir.' She reaches across the table, touches his hand to still his voice. 'I'll tell you what the Earl of Warwick intends.'

He looks at her, mute though open-mouthed.

'He intends to make the King his puppet and rule through him. And if the King won't acquiesce to that, he'll kill him. He's already married my son George to his daughter. He'll make George king in Edward's stead.'

She has feared it since she saw them standing together on the quayside at Sandwich, known it for certain these two days past; cursed herself for believing her fear too fanciful, such treachery too extreme. She's been a fool. She knows what men are. She watches the mayor's face grow pale and presses her case. 'And what do you think will happen to the Queen then?' she asks him. 'And to my granddaughters?'

'Lady, it's hard to give the Earl of Warwick nothing when he stands with an army at your door.'

'Then give as little as you can.'

He rubs a hand across his chin; she can see him weighing possibilities and decides to tip the scale.

'Tell him no one can hold authority in the King's name unless the King grants it. The King does not. Cannot, for he isn't here. If Warwick defends the King's rights as he says he does, he can't gainsay you.'

He nods.

'Tell him the Queen has taken sanctuary. Not here. Don't tell him where. And tell him you have no men to give him, that the men of London have gone north already to fight for the King.'

The mayor's brow is furrowed deep. 'But should we not equip him to put down the rebellion in the north? He says he'll aid the King in that. Perhaps he . . .'

'Sir, think,' she taps his hand again. 'Whose is the most powerful family in the north?'

'Well, Warwick's, I suppose. The Nevilles . . .' Realization begins to dawn.

'Indeed. And I'll wager my soul that the rebellion in the north is all of Warwick's making. A diversion to draw Edward up country while he takes England from the south.'

'Dear God.' The mayor sits back in his seat. She can see his world is reeling. 'He's asked for weapons from the royal armoury.'

'Which he will use against the King.'

'I . . .'

'Tell him you've no authority over the royal armoury and can't open its doors to him. But,' she concedes, 'you will loan him money to buy arms. It is, as you say, hard to give the Earl of Warwick nothing.'

He nods. 'How much shall we lend?'

'As little as you can and at as high a rate of interest as you dare.'

Two days later Warwick is gone, with less than he hoped for but enough to make trouble. His army is five thousand and well-armed. It will grow. And in the north he has men unnumbered. It makes her mouth dry to think of it. She sent messages to her son George; it's not too late, they said, repent, leave Warwick and come to me. She received no reply and when Warwick rode away, George rode beside him, pace for pace.

'So be it,' she says. But she can't forget the child he was; how she lost two sons that came before him, then wrestled with angels to keep him alive. She wonders if those lost would have betrayed her so, then shakes her head at such a pointless thought. They died, George lived, that's the way of it. And he's been hard work ever since.

In the days that follow Jacquetta writes: 'Should I come to you in London? Should I go to my daughter the Queen?'

'Stay where you are,' Cecily writes. 'Safest.'

For God's sake don't come here, she thinks. For I'd be tempted to take up a poker and beat you blue. Yes, you and your worthless daughter that now two of my sons have made themselves such fools for.

23.

No Woodville head is safe in England now. Lying sleepless
through the short summer nights, smothered by the stench of
her sweat and deafened by the beat of her heart, Cecily has
imagined the Queen's fear and measured it against her own; the
grinding of the guts that sends her rushing to the privy, the
struggle to breathe against the ball of dread in her throat,
the vision of Edward constantly before her, broken, bloody and
dead.

In the single hour of deep dark she even finds pity for Elizabeth,
alone in Norwich with no one but her daughters and knowledge
of a blade at the throat of all she loves. But, in the early dawn,
when Cecily has called for her women, when they have got her up
and dressed her, when she has heard mass and made a face that
she can show to the world, when she is armoured in velvets and
pearls so that she can carry on the business of being the King's
Mother; then her pity dissolves. You made yourself queen, she
thinks. Get on with it.

With whatever accuracy she has measured Elizabeth's fear, she
hasn't reckoned the rage that masks it. Five days after Warwick
rides north, the Queen comes to Westminster. Cecily hurries to
meet her and finds her in the courtyard, being helped from the
back of a lathered horse by her brother Anthony, while the men
who have guarded them throw legs over pommels and slide
gratefully to the ground. Grooms and servants rush forward to
help, and the Queen's youngest, who has been bawling against
her mother's shoulder, is handed off to a maid without a back-
ward glance. Elizabeth, with no word for anyone, heads indoors,

stiff-legged, as blown as her horse, with her brother hurrying after.

Cecily takes time only to notice that the other princesses and their nurses are being tended before following them. When she comes to the Queen's chamber its door is open and the Queen's ladies, who have been idle and anxious for days, are milling and fussing about their mistress. One draws the cloak from her shoulders, another offers wine in a glass.

'Your Grace,' Cecily announces herself above the clatter and Elizabeth turns to her, her body rigid with fury. Her hands are fisted at her side and her eyes, reddened by the dust of the road, spark like flint. Her lips, most often bowed and carmined, are drawn back, pale, from her teeth. 'You swore,' she snarls. 'You swore you would not suffer your family to disparage me.'

Cecily has no answer to that, for indeed, she did swear and yet here Elizabeth stands, in every way disparaged. The King's Mother isn't used to being unable to do the things she says she will do. It is a humiliation, and like every humiliation she has ever faced, she has admitted and borne it. But to be reminded of it now, to be accused by Elizabeth, however justly, wakens her own cold anger. The Queen's women, shocked to see the great lady so upbraided, stand open-mouthed.

She signals to them, sharp, and says, 'Go and prepare food and a bath for the Queen.' They are gone in an instant and the room is quiet except for Elizabeth's sawing breath.

Cecily waits a beat or two and then, 'I told you to stay in Norwich. And yet, here you are, riding across the country at great danger to yourself and to your daughters.'

Elizabeth's voice climbs. 'You told me? Madam, I take no orders from you! And from whom am I in danger?' She staggers across the room until she stands face to face with Cecily. 'From your family!' she accuses. 'Your nephews and your stupid, vicious son!' She beats a fist, once, hard against her own breast. 'They won't rest till they destroy me!'

Her voice breaks and tears threaten. She gasps and reaches again for her anger, shakes with it, rages. 'They're your people and yet you do nothing, nothing to stop them!'

'You have no idea what I do.' Cecily's voice is cold as stone and she has drawn herself to her full height.

As if this very calmness offends her to the core, Elizabeth bends her body almost double and screams, 'I am your queen!'

And now, Cecily's voice rises above hers. 'Then for God's sake act like it!'

There is silence in the room. Elizabeth recoils as if slapped; as if this reminder of how far she is, in this moment, from what she should be, has fallen upon her like a blow. A screaming woman, filthy from the road. She draws back her shoulders, steadies her breath, unclenches her hands and clasps them before her. It is the practised stance of queenship and there, with a defiant lift of her chin and despite all her dishevelment, she is herself again.

'We will begin afresh,' she says, her voice barely trembling. She holds her hand out and down, commanding an obeisance. 'Lady Cecily.'

Given the state of things, it is an act of courage, Cecily supposes, and so she rewards it with a bow. 'Your Grace.'

When Cecily rises, Elizabeth nods, swallows and, with effort, speaks again. 'My brother here,' she gestures across the room to where Anthony stands, exasperated and staring, 'parted from my husband the King two weeks ago and has news that may be useful to us.'

Two weeks, Cecily thinks, her heart leaping. Two weeks ago, Edward lived. Fourteen days and as many nights. So short a time ago, he spoke and breathed. It brings a wash of relief. But a man may die and breed maggots in two weeks. She swallows down the thought.

'Then shall we sit and hear it?'

Anthony Woodville looks no less road-worn than his sister.

He sits splay-legged between them, runs blistered fingers through sweat-matted hair, rubs sore eyes with the heels of his hands and heaves a breath before he speaks of all that happened two weeks ago.

Edward's company, he says, had reached Nottingham when news came to them of the size of the rebel force. Loyal men, who'd watched it gather, rode hard to bring them word. No peasant army this, they told the King. No village malcontents with rusty blades and clubs. This is an army, three times the size of yours.

Anthony sighs. 'And the man who calls himself Robin of Redesdale? He is husband to Warwick's cousin and master of his castle at Middleham.'

'Of course he is,' says Cecily, bitter.

'And those same messengers brought us Redesdale's manifesto. It reads much like Warwick's own, which I've seen since. Penned by the same hand, I'd say. It lays the ills of England at my family's door and calls for the Woodvilles to be put down. It says our king is no better than mad Henry who came before him, and worthy of no better fate, for he puts aside those lords who are of his own blood in favour of grasping favourites and upstarts, who he enriches at England's expense.'

He stops a moment. Licks his lips with a dry tongue and clears his throat. Cecily reaches for wine, pours and hands it to him, while Elizabeth sits quiet, her eyes on her hands tight-clasped in her lap. Anthony drinks in long gulps and wipes his mouth against his dusty cuff.

'What did Edward do?' Cecily asks.

'He cursed his blasted mother for always being right,' Anthony tells her.

Cecily lays a hand over her eyes.

She hears the hiss of Elizabeth's voice. 'I've warned him against Warwick a thousand times.'

'Sister . . .' cautions Anthony, while Cecily thinks, dear God, woman, shut up or I'll take you out and drown you. From the dark behind her eyelids she nods for Anthony to speak on.

'I don't think it was that he didn't believe your warning when it came,' he placates. 'More that he didn't want to. His cousin and oldest ally? His brother? Even then, with Redesdale's manifesto in his hands, he didn't.'

When Cecily looks up askance Anthony spreads his hands.

'Well, he'll have seen Warwick's own manifesto by now and will be out of all doubt.'

'And why were you not with him when that arrived?'

A look of shame mars Anthony's features. 'He said it was too dangerous to take Woodvilles further north, so he sent us away. My father and brother John into Wales, to William Herbert, with an order to raise Welsh troops. I to my lands in Norfolk to raise my own people.'

He pauses a moment before he speaks again. 'And he told me, "If you can, find my queen and take her to my mother in London, for her safety."' He looks sideways to Elizabeth. 'So you see, sister, his first thought was for you.'

She tuts and looks away.

'My son Richard is still with him?' Cecily asks.

'Yes . . .' he hesitates. 'He seemed less surprised, but no less grieved, by Warwick's . . .'

'Treason?'

'Treason. Yes.' He looks up. 'But Lady, you must have hope. One army must already be on its way to Edward's aid from Wales. Lord Herbert won't fail him. And another from the west country brought up by the Earl of Devon.'

She nods.

Now he puts his hands to his knees and pushes himself to stand. 'And I myself should be gone. I have men mustering. I must join them and ride hard.' And though it's late afternoon and he looks like a man who hasn't slept in a year, he takes time only to change his clothes and sketch a prayer before he goes. 'There are hours of daylight left,' he says. 'I can waste none of them.'

She leaves the Queen to her women once he's gone. She writes to Jacquetta, to say her daughter is safe, for she can't imagine Elizabeth taking time to send such comfort. But, when the sun begins to set, she finds herself wandering, and her feet take her to Elizabeth's door, where, upon announcing herself, she is granted entry.

Elizabeth sits in a low chair by an open window. Two of her women kneel behind her, wiping squares of silk down her drying hair, which falls to the floor, a sheet of silver gilt. She is fresh from her bath, clean and scented, lightly robed, and her face, though tired still and pinched, has regained its moon-like beauty. She stands when Cecily approaches and her hair ripples to her hips.

'When my family is in danger,' Cecily says, 'I find it helpful to go to prayer.'

'Are you asking me to pray with you?'

Cecily carries on as if Elizabeth hasn't spoken. 'And to do so publicly. It reassures the household that we're confident of God's favour. And, if you and I go together – Queen and King's Mother – it will be seen that we are at one. That you are my family, as I am yours. From that they will infer that those who stand in opposition to you, stand also in opposition to me. That our enemies, whoever they are, are held in common.'

Even my brother's sons, she reminds herself. Even my own son.

So Elizabeth orders her women to bind up her hair, to paint her lips and put rubies at her throat. When that's done, they call both their households to follow them to the chapel, where they hear compline and a mass. As the priest lifts Christ's body before their eyes, Cecily urges God to observe her actions, and to find in them her most earnest prayer.

'I have humbled myself,' she tells Him. 'I have pledged myself to Elizabeth.' Then she frees her mind to fly across fields and rivers and byways to wherever Edward is. She holds him up, his body and soul no less precious to her than Christ's, and says, 'I do it for him. So that you won't let him die.'

Beside her, the Queen closes her prayers with a soft Amen.

24.

August 1469

They keep the offices of prayer together daily now. It marks the time of waiting. Otherwise, they keep to themselves. Chancellor Stillington scuttles between them, with little else to say except, no news yet. No news.

Beyond the walls of Westminster, London's business carries on. The traffic on the river is no less than before, its summer stink no less vile. Cecily would like to be at Baynard's. Or, better yet, her manor in Kennington, with its warm scents and water-rilled gardens. It was Edward's gift to her last year. They walked its espaliered paths in the autumn, just as the stone fruits were ripening.

'You'll get a bit of peace here, Captain Mother,' he'd said, reaching to pull plums from a bough.

'What? Are you retiring me?' she'd asked crossly. She was still missing Meg then, heartsore.

'These are good. Look.' He threw a plum to her, which she let fall, not deigning to remove her hands from her sleeves to catch it. He grinned at her, plum juice glistening on his teeth. 'Retire you? I wouldn't dare. Look, it's an hour from Westminster, two from Windsor,' he shrugged. 'Anyway, I give up. Come and go as you please, you usually do.'

If she closes her eyes now she can feel the grass give beneath her feet, its moisture soaking the soft leather of her soles, leaving dewdrops on the hem of her gown. If she reached out she could thread her arm through his and he'd say, 'Come now, Captain Mother, walk with me and admit how much you like it.'

She wishes she had, instead of keeping her distance, feigning indifference to him and his gift.

Today, the floors of Westminster are hard stone and the grass of its gardens baked dry. Edward usually takes his queen to Windsor for summer, or to Greenwich. But she and Elizabeth have decided without speaking of it that they should stay here for now. The Tower, their last defence, should they need it, is only two river miles away.

It's been fifteen days since Warwick marched north. Twenty-five since Anthony saw Edward living. And Richard with him, of course, who has so far only played at fighting and kept notes of his bouts in a book. He'll be seventeen in October, if he lives so long. She's lost one son that age to battle already, doubts she could bear it again.

They are coming from matins, she and the Queen, their people about them. They are ready to turn their separate ways, when Stillington comes striding, a sweating messenger at his heels. He bows to the Queen, leans close to Cecily and speaks low and urgent. 'From your son,' he tells her, 'from Richard.'

The name, overheard, sends ripples through the crowd.

'He doesn't write to me?' Elizabeth, questions, imperious.

'I'm his mother, Elizabeth,' Cecily can't help but chide. 'And he probably doesn't know you're here.'

Elizabeth isn't listening. 'Is there nothing from the King?' she demands of the messenger.

The poor man shows his empty satchel, its single square of parchment already in Cecily's hand. 'This is all I have . . .'

He's a relay rider, one of a network Edward has established to move news at speed about his kingdom. His hands are among many that Richard's letter might have passed through. He can tell them only that it was handed to him at Highgate this morning, that it came from the north. No, he isn't sure exactly where.

'The answers to your questions are likely in the letter,' says Stillington, painfully patient.

'Then let's read the thing,' says Cecily. She steps back into the chapel, knowing they will follow, calling to the messenger to wait.

'Edward lives.' The first words she reads aloud draw a relieved gust of breath from Stillington, and send Elizabeth's hands, steepled, to her mouth.

'But is the prisoner of the Earl of Warwick.'

'Christ.' Stillington can't help himself. Nor Elizabeth, who whimpers low.

'Mother,' Richard writes, 'know first that I think he is in no immediate danger. He became a prisoner willingly, says he's certain Warwick will do no violence to him. That he'll give him no reason to do so. He says also to tell you that he's taken your advice; that he's fighting first with his head. You'll know what he means, I suppose. You always do.'

Richard parted from Edward, she learns, at July's end. 'Not willingly,' he writes. 'But at my brother's command. I'm with Will Hastings, though it's best I don't tell you where, and pointless, anyway, for we must each be somewhere else tomorrow. Pity my horse. Our given task is to make England ungovernable.'

And on he writes, 'The news I can't help but give you is . . .'

'Oh, dear God,' breathes Cecily.

'What? What?' Elizabeth demands between splayed fingers.

'William Herbert is dead, and the Earl of Devon. Their armies destroyed by Redesdale's men.'

'Warwick's men!' spits Elizabeth.

'Yes,' Cecily concedes. 'Warwick's men.'

Herbert and Devon. The armies Edward had waited for. His hope to make a stand.

'We were heading south to meet them when the news came,' Richard writes. 'And no surprise that most of our small force deserted on hearing it. Then my brother said, "When you can't fight, you must think of something else to do." So he sent us off, Will

Hastings and I, others who had stayed. Then he rode on into Warwick's arms. With Hastings, I held back long enough to see him taken. They'll take him to Coventry, I think. And try to rule England in his name. We who remain free will do all we can to make that difficult. If we do our work well, Warwick will find it impossible to raise men or rule. And you must do what you can to help with that, Mother. If orders come from Edward, know they were given by Warwick. Make sure the council knows it too. Make sure everyone knows it.'

'What?' says Elizabeth. 'What does it mean? What are we to do?'

Cecily gasps. She has thought, sometimes, that Edward learned nothing from his father. But he's learned this at least; that in chaos people crave certainty, and for nearly nine years now, Edward's been that; since Mortimer's Cross, since Towton, since he put mad Henry in the Tower. Take away the discipline of good rule and people will say, 'Give us our king back.' And Warwick, even Warwick, can't gainsay all England.

Cecily reaches out and grasps Elizabeth's wrist. 'Call up your secretaries,' she says. 'We have letters to write.'

They work together, and word goes out to every noble house in England, every household that commands men; that the King is taken against his will, that any orders that come in his name are Warwick's, that as servants of the King, it is their duty to ignore them. 'Unless you want to be ruled by Warwick, of course,' dictates Cecily.

'Who will put you in bed with the French,' adds Elizabeth.

'Yes. Write that,' adds Cecily. 'That'll put metal in them.'

By the time the last of their messengers is saddled and gone, and their secretaries have gathered up their inks and left, nursing sore fingers, evening has come. A day of bright heat turning muggy, the blue of the sky falling to a weary grey sigh. Cecily, relieved of the need to speak and move, realizes how tired she is, how her jaw aches and the band of her cap bites into her brow.

The hand she lifts to ease it comes away damp with sweat and her lips, when she tests them, taste of salt. She turns to the table. There is small beer and she pours two cups, walks to the window's embrasure where Elizabeth looks out and puts one into her hands.

'Here,' she says.

Elizabeth looks at her as if she doesn't know what drink is. Her eyes are wide, like those of a man struck by an arrow who doesn't know yet that he'll fall. Richard's letter had ended with a word for her. 'If the Queen is with you, tell her that her father and brothers still live, so far as we know. And that Edward sends his heart's love. He would have written himself, but time was so short. He says he trusts you, Mother, to keep her safe.'

Absurd that this task should fall to her, who has wished her daughter-in-law dead a thousand times and never more so than in these last weeks. Oh, not dead, she supposes, that's harsh. Just never born. Not back to God, only never gone from his company. But, she concedes, Elizabeth has worked today. She has kept pace, dictated letter after letter, her words fluid and fast. But that occupation now done, she seems suddenly adrift. It is, Cecily supposes, not surprising. She's adrift herself. So she wraps Elizabeth's hands around the cup and guides her to the window seat.

'Sit down,' she says. 'Before you fall down.' She takes a place opposite, leans her back against the cool stone and closes her eyes. 'You should drink.'

And Elizabeth does. Then, in a little while, she asks, 'What will Warwick do with my daughters, if he wins?'

'He won't win.'

'But if he does?'

Cecily decides there's no point lying about it. 'Sell their wardships, I expect. They have royal blood. That counts for something. Middling marriages, in time.'

'He'll take them from me.'

'Yes.'

'And me?'

Elizabeth has no blood to make her worth anything to anyone. No land or titles but what's been given by the King and can be taken back. 'A religious life, most likely. Reclusive.'

'I think he wants me dead.'

She reaches to touch Elizabeth's hand. 'You must know, I'd never allow that.'

'Oh? We've learned, I think, how little influence you have over the Earl of Warwick.'

It stings, to be reminded. She feels shame, and a flood of irritation.

But Elizabeth only shakes her head, as if to rattle that thought out of it to make space for another. 'He would show, I think, no such mercy to the men of my family. My father. My brothers.' She ends on a whisper, 'My sons.'

Ah yes, her sons by . . . dear God, what was that man's name? They come with Elizabeth to chapel, her Grey boys, sit pale-faced behind her with their tutor. Not fighting age yet, but on the cusp of it. Which makes them dangerous enough to Warwick.

Well, no point lying about that either. 'No. He wouldn't.'

The silence that falls then is thick and heavy. Cecily bows her head to ease the ache in her neck and swallows drily. The beer hasn't quenched her thirst and its taste is bitter in her mouth. The room is growing dim. She should get up, call a servant to light candles. She's about to do so when a falling cup rattles across the floor and the keening begins. A single note, breathless and high, panic and dread singing in the throat. Cecily looks up and sees Elizabeth lost to a grief that hasn't come yet, her empty hands raised before eyes wide open to all possible horrors.

Oh, dear God, Cecily thinks. Not now. She kneels before the Queen, takes her by the shoulders and shakes. 'Stop it. It hasn't happened. I know what you fear, but it hasn't happened yet.' The cries rise, strained to breaking.

'Look at me, Elizabeth,' she shakes her again. 'I've lost a son and those that remain to me are out there in danger equal to yours. Am I weeping?' Another shake. 'No. Look at me. Dry-eyed.'

At last Elizabeth's eyes focus on her face, her hands grasp Cecily's wrists and the keening gives way to shuddering sobs.

'That's it,' says Cecily. 'Don't waste time with tears. Be practical. Today we've done much that's helpful. Tomorrow we'll do more. There's always something you can do, Elizabeth.'

At last Elizabeth quietens, nods and says, 'Yes. I'm well now, I'm sensible.'

Cecily leads her to her chambers and hands her to her women; to Joan Peasemarsh, who is caring and discreet. Joan returns to Cecily an hour later with the assurance that Elizabeth is calm now and sleeping.

Good for her, thinks Cecily, whose eyes are gritty with the lack of rest.

When Joan is gone, Annette looks up from her sewing. She's there every evening now, in Cecily's chambers, busy with something ordinary, as if the world isn't falling apart. It's a blessing. She nods at the closing door and speaks of the Queen. 'She's strung very tight, that one.'

'Yes, well.' Cecily watches Annette's steady needle, out and in. 'These are tightly strung times.'

'Not just now. Always has been. It just shows more, now she's tested.'

Cecily shrugs and sighs. 'What of it?'

A stitch, a stitch and then another. 'Pity her first husband died. She might have been happy, living a quieter life. A country lady.'

'Don't be naïve, Annette.'

The nurse smiles, lifts her work to check the neatness of the stitches. 'I'm sure you're right. Anyway. Too late. She must stick at it now. You must keep her steady.'

'Elizabeth will stick. She'll cling on by her fingernails.'

For what else can you do, once you're a queen? The pinnacle Elizabeth has climbed to is high and teetering. And once you're up, standing in the wind, they take the rope away. You must strain every sinew to keep your place. And if you fall? Well. Blood on the cobbles. And a throw of cold water to wash the mess away.

25.

There's blood on the cobbles already in Coventry. The heads of Elizabeth's father and her brother John have rolled into pools of it. Their luck ran out three weeks after they parted from Edward. Captured at Chepstow and dragged across the country to Gosford Green, where no charges were brought against them and they were submitted to no trial. Just the order given for an axe to the neck, signed by the Earl of Warwick and George Duke of Clarence, issued in the name of the King. A copy sent to Stillington. For the record.

'I should have taken it to the Queen first,' he says, sheepish, 'but I thought you'd do it better. You'd be more . . .'

'Women's work, is it? News of dead family.' Cecily supposes it is and takes the paper. Best get it done.

But Elizabeth, when she reads it, seems beyond tears. She folds the paper to the table and herself into a chair, and says nothing.

'I'm sorry,' says Cecily, and she is. Truly. But Elizabeth holds up a hand that trembles and turns her face away. Cecily perseveres, 'I had hoped . . .'

'Go away,' Elizabeth says. 'I want nothing from you.'

So Cecily calls Joan to sit with her mistress and leaves, but when the chamber door is closed she listens outside it, until the silence is rent by bitter sobs. When she turns to go, she's surprised to find her own cheeks wet. Weeping for the golden Woodville? No, not for him. He was a chancer all his life and has had a good run. No, her tears are for Jacquetta, newly made widow and robbed of a son. She's known her nearly forty years, been irritated by her for most of them, angry with her since this marriage between their children that has caused so much harm.

But Cecily has no one left alive now, bar her family, who has known her so long. Jacquetta was there when Edward was born. Held her hand when his infant life was almost lost. She must write to her. She wants to say, this is your own fault; none of it would have happened if you hadn't married your daughter to my son. But what would be the point? No. If her old friend were here now, she'd take her to the hearth, draw down ashes for their heads, and hold her through that first, terrible riptide of grief.

Her doleful letter can barely have arrived with Jacquetta when one comes for Cecily, delivered early morning by a messenger who has ridden through the night. It isn't from Jacquetta herself, but from her steward at Grafton, written in haste, urgent and alarmed.

'Grief on grief,' he writes. For Warwick's men came yesterday with the King's warrant and arrested his mistress.

Dear God.

'Before they took her, she bade me entreat for your help. She is desperate.'

The charge is witchcraft and soon will be made public. Leaden images have been found: a man and a woman, a king and a queen. By these, the charge says, Jacquetta brought about her daughter's marriage by sorcery. And another figure, an armed man pierced with a wire. By this, she sought to bring about the Earl of Warwick's death.

'Hasn't worked then, has it?' Cecily sneers beneath her breath.

She has barely finished reading when her door opens and the Queen comes, shaking with agitation, Joan Peasemarsh trailing red-faced behind.

Elizabeth, she can see, has received her own letter. It's in the hand stretched out before her as she crosses the room. Cecily hasn't seen Elizabeth since she was sent from her two nights ago. It's without precedent that the Queen comes here to her rather than sending a summons.

Cecily holds up her own letter.

'You've seen it then.' Wild-eyed Elizabeth is back, brittle and sharp, angry and afraid. 'What must we do? What must we do?'

Cecily comes around the table. 'Sit down, Elizabeth, please. We'll find what help we can for your mother . . .'

But Elizabeth only shakes her head. 'They've named me witch, too, in their talk. Your damned nephew and your vicious son. They'll come for me next!'

Ah, thinks Cecily, so that's your concern. She decides to be practical. 'No, Elizabeth, they won't. It would be too difficult. London wouldn't give you up. They'd need an army, and they don't have one to spare, or the time for a siege. You're not, for the moment, their most important consideration.'

Reports have been coming in for days now of risings up and down the country. A breakdown of law and order, civil disobedience that no one takes action to put down. Warwick's resources must be stretched to the limit. That's Hastings's work, Cecily knows. Good man. Hastings and my son, Richard.

Elizabeth isn't convinced. 'They won't rest till I'm dead!'

Well yes, thinks Cecily, that would give us all a quiet moment.

'They don't need you dead, Elizabeth,' she tells her, and it's the sad truth. 'They'll find your mother guilty and use her guilt to annul your marriage. You'll be dead enough for them then. Then Edward can marry someone else of their choosing. Someone French, probably.'

'And he'll do it!'

'Edward? Not willingly.'

'But he's going along with all of this, isn't he? Of course he is, or they'd have killed him!'

'Be sensible, Elizabeth. What choice does he have? Would you rather he put his foot down and found himself a corpse?'

Elizabeth shakes her head. 'I . . .'

'Would you?' Cecily insists.

Elizabeth looks suddenly bewildered, exhausted and thin. She's been pacing, but now she sits. 'No. I don't know. I don't know how all of this is happening. Edward said . . .' she casts about, 'Edward swore . . .'

'What did he swear?'

'That he'd always keep me safe. But my father and brother are dead and my mother will be burned for a witch.' The anger is gone and tears stand again in her eyes. 'My mother told me this marriage would be the making of us all. But she was wrong. It's our destruction.'

Perhaps Annette is right and Elizabeth isn't made for this. It's too much. For, balanced on her high pinnacle, she must keep not only herself aloft, but her whole family; their titles and careers, marriages and ambitions. Their very lives, now. And as she teeters she feels their shifting weight and their desperate hands scrabbling at her skirts.

'Oh, Elizabeth . . .'

'I don't know if I can bear it. I just want this to end.'

Cecily takes pity, kneels before her, grasps her hand and holds it tight. 'So do I. And it will, one way or another. Soon.'

Elizabeth looks at her askance. 'How?'

'They've called a Parliament. Warwick and George. In York at September's end. At it, Edward will be made to ratify Warwick's power, to annul your marriage, condemn your family and put Nevilles into every position of power in the country.'

Elizabeth is aghast. 'Then we'll be finished.'

'Except it hasn't happened yet,' says Cecily, looking hard into her face. 'The game isn't over and we still have pieces in play.'

She turns, and lifts from the table another letter. 'This came last night from Richard. I'd have told you of it this morning but, well . . .' She gives it into Elizabeth's hands. It carries rumours of a Lancastrian uprising on the Scottish border; old diehards that won't give in and have been waiting for a chance. 'This uprising isn't just a threat to England, Elizabeth. Or to us,' explains Cecily carefully. 'It threatens Warwick, too. The rebels' plan is to force

Warwick's hand to put Edward down entirely and mad Henry back on the throne.'

Elizabeth is at a loss. 'This is good news?'

Cecily sighs. 'Elizabeth, do you play chess?'

A shake of the head.

'I thought not.'

So she explains. 'Warwick doesn't want mad Henry and Marguerite. He wants a chastened Edward doing his bidding. Or, if not that, his new son-in-law doing the same. So, he needs to put this uprising down. But, you know, he's short, now, of men and resources. Overstretched, as I've said.' She points again to the letter in Elizabeth's hands. 'Richard says Warwick is sending out calls for men, but the lords of England will send none. They say, "Is this order really from the King?" They say, "If you want us to fight for the King, let's see him."'

'So, you mean, we want this Lancastrian uprising to happen?'

'Very much. And before September's end.'

'And Richard and Hastings are doing all of this?'

'Richard and Hastings, and the other men Edward sent out before he was taken. And we, with the letters we write. And we must write again, Elizabeth. We must remind people that, when first my family was fighting mad Henry for the crown, it was Edward who won at Mortimer's Cross and at Towton. And Warwick who lost at St Albans. If they want a winner, they must be reminded who to back.'

'This is a very dangerous game,' says Elizabeth.

'Yes. And played for very high stakes. So we must hold our nerve, Elizabeth. As Edward is holding his. And in the meantime, we must do what we can for your mother.'

26.

Westminster

'Do you imagine I've time for Margaret Beaufort now?'

Young Henry Tudor's mother has begged a moment's attention and waited, already, a patient hour until Cecily's steward
deemed it safe to interrupt his mistress's work. Cecily is dictating
letters, as she always is these days. This time on Jacquetta's behalf.
Urging women to urge their men to have no part in any trial she
might be brought to, or commission set to test her. There's a con-
federacy among women when it comes to charges of witchcraft,
for they know them to be easily brought and hard to refute; that
they are the vicious tools men take into their hands when they
wish to draw women into the maelstrom of their violence.

She has written to Warwick's wife saying, 'What is your husband thinking of?' To Warwick himself asking, 'Do you think it
is to your honour to make war on women?' And to her son,
George, she has sent a warning, 'Edward won't forgive an attack
on his queen's mother. And you'll soon be very much in need of
Edward's forgiveness. Mine, too.' She reminds them all of the
laws surrounding such accusations; that there must be a commission of investigation, that all must be above board, that witnesses
must be found and questioned, their testimony examined by state
and church. She's playing for time, she knows, but that's the only
game in play at this moment.

As one letter is finished and before another can be started, her
steward says, 'The lady asked first if George, the Duke of Clarence, was here.'

If he has learned anything in his long years of service, it's how to get her attention.

Cecily looks up from her papers. 'And did you tell her he was not?'

He nods. 'She seemed . . . relieved. Then asked for you.'

She humphs. 'Second to my son George, am I?'

His smile is wry when Cecily sighs and says, 'Tell her I'm coming.'

She's grown to like young Henry Tudor's mother in the years since Edward's crowning. She gives no trouble, which is something these days, and when she comes to court is good company. On occasion, Cecily has visited her manor at Woking, where she keeps a good library and breeds sharp hawks. Margaret has attended the Queen's last two childbeds, which Cecily thinks is generous, given her history. Or perhaps just politic. Either way, commendable. She keeps company with the Queen sometimes and Cecily has found on occasion that, if she needs Elizabeth to understand something without seeming to instruct her, it is useful, first, to tell Margaret Beaufort.

Cecily looks over her secretary's shoulder as he sands the last missive and takes a moment to think. She can imagine, well enough, why Margaret is here. Her son is William Herbert's ward. And William Herbert is dead. 'Have them ready for my seal,' she tells him and steps away.

Margaret's obeisance is deep, and when Cecily raises her and kisses her on both cheeks, she sees that her face is pale and the skin beneath her eyes shadowed blue.

'I'm sorry to trouble you,' Margaret says, 'when there must be so very much that demands your attention.'

'A visit from you is always welcome, Margaret.'

'I'm afraid I'm less visitor, more petitioner today.'

'I imagine you're here about your son?'

Margaret looks up wide-eyed, falling on Cecily's words like a merlin on a rabbit's neck. 'You've news of him?'

'I'm sorry, no, none at all.' She leads her to the room's tall window and sits her down in its embrasure. 'Have you reason to believe such news would be bad?'

Margaret lowers her head. 'I've been in some distress.' Her fingers twist in her lap, but her words remain calm, measured.

Henry is twelve now, old enough to squire for a knight. And in that capacity, William Herbert took him on the campaign to dent the head of Robin of Redesdale. A good first outing for a young lad, or should have been. No one expected it would get so serious.

'He was present at the battle?'

Margaret nods. 'Yes. At first, I could find out nothing and feared that . . .' She takes a breath. 'But I've learned he was taken alive from the field by one of Herbert's men, a relative of his wife, I believe. I've written to her but . . .'

'At Pembroke, no doubt?'

'Yes.'

'Good, well, so far I can help you – she's not there. I've had notice that she's taken her household to her brother's home until the outcome of this current . . . difficulty . . . is clear. I imagine Henry has been taken there.'

'Oh, I pray so!' says Margaret with new hope.

'Then be at ease.' She takes Margaret's twisting fingers in her hands, calming. 'We'll write today and discover. If I can put one woman's heart at rest about the fate of her son, I'm happy to do it.'

'Thank you. And I'm sorry. You must be in such fear for your own.'

She'll never admit it. 'I've no fear for Edward. He's a man of great resource and I'm sure all will be well soon enough.' She takes back her hands, makes a calm show of smoothing her sleeves. 'I hear you asked first for another of my sons, George.'

'I asked if he was here.'

Cecily nets her fingers. 'Because you're in fear of him? Or because you wanted his attention?'

Margaret looks away.

'You must understand, Margaret, that my son George and I are not, at present, great friends.'

Margaret turns back to her and speaks with quiet urgency. 'If you suspect me of having sympathies with him, or with his cause, I assure you, I have not.'

'Then?'

'I was told he held authority here in Westminster.'

'Ah. He'd like to. But he doesn't.'

'So I see. But, had I found it to be so, I confess I would have sought his help, as I've sought yours.'

'To discover the whereabouts of your son?'

Margaret nods, tight, her lips pressed closed.

'Perhaps you'd have asked more? You might have asked for your son's custodianship. For the restoration of his titles.'

Again Margaret's head dips. 'Though I've no call on the Duke of Clarence's friendship.'

'No, indeed. So you might have had to offer him something in return. Your support for his cause. Your husband's men at his disposal.'

Margaret's reply is slow but, when it comes, quiet and emphatic. 'I'm relieved not to have been so tempted.'

Cecily leans back and a distance opens between them. 'You are, at least, very honest.'

'I see no reason to lie to you.' Margaret slides from her seat to her knees, puts her hands within Cecily's and bows her head over them. 'Lady, you've dealt fairly with me. My son has been safe. Happy, even. I've had hope, and been content. My loyalty is to your house. I trust I've given you no cause to doubt it. But, my son. My son commands my heart. If your Edward's rule topples, and I must deal with another to secure Henry's safety, I'll do it. Though I swear to you, it's not my wish.'

She looks up into Cecily's face and her fine eyes brim with tears. 'It is my daily prayer that I may one day see my son Earl of Richmond, a friend to King Edward and a comfort to his mother.' She laughs, shallow and shaky. 'I wear out my knees in hope of it.'

She's so small, so earnest, and still so young, that Cecily can't help but be moved by her. She leans towards her again, lays a hand against her cheek and, with a thumb, wipes away the single tear that has escaped her reserve. She smiles and teases, gently, 'Whenever we speak of your son, you end up weeping.'

Margaret screws her eyes, blinks them dry and says, all openness, 'He is my singular treasure.'

And he is. Though she got him lovelessly enough and the birthing of him broke her; though, since he was born, she can bear no man's touch for fear of what it might bring. She would brave anything for him. It's as if, Margaret sometimes feels, that by some magic he lives both in the world and in her body still, so that she must measure her every step for his safety and husband every breath for his nourishment.

Cecily looks down at her; what should she do? 'I'm surprised,' she says, 'that you come to me for help today, and not to the Queen, who is, surely, a friend to you.'

In this, as in all Margaret's answers, there is certainty and no guile. 'The Queen doesn't love her sons as we love ours.' And then, to explain, 'She's not felt,' she taps a finger at her heart, 'this binding.' She takes a slow breath, it requires courage to say it. 'You have, I know. I've seen the way you are, with Edward.'

Cecily feels her breath catch. She imagines, always, that nothing of herself is seen but what she wishes to reveal. But it's as if a chord has been touched deep within her, and she lets her breath fall on its thrumming note. 'Our sons are all very far away.'

'I pray we'll have them soon restored to us.'

This must end, determines Cecily, or I'll find myself weeping too.

So she sits back, signals Margaret to do the same, and returns her hands to her lap. 'Here's what I'll do.' She watches Margaret's careful intake of breath. 'I'll write to Herbert's wife. Our first sensible step is to determine that your boy is safe. If he is, I'll let her know your wishes for his future.'

'Thank you.'

Cecily raises a finger, a caution. 'But I'll not force her hand. She's lost a husband. I'll take nothing more from her that she doesn't wish to give. You must know, she has imagined a marriage between her daughter and your son.'

'No,' says Margaret. 'She has imagined a marriage between her daughter and the Earl of Richmond. Until my son is that, she'll make no pledges.'

Cecily chuckles. 'You're a sharp blade.'

Margaret inclines her head, it's not a denial. 'And, you know, I can imagine a time when Edward might reward Herbert's wife by making my son worthy of her daughter. But, forgive me, until Edward is secure again on his throne, I am all uncertainty. And please, forgive again, should Warwick win . . .'

A change draws Cecily's eye to the open window beside her. An east wind has thrown a ripple of light across the Thames and she feels the air freshen for the first time in days.

She blinks slow and lets the light play a moment behind her eyes, then she turns again to Margaret. 'Listen, you're right that your son's safety, and all his hope of a future, lie in Edward's rule. Now here's my promise, given in good faith, as certain as if God gave it to you himself. My Edward will return in strength.'

27.

September 1469

September brings relief from the heat, but not the waiting. Though Cecily is, at least, able to call Margaret back to her with news that her son is safe. 'He's taken no harm,' she tells her.

Margaret contrives not to weep, but thanks Cecily on her knees and begs her to share prayers. So they go to the chapel together, where, with fervour, Margaret urges God towards the further restoration of her son.

It's good, Cecily supposes, to have done a small kindness for someone. She reminds God of it and he chooses, perhaps, to reward her, for only days later she has good news of her own sons. Another of Richard's hurried missives, delivered at first light, tells her he's riding north again in haste, that their plan has worked, the Lancastrian rebels are up and, faced with them, Warwick can no longer hold. Edward is free and in charge again.

'I'll meet him in York,' Richard says. 'He's calling up men. I've five hundred of my own and I'll gather more as I go. Now, there's going to be some fighting, Mother. But don't worry,' his words remind her of his father's wry smile. 'Edward's good at that, and I'm learning.'

Of the rebels among their own kin, Richard says nothing. Only closes with words for the Queen: 'Tell her for her comfort that Anthony is well and I expect to see him in York. And that her mother is freed from Warwick Castle. An honour guard escorts her to you in London. Tell the Queen, Edward would make no other move until this was agreed and done.'

She doesn't run exactly, but her steps have rarely been brisker. Her veils lift in the wind of them and servants turn to gawp. She points to one and, without slowing her pace, commands, 'Tell Chancellor Stillington to meet me in the Queen's chambers.'

She doesn't wait to ask admittance, just looks at the door guards with such fierce expectation that they almost fall over themselves to open. Elizabeth looks up from where a maid, on her knees, is binding a jewelled rosary about the narrowness of her waist.

'Edward's free,' Cecily says, marching towards Elizabeth with Richard's letter in an outstretched hand. 'The fight's on.'

The maid has only a moment to lean back as the Queen's legs fold beneath her and she sinks to the floor amid her skirts. Cecily can't help but laugh, and Elizabeth too gives way to a gasp of relief as Cecily reaches an arm, leans in and says, 'Your mother, too.'

By the time she's pulled Elizabeth to her feet again there is the sound of a man's footsteps coming fast. 'Stillington,' says Cecily. And here he is, with letters of his own in either hand.

'From Warwick,' he holds up the first, and then the second, 'and from the King himself, lest there be any doubt.' His grin threatens to split his face. 'There will be no Parliament.'

No Parliament but, as Richard has said, a fight coming. And Edward at its centre. Well, good. Cecily feels the thrust of muscle as her son finds his stride again, the powerful swing of his fresh-metalled arm. She relishes it: this release of energy, this forward motion, the channelling of his will into the body, into the long stretch of his sword. She looks down at her own hand, curled about the knife that cuts her meat, and sighs. For the moment her own work is done, the impetus of action passed to him. And all the uncertainties of their future, his to fix.

The Queen, it seems, envisages none.

'When Edward has put down the Lancastrian rebels,' Elizabeth says, paring flesh from bone, 'he'll turn to those that bite his own bosom. Warwick and his brothers. The Duke of Clarence. He will avenge my family's slaughter and my mother's humiliation.'

She speaks with conviction, as if her tongue had an edge to sever heads.

Cecily says nothing. Only looks from her plate to Jacquetta, who averts her eyes and fiddles with crumbs. It's easier, Cecily has discovered, to pity Jacquetta when she is far away than when she sits across the table from you while her daughter describes a vengeance that encompasses your own son. She's angry enough with George to take a blade to him herself, but isn't ready yet to let Elizabeth do it.

She's about to speak when Jacquetta lays a soft hand on her daughter's sleeve and says, 'I'm sure Edward will do all necessary to secure both England and our honour.'

After dinner, Jacquetta comes to her alone. Cecily has left them to each other, the Queen and her mother, since, two days ago and three behind Richard's letter, Jacquetta tottered from her carriage ashen-faced and unsteady on to Westminster's cobbles. She looks better now, refreshed at least, but the brightness that's been hers from youth is extinguished and the folds of her face draw heavily down. Cecily brings her to sit by the fire; the evening is cool enough at last to make one welcome. She puts wine in her hand and lets her speak in her own time.

'I'd not imagined,' Jacquetta says at last, 'that my family would be so hated.'

'Hadn't you?' Cecily, already tired, is torn between vexation and pity. 'Even when you reached to pluck the most coveted of prizes and it fell into your hands like an apple?'

'No.' An honest answer. 'I suppose I saw only the ripeness of the fruit. My daughter a queen. My family . . .'

'. . . raised to the heights? Well, you've had all that. A little hatred, a little envy, is the price of it.'

'The price is already,' corrects Jacquetta, her voice breaking, 'a husband, and a son.' She breathes in courage to look at Cecily with eyes once blue, turned dull and milky. 'And may yet rise further.'

'It may. And I pay it too. A son estranged. A family divided. For your daughter's marriage, I'm at war with my brother's sons. With my own son.'

Jacquetta's eyes lower. Her hands in her lap flutter. 'I'm sorry.'

Cecily shakes her head. 'What can I do with such an apology? It blunts no swords. Besides, I think you wouldn't wish the apple back to the tree.'

A shrug, an admission. 'No.' Her brow furrows deep. 'Elizabeth's first marriage . . .'

Oh, thinks Cecily, I'm to hear of this now, am I? Elizabeth's first husband was a nobody whose death no one mourns.

'. . . it was the best I could do for her then. But it was nothing. Who could see how beautiful she is and not believe her worth more? So, when Elizabeth caught your Edward's eye . . .'

Cecily looks away. It is pitiful. 'You mean, when you brought Elizabeth into Edward's eye.'

'You'd have done the same,' Jacquetta admonishes.

'Your marriage to Richard Woodville made good marriages for your daughters hard to get. I'd not have done that.'

'No. You wouldn't. But I find I can't regret that, either.' Her eyes are thick with unshed tears.

Cecily sighs, relents a little. 'I suppose there's no point, now, in regret. No time for it either.'

Jacquetta shakes her head. 'No.'

'At least now we both want the same man to win.'

'Certainly. We pray for the same outcomes.'

'Your daughter doesn't, quite.'

Jacquetta hesitates. 'What she said tonight, was . . .'

'Not unreasonable, in the circumstances. But it'll do her no good to bay for blood.'

'Surely, Warwick at least must be brought down?'

'Well, yes, he must be stopped.' Certainly, Cecily can see no good end to this that leaves Warwick alive. 'But it's not like he's a cutpurse whose hand you can lop and have done. His fingers are in every pie in England.'

Even now it wouldn't be easy to destroy Warwick without bringing the country up in arms. And even if it were, there is Edward himself, whose weaknesses she knows well enough. Warwick has released Edward, so Warwick must, however reluctantly, have surrendered to him. Could Edward, who threw forgiveness over even Henry Beaufort's penitent shoulders, call his fellow pirate a traitor if he came to him on his knees? And how could he condemn Warwick, without condemning his own brother, too?

There's no way to explain this to Jacquetta, so she only pours for them both and turns again to the fire. 'You should know, Jacquetta, and you can break it to your daughter in whatever way you like, I'll save George if I can.'

Jacquetta's answer is immediate and unfeigned. 'Of course you will. What mother wouldn't?'

And that's Jacquetta, she thinks, soft in heart and head. They watch the fire a while till Cecily speaks again. 'I'd geld him perhaps. Drag him twenty miles behind my horse. Beat him with sticks. But I'd not kill him.'

It raises a sad smile from Jacquetta.

The warmth and the wine and the sadness make a way for reminiscence. 'Do you remember,' says Jacquetta, wistful, 'those summers in France?'

And Cecily finds that her pity for her old friend's loss extends just so far that she'll let her words open a door on days long gone; when her own Richard was Lieutenant of France and the golden Woodville among his captains. When their husbands were young and had all before them, and their children toddled and played together on Rouen's broad lawns.

'We were always pregnant,' says Cecily, rueful.

'Yes. And wanted nothing more for our babies but that they live, and be happy.'

Cecily squints a little into the fire. Did we? Is that all?

28.

October 1469

The Mayor of London sends four hundred citizens to meet the King on the road, and the aldermen in scarlet and the guildsmen in blue stand in place outside St Paul's, collaring their furs against a stiff October breeze, until he comes and brings the sun with him through the bannered streets. He takes his queen's face in his hands on the cathedral steps, scans it hungrily, kisses it and calls her his sweet, then over her shoulder grumbles to his mother, 'What's all this fuss about?'

'You've won a battle, haven't you?'

A quirk of the lip. 'Minor skirmish.' Then he shoulders his way inside with the Queen beside him, stiff-backed and silent but holding fast to his hand. 'Let's get this done then.'

It's left to Richard to lead her in, and he winks at her as he does so. Jacquetta follows in their wake, heavy and grateful on Anthony's arm. The cathedral fills behind them and its rafters lift with song There's much to give thanks for. The Lancastrian rebels are down and their great purpose brought to nothing, except the use her house has made of it. So Cecily gives thanks, both for the defeat of the rebellion and for its happening at all; for the voices raised about her, the great lords who stood firm and fought for Edward, the men of London who, when Warwick knocked, left him standing at the door. But Cecily has as much to say to God in petition as in gratitude. For in all of this great crowd, where is the Earl of Warwick? Where is her prodigal son?

'Each in their own homes, Mother,' Richard tells her. 'Where Edward's sent them to cool their heels.' The King and all his company have come back to Westminster. Richard's bath has taken the sweat of the road off him and, because she has sent his servants away so that she can speak to him, he must swipe at his own damp hair, which kinks and swipes back and won't set straight. His robe is tied loose about him and his narrow feet are bare. He gives up, throws the comb on to a table and himself into a chair. 'I'm surprised he hasn't told you so himself.'

'Well. Of course, he's with the Queen.' She hears the sulkiness in her own voice.

'Oh. Well, yes, I suppose he is.' Richard grins that slow grin that was his father's. 'They've been apart a long time.'

'I'd have thought he'd take a moment first to explain himself to his mother.'

'Perhaps he's practising for that by explaining himself to his wife.' Then his face turns serious. 'I don't imagine he'll find it easy.'

'She's keen to see her father's murderers dead. Perhaps I am too.'

'Edward won't do it, you know that. Nor would you.'

'I'd like to see them hung up by their pizzles.'

He grimaces. 'I'm fairly confident he won't do that, either. He'll pardon them. If he can.'

'And that'll be an end to all this, will it?'

He spreads his hands.

'Come on,' she says. 'You've spent more time with Warwick than most in recent years, is he amendable?'

'Not this past year, I haven't. I'm out of his orbit.' He nets his hands, turns his palms and pushes them away from him, a gesture so like his father's it stabs her heart. 'And glad to be so.'

'Your brother George is in it still.'

'It'll be a hard trick to break him from it. But it must be done.' He rolls his shoulders, releasing a crick. 'George has a suggestible nature. He's vain and has a weak head. That apart, he's my brother, and I'd like to think well of him.'

'And do you think well of Warwick?'

He sighs and leans back. 'I think as you do, that he's the brightest star in Edward's firmament. Brilliant and bold, just as Edward is. I'm just not sure there's room enough for them both in a single sky.'

She sighs and sits down opposite him. 'But your own choice is made, Richard?'

He looks at her, incredulous. 'Do you doubt?' He shakes his head. 'I told you long ago and nothing's changed. I suppose I'm a simple man, Mother. My brother is King of England. I love him, and I've given him my oath.' He shrugs and lifts his face to her again. 'That's it.'

She nods and finds herself just staring at him, the planes of his cheeks, the squareness of his jaw, the bronzed skin of face and neck giving way to tender white, where clothes or armour have concealed him. He's had a hard summer, she imagines, most of it in the saddle, much of it with a blade in his hand. As he reaches a hand to swipe again at his hair, which is dry now and falling all ways, the sleeve of his gown falls back to reveal a forearm that, though pale as his breast, is fine-boned and muscled. Her youngest. No longer a boy.

She'd like to lean forward, take his messy head between her hands and kiss it, but she only nods and says, 'I'd better let your man come back and sort that out.' Then squeezes his shoulder as she passes to the door.

That night, at the homecoming feast, Richard's brother the King doesn't scruple to kiss him, nor to throw a meaty arm about his slender frame as he presents him to the room. He calls him his true brother, the great prop of his reign. Then pulls him round to face him, hands on either shoulder, and says, 'And now High Constable of England, too.'

The room erupts in cheers, though Richard himself turns pale while men crowd to congratulate and clap him on the back.

He didn't see it coming, thinks Cecily. Well, nor did she. It's high office indeed.

While his brother is fêted, Edward steps to his mother and says, with a grin, 'Well, what do you think?'

'It's a lot for a boy barely seventeen.' England's Constable has the security of the realm in his remit and is architect of its military strategy.

'Oh, he'll grow into it, I'll put men alongside him for now. Anyway, I know you don't think much of him, Mother, but he's clever, and as fierce a fighter as you'll ever see. I wouldn't pick a quarrel with him when he's got that bloody axe in his hand.'

'You've no idea what I think of him,' says Cecily. 'In fact, I'm very interested in the careers of both your brothers.'

He grimaces. 'I'm sorry I've had no time to speak to you yet, Mother, but I'll come tomorrow and tell you all. I know what you've done, and the debt of thanks I owe you.' He nods across to where the Queen sits, straight-backed and unsmiling in her high chair. 'Not least your care of Elizabeth.'

'Well,' she says, smiling sly, 'I'm very happy to return her to your hands now.'

When he puffs out his cheeks and expels air she flicks a hand against his breast. 'She has suffered, Edward. You might be ready to forgive, I'm not sure she will be.'

'I don't know what I'm ready for,' he says. 'More trouble, probably.'

29.

March to June, 1470

London

Never any shortage of trouble. It springs up as the ice gives way on England's rivers and the first green blades of a still far-off summer drive sharp through loosening soil. In the flat lands of Lincolnshire, Lord Welles burns his neighbour's house and steals his goods. A private war, it might not seem to matter much, but since the neighbour is Edward's senior officer in the county, it does. So Welles is called to Westminster to explain himself, at length and on his knees. On his promise of reparation, he's pardoned, but when news comes that Welles's hot-headed son is gathering an army to protect his father from his king, Edward decides to deal with it himself. It's been a long winter after all, mostly spent wrangling in council chambers, so the chance to warm his muscles in a fight isn't unwelcome.

He goes to Baynard's to farewell his mother, and finds his brother George there.

'You can't be entirely surprised,' Cecily tells him. 'I've been trying to get the two of you in a room together for months.'

George has been pardoned for last year's revolt, and Warwick too, after displays of remorse both public and painful. But the three men have kept their distance since. Licking their wounds, testing the depth of their hurt. Like pushing a tongue into the gummy hole of a tooth newly pulled. Salty, miserable, irresistibly stinging.

'Swear your loyalty and you'll lose nothing of what you had

before,' Edward told them in a display of steely-eyed magnanimity at the turning of the year. 'You'll be as you ever were. I'm not a vengeful man.'

It isn't entirely true that they'll lose nothing. Both have lost honour, and Warwick's family no longer dominates the north. Edward has taken the earldom of Northumberland from John Neville and given it to Harry Percy. Percy's people held it of old, and have no love for the Nevilles. It's an irony that John, of all Warwick's brothers, didn't take Warwick's side in the rebellion. But he didn't take Edward's either. Just sat on his hands. Still, his earldom is a lynchpin of Neville family power, so the family loses it, and he's made Marquess of Montagu in compensation. A grand title but with little money to support it. 'It's like being tipped from a castle to a magpie's nest,' he complained to Cecily, then said no more. Just shrugged, sealed his lips and got on with it.

Faced with the oath, George took it and stepped away, but Warwick looked up from his knees and said, 'I've lost enough already, having forfeited my kingly cousin's love.'

Edward leaned forward then, grasped Warwick's shoulder and said, in a gravel-slaked voice, 'Earn it back then.' And Cecily, watching, had thought for a moment they'd fall on one another's breasts and weep. But Edward checked himself, drew back his arm and came to his feet as Warwick bowed himself from the chamber.

'We're in perfect amity, my cousin, my brother, and I,' Edward told the world. But that night, in his cups before Cecily's fire, he looked for a moment, lost. He sighed and said, 'My cousin Warwick. My own brother,' then scrubbed at his eyes before rolling his shoulders and saying, 'If they try it again, I'll kill the fuckers.'

Cecily greets Edward now with a kiss to both cheeks. George greets him by sinking to his knees and repeating his oath of loyalty.

'Haven't we done this already, George?' Edward asks, cautious.

'Oh, get up, George,' says Cecily, pushing at his shoulder with an outstretched hand. 'There's no one here to be impressed by your humility. You're the King's brother in my house, not his subject.'

'Strictly speaking he's both, wherever he is. But yes. Get up, George.' And Edward reaches a hand to pull his brother to his feet. George takes it and they are, at least, smiling.

'Now, do you think you can eat a meal without sticking knives in each other?' asks Cecily over her shoulder. She's leading the way to the next room, where the smell of roast meat bids them warm and welcome.

They talk about everything and nothing, and her boys drink more than they should, George going hard at that sweet Portuguese wine he favours, so thickly dark it coats his lips and tongue. Edward keeping pace with a drier drink and wearing it better.

'So you're going into Lincolnshire to put down this Welles business?' George says at last, on a stretch.

'Want to come with me?' says Edward, testing.

George shakes his head, slow, and smiles. 'No. I'm keeping my sword in my scabbard and myself out of trouble,' he tips his cup towards his brother, 'as you told me to do. No fighting for me unless you command me.' He blinks, as if an idea just occurred to him, 'Are you commanding me?'

Edward looks at him several moments; Cecily can see he's wondering if he should, if he could bear his company so long. 'No,' he says, turning his cup in his hands. 'Don't trouble. I'll take care of this.'

'George is going home to his wife tomorrow,' says Cecily. 'She'll have a babe in her arms before summer comes, please God.' Isabel Neville, she thinks. I was there when she was born. Can it really be twenty years? Her men are not alone in feeling the losses of recent months, this wounding severance of kin.

'I should spend time with her before she begins her confinement,' says George, shrugging. 'So my Lady Mother says.'

'You'll have to keep both swords in your scabbard then,

George,' says Edward with a gesture. And then they're both giggling, like green boys, embarrassed and delighted with themselves, their hands across their eyes and their shoulders shuddering.

'What fools you are,' Cecily chides. 'And now you should go home too, Edward, if you're to be fit for the riding tomorrow.'

'Aye,' he comes to himself, stretches and stands. 'Share my barge, George?'

'I'm staying here tonight.'

'Are you now?'

'Under his mother's good influence,' says Cecily.

It's full dark as they come to the river steps, the torches in their sconces reflecting fire on stone still wet from an evening of drizzle. Edward's barge is waiting, its oarsmen huddled against the cold. The wind is blowing up the river and, at this moment, you wouldn't believe spring to be on the way. She pulls Edward's fur-lined cloak closer about his shoulders and lets him kiss her, relishing the warmth of his lips on her brow and the smell of wine on his breath.

'I'll be there in the morning to watch you ride out,' she says, 'just as I always am.' He's going off to fight again. She'll never grow used to it.

'All right,' he says. 'But this is nothing. I'll be back before you know I've gone.'

'Of course you will.'

She pats his breadth of shoulder and he's off, trotting sure-footed down the steps. But just as he reaches the boat she finds herself hurrying down to him, leaving George at the door. She takes his gloved hand and holds it to her breast. 'Better times ahead, Edward. A good start tonight and more to come. Your father would have hated to see his sons at odds.'

'I hate it myself, Mother.' He takes her bare hand between his and kisses it. 'I'll be a good brother to him, for Father's sake and yours. If he doesn't cross me.'

He lets go and steps into the barge.

'He'd have come with you tomorrow, you know, if you'd asked.'

She wonders if he's heard this last but as he takes his seat he raises his hand, nods and says, 'I know.' And as the oars pull him into the river's flow he raises his voice. 'God keep you, George.'

She turns, lifts her skirts from the wet, and makes her careful way back to her troublesome son who stands, shoulders hunched against the wind, watching his brother disappear. 'Your good luck's held, George,' she tells him as she walks ahead of him to go indoors. 'I hope you're thankful for it.'

That night, in her bed, the thought of George asleep under her own roof keeps her wakeful. It's a rare enough event, she supposes, now he's a man. She'd like to go and watch him sleep, as she did in his infancy, as she did with all her children, for nothing but the pleasure of seeing them breathe, feeling their restful pull on her heart. She blinks, and finding her eyes gritty with sleep-lack, gives herself to the memory of his birth; that long ago lying-in in Dublin when she pinched herself to wakefulness for three long nights, watching his new-born breast rise and fall, willing the life to stay in him. She can admit now, but only to herself and in the dark, that it wasn't done for love, only that she didn't want to lose another son and dared God to his face to take this one from her. Were she honest, she'd say that even then, before his eyes could focus and when his hands could only grasp, George's pull on her heart was never restful. That it was a trouble to her. And that the trouble sprang from an irrational but certain knowledge that one day he would wrong her and wound her to the core. She turns her face into the pillow, squeezes her eyes tight shut in shame.

What sort of a mother is she?

A week later, a letter from George brings more worry than comfort. It tells her he's decided to aid his brother after all.

'I'm resolved,' he writes, 'and with Warwick too, to bring an army to him, that we might defeat his enemies together.' She finds the idea of George going anywhere with a sword at his hip and men at his back to be no reassuring thing. In her heart she'd like to believe his intentions good. The ice in her bones tells her otherwise.

'Stay where you are,' she writes. Damn fool.

The next day, she knows to trust her bones. If George is in the saddle, he rides against his brother, not to his aid. Word comes from Edward about the men of Welles's army. 'Before I kicked their arses at Empingham,' he writes, 'they called out full-throated for Warwick and Clarence. Well,' and she can hear the bitter anger in his voice, 'they called out louder for Christ's pity when we came at them. When they turned their shit-stained tails and ran.' He has sent messages to Warwick and to George to put down their arms and come to him, to explain themselves, to make their intentions plain, and to redeem their honour, if they can.

Cecily lays out paper, begins to write: 'George . . .'

But what can you say to a son who calls down swords against his brother, war upon his house? And what do you ask of God for him? Turn his heart? Strike him down? Bring him within my arm's reach so I may deal the bloody blow myself?

But George, and Warwick too, are beyond her reach. Welles, captured, has confessed that all he did was at their order and with their aid. He himself but a decoy to draw Edward to his death.

So the Earl of Warwick and George Duke of Clarence are declared traitors. Rewards are offered for their arrest. They protest their innocence. Swear they've done no wrong. They'll come before Edward in the north country, explain themselves and beg his pardon. With a mother's heart, Cecily knows they won't come. With a brother's heart, full of rage and anguish, Edward rides to the appointed place and finds she's right. They're flying south and west towards Clarence lands where their women wait, and to the coast, where Warwick's ships lie at anchor.

Cecily doesn't need Edward to tell her what they plan. They'll head for Calais, where Warwick is captain, where he has authority to call up men, and money to buy mercenaries. 'I've sent word,' writes Edward, 'to bar them entry to the port.'

Cecily writes to Meg in Burgundy. 'We're at war,' she tells her. 'Have your husband raise his fleet. If your rebel brother tries for Calais, drive him back or take him.' She thinks how this will grieve her daughter, who on her last night in England could speak only of her fear for him. Meg's grief is an echo of her own. At night she wraps her arms about her body and wonders how it could have so betrayed her. How her husband's good seed planted in it could have borne this sick and rotten fruit.

For Edward then, a mad pursuit and a desperate scramble. Long rides across foul ground on blown horses. For Cecily, a seething wait, endured in the company of Elizabeth, who looks at her through scalding eyes and reminds her, every hour, how Cecily's family wrong her. When at last Edward clatters into Exeter, it is to learn that his brother and the Earl have been and gone. 'Taken to the sea,' he writes. 'And their women with them.'

It is possible, Cecily discovers, to feel pity for Warwick's daughter, George's wife. Poor Isabel, what kind of a birthing can it have been? In a ship's cabin, on a rough sea, driven from Calais by cannon fire, harried by Burgundian ships, her child born gasping, and dead within a day, its useless body swallowed by the sea.

'I hope the fish feed on it,' grumbles Elizabeth to Cecily. 'I hope demons gorge on its soul!'

They're arriving at Canterbury, tired and tetchy, where tomorrow Edward is expected and the council will meet.

'It was my grandchild,' Cecily reminds her. Though in truth she wonders what good could come of any son of George's. Perhaps it's best the creature's dead.

'I've given you grandchildren!' Elizabeth snarls. She looks queasy, ill. Hardly surprising. Last night, as they travelled, Jacquetta confided that Elizabeth sickens in the mornings and is likely three months gone.

'Then she should have stayed at home,' said Cecily. There could be no worse time. Tomorrow's council must make urgent plans to repel invasion, for Warwick's desperate flotilla has landed in Normandy, where Louis himself came out open-armed to greet him. Louis, who has waited a patient decade to stir up trouble in England, and has polished Warwick into a ready tool, handy for that purpose.

30.

June to August, 1470

Canterbury

The obvious things are done. With the council's support, Edward strengthens sea defences on the south coast and Kent, where an invasion landing is most likely. Loyal Anthony Woodville is given Warwick's old title of Admiral of the Fleet and sent to patrol the Channel. Men of Warwick's, stragglers caught in the last desperate rush from England, are made an example of, their mutilated corpses staked upside down to the ground, their severed heads mounted on their arses and staring out to sea. 'See what's waiting for you,' their twisted faces say. 'Come and get it.'

'Had you done the same for your cousin and brother last year,' Elizabeth snarls as Edward hands her into her carriage, 'we wouldn't be threatened as we are now.' The women are heading back to London, Edward to shore up the coastal defences, Richard with him.

'You'd have relished the sight, Elizabeth. I'm sure,' says Edward in his dangerous voice; the one that's a thin skin stretched and flaming over a boil of anger.

'I live in anticipation of it.' She taps a finger, sharp against her brow. 'I conjure the image hourly in my mind.'

'Beware, madam. Such blood-filled thoughts might mar the child you carry.'

Cecily, mounted on her mare beside them, reins in close and leans from the saddle. 'Is it wise, do you think, to part bickering at such a time?' She leans closer still and hisses, 'And so publicly?'

Elizabeth straightens in her seat. Edward nods to his mother then turns to say something, more softly, to his wife. Cecily sees one white hand reach out to grasp his, the other laid protectively over the slight swell of her belly. She moves away to give them privacy.

In a minute or two he comes to her, leans a shoulder on her horse's wither and sighs. She watches him as the horse shifts and he adjusts. He looks tired. A little shamed.

'She is, of course, not wrong,' he says.

'No,' she admits. 'But I tire of being reminded.'

As the guards square up behind them, her mare skitters sideways. Edward steps back as her firm hand stills it, but she can't hide a grimace at the sharp twinge in her back.

'Will you be all right?' he asks.

She's stiff and has been sitting too long these past days, while the men talked. She feels her age when she isn't moving. 'Of course. The ride will loosen me.'

'You could share Elizabeth's carriage, you know.'

'Dear God, Edward, do you wish me in purgatory?'

A wry smile. 'You'd soon talk your way out of it.' But then he turns serious, lays his hand over hers on the rein. 'When you get back to London, lodge in the Tower. Elizabeth and the girls with you. And Elizabeth's Grey boys. Safest place.'

He means if Warwick comes. He means, if he loses.

He can't look at her, and makes, instead, a study of her horse's mane, twisting its strands between strong fingers. 'The new child might be a son . . .'

She's thought of this. And of what Warwick might do to it.

'. . . and you'd know what to do,' he says.

'Then I was right,' she replies. 'You do wish me in purgatory.' But this time she can't raise him with a joke, and suddenly she's fearful. The skin of his neck, as she looks down on his bent head, is so soft. 'Edward,' she says. He looks up at her again, squinting against a sudden break of sunlight. 'You've never parted from me in anything but certainty of victory. You always say, "Captain Mother, I'll be back before you know it."'

He straightens his shoulders, pulls himself up. 'This time will be no different.'

She leans down, closes a fist against his cheek, a handful of golden hair. 'Remember that the sun rises for you.' Then she looks up again and nods behind him. Richard has come up to make his goodbye and stands a discreet yard away, fiddling with the dagger at his waist. 'And you have the best of brothers at your side.'

She says it so that Richard can hear, and he grows an inch in the moment. 'Come bid me farewell, Richard,' she commands him.

He kisses her hand and asks for her prayers. Still so earnest.

'I will keep you constantly before God's face,' she promises, matching his solemnity. 'I'll give Him no rest.'

Little rest for anybody. The summer is hot, the coast ominous, the country restless. Pockets of trouble here and there, skirmishes and sudden quarrels. Edward is kept busy and always on the move. Cecily, with Elizabeth, holds London from the Tower.

Charles of Burgundy has spies in the French court. Well, of course he does. In July he writes that Louis fêtes Warwick and George at Angers, where there are private talks and public feasting. Then they're back in Normandy and sitting tight. Louis moves on to Amboise and who does he meet there? Well, who do you think? His cousin Marguerite, of course. Then back to Angers go Louis and Marguerite both, and Warwick is called to them, but not George, and Marguerite sends for her boy, Edouard, as she calls him in her sibilant French. Almost seventeen now, tall, fine-legged, with a jutting chin. A ripe enough heir to England, if only someone could win back his father's throne.

That someone might be Warwick. Marguerite commands her old enemy to his knees and keeps him humbled there a quarter hour, while Louis reads out first her terms, then Warwick's; details of a deal Louis would like them to make together, and what he himself will do to support it. At the end, her face as cold as judgement and basalt hard, she bids her old enemy to pull himself to standing, kiss her fingers and swear his oath on Edouard's as yet unblooded sword.

'I'll reconquer England,' Warwick swears. 'I'll free Henry your husband from the Tower and put him back on his throne. And Edouard, your true son of Henry's blood, will be heir to it.'

'Not George of York,' she demands.

'No. Edouard of Lancaster.'

Days later Warwick swears it all again, on a shard of the true cross in the cathedral at Angers, where, to seal the deal, Edouard takes Warwick's daughter, his youngest, Anne, to wife. And when the girl, leaving the church, stumbles and shakes, her mother takes her wrist and says, 'No weeping now. Your father's making you a queen.'

At home Elizabeth rages. Cecily resists the urge to slap her and says, 'If you stop shouting, you'll see there's cause for hope.'

'If that's so for God's sake tell me,' says Edward, who has ranted no less than his wife. He's come back to London and, before he meets with the men of his council, speaks with his mother and, because she won't be left out from their talk, his queen.

'Well, they're divided now, aren't they?' Cecily explains. 'Warwick and your brother? It's to our advantage. George went with Warwick because he promised to make him king. Well, that promise is broken, isn't it? What might George be now? Nothing much. Brother-in-law to a prince who despises him.'

'And subject to a queen who would revel in his blood . . .' says Edward, catching her drift.

'He's that already,' says Elizabeth. 'I'm a queen. I'd revel.'

'. . . He'd be better off with me.'

'Indeed,' Cecily confirms.

'Can Meg get word to him?' Edward asks.

'I'd think so, yes.'

He nods. 'Have her tell George he'll have full forgiveness if he returns to fight for me. Restoration of his titles, his place at my side. He need only turn his back on Warwick.'

'Yes. Now,' says Cecily, 'a second advantage. Warwick's promised he'll conquer England. Well and good. But he'll do it with a French army, for a French queen, and for her son who speaks English with an accent.'

'And he'll embroil England in a French war,' nods Edward. For now the terms of Louis's deal are known: France will provide the money, the troops and the ships to invade England, to make Henry king again and Warwick his general. But in return, Warwick has promised that, when Henry rules in England, or Marguerite rather, let's not delude ourselves, England's money, arms and men must be given to destroy Burgundy for France.

'There isn't a man alive in England who'll stomach it,' says Edward.

'So we must tell them about it,' says Cecily. 'This will be, at least at first, a war of words.'

'Well, that's your forte, Mother.'

'So we must take up our pens again,' says Elizabeth. 'We must call up our secretaries.'

'Yes,' says Cecily. 'There's much to do.'

'It will still come to a fight, Mother,' Edward cautions. 'You do know that.'

'Of course. But we've spoken so far of two advantages. Perhaps there are three.'

Edward waits for her explanation.

'Warwick's heart isn't in this. How can it be? Marguerite killed his father. Killed yours. Would you take her side?'

'I'd rather burn in hell.'

'Quite. And all Marguerite's generals who've shared her exile in France: Edmund Beaufort, Henry Holland, the Earl of Oxford. Jasper bloody Tudor. Every one of them despises Warwick at least as much as they despise you. More, perhaps. Do you think, once Warwick has won England for them, they'll allow him to live? They'll turn on him. They'll feed his liver to their dogs. Surely, in his heart, he knows this?'

'Then why is he in league with them?' Elizabeth, who has never learned chess.

Stretching her patience, Cecily explains, 'Kicked out of England, barred from Calais. Warwick's isolated and he's desperate. He's finished without Louis's support. And the price of that support . . .'

'. . . is mad Henry back on the throne,' says Edward.

'But once that's done,' Cecily shrugs. 'Louis has made Warwick his tool, but he'll be content to see him broken once he's had the use of him.'

Edward shakes his head. 'Then he, too, would be better off with me.'

'You'd not forgive him?' Elizabeth says aghast. 'Not again!'

Edward raises a hand. 'No, Elizabeth. There's no forgiveness now for the Earl of Warwick.'

'Though you might let him think there could be,' says Cecily. 'When the time is right.'

He nods. 'Yes.'

By August, Edward's back in the saddle heading north, where it's rumoured men of Warwick's affinity are gathering under mad Henry's standard. But before he goes, and because Warwick's invasion is expected any day, he fortifies the Tower and bids his family stay there.

As he rides, there appears behind him a rash of papers on church doors, moving up the country in his wake like fleas on a dog's back. Warwick's manifesto. It calls on his countrymen to re-crown Henry the rightful king. As well as rebel and usurper and other foul things, it names Edward a base-born bastard with no right to rule. 'For his mother, you must know,' the text goes, 'took an archer to her bed while her husband fought in France, and Edward is the fruit of it.'

Cecily looks up from reading a copy of it to find Elizabeth staring as if she expects an explosion of rage. Cecily only sneers and tosses the paper aside. 'My Lord of Warwick is so unoriginal,' she says. 'An archer. What an idea. Perhaps Marguerite came up with it. She knows all about adultery.'

Elizabeth's eyes widen.

'What? You don't think mad Henry put that boy in her belly, do you? Edmund Beaufort's father did it. And let no one tell you otherwise.'

Warwick's words are torn from the doors and fresh proclamations put in their place. 'The Earl of Warwick is a traitor, who threatens invasion of this realm with a French army,' people read. 'For a French queen, whose son is the late Duke of Somerset's bastard.'

'Tip for tap,' says Cecily.

31.

September 1470

The Tower

The weather in London stays fine as September comes in. In the evenings Cecily walks the Tower's walls. From their height she looks south to the teeming wharves of Southwark, then turns west, to look beyond the bridge, towards the quiet walls of St Mary's Priory and its riverside orchards heavy with fruit. It's restful, and she needs rest. She leaves Elizabeth to her mother. The Queen is seven months gone now, carrying high and robbed of breath. This spiralling climb would defeat her. She says it was never like this before, with her other children. Yesterday, Jacquetta suggested it might be because this time she carries a son, but, as she leaned affectionately forward to touch the swell of her daughter's skirts, Elizabeth batted her hand away crossly and said, 'I've borne sons before, Mother.'

Not when it counted, thought Cecily.

In the Channel, the weather is not so kind, and when an autumn storm snarls its way up Normandy's coast, Edward's guard on the Seine's mouth is scattered by the lash of its tail. In the lull that follows, Warwick's invasion force slips through. It lands in Plymouth on the seventh of the month. News of it reaches Cecily a week later, by which time its men are marching, their numbers growing by the day.

'How many and who?' she asks.

They are Warwick, of course. The Earl of Oxford. Jasper Tudor and the men of sixty ships.

'Not Marguerite or her whelp?' she presses. 'Not Edmund

Beaufort? Not his brother John?' They are the last of the Beaufort men, and she hungers for their blood. The messenger shakes his head.

'No,' she scorns. 'They send Warwick their dog ahead of them slathering for the bones of England. They'll turn up after and rip them from his jaws when he's done.'

The messenger screws his cap in his hands, fearful of her anger. 'Lady, your son, the Duke of Clarence, rides with Warwick. And his men of the west country rally to him.'

'Well, that much I'd guessed!' The lash of her voice almost takes the knees from under him. She's had no word from George since her messages were sent, though Meg says she has.

'He'll turn, Mother,' her letters say. 'I'm as sure of it as I am of salvation. When it comes to it, George will fight with us.'

He's showing little sign of it so far.

'George won't turn,' says Elizabeth now. 'And Edward's so far in the north.' She's breathless, panicked, but striving to be calm, her arms wrapped about her belly, her body shielding. 'They'll come here and we're helpless.'

'They won't and we're not,' says Cecily. 'Warwick of all people knows I'll hold London against him, and he hasn't time for a siege.'

But she's far from sure. So she calls London's mayor to her, John Stockton. He's new in the post and, though he's wanted the job all his life, looks to Cecily at this moment as if he'd cheerfully give it to his dog. 'Come now,' she says. 'We must call up men.' When he turns his face to her it's the colour of whey. She steps to his side and speaks low. 'Take heart, sir. Stand firm with me now and when the King comes he'll clap you on the back and say, "Good Mayor Stockton, who held the city in my name."'

She knows how to put courage into a man, even when her own is close to failing.

At her word, he calls up a reserve of three thousand. Cecily, with Elizabeth and Jacquetta beside her, watch them line up along the city walls, arrows fletched and ready, pikes glinting in a gold-spun sun.

'I've done this before, remember,' Cecily reassures Elizabeth. 'Ten years ago Marguerite sat an army outside London's gates and I kept them closed until Edward came and chased her like a terrier after a rat. I can do it again if I have to.'

When night comes she climbs the walls to feel the solid bulk of soldiery that stands between her and a threatening world. To stretch her eyes between their muscled shoulders and look north, where fleet-horsed messengers ride with word for Edward. 'Turn back. Warwick comes.' She feels in her body her son's resolution and rage, the tight turn of his horse on its haunches. She strains for the sound of hooves and hears nothing; only the shallow breath of the city below her, its sleepless stirrings in the dark, its fretful prayers in the morning and, every hour, the doleful tolling of its bells.

Four such days and nights, then news comes that the city is reprieved, at least for now. The rebels are following the Severn inland to Warwick's rich recruiting lands at England's heart.

'They're looking for a fight,' Cecily tells Elizabeth. 'And Edward will give them one.' He has good men with him and more will come. 'Soon there'll be news we can rejoice at.'

It's easy to be brave in daylight, and for the sake of Elizabeth and Jacquetta, who lean on her strength. But the nights are another matter. She spends them wakeful, testing her heart against the pain and grief to come. Soon her sons will set savage blades each against the other, and at least one of those sons will lose. How can you say, 'I hope it will be this one,' and not feel a tear to your heart? How can you pray for such a thing and not be damned?

The hours follow on like rosary beads, each one heavy with her sinful prayer. Stillington comes most days, says, 'No news,' and goes away again. Cecily and Jacquetta watch as Elizabeth's belly grows rounder, though her face is gaunt and food revolts her. The Queen's days are agitated and tearful. Scorning company, she walks for hours together beneath the towering walls of the inner ward, touching and leaning against them, as if measuring the depth of their protection, the height of her confinement. She walks till at last she must sit, gasping, then they bring her inside and lay her down. They dose her with borage and bugloss flowers, herbs of Leo to steady her heart. But as soon as her breath settles, she's walking again.

They begin to think of a lying-in at the Tower and order Elizabeth's women to prepare a room, the one Elizabeth slept in the night before her coronation. Cecily's daughter Anne says she'll come and be with the Queen when her time comes. They send to Westminster Abbey for the Virgin's girdle; the gift of the Holy Mother that strengthens queens in childbirth. They lay up oil of roses and sage, distillations of lavender, and the Queen's women are stitching. Tiny shirts and swaddling. Muslin sheets.

When they show her the room and all their industry, Elizabeth says, 'Am I not sequestered enough?' And yet she takes to spending her days there, curled and listless, watching the women sew.

'At least she's quiet,' says Cecily to Jacquetta. For the pacing and fretting wore on her nerves.

And here comes Stillington again. No news.

At mid-month, Margaret Beaufort comes. She brings books for Elizabeth: a life of St Margaret, one of St Elizabeth, each of their namesakes. Comfortable reading for a woman coming to childbed, stories of deliverance and the birth of longed-for sons.

'She'll be happy to have them,' says Cecily. 'As I am to see you. Though, I admit, I am surprised.'

'Are you?' asks Margaret. 'Why?'

'I'm not sure you should be a friend to us right now.'

'Now why do you say that?'

'Marguerite as queen might give you your son back. Your boy is mad Henry's nephew.'

Margaret puts her head on one side. 'Don't imagine I haven't thought of it.' Then she shakes herself. 'But Marguerite isn't queen yet. And it would be a reckless gambler who bet for Warwick against your Edward.'

Cecily's smile is tight but grateful. 'Of course, you're right. But, for your comfort, should she win, I promise not to tell her you were here.'

They go to the Queen and find her with her mother in the room that is made ready. Not quite sequestered, but almost. The door still stands open and the narrow windows still let daylight in. If Margaret is shocked by Elizabeth's wan face, or the tremble in her fingers as she leafs through the books' pages, she doesn't show it. She only says comforting things about the certainty of Edward's victory, the disadvantages of the invader.

'You should know,' Margaret says at last, sitting prim beside Elizabeth's bed with her small hands folded in her lap, 'I mean, I should tell you, that Marguerite has written to my husband asking him to bring the men of his affinity to her cause. To remember his old loyalties to Lancaster.'

It's a startling admission that leaves Elizabeth open-mouthed, brings Jacquetta's hand to her face and causes even Cecily to stare.

Margaret goes on, 'He won't, of course.'

'I'm astonished,' Cecily says. 'Not at the request, but that you speak of it so openly to us.'

Margaret turns eyes on her that are clear and unblinking. 'I want you to be in no doubt of where my loyalties lie.'

'We are sure, my dear.' Jacquetta leans forward, squeezes her hand. 'We're very sure of you.'

'Now. To happier matters, perhaps,' says Margaret, looking from Elizabeth's swollen body to the comforts of the room, the signs of preparation, the crib standing ready. 'I think soon there'll be a new child to show the King when he comes home.' She turns a soft smile on Elizabeth. 'If, when your time comes, it would help to have me here, I'll come most willingly.'

'I'd welcome it,' says Elizabeth. 'It will be soon enough.'

When evening comes Cecily walks Margaret to her carriage, sees her safely inside, then leans in and asks, 'I assume your lord has not told Marguerite, no?'

Margaret turns from the settling of her skirts and her small teeth shine in the half-dark.

'It would be very foolish,' she says, 'to declare ourselves so utterly.' She pulls on gloves; autumn is beginning to bite. 'You and I are something alike, I think. Loyal but also politic.' She smooths kidskin around supple fingers, flexes her hand. 'My lord delays. He vacillates. He is frugal with words. But he won't fight for Warwick.' She lets her man close the door between them, then leans forward again. 'You have my word.'

Elizabeth says November, for the child. Early in the month, most likely. She has counted, and says she could name the day of conception if it was asked of her, though she doesn't care to bring it to mind. It was in February, after the council met and granted clemency to Warwick and Clarence. Edward had signed their pardons, seen them sealed and sent them hence. He came to her late, teasing and amorous. Not sober. He slid his hand down her hip and said, 'Are you ready to be a good wife to me?'

'Why?' she asked, bitter. 'Have you been a good husband to me?'

But she let him undress her and lead her to the bed and, when he came in her, she pulled him deeper, letting him think it was passion. Later though, when he looked to her for lazy talk and kisses, she turned her face away and wouldn't speak so that, after a little while, he left to seek warmth in his own bed. Then she drew up her legs and tilted her hips to hold his seed inside her, praying he'd left something that might be the makings of a son. A fortnight later, she'd woken nauseous and her bleeding, that month, didn't come.

So, in the last days of September Elizabeth hears a mass, makes confession, kisses her children and steps into the room made ready with no more thought of leaving it. Jacquetta and Joan Peasemarsh cover the windows, turning the day into a candled twilight, and settle themselves at her side. Soon Anne will come and Margaret be sent for, but before much thought can be given to such things, news comes that shakes them as if the foundations of the Tower were crumbling.

Treachery has driven Edward from England. John Neville, Warwick's indecisive brother, has turned his coat at last and brought an army down upon his king. Edward, pulled from his bed, had barely an hour to rise up and run for the coast where, though King of England, he was forced to barter the clothes off his back and the coin in his pocket for safe passage across the sea. He has sailed into a storm with the few friends left to him. God knows where.

Now, free of him, Warwick has turned his army south towards London.

It's barely light, raining hard, and a wind from the east is pushing waves against the water gate as Jacquetta and Cecily bundle Elizabeth, wrapped in furs and a guard's borrowed oilskin, into a barge that buffets and kicks. 'I'll drown,' she cries. But no one listens. There's no time for it. The city won't hold for a king that's fled his country. When Warwick comes to London, its gates and all its power will be open to him. They must flee.

Jacquetta stumbles, landing heavily in the boat as Cecily hands Elizabeth's daughters down. Baby Cecily is passed screaming into Jacquetta's arms, while Lizzie and Mary cling to one another and to their nurse's rain-soaked skirts. When they are safely under cover, Cecily orders the oarsmen to pull away before she, with Elizabeth's Grey sons and Stillington who brought the news, takes the second boat, which lurches into the current and follows the swaying lanterns of the first.

They meet again at Westminster's Abbey door and are greeted by good Abbot Millyng, who grants them sanctuary of church.

In kindness, he gives up to them rooms of his own lodging. There are two, one leading from the other, high-windowed and cold, with an anteroom and a tiny chapel. Just one bed in the furthest room, little other furnishing but what God would approve. As the women stare at their austere comforts, rainwater dripping from their cloaks, the space seems already full.

'You can lie in in here with your mother,' Cecily tells Elizabeth. 'We'll bring cots next door for the rest.'

'I can't take you all,' the abbot flusters, as if the admission shames him. 'The Queen and her daughters, I thought, and her mother. There are sanctuary houses of course . . .' Not houses perhaps, but lean-tos and hovels, bare cells against the precinct walls, where killers and debtors and all manner of thieves scrape along on God's mercy.

'I've no need of sanctuary, Lord Abbot,' says Stillington.

'Don't be a fool,' snipes Cecily. 'There are men Warwick hates and you're among them. You can do nothing for Edward if you're dead. Take the Queen's Grey sons to St Martin's-Le-Grand, claim sanctuary there. And take care of them. They're at your charge, and you shall answer.'

He nods, knowing she's right.

'You'll stay with us?' Jacquetta reaches a hand towards Cecily as she lowers her shivering daughter to a chair.

'Of course not,' she says, 'I'm of no use here and Warwick daren't kill me. I'll go home to Baynard's. He can find me there if he wants me.' She clasps, for a moment, the outstretched hand. 'I'll do what I can.'

32.

October to November 1470

London

Warwick comes to London, and brings mad Henry out blinking into the light. He makes a sorry sight. In his five years a captive in the Tower, Cecily has visited him from time to time. Sometimes he knew her. More often he didn't; neither her nor the guards that shielded him, nor the servants who shaved his face and hung clothes on his spindled frame. Once he invited her to play chess, but couldn't remember how to arrange the pieces on the board. On the day he asked how her good lord husband was, it had stopped the breath in her throat.

'Long dead, sir,' she told him and watched his mouth fall open in grief, his palsied fingers lift to tap his grey-wisped brow.

'Then who keeps my crown for me?' he asked, plaintive.

'My son, sir. It's his now.'

He'd smiled, consoled. 'Good man.'

He made a pledge to pray for Edward and looked set to be about it, but before his hands could clasp, his rheumy eyes had lost their focus and he asked again with spittle-strung lips, 'How does your lord husband?'

She'd left him then, to the forgetfulness of his untethered mind, to the care of men who were, she hoped, mostly gentle.

She'd been unsettled after.

'I don't know why you go,' Edward had said.

'To remind myself what we saved England from,' she told him. Not an honest answer. Truth is she'd have been hard put to say why, except that it both fascinated and repelled her to see a man so weak, so unmade, who once had power of life and death over her.

And look at him now, she tells herself, as he's brought through London's streets to St Paul's, where the weight of a crown will be pressed upon him again. Absurd. If even God couldn't make a king of him, it's surely beyond the Earl of Warwick.

And yet Warwick seems set to try. He's put him on a horse and rides close beside him up Cheapside. Cecily imagines he must have tied Henry's feet to his stirrups to stop him falling, that beneath his gold-shot cloak the poor man's hands are lashed to his saddle's pommel.

She has come out from Baynard's to watch. Dressed in all her finery, and surrounded by men at arms, she has walked the streets to the gate that guards the cathedral precincts. Her party – a shock of steel and colour against a drab London day – draws every eye. Warwick's for certain. As he notices her, she lifts her head and her snarl of derision turns his face scarlet. There are no cheers for mad Henry as he passes, only sniggers, shaking heads, and men hawking spit into the street. Behind Henry rides her son, George, who notices her late and turns in his saddle to stare, while his high-stepping horse trots on and fights the bit. Just like George, she thinks. Looking one way, pulled in the other.

When the procession has gone and the cathedral door is closed behind it, Cecily smooths her skirts and turns into the still open space of the road, as if it had been cleared for no one but her, and walks stately back to Baynard's. As she goes men raise their voices, cautious, and say, 'God save King Edward,' and, 'God preserve the house of York.' She nods her head in thanks as her guards hand out cloth badges bearing Edward's sun in splendour.

'To wear when he returns,' she tells them. 'Save your cheers for that day.' And nods to the women who lean laughing from windows, who cock their fingers and cry out, 'Give us back King Edward, he's lustier than this one.'

Back at Baynard's she sits before her mirror as her women

unpin the high henin from her head and lift the heavy jewels from her neck: the collar of white roses and golden suns that are the mark of her house. It's a relief. She's cold, her back aches from standing, and the face that looks back at her, though it has lost none of its hauteur, is gaunt and grey and lined.

'I hope it was worth it,' says Annette as she coaxes the fire's flames to warm her mistress.

'It made me feel better.'

'Hmm. No doubt it will rile the Earl of Warwick. Is that a luxury you can afford?'

'He daren't touch me,' she tells Annette. But now she sighs. Her old friend is right. Today her actions were public and provoking. And what will it matter, really, if a few old men go home and say, 'The runaway King's mother was there, you know, handing out favours in the street'? What difference, if Edward's sun in splendour slumbers in a handful of secret cupboards?

She raises her chin and looks herself in the eye. It will matter, she thinks. They'll look at King Henry and remember King Edward and see how badly they've been robbed. And when Edward fights his way back – as dear God he surely must – they'll turn out and fight for him.

And so she works to keep hope alive. To undermine Warwick in whatever small ways she can. And is consoled to know she doesn't work alone. Richard didn't board the boat with his brother. He turned back on the very shoreline, against Edward's order. A man alone, masked in chaos, slipping past an enemy army that would have skewered him like a pig. He's somewhere in England now, going about dangerous business; business he's familiar with and good at. She learned this from a grubby paper passed to the hand of one of her household men as he came along the river wharf, by a fellow who drew up his hood and slipped into the crowd like a fish into a shoal. She has burned it for safety, but committed every word to memory.

'Edward makes for Burgundy to seek shelter with Duke Charles. Mother, get word to Meg. Tell her to make sure her husband understands the threat his country will face from a France united with Marguerite's England. No time for his two-faced games now. His best hope is to arm Edward well and send him home. Tell her I'm sorry we've brought this trouble to her door, but we need her now as we never have. I'll stay in England as long as I can to put our friends on alert; to make sure that, when Edward returns, pray God, men will rise for him, armed and ready. As for George, I don't know what you can do, but please try. And guard the Queen. I'll not write again for safety's sake. God keep you, Mother.' And signed with only his initial, that looping R with its bent-back spine. Richard.

In Burgundy, Duke Charles dithers and turns his two faces this way and that. He declares himself content enough with England's restored King Henry. He wants, he says, no row with France.

'Idiot!' declares Cecily and slaps her daughter's letter against her skirts.

Burgundy's ambassador shouldn't come to Cecily's house now. His business is with Henry, and with Warwick. But he does come, in darkness and in secret, to carry news from her daughter and to wait in shadows for her reply.

Edward, Meg writes, is safe, but lodged in The Hague far from Burgundy's court. 'Charles does with Edward as he did with George and Richard ten years ago. He keeps him in his pocket till he sees which way the world turns.' Cecily can read Meg's frustration in every stroke of the pen.

'Tell him it turns against him,' Cecily writes. 'Louis declared his alliance with Marguerite the day after Henry took his crown back. Its terms lay out plans for Burgundy's destruction and offer pensions to the great men of England if they'll join the fight against your lord.'

'He knows that, but fears to commit himself,' writes Meg next.

'And he doubts Edward can win. He says when a man escapes his house through a window he'll struggle to return through its door.'

'Tell him he's never been more wrong,' says Cecily. 'There isn't a fight my Edward can't win.' She forces herself, every day, to believe it.

All through October this exchange of letters continues. As do Charles's prevarication, Meg's frustration and Cecily's fears reined in by prayer. She wonders how Elizabeth bears it, in those cramped rooms, cut off from all news and intelligence. Warwick has placed a woman with her, Lady Scrope. He says to aid with her lying-in, in fact, to spy and keep her ignorant. Part of Cecily's own agreement with Warwick is that she'll neither visit nor correspond with her daughter-in-law, and she's been faithful, at least in that. But on the second day of November, when the abbot sends word that the Queen's labour is well progressed, she takes a boat to Westminster and the Abbey. Her promise was to Warwick, she reasons, and he's gone about the country, leaving the city in George's charge.

'And I've made no such promises to him,' she tells Annette.

Cecily arrives to find the Queen's daughters and their nurses sitting in a dull huddle by a low fire in the outer room. Only little Lizzie rises to greet her, reaching out her arms to be held.

'This child's hands are cold,' says Cecily, sharp to the nurse. 'Some more wood on that fire, I think,' and the nurse nods and places it, a small log from a meagre store.

'I'll send more,' says Cecily, as she gives up chafing Lizzie's fingers and pushes her back towards the others.

'You can't come in.' Lady Scrope shields the threshold of the inner chamber with her body. A woman of Cecily's age, though she looks older.

'You surely won't keep me from greeting my grandchild?' says Cecily, charm over steel. 'What harm can it do?' Then, more confidential, 'And Warwick isn't here to know of it.'

The woman wavers. 'I'll hear all your conversation.' The door is cracked open a fraction more, enough for Cecily to pass through into the smug of the blood-scented room.

'We will speak only of babies and swaddling, I swear.'

'Talk some sense into her, if you can,' Scrope hisses, nodding over her shoulder to the bed.

'A son,' says Jacquetta, stumbling from Elizabeth's bedside, wiping her hands on a blood-flecked apron. 'After all this time, a son.' The afterbirth still smoulders on the smoking fire and a wet nurse, sent by the abbot's kindness, has breast and blanket ready. 'But she won't give him up,' Jacquetta flusters, 'not even to be fed.'

Cecily crosses to the bed where Elizabeth, tangled in sheets and her own sweat-soaked hair, is curled about her newborn, his blood-smeared head cupped in her hand, his reaching hands against her face, his mouth working. Cecily lowers herself down beside her.

'He's strong, Elizabeth,' she says. 'Warwick will run from the very idea of him.'

'He'll kill him,' she says in a voice made rough by crying.

'He will not.'

'He'll poison him.'

'I think not even the Earl of Warwick can poison milk in the breast.'

The child gives out a whining cry.

'He's hungry. Now give him to this good woman. Let him be washed and fed and have a chance at life.'

It takes a while, but at last Elizabeth passes the child to the nurse and, while Jacquetta fusses to straighten the bed, to pull back the hair from Elizabeth's face, Cecily watches him feed, feeling the deep sucking pull within her own body. Edward's son. Heir to a kingdom wrenched from his father's hands, with no protection but what she can offer. In her heart she whispers her solemn oath: I will keep you safe. I will preserve your life and the crown that will come to you.

Elizabeth won't have her son taken from her for baptism, so they call Abbot Millyng to come to them and there, in this borrowed room, Edward's son is welcomed to God's family.

'What name?' the abbot asks.

'Edward,' says Cecily. Then looks to Elizabeth, who nods agreement. 'One day, Elizabeth, he will be King Edward the fifth.'

She stares at Lady Scrope, daring her to gainsay it.

Later, when the baby sleeps and even Scrope dozes, Elizabeth turns her face to Cecily and whispers, 'You believe it?'

'That your son will be king? Of course.'

Quieter still, 'Is it true, that Edward lives? That he's in Burgundy?'

Cecily looks at her, quizzical.

'The butcher, who brings meat, brings city news,' Jacquetta explains. A nod at Scrope. 'And she's not as close-mouthed as she looks.'

'I'm glad of it,' says Cecily. 'Yes. It's true. And he'll come back.' A finger to her lip. 'I can say no more for now.'

Elizabeth nods, can't help but ask. 'Do you believe he can win?'

In the dark nights, when she has sought God's comfort and found only dread, Cecily has asked herself that question. She has calculated the odds and quailed. But then she remembers the three suns God set in the sky to mark her son's first victory, when he was a green boy fighting in the frost at Mortimer's Cross and all the world against him. Three suns. Heaven's promise, harnessed to his will.

She finds a smile for Elizabeth now, dusts a finger over the downy cheek of the sleeping child. 'He is Edward. Do you imagine he can lose?'

33.

Late that night, George comes to Baynard's. He stands before her, his face petulant and wrung. The smell of drink strong on him.

'She's had a son,' he snarls. 'The Woodville bitch. Did you know?'

She takes a breath, affords a moment to smooth her sleeves. He has answered none of her letters, sent not a word to her these long weeks.

'That Edward's queen has been delivered of a prince? Yes. I know.'

'Then you can't give back all I've lost, can you? For all your promises. You can't make me Edward's heir again.'

He circles her, breathing heavy, fists clenched, coming close then stepping back, thrusting and threatening.

She stands her ground. 'Is that such a loss? What are you heir to now?'

'To England, after Henry.'

She looks away from him, corrects a pleat at her wrist. 'After Henry's son, you mean.'

'Marguerite's bastard you call him.' A finger in her face, jabbing.

'As indeed he is,' she forces a smile. 'But you'd have a fight on your hands to prove it. No, you might have to kill him. Will you kill everyone?'

Still, he circles, flexing his hands then tightening them to fists. Looking like he might use them.

Punch me and I'll punch you back, she thinks. 'George, will you sit down? You make me dizzy.'

He slumps into a chair, splay-legged, foot tapping. She pours wine for him, waters it well and watches him slurp. He's a disgrace.

He pulls a sleeve across his mouth. 'I'd kill Edward.'

'Really? Your brother?'

'I'd kill Warwick.'

'Now there you'd be doing me a favour.' She takes a seat opposite and watches him, his glassy eyes, his wine-stained lips. She sighs. 'Tell me, son. Who's wronged you most?'

'Warwick.' He shakes his head, lolling. 'Edward. You.'

'Me?'

'You.' He lashes a hand towards her, the dregs of his wine cup spill. 'It's always Edward, with you.'

Ah, she thinks, is this the source of his trouble? 'Well,' she takes the time to speak slow. 'He is my oldest son. And he is the King.'

'Warwick says he's a bastard. You fucked an archer.'

'Warwick said he'd make you king. Do you think his word reliable?'

Tears leak from his eyes then, he blinks them loose, brings his fist to his head and strikes his brow. 'He plays me for a fool.'

'Yes. He does.' She lets him cry a little. Snot on his lip.

'Why don't you come back to us, George?'

'What for? What would I be with you?' A child holding out his hand for comfits.

'You'd be the King's brother. Duke of Clarence, Lieutenant of Ireland. Whatever you were before. Though not his heir, I grant you.' She takes a breath. 'And you'll be my son.'

'You've never cared for me.'

Dear God, she thinks, be a man. She rises from her chair and kneels before him, is forced to speak to his bowed head for he won't look at her.

'Before you, I lost two sons. One.' A click of her fingers. 'Another.' Click. 'Just like that.' She takes his hands, their clammy heat, their ineffectual fingers, and wraps them in her own. 'When you were born I sat three days and nights praying for you. I dared God and the Devil to come and fight me for you. I'd have taken either of them down if they'd tried it. If you have life now, it's because I bound you to it. How can you imagine I don't care?'

His shoulders slump and he weeps in drunken earnest then, he clings to her and she lets him. When he's done at last, she puts him to bed, feeds the fire, lights candles to guard against the dark. She draws a chair to his bedside and sets herself to watch. His mouth is slack in sleep, his hair curls damp at his temple. She puts her fingers to it, combs its tarnished copper till it lies smooth. If only it were so easy to unravel the mess of her feelings for this child. The disgust and pity. The warring urges to push him away and pull him to her breast. She wonders, if the devil came for him tonight, would I still fight for him? She lays her head beside his on the pillow, feels his breath against her face, and lets herself imagine for a moment that its smell is not stale wine and sourness, but breast milk and salt. That he lies here a babe again, with a life before him and a chance to shape it better.

She isn't sure what wakes him. The lightening of the room or the sound of morning traffic on the river beneath the window. But he screws his face, turns on his elbow and looks up at her through slitted eyes. 'Have you been there all night?' he asks, querulous.

She doesn't answer, only says as she gets up to go, 'I'll send water, and a man to help you dress. Breakfast with me when you're ready.'

When he arrives at her table he doesn't look so bad. His face a little pale perhaps, his eyes a little swollen, but otherwise well enough.

'I imagine your head aches,' she says.

He shrugs. 'Not so much.'

'You must be used to it then. The drinking.'

She has sent the servants away and they're alone. He sits, and she watches as he pulls bread towards him, cheese, a little dish of honey. He looks at it as if eating is a task he must perform but doesn't relish. 'Have you no wine?' he asks.

She rises, brings the jug, sits again and watches him pour, resists the urge to tell him to water it. Instead she asks, 'What will you do now?'

He picks up a knife. 'Eat my breakfast. And be about my business.'

'I mean, will you leave Warwick and his treason?'

'Hard to say. At the moment, Warwick's winning. You say Edward promises to restore me. But he's in no position to do that, is he? Sitting on his arse like a beggar in Burgundy.'

'You do know he'll come back?'

'It's all the talk.'

'And you know, he's never lost a fight?'

'Can't see him winning this one.'

'And from that, you conclude you're better off where you are, do you?'

Again, a shrug.

She slides butter over bread but doesn't eat.

'Let me make you a prophecy, George. If Warwick wins for Marguerite, he'll not live beyond a year. He's her sword now, but when the fight's done she'll have him melted down for horse nails.'

'You don't think she'll be grateful?'

Her barking laugh surprises even herself, and silence follows it. The bread on his plate is rubbed to crumbs and his cheeks flushed.

'You'd likely be melted down with him, George. And, even if you're allowed to live, what will you be? Your lands and titles will be given back to the Lancastrian lords we took them from. You might get a post as Prince Edouard's pot boy.' She makes a drawling French mockery of the name.

'I'm to be Duke of York,' he says, surly.

'I heard. It's a grand title. How long do you think you'll keep it?'

He shifts in his chair, looks as though he'll rise, but then thinks better of it.

'George,' she goes on. 'Marguerite will rule in Henry's name and, when he's dead, her son. She'll surround herself with men of her own choosing. The Beauforts, Oxford, Henry Holland. There isn't one among them who wouldn't slide a blade between your ribs as smoothly as I spread butter.' She lays her knife across her plate. 'But I don't need to tell you this. I think you know already.'

She wipes her hands, casts the napkin aside. 'Besides, all this is moot. Edward will win. I'd like you to be at his side when he does. I'd like you to have your life back.'

'What does he want? Me or the men I'd bring with me?'

'I'd say he needs the men. He wants you.'

'Does he now?'

'You're his brother.'

'He'd never trust me.'

'Not at first, perhaps. But you could earn his trust, couldn't you? Anyway. How much do you trust Warwick?'

This time he does rise. 'I'm going,' he says, turning to the door.

She joins him there and asks again. 'What will you do though, George?'

Even now, he can't look at her. 'It's too soon to say. Let's see if Edward can put a force together. Let's see if he can even get as far as England. If he does that then . . .'

'All right.' She lays a hand on his sleeve. 'Might I send word to him that, when he lands in England, you'll bring your force to him?'

His hand is to the latch, his brow low over his face. She can't let him leave without a promise.

'George . . .'

'I don't know.'

Then the door's open and he's off, striding down the corridor as if desperate to be gone.

'Then I wish you good luck with Warwick,' she calls after him. 'But don't come crying to me!'

He turns the corner. She hears the clatter of his boots on the stair.

34.

November 1470

In the Parliament at month's end, George is confirmed Duke of York, and all the lords of Lancaster have their titles restored, including those that used to be George's, so he's lost more than he's gained. Edward is attainted, named usurper, Henry's new reign decreed to have begun the day he fled. And Warwick is named Protector of the Realm. It cuts to the quick, but Cecily shakes her head at it, forbids tears. It's nothing she didn't know already. Only now it's scratched out on vellum, sealed up in Parliament rolls.

Meg writes that Richard is in Bruges now, with Edward. The Earl of Oxford's men had almost caught up with him and he'd had to make a run for it. A setback, she admits. But at least he's still alive.

Henry Tudor is reunited with his mother. So at least Margaret will be happy. Cecily hears she brought the boy to court, presented him to mad Henry who, once reminded who he is, made him welcome, let him kiss his hand. But perhaps Margaret isn't as happy as all that for, in the end, Henry gave the boy's wardship back to his uncle Jasper, who will take him again to Wales. And when Margaret asked about her son's restoration to the earldom of Richmond, Henry lost interest.

'Who holds that title now?' he pondered. Well, that would be George, the new Duke of York. 'Oh, well,' he said, waving her away. 'You must speak to him about that.'

So Margaret comes to Baynard's.

'I'll say this for you,' Cecily tells her. 'You'll talk to anyone. Even one so down and out as me.'

'Oh,' says Margaret, taking off her gloves. 'I don't think you're quite finished yet.'

Cecily smiles. 'Sit down, Margaret, drink some wine. It's been a long time since I had intelligent conversation.'

They agree to temper their talk. To respect one another's secrets. But Cecily can't help but ask, 'Your husband. What does he say now about fighting for Marguerite? Is he still, how did you put it? Frugal with his words.'

'He's a very cautious man. Besides, there's no one to fight yet, is there? Not while Edward's still in Burgundy.'

'So you'll watch and wait?'

'Chess. Isn't it?' Margaret looks into her wine cup. 'The long game.' She steadies it in her lap. 'I'll be honest with you, as I'd be with few others. My interest is my son. I want him to live, whoever rules England. For now, that's King Henry, Warwick and your George. It doesn't much matter if I wish it otherwise.'

'You'll work with what you have?'

'As you do.'

'My loyalties are carved in stone.'

Margaret cocks her head on one side, balancing narrowed eyes with a tight smile. 'I think your loyalties are much like mine. They're with your son. My ideal would be to find a way that both your son and mine could survive and thrive.'

'So, your question is, if Edward wins, would he restore your boy?'

'Would he?'

'You have my word on it.' She lifts a finger. 'If your husband, when the time comes, fights for us.'

Margaret raises her cup, a toast. 'Depend on it.'

Cecily shakes her head and smiles. You have to admire her.

'But, it would be remiss of me,' says Margaret, sombre again, 'not to make every effort to secure what I can for my son now.'

'From mad Henry? You've had precious little so far.'

'I don't know. A fortnight in my son's company. Recognition of his place within the house of Lancaster. The protection of Jasper, the King's brother . . .'

'The King's half-brother.'

She shrugs. 'The only one he has.'

'Nothing to live on though. No title.'

'I'm told to ask your George about that.'

Cecily laughs. 'You think George will give up his earldom of Richmond?'

'He's had to give up so much already, would he even notice? And the King has virtually ordered it.'

'Not what I heard.'

'I'm not even going to ask how you hear so much.'

They smile at each other. A pause.

'Let's ask him, shall we?' says Cecily.

'I was hoping we might.'

'He'll say no.'

'Perhaps. But you could remind him of the bind he's in; the dangers of swimming against the relentless tide of Lancaster. And for yourself, wouldn't you like to see him have to give up a little more? Be a little less content with his lot. I'm sure you're trying to tempt him back to Edward's side.'

'You have a remarkable grasp of strategy.'

She inclines her head. 'I learned it from you.'

Cecily sends her man with a message for George.

'Margaret's in favour with King Henry, George,' she tells him. 'For your own sake, you'd be foolish not to meet her. So do it on neutral ground. Come to Baynard's.' And two days later, he comes.

Margaret makes herself the supplicant: the earldom of Richmond for her son, the King's nephew.

George's response begins with table-thumping, a leap from his chair to the door and, 'Over my dead body.'

Cecily rises and follows him. 'George,' she calls him back. 'Hear the Lady Margaret out.'

She refastens the latch, threads his rigid arm through hers to bring him back to the table and, out of Margaret's hearing, takes her chance. 'See how they all want a bite out of you?' A low whisper only he will hear, 'Gobble, gobble, gobble.'

When they're seated again Margaret speaks, cool and level. 'The King has expressed it as his wish.'

Not quite, thinks Cecily. And, if he had, he'll have forgotten by now. But let it go.

'Did you get that in writing?' George, through gritted teeth.

'I shouldn't need to,' says Margaret. 'But no matter. If you won't satisfy me, I'll take it up with Queen Marguerite when she comes. I'm sure she'd be sorry to see you obdurate.'

He almost snarls.

'George,' says Cecily. 'It seems to me . . .'

'Don't speak, Mother.'

She opens her hands. Well.

The conversation passes through every stage of 'perhaps' and 'on condition' and ends with an offer of compromise likely to satisfy no one except, perhaps, Cecily. Henry Tudor will inherit the earldom of Richmond on the death of George, Duke of York.

Margaret bridles. 'You're a young man yet. That's likely to be far off.'

He is immovable.

'You may have sons of your own. I'd need guarantees that the earldom would be excluded from their inheritance.'

He shrugs. Concedes. But will do no more. He is thrumming with anger. Margaret the same, but hiding it better.

Cecily looks from one to the other. 'Well, I think we can go no further today. George, I'll walk you to the river steps. Margaret, will you wait?'

She keeps with his rapid pace, says nothing till they come

outside. At the top of the steps, before he can descend to his barge, she lays a hand on his elbow. 'George.' He turns to her and she looks calmly into his face. 'Surely now you see how it is.'

The muscles of his jaw are working and his breath hisses through his nose. He looks down the river, up at the house, anywhere but at her. 'Tell Edward . . .'

'What?'

'Tell him I'll do it.'

'Good. Yes. Welcome back, George.'

He rattles, fast down the steps. Thinks again and rattles back.

'He'll be very much in my debt,' he snarls.

For a moment she doesn't trust herself to speak.

'Yes,' she says. 'I suppose he will.'

'Tell him I'll expect gratitude. Beyond restoration, there must be reward.'

'I'm sure he won't disappoint you.'

When he's gone, she walks back to the house. She thinks perhaps her son is as mad as King Henry, in his way. All the same, this is a win. She's had few enough of those lately.

At the door she takes a moment to arrange her face, to loosen the rigid twist of disgust from her lips and put on smoothness. She finds Margaret readying herself to go.

'I'm sorry,' she tells her. 'I did warn you.'

'It hardly matters.' The way Margaret pulls on her gloves makes it clear that it matters very much. 'Marguerite will do it.'

'Probably. But, like Edward, she's not here.'

'A race, then. Who do you think will get here first?'

'Place your bets?'

At the door Margaret stops, there is colour high in her cheeks.

'Why do I still feel, after all these years, that there are moves in this game that you know and I don't?'

'Not at all.' She leans in, lets their cheeks touch. 'I think we're close to even.'

35.

January to April, 1471

For Marguerite, it seems, this isn't a race. Despite all of War-wick's preparations, his pleadings and assurances, she says she won't come to England until Edward is dead, nor risk her son in any battle staged to bring that death about. 'That's a job for you,' she tells him. 'Let me know when you've done it.'

But Warwick can't kill Edward if Edward won't come. And Edward can't come unless Charles arms him and Charles won't risk that till he sees evidence, hard evidence, mind, that France and England plan to move against him. And Louis says, 'War-wick, where's my war with Burgundy?' But Warwick can't go to war with Burgundy because he hasn't the men and he hasn't the money and every man and merchant in England he speaks to of it looks wide-eyed at him and says, 'War with Burgundy? Why?'

'He's never been as good at this as he thinks he is, you know,' Cecily tells George.

She gets much of her news from him now, in snippets and bits as his fickle mood takes him, or from London's mayor who, secretly, still dreams of the day when bold King Edward will slap him on the back and say, 'Good Mayor Stockton.' And from Meg in Burgundy, of course, who's as driven mad by it all as she is, becalmed in these winter-dark waters while the ship of their future lurches towards the rocks.

Until, at last, comes a day when Meg's able to write and say, 'Mother, wind's up.'

Who'd have imagined it would be Louis who finally sets shoul-der to the sail for them? In the dark days of February he sends an impatient embassy to England with orders not to return till they have in their hands Warwick's plans for Burgundy's invasion and a date set for its sailing. For Charles, at last, that's evidence enough of ill intent. Within days, Edward and Richard are guests at his court.

'And I was able to greet my brothers again,' writes Meg. 'And tell them their long wait is over.'

Cecily imagines the preparations. The gathering of a fleet, the signing on of men, the victualling and arming, the caulking of timbers and oiling of sails. She worries about the winter crossing. Dreams of storms and wakes drenched. Beyond fear of drowning lies the terror of landing. The razored rocks and cliffs of England. The shores watched and guarded by men ready to fillet them like fish, or to beat them bloody back into the sea.

'He'll likely land in Norfolk,' says Burgundy's ambassador. 'Any day now.'

He meets her at the chapel door in the darkness after compline, whispers in her ear that Edward waits only for a lull in savage March winds. 'Look for his coming from the east,' he says, shoulders his cloak and is gone.

Rumours fly the Channel. London's streets are abuzz with speculation and the country hums with the sound of blades set to whetstones. George sends a hurried note. 'We think Edward's coming,' he writes. 'The Earl of Oxford leads men into East Anglia. I go west to bring up my force.'

Yes, well, Cecily thinks. Just remember who you're bringing it for.

Her sister Katherine writes that her grandson, who is Norfolk's duke, has been brought to London under guard. 'And Norfolk men who would fight for Edward are in Oxford's eye. If you've any way to warn him, tell Edward to land elsewhere.'

She has no way, of course, bar shouting into the wind, which is rising again, so that the Thames fights with itself beneath her windows. She stands on the river jetty to let the power of it buffet her.

'Never let a storm wave hit side on,' she remembers Edward telling her once. 'You must set your ship into the wave and let its prow split the force.' She turns her face east and feels it lashed with rain, imagines above her head the swell of sailcloth, beneath her feet the gut-fall pitch of a hull.

Somehow he gets word. His scattering of ships battles its way up England's eastern coast. Mayor Stockton brings news of a rough landing north of the Humber. It's not where he'd wish to be. He'll have to move inland or take ship again to cross the ravenous river's mouth. And Warwick keeps a canny watch at Coventry, barring his way to London.

'And John Neville holds Pontefract,' reminds the mayor. 'He'll have to get past him first. And Warwick's ordered Oxford to bring the eastern forces up now, and Jasper Tudor with the Welsh.'

She swallows bile, nods. A storm on land then, as well as at sea, and Edward riding south to set his prow against it.

'Where's Edmund Beaufort?' she asks, for surely he'll come to England now. The mayor shakes his head. Doesn't know.

Margaret does. 'He's with me,' she writes from Woking. 'Or was. I'll tell you myself before you hear it from elsewhere. He wants us to fight for Marguerite when she comes. We haven't said no. We haven't said yes either.'

Not yet, thinks Cecily. But she's under no illusions. Margaret will bide her time, then back the man likely to win. At the moment, that doesn't look like Edward.

'I can tell you York opened its gates for Edward.' She wolfs down Margaret's morsel of good news like a starved dog. 'He's past Doncaster now and raising men as he comes.'

'And Marguerite?'

'Louis grows impatient. Insists she should be in England for her victory. Edmund says she'll come any day. And a fresh force with her.'

One terror-filled week, and then another. April comes, but no news nor sign of spring. Then Palm Sunday with its acclamations and expectations of death. She calls on the power of Annette's prayers to the Holy Mother, and makes her own demands of

Michael Archangel, whose bright sword strikes first against the enemies of God.

'My enemies are your enemies,' she tells him. 'Bring them down.'

Next morning, her servants report a bustle in the city, the movement of soldiers and the closing of the gates. So she takes herself to Mayor Stockton, who can barely afford time to speak, but says the city is to be fortified against the coming of Edward.

'Edward?' she gasps.

'I know little, except he's passed Pontefract and Coventry. And that Warwick didn't fight him.'

The shock of it, the relief, almost fells her, till he dares a hand to hold her steady and whispers into her incredulous ears, 'He moved too fast. Warwick wasn't ready. He was depending on your son George's reinforcements, but I hear that, when he looked out from his high walls one morning, he found them standing all against him, and your three sons shoulder to shoulder at their head.'

She can barely believe it. 'So he let them pass?'

'Aye. But follows hard on Edward's heels and hopes to fight another day, when Oxford comes, and Tudor.'

She's thinking fast, though her body shakes. 'But if Edward could reach London. If he could take it ... .'

'It would be a mighty step forward,' he concedes.

'God, yes. Do you know where he is now?'

'Close.'

'Who holds the city?'

'Archbishop George Neville. Till his brother Warwick comes. I'd say he's putting a brave face on it.'

George Neville's brave face is that of mad King Henry who, next day, he ties into saddle and parades around the city. No one even pretends to cheer and men in the street call out for King Edward, and jostle to show the sun in splendour sewn defiantly to their sleeves.

So that night, Cecily puts on her finest, goes to George Neville and says, 'Well, you see how it is. Edward's in St Albans already. I had a letter from him this morning. Copies sent to the mayor, the city magistrates and the Queen. He calls for mad Henry to be secured in the Tower and the city made ready for his coming. I dare say you've had one too?'

George Neville wipes an unsteady hand across bloodshot eyes, lifts a paper from his desk and places it face up, so that she can see the bold signature at its foot; Edward, R. 'Yes.' Another paper. 'And this one from my brother saying the city must hold for King Henry. And for him.'

'Well. A dilemma. What will you do?'

He shakes his head, as if he genuinely doesn't know.

'Depends who you're most afraid of, I suppose.' She sidles up to him, whispers in his ear. 'You've seen Edward fight. He'll tear you limb from limb.' She smiles to see the jumping pulse at this throat.

'Do you imagine my brother wouldn't do the same?' His voice shakes.

'But your brother Warwick is days away. And Edward's almost at your door. He is, I think, your more immediate problem.'

'Dear God . . .'

'Choose, Nephew. Or if you daren't, let the city decide. Then at least you'll be able to say, "It wasn't me."'

So next morning he goes to the city authorities and asks them their will. Cecily, who has spent the night talking to them of it, knows already what their answer will be. She waits at the entrance to receive their bows as they file out, to let a bold few kiss her hand. Mayor Stockton is last among them. He stands beside her and lets out a breath. 'King Edward'll be here tomorrow, I should think.'

It's been more than a year since she saw him. As he climbs the steps of St Paul's he looks leaner, fitter, ready for a fight. The poor have come for their Maundy money, and he throws coins to them from his own purse. She feels the joy of him close her throat, and gasps. But there's no time yet for relief or thankfulness. This is no triumphant return. Just a bit of a show before they get down to business. When he lifts her from her deep obeisance and kisses her brow, the crowd, subdued so far, gives up straggling cheers. She steps back a moment, expecting him to turn and take the welcome with his usual young man's swagger, but he only draws her close to him again, looks deep into her face as if committing it anew to memory, and raises a metalled fist in the air for the crowd at his back to see.

'Will you win for us then, Eddie?' a bold voice, a challenge taken up by the throng. She watches his eyes narrow, just before he turns.

And there's the grin and the bold stride, the challenge thrown back, 'Don't I always?' The day is in his hands again and the streets roar.

He returns to her, serious once more. 'Where's my wife, Captain Mother?'

'Well, you know,' she cocks her head to one side. 'She says she won't come out from sanctuary till you fetch her.'

He grimaces. 'Best be about it then.'

At the doors of the abbot's lodging, Elizabeth stands, her daughters ranged about her, her mother at her back, and in her arms her royal son, bundled against the cold. She's dressed like a queen in a cloak of silver fox, and the veils of her henin lift in a brittle wind. Well, thinks Cecily, she looks the part.

As her husband strides towards her Elizabeth lifts her chin and turns her body to show the tiny face held tight in the defence of her arms. When he holds out his arms, she gives the child up to him.

'Your son,' she says. As if delivering a message. Proving a point. She lets him kiss her hand, then carry it high in his as they walk the path through King's Gate to the abbey, but she keeps a sword's length of distance between them, and whatever smiles he has are for the child in his arms and the little girls who cling to the women's skirts. Elizabeth smiles for no one.

There's time only for the crown to be lifted from the altar and pressed briefly to his head, to make a show of it for the people gathered; the soldiers and captains who came with him, the mayor and aldermen who rode from St Paul's in their train. Then to horse again, to the safety of Baynard's, the council table and planning for the fight to come.

Cecily rides there behind Edward and Elizabeth, flanked by her other sons. She watches their faces as they go, wind-chapped, tight-jawed and tense. She can feel already the bunching of their muscles, their juddering heartbeats, their itch for the fight. She notices that Richard's watchful eyes slide often to George, as if anticipating his brother's actions has become a habit. George looks at nothing and no one, except the brother who rides ahead of him, the Queen at his side, the son in her arms.

36.

13 April 1471

The Tower

It's rained fitfully since the small hours, rattling at her window like a man with a quarrel. She could tell herself it's what's kept her awake all night, but it would be a lie. So, when she hears men stirring in the courtyard, she gets up and sets herself to watch from the window. They're back within the Tower's stout walls, where Edward brought them for safety's sake last night when scouts reported Warwick's army closing on the city. Now the rain has slowed to a drizzle and the grooms are bringing up horses, each with an oilskin cast over its harness, so that at least her sons will ride to war with dry arses. Though little else if this sky doesn't clear, she thinks, squinting into the thin grey morning light. Time to go down.

Her daughter Anne is waiting for her when she leaves her chamber. It doesn't look like she's slept either. She came to them late as the Good Friday vigil ended, a simmering cauldron of resentment and fear. Many years ago, when Anne was a child, before the battle lines of York's long war with Lancaster had been drawn, Cecily married her to Henry Holland. She did it for his dukedom, has regretted it since. He's shared Marguerite's exile since Towton, leaving Anne nothing to remember him by but a single daughter, who looks too much like him to make her comfortable, and a cloudiness in her right eye, from the time he smashed her head against a wall. She's lived free of him these ten years and content, but he rides now with Warwick, and Marguerite has promised him restoration of his property, his titles, and his wife.

'I'll not be at home when he comes,' said Anne when she came to her mother last night. 'I'll cut my own throat before he touches me again.'

In truth, this is what's kept Cecily awake. Listening to the weather in the dark, she has calculated the price of losing, and by whom it will be paid; by her daughter in the bed of Henry Holland, and by her sons in their blood. She has measured, too, her impotence to prevent it. For all her politicking and the strength of her will, the future will be decided by chance in a battle she can't fight; by the stroke of a sword, the flight of an arrow, or the stumble of a man's horse in the charge. Tomorrow she might be King's Mother again. Or just another broken woman, with her children dead at her feet.

Now, as she steps into the courtyard with her daughter, she straightens her spine and puts the foolishness of the night behind her. It's strategy that wins battles, she chides herself, not chance. The rain has stopped, the grooms are pulling off the oilcloths and, if she looks west, she can see, high above the Tower's walls, thin wisps of blue.

'You won't be going back to Henry Holland,' she tells Anne. 'Not a chance of it.'

Richard is the first of her sons to appear from the base of the White Tower. He's still only eighteen and the squires at his shoulder look older than he does, but in the coming battle he'll command the right flank, while Edward takes the centre and William Hastings the left. It will put him at the very front of the fighting.

'Are you sure?' she asked Edward yesterday.

He nodded. 'Oh yes. You would be too if you'd seen him fight.'

Richard sees her and, after giving instructions about the stowing of his gear, comes across. He can't quite manage a smile, but he's walking loose on his toes and his face has colour in it. He's not cowed. He kisses his sister's cheek and then her own hand. 'Mother.'

'Have you checked your armour?'

His eyes are solemn. 'Yes.'

'Yourself, I mean. Not left it to others.'

It's a discipline she's imposed on all her sons. Every strap, she's told them, every buckle, every slide of plate. When her husband was alive she'd watch him do it, his long fingers testing. Then, when he'd moved on or wasn't looking, she'd check it again herself. She can't impose so far on her sons.

'Of course, Mother.'

Then Richard looks beyond her shoulder. Here comes George, with Will Hastings and Anthony Woodville either side of him, as if holding him to account.

'George!' Richard calls. 'Mother wants to know if you've checked your armour.'

George laughs, high and boastful. 'Don't need to,' he says. 'Blades bounce off me.'

'Do they now?' she says once he stands before her. 'What a miracle you are.'

A sharp bow. 'Mother.'

'George.'

He'll have no battle command, but will fight in the centre with his brother the King.

'Keep him where you can see him,' she told Edward yesterday. 'Keep him under watch.'

Men are mounting now, everywhere the creak of leather, the chink of steel. Only a hundred or so here, but an army of ten thousand waiting beyond the city walls. Cecily has listed every lord that has brought men out to fight for them; carries in her mind the quartering of every standard. She makes it her business to know such things. She has added Henry Stafford's name to the roll. Though he's one among many, it pleases her that Margaret Beaufort has at last placed her bet.

Edward is last to come. He has Elizabeth by the hand, who looks pinched and cold, her high cheekbones sharp as knives.

'I've kept you all waiting,' he calls. 'I've been saying goodbye to my son.'

Richard bows to his queen. 'God keep England's heir safe in your care, Your Grace.'

Elizabeth smiles, tight, and gifts him her hand to kiss. Haughty this morning, thinks Cecily.

'We should be gone, Edward.' George's hand is already reaching for the bridle; his groom stands ready to boost him to the saddle.

Edward's voice is low. 'Farewell your queen, George.'

The groom stands back and George turns. An impatient nod. 'Madam.'

She proffers no hand. He gives no loyal kiss.

'And our mother, George.'

She'll have none of this nonsense. She takes his head between her hands and looks deep into his face, into the bronze-flecked hazel of eyes that dart and skitter. 'God keep you steady, George.'

He nods once, and pulls away. Then Richard's lips are pressed against her cheek, and Edward's hand laid steady on her arm.

'Forgive me, gentlemen, a word with my mother before we go.' Edward pulls her aside, shifts on his feet. 'I'm sorry it's come to this, Mother,' he tells her, his face earnest. 'That I must go and fight your brother's sons, I know it wounds you, and I'm sorry.'

It's unexpected and takes her like a blow. It's been many weeks, she realizes, since Warwick and his brothers ceased to be her kin and became only her enemies. If she had them before her now and a knife in her hand, she'd take care of business herself. Nor has she forgotten what brought them to this place: the foolishness of Edward's marriage, Warwick's reckless vanity, George's envy and dangerous pride. But there. We are where we are. And she can't let regret slow his sword.

'You mustn't think of it, Edward,' she tells him. 'It would only grieve me to see them living.'

★

A messenger comes at midnight to say Edward has drawn up his battle lines north of Barnet, ten miles from the city.

Another sleepless night. At last she gives up waiting for dawn to light her window and goes to seek it out upon the walls. The stones are coldly wet against her hand and the walkway, between lonely guard posts pooled in torchlight, is treacherously shadowed. She looks east and waits again, until at last, a thin smudge of milky whiteness marks the distant horizon. Nothing like morning yet, but the promise of it.

Now, she knows, the camp will be rousing, her sons rising from camp beds by lamplight; making confession, breaking their fast. Her husband once admitted he could never eat before battle, nor drink much for fear of pissing himself. She wonders what it's like, to feel such fear in the body, to master it and fight. They'll be calling their squires to arm them now. They'll stand, chin up, legs wide, the pinions of their arms lifted, so that naked flesh can be wrapped in leather, encased in steel; their vulnerable flesh hidden, their pulsing veins buried deep.

Still, the sky doesn't lighten. The day seems weighted and the air thick and cold, but she hears the tolling of the bell that marks the hour and knows that, even now, they'll be stepping from their tents on to the dew-soaked grass, visors raised to scent the air. They'll test the slide of swords from scabbards, the hang of daggers at the hip. Their captains will come up for final orders, signed off with a dry-mouthed prayer.

The darkness fades to grey, but no sun comes. A mist lies thick upon the river, so that even the wharves of the opposite bank are lost to sight. She blinks, and beads of moisture fall from her lashes; she touches her face and brings her hand away wet.

Now they're mounting to ride to their command positions, she hopes they'll embrace before they go. She strains her eyes and wonders whether fog rolls over the battleground, whether death will come for them unseen. She feels the restless shift of horses at the early cannon's volley, the windy rush of the first arrows' flight. Her heart hammers as the charge begins, as limbs stretch in the gallop and swords lift in a swing. Not ten miles from where she stands. She could find a horse and be there within the hour. She's down the steps already, walking fast to the chapel, where the air hangs heavy with incense and the women wrestle in prayer.

37.

Easter Sunday, 14 April 1471

Five in the morning. The first messenger comes to say battle was joined an hour ago. He was ordered to ride as the first volleys were fired. Cecily wants details, numbers. He doesn't want to give them, but confesses at last that Warwick's strength is half as great again as their own and that they fight in a snarling fog. She sends him back on a fresh horse.

'Come again when you've better news.'

At six comes Archbishop Bourchier, to console them with a mass for the risen Christ. He reminds them that, in that holy time, women waited vigil just as they do now, and were rewarded with salvation and the promise of Heaven. 'Whatever today brings, that promise stands,' he says. 'The kingdoms of this world are as dust, but the kingdom of God stands forever.'

Jacquetta sobs and thanks him for his comfort. Cecily excuses herself his company.

'I'll rejoice in God's kingdom when I arrive in it,' she tells him. 'Today I care only for my son's.'

As she leaves, Elizabeth hurries after her. They go to the great hall, where Elizabeth takes the royal seat and Cecily sits beside her; where they watch the unmoving sky through high windows and wait for a footfall on the stair.

At ten there's news of soldiers straggling into the city. Men of Hastings's command who speak of a rout. Cecily sends for Mayor Stockton, who says, 'No, no. They are no more than a dozen.' His own intelligencers, he assures them, say the battle goes on, Hastings falling back, but Edward holding the line.

Elizabeth orders her son brought to her and paces the hall

while he frets in her arms. The noise of it sets Cecily's nerves grinding, like the teeth of a saw against bone.

'When your husband was killed, you sent your own sons out of the country,' Elizabeth challenges her. 'Will you send me and mine? Can you get us away? Did Edward make a plan?'

'Of course he did,' Cecily snaps. 'We'll get you out if we need to.'

Though she isn't sure how. She's had a ship standing ready since yesterday. But today there's no wind to shift it and nothing to be done about that. 'Pray God we've no need to.' But she herself can't pray, so she sends for Annette who speaks to God for her: the Ave, the Pater Noster, Thy will be done. For the first time the old nurse's prayers irk her.

'Not that,' she hisses, grasping her shoulder. 'Not submission. Not entreaty.'

Not His will, she means. Mine.

Another hour, and the child won't stop crying. Six months old, new teeth breaking through his jaw, his face teeming tears and snot.

'Dear God!' shouts Elizabeth at last, pulling him from her shoulder and shaking him at arm's length. 'Shut up, shut up, shut up!'

And she pushes him to the waiting wet nurse, who quiets him with feeding and grimaces in silence when he bites. Elizabeth comes back to her high chair, her breath shallow and squeezing, her knuckles white against her mouth.

Cecily knows she should comfort her but can't bear to, so watches her instead through narrowed eyes; the knotting sinews of her long neck, the teary blinking of her frightened eyes.

'Feel it,' Cecily whispers out of her hearing. 'We wouldn't be here but for you.'

The waiting is forever and endless, but at last, a clatter on the stairs and the morning's first messenger comes back at a run, ending on his knees, breathless and blown.

'What?' Cecily is on her feet. She's desperate for any word, and ready for the worst.

But when he looks up, his face is riven by relief. 'Not yet midday,' he says, 'and the battle won.'

There are a thousand questions. He can answer almost none.

'Does the King bear any injury?' asks Cecily.

'None that I could see.'

'Do all my sons live?'

He shakes his head. 'I don't know.' Her face must speak her exasperation. 'There was no time, Lady. The King would brook no delay.'

The order for him to ride was the first Edward gave, as he pulled off his helmet and shook sweat from his hair; as his squires swarmed, pushing and probing to be sure that the blood he was drenched in was none of his own.

'Just tell them it's done,' he said. 'More news when I have it.'

'Is Warwick dead?' Elizabeth, who hasn't spoken yet but sits, still trembling, has only one question. 'Is he dead?'

'So they say, Your Grace. Though I've seen no body.'

Next morning it's there for the world to see, Warwick's body, brought from the battlefield to the nave of St Paul's. He's still, as he never was in life, and white as bone. Except where the livid bruises mar the flesh and, of course, the battered face, the cudgelled skull. He was killed in the rout, so Cecily has learned, when he saw that all was lost and tried to flee. It's easy to see what happened. She lowers herself to one knee to examine it better, holds her candle close. He was pulled down as he ran, his helmet torn from him and then . . . Well. The left eye is gone and the jaw bone on the right swings loose, mouth gaping, teeth smashed. The eye that remains is blood-filled and sunken. But there's no mistaking him. That gold-red beard, that breadth of chest. But, to aid those common men who are less intimate with his looks, and who queue outside to view the fallen rebel, his banner hangs above him. The fierce bear, its brutal staff, lifeless in the chill air.

'I ordered him to be brought to me alive.' Edward's voice

above her head is thick and mournful. 'Now no man will claim his killing.'

'Can't say I blame them.'

Last night, when William Hastings had whispered the tale to her while Edward, ten feet away, gave orders to the Dean about the display of the body, she saw his eyes shift towards his king. She leaned close and whispered, 'Dear God, William, was it you?'

He flexed his neck, a gesture that signalled necessity. 'Would you risk him being forgiven again?'

She laid a hand on his sleeve. 'Never tell Edward.'

Now she turns the light of her candle on to the second body, laid out beside the first on the dark stone pavement. John Neville. Warwick's brother. There's no mark on him, but for the slash that runs across his hip and into the groin, where the great vein runs. And, of course, he too has lost an eye. She knows how it goes. A rondel blade through the visor is the surest way to finish a man who's been brought down but isn't dead; who writhes on the battlefield or struggles to remount. Poor John. She's been told that, when they stripped his body, they found Edward's badge, the sun in splendour, hidden beneath his gambeson, turned inward against his heart.

'I'll not have their bodies broken,' says Edward. 'Keep them here a week so all can see, then let their families bury them. You'll see to it, Mother?'

'Elizabeth wants their heads on London Bridge.'

'Aye. Sometimes I think she wants mine there too.'

'Probably. Watch out though,' she says. 'If I start lopping heads I might never stop. And your wife's might be first among them.'

He huffs, thinks she isn't serious. Well, mostly she's not.

'I'm surprised she isn't here to see this for herself.'

'Been already. Do you think she could wait? I let her come alone. She wanted to bring our daughters. I forbade it.'

Dear God. 'Well,' she pulls herself to standing, less easy than it used to be, straightens her skirts, 'I've seen enough.'

She takes the hand that Edward offers, tightens her thankful fingers around its living warmth, and sets off towards the north door. As they go, she hears the southern door thrown open and the first of the eager crowds passing in.

Bodies shown and bodies hidden. A terrible thing, this exposure in death. Warwick and John, beaten, lie naked for any man to see. Not just the wounds that prove them dead, but the private things. The scattering of dark moles across John's chest, the soft beginnings of a paunch at Warwick's belly, the curled smallness in his groin. She imagines men whispering and sniggering behind their hands. 'Not much of a staff on that old bear,' they'll say. And their wives will squeeze their arms and titter.

Last evening she saw something long hidden in a body of her own making. When, after dark, Edward returned to the city and came to St Paul's for the thanksgiving, riding up Ludgate through a river of torchlight, George was the only brother at his side, smiling and waving as if the crowd loved him. It caused her heart to falter, though she'd been told by then that all three of her sons lived.

'Where's Richard?' she asked as Edward stepped up to kiss her.

He grimaced. 'Injured. I didn't want him to endure all this . . .' he lifted his arm, '. . . fuss. So I sent him straight off to the Tower. You'll see him there once this is done. Don't worry, he's well enough. Walking wounded.'

So when they returned to the Tower, she went first to find him. To see for herself how bad it was, to feel his living heartbeat under her hand. She was told which room and didn't think to knock, but when she stepped inside he was just rising from the bath placed in its centre. His back was to her, a squire hovering with a towel. She didn't notice first the slimness of his hips, or the bandaged hand held stiffly away from himself. No, she noticed the lift in his right shoulder and, as he straightened, shedding water, the snaking curve of his spine. The squire had been quick, lifting the bath sheet to shield him from her view, but he must have heard her gasp for, when he turned, his face was marked first by surprise, then recognition and sudden shame.

At length he let her look at it again, when he'd sat her down in the window embrasure and she'd recovered herself. When he had sent the squire away and pulled himself into a robe. He leaned his head against her shoulder and let her push the fabric down, so she could trace her fingers along the unnatural twist of bone. How men would spit at this, she thought. How they would gawp and point and cross themselves. She swallowed hard on her own revulsion.

'Does it hurt?' she asked.

She felt the roll of his brow against her shoulder. 'Barely at all.' He eased himself up, pulled the robe back again, awkward, one-handed. 'It barely makes a difference. I can do anything I'm needed for. Walk, talk, think straight. Ride hard. Draw a sword.' He tried to catch her eye, to tease a smile. 'Even my brother says I'm handy with an axe.'

'He says you're the best fighter he has.'

He smiled a little at that. 'Well then. I have my uses. And I think myself no more sin-ridden than the next man, so . . .'

'You've never said a word to me.'

'I hoped you'd never know.'

'Did you imagine I'd think less of you?'

He shrugged. 'There are many who would.'

Then she felt shame. Truth is, she has always thought less of him. Richard the short son, the dark son. The one who came last and made her so ill, as if he leached all strength from her body. He was sickly as a babe, fretful and slow to thrive, but straight-limbed enough.

'You weren't born this way. Is it some injury, some hurt?'

He shook his head. 'No. It just happened.'

'When?'

'It began in my thirteenth year. While I was in the north. It gets a little worse, I think, as time passes.'

'Does Edward know?'

He nodded. 'Yes. Edward knows.'

'And didn't tell me?'

'I asked him not to.'

'Who else?'

'The men who tailor my clothes. My armourer. My body squires, as you saw. I choose them carefully.'

'You were with Warwick then. Did he . . .'

'Warwick knew. He was kind about it. He brought in physicians.'

'I'll bring better ones.'

'There's really no point. I don't think anything can be done.'

'Then what?'

'I'll continue as I am. I live clean, for the most part. I keep my body strong. I make confession and honour the saints' days, pray for my dead. I'm loyal to my king and faithful to my God and I trust neither will fail me. God will not test me beyond what I can bear.'

'If you're lucky.'

He grimaced. His hair was drying now, in waves and kinks and knots. He ran his good hand through it, noticed the other and held it up before her eyes. 'My feelings are hurt. You haven't even asked about this. My first war wound.'

'It looks like it won't kill you. What is it?'

He shook his head. 'Laughable, really. The very tip of the smallest finger gone. Mashed against the hilt of another man's sword, so the surgeon cut it off at the knuckle. Bled like a pig and hurt like Hell. I hope I never suffer worse.'

She decided to be practical. 'Will it affect your sword grip?'

He shrugged. 'I'll adjust.'

38.

He'll have to adjust. And quickly.

Two days later, while Warwick's body bloats, news comes that Marguerite landed at Weymouth on the very day he died. Her son is with her, Lancaster's heir, fighting age now. And Edmund Beaufort met her with a force. He's the best of her captains since his brother Henry's head toppled rotten to the river from its spike on London Bridge.

'What now?' asks Cecily.

'She'll turn east and join up with Warwick's Kentish men,' says Edward. 'Those fuckers are still itching for a fight. Or push north and hope Jasper Tudor will bring up his Welshmen.'

'Which he will,' says Richard.

'Which he will,' Edward agrees. 'Either way, we have to catch her first.'

'She'll trip on her skirts running from us,' jeers George. And here he comes, tottering across the room like a girl in startled fright. '*Aidez-moi, aidez-moi!*'

'Don't be a fool, George,' Cecily snaps.

But when Edward's mouth turns up at his antics, the wrenching fears of recent days turn to cold anger. She puts herself before him, speaks hard into his face. 'Don't imagine, Edward, that because Marguerite is a woman, she's anything less than a match for you. She'd tear out your throat in an instant.'

'She won't get near us,' George mutters behind her.

Cecily ignores him, speaks only to Edward. 'She has a son no less to her than you are to me. Think,' her hand is a fist against his breast. 'Whatever I'd do for you, she'll do for him. She'll call up the powers of Hell to bring you down. And if she joins with Jasper's Welshmen . . .'

He takes her fist, uncurls it, nets her fingers in his. 'I know what she's capable of, Mother. And what drives her.'

She pulls her hand away. 'Then for God's sake catch her, before she meets with Jasper. And finish it this time.'

Now the brothers are back in the saddle, men mustering at Windsor, and Cecily is left again to the company of women: the Queen and her brood, the Queen's mother, and Cecily's own daughter Anne, whose husband is, for all her wishing it, not yet dead. The Queen's brother, Anthony, is left behind to guard them. He's not up for hard riding. The last battle left him with a leg pike-gouged and black from hip to ankle.

The first evening, Margaret Beaufort comes. They're glad of her company, but not of her news. Her husband didn't return with the army from Barnet, his injuries so severe his men lodged him in the town.

'I'd had no word,' she tells them. 'I had to send riders out myself and heard only today that he lives. I go to him now. I'll fetch him home to Woking if I can. Be with him if . . .'

Even Elizabeth is moved to sympathy and offers a royal escort for her journey. 'I'm sorry,' she tells her friend. 'He fought for us and we've done nothing for him. But it's been . . . you've no idea how it's been.'

And Margaret, despite her own distress, must comfort her queen in her weeping.

The escort is ordered and next morning, early, Cecily walks with Margaret into the courtyard to meet it. The weather is better, the sun even has some heat in it, and Margaret's guard is forming up around a carriage whose door stands open. Cecily hands Margaret in, helps her settle, small but straight-backed in the shadowed interior. 'I hope your husband lives, Margaret,' she says.

Margaret reaches for her hand, squeezes it in thanks. 'I will, you know, do all I can for him. He's been . . . he is . . .'

'A good husband?'

'Not as you would count it perhaps, but yes.'

'I'm very sure. And you care for him. You wouldn't risk going to him otherwise.'

Margaret looks up, surprised. Cecily leans in. 'It's still possible you'll need to find favour with Marguerite. If things go badly for us. That might be harder to do if you're seen to be nursing a man who fought for York. Or mourning him.'

She can see that Margaret hadn't thought of that. 'Oh, I don't know. Surely Marguerite understands what women do for their husbands.'

Cecily's smile is rueful. 'Oh Margaret, be advised by one who knows her better. Marguerite, in all her life, has never done anything for her husband.'

Nor he for her in all fairness, Cecily acknowledges as she walks alone back to the Tower and its fretful days. Marguerite was not quite fifteen when Cecily first met her, and she remembers that her feelings for her then were pity and a grudging respect. Marguerite's family had married her to mad Henry, who was King of England then. She was handed to Cecily for delivery like a parcel, and hosted by her at Rouen before she sailed for her new home. Marguerite could have had no idea what she travelled to, though Cecily knew well enough: a man who had no earthly use for women and thought children were got through prayer.

And God knows that Marguerite, a hated French queen who brought no dowry, no influence and not an inch of France, needed a child. Now the one she has is life and breath to her. Her hope, her safety, her weapon in war and the cause that drives her. She fights, not to put mad Henry back on his throne. Who'd want him? But to put her son there. And to be, at last, unassailable as she's never been in all her life. To be, as Cecily is now, King's Mother.

But that son of hers, Edouard, is no royal get. Cecily, in that long ago time, taught Marguerite a lesson, one she'd need at Henry's court. When an impossible thing must be done, she'd told her, you must find a way to make it appear to be done. And so Marguerite made it appear that the King had an heir. But it was Edmund Beaufort's father that put the thing inside her, and simple Henry, when presented with the sad scrap, said only that it must have been begotten by the Holy Ghost, and that his prayers had been answered.

And for the sake of that bastard child, Marguerite has fought Cecily ever since.

And I've lost a husband in that fight, she thinks now as she climbs the steps to the Tower. My son Edmund, too. It's been ten years, their blood will have dried to dust, but the wound to Cecily's heart still bleeds and she's no less bitter. Now Marguerite comes again. And Cecily must set all her sons against her.

A week, and word comes that the army is moving west from Windsor at pace.

'Marguerite's left Exeter,' writes Edward. 'For my guess, they'll head north to meet with Jasper coming from Wales.' Nothing certain though. Cecily's finger traces the route of the Severn as it curves inland, its wide mouth narrowing, drawing Wales nearer to England.

'The river crossings are here,' Cecily points them out to Elizabeth. 'The bridges at Gloucester and Tewkesbury. Edward must fight Marguerite before Jasper crosses them and makes her invincible.'

'If he's right,' Elizabeth scorns and points. 'From Exeter she could as easily turn for London. He's not infallible you know, your son. He's been wrong before.'

It's true. He has. Wrong, out-manoeuvred, taken by surprise. Made a prisoner, forced into exile. Cecily's eyes scan the inky country between Windsor, Exeter, the Severn and its crossings.

On the map she can span it with her hand, in her mind she can fathom no inch of it, nor plot the route of armies moving blind.

News is thin and patchy. Edward comes to Abingdon, then Malmesbury. On May Day Marguerite dithers, this way or that? Then she's in Bristol. The armies, it seems, will meet at Sudbury. Then, not Sudbury.

'She's running north,' writes Edward. 'And Jasper and his Welshmen are on the move.' Cecily feels frustration flood his body, the strain on the bit as he pulls his horse about. The race is on, the Severn narrowing.

The map taunts her. Gloucester and Tewkesbury, their towering abbeys and wet river plains. Their bridges and the many miles to reach them. The days drag, the sun rises early, grows hot, then hotter. Her mind marches every hour with Edward, driving on at a murderous pace, his horse slathered and blowing beneath him; his sweat blinds her, his thirst tears at her throat.

'How many miles?' she asks Anthony. 'An army at best push in this heat?'

'Fifteen is good in a day. Twenty barely possible.'

Across the murderous map two armies push towards a single point on the river. Impossible that he will fail to reach it. Cecily's will drives him forward, her lungs straining for his breath, her body tense against the blow that's sure to come.

When it lands it almost fells her, a great pillowing bludgeon of relief that sends her to the floor.

'Battle done.' A scribe's hand, but Richard's signature, his very own.

At Tewkesbury. She will go to its abbey, she will give thanks on her knees. Even Elizabeth is laughing, gulping, gasping at the reprieve. They've done what Anthony deemed impossible; marched fifty miles in two days, beat Jasper to the river, fought and won. A third of Marguerite's forces are dead. And among them, her Edouard. Her hope.

'He fought in the centre with the Beaufort brothers,' Richard ends his letter with this news. 'And was brought down in the rout. Now God keep you, I must sleep.'

'And we must work,' says Elizabeth, taking Cecily's hand. They send word to Mayor Stockton and the city authorities. They set scribes to work to make copies of the notice of victory and send messengers to take them far and wide. When dark comes and they can do no more, they go to chapel to take mass and give thanks on their knees.

When that's done, and the other women go to their beds, Cecily stays behind to light candles. One for each of her living sons: Edward first, George and Richard lit from him. One for her husband lost, another for Edmund. Bright flames, the wax soft and supple between her fingers.

'I've done my penance, Edmund,' she tells her long lost son. 'Edouard's death for yours. Marguerite's grief for mine.' Edmund and Edouard, both seventeen, dead ten years apart, each in their first battle. She sits back on her heels, closes her eyes and lets the candlelight blur and redden behind them. She wonders where Marguerite is. Whether she has seen Edouard dead. I would drag him in and show you, she thinks. Every sword stroke, every bruise and bloody smear. There. See how you like it.

Another day, another letter from Richard. John Beaufort, it tells them, died in the battle. His brother Edmund, with fifteen of Marguerite's captains, fled, begged for and were granted sanctuary at Tewkesbury Abbey.

'But,' he writes, 'Edward insists Tewkesbury's not a sanctuary church. Strictly speaking.'

'Strictly speaking?' says Elizabeth.

'A church must have a sanctuary licence,' Cecily tells her. 'Not all do.'

'I'm not sure God makes the distinction,' writes Richard. 'The abbot didn't. But Edward did, and he's king, so he had them dragged out by their hair. Now he's given them to me and, because

I'm Constable of England, I must try them for treason. Well, they're guilty of that for certain and, if the church can't shield them, I can take off their heads in good conscience.'

Do, thinks Cecily. I've waited long enough.

'And Marguerite has surrendered. We have her in our keeping. She's a sad sight, though I'm sure you'll have no pity for it.'

None at all.

'Warwick's daughter was with her.'

He means the younger, Anne, who was married to Edouard and to whom Cecily has given no thought.

'She'll need a little kindness, I think.'

If anyone has time to give it. Two days later, just as Cecily's heart remembers how to beat, she's woken early by the sounds of the Tower garrison arming and Anthony hammering at her door to say that a rebel fleet lies at anchor in the Thames and an army has raised mad Henry's standard at London Bridge.

39.

12 to 21 May 1471

The Tower

'Surely they must know mad Henry's cause is lost?'

Elizabeth's voice is level, but her body trembles with the effort of keeping it so. She has left her children in the nursery with their minders, locked the door and hidden the key among her skirts. As if that would help, thinks Cecily. As if a man can't simply hack down a door with an axe.

'Your Grace,' Mayor Stockton addresses the Queen. He's only a little steadier than her, his skin grey as old cooked mutton and sweat standing on his brow. 'His cause can't be counted lost when ten thousand men stand ready to fight for it.'

'Ten thousand.' Anthony wipes a hand across his face and pegs stiff-legged around the table to the mayor's side. 'So many?'

The Earl of Warwick was always a pirate, and when he went to war he left his cousin Thomas Neville in charge of both his fleet and the Calais garrison. Now Thomas has brought them up to London, the wild men of Kent, too. He stands with them across the river in Southwark and says, 'Let me in.'

'Tell him to burn in Hell,' says Cecily.

Mayor Stockton, who must surely tire of armies arriving at his door, holds out his hand. 'He says he wants only to pass through the city. That he goes north to offer battle to King Edward.'

'You believe that, do you?'

Mayor Stockton, who has learned by now that Cecily's thinking is several steps ahead of his own, looks anxiously from her to Anthony. 'I . . .'

'She's right,' Anthony tells him. 'Edward's in the middle of the country. If I were Thomas and wanted to fight him I'd land in Kent and skirt north. Better still, I'd come ashore in the Wash. No, he's come to the Tower because the Tower's his target.'

'Dear God,' says Elizabeth, her voice fluttering through frightened fingers steepled at her mouth. 'He comes for me.'

No,' says Cecily, firm, for she's guessed that Thomas plans to finish what Warwick started and rule England through a puppet king. She looks at Elizabeth, now rigid with fear. 'Mad Henry's here in the Tower. He comes for him, not for you.'

'Then give him to them,' she snarls, murderous, 'give them his corpse.'

'Kill him?' says the mayor, horrorstruck.

'Elizabeth,' warns Anthony, 'whatever Henry is now he was once God's anointed. What man would dare?'

I would, thinks Cecily. Pass me the knife. But these men won't risk their souls for it, nor will the city sanction it.

She turns to Mayor Stockton. 'We will not kill a man who once wore England's crown. Now, Thomas Neville waits for your reply?'

He nods.

'Good, then we can buy a little time.' She draws him to a table, sits him down and takes a seat beside him, close. She must shore him up. 'Mayor Stockton, I think Thomas Neville underestimates your courage. Or our information. Perhaps he imagines us still ignorant of Edward's victory at Tewkesbury, and so concludes you will be cowed into giving the city up?'

'That might be so,' he says.

'But we are not ignorant, are we? And you are not cowed.'

He looks it, but shakes his head.

She leans in. 'You and I will not be tricked by his bluff and bluster.'

'Bluff and bluster!' cries Elizabeth. 'He has ten thousand, and a fleet!'

Cecily holds out a hand, sharp, to silence her, but keeps her eyes fixed on the mayor. 'We will not be tricked.'

'No.'

So they call up a secretary, and frame a letter that urges Thomas's duty to his cousin King Edward, so much more deserving than the Earl of Warwick ever was and, most importantly, still alive. 'Now, having triumphed over all his enemies,' dictates Cecily, 'he is drawing towards London, even as we write . . .'

'But he's miles away,' whines Elizabeth, only to be shushed by her brother.

'As we write, Mayor Stockton,' Cecily urges. 'So, Sir Thomas, you must withdraw.'

'Yes.' The mayor nods, emboldened, then scratches his head, no more to say.

'Good man,' says Cecily. 'It will do.' She draws back, pushes a fresh parchment under her secretary's pen. 'Now. Write this from me and I will sign it: Sir, if for nothing else then for the love and service you owe to your dead father, who claimed and favoured you when he need not have, I urge you to abandon this futile purpose and whatever sad delusions fill your head.'

He scratches, she signs, feeling Elizabeth's eyes on her as she writes, 'Cecily, the King's Mother.'

The letters are done. Her own enclosed with the mayor's. He takes them and goes, and as the door closes on him, Anthony speaks. 'We must anticipate that Thomas Neville may not respond as we would wish. He has begun by asking for our surrender. Next, he will demand it with violence.'

'Yes,' says Cecily. 'We must hope the mayor's courage holds. And ready ourselves for attack.'

With a nod, he goes about it. Then, when the secretary and servants have bowed their way out, Cecily and Elizabeth are alone.

Soon noises draw them to the window, the rumble of metal heavy on cobbles, as cannons and bombards are dragged from the Tower to line the river bank. Under the shouts of their captains, men strain their backs to pull, while others stride out to set hammers to river walls so the gunners will have clear range across the water. They strain their eyes west towards the bridge, to the mass of enemies that fill the streets of Southwark and crowd its wharves, to the mounted men beneath their flurry of banners, Thomas Neville among them, waiting for the city's answer. And that must be Mayor Stockton's messenger now, striding lonely across the barricaded bridge to give it. 'Who is this man Thomas Neville anyway?' worries Elizabeth. 'Who was his father?'

Turning, Cecily sees that Elizabeth's eyes are fixed and staring; that a blue vein pulses at her throat. She's at the very edge of terror. Well, Cecily understands that. She feels the beat of her own heart rapid and jittery, the cold empty space that opens in her chest when she's afraid. She licks lips that are cracked and dry so that she can speak and distract them both.

'My brother William was his father. A good man. You wouldn't know, he died before your marriage. Thomas was his bastard.'

And, because William had no other son, he'd loved him, but couldn't give him his title or his place in the world. So Thomas isn't Earl of Kent or Baron Fauconberg as his father was, but the Bastard Fauconberg, a man who must make his living as he can.

And while Cecily recalls William's grief for that, she watches Elizabeth's face curl into a venomous snarl.

'Dear God, madam. Your family.' Elizabeth steps away from her, as if from a contagion. 'Can you breed nothing but villains and traitors?'

'And yet, madam,' Cecily keeps her voice low, tamps it as she would a fire, 'you contrived a great deal to marry into it.'

Elizabeth throws up her hands. 'Oh well! Had I but known!'

'Really?' Cecily, her back to the window, watches Elizabeth circle the room, her pale face now flaring colour, her lips drawn back from her teeth. Ugly, in this moment. She wonders if Edward has seen her like this and how he's kept his hands from her throat. 'I doubt it would have stopped you.'

'What?'

'You'd have fucked Satan himself to get a crown on your head.'

She watches while Elizabeth rounds the table again to stand before her. She knows she's said too much, but can do nothing, now, other than say more. 'And your own glorious family all lined up behind you, pushing.' She thrusts a hip, provocative, vulgar.

Elizabeth falters, stumbles as if reeling from a blow. 'How dare you?'

'How dare I? Oh, madam, I've danced around you long enough.' It is so freeing, this anger, as if armies would break against it.

'My family . . .' says Elizabeth, recovering.

'What of them?'

'My family, who you so disparage . . .'

'Oh Elizabeth, the whole world disparages your family!'

'. . . answers to me.' She is drawn to her full height, her teeth bare and glistening. 'I, madam, can command my family, as you so clearly can't command yours. My family is loyal to me. And, because of me, to my husband, your precious son.' She flicks a skirt, turns away towards the table. 'Little as he deserves it.'

'Oh, Elizabeth, because of you? Really?' Cecily pursues her across the room. 'Because they live on his back like leeches more like. You're just the stool they use to climb on to him. Yes, like leeches, sucking and slathering and growing fat.' She throws the taunts at Elizabeth's back. 'While better men . . .'

'What?' Elizabeth rounds on her. 'Better men like Thomas Neville? Like the Earl of Warwick? Like your vicious, treacherous, idiot son George?'

Enough. Cecily strides forward, her arm raised, but then comes the crunch of the first cannon ball against the Tower's curtain wall, and Anthony Woodville lurches into the room and says, 'It's begun.'

By sunset, buildings on the Southwark side of the bridge are alight, but the barricades have held and, though pounded by cannon, the walls of the Tower are unbreached. Next day, the Bastard turns his army round and marches up river.

'He'll cross at Kingston,' says Anthony, 'bring havoc to Westminster, then us.' He scrambles boatloads of men, who travel faster than an army on foot, and the Bastard turns back.

Next morning the Bastard's army batters the bridge again, and by midday the buildings along its length are burning, acrid smoke rolling towards the Tower on an easterly wind.

'You can't cross the fucker if it's on fire!' the defenders taunt.

But further down river, beyond the range of cannon, the Bastard has used his ships to land parties of men, which march now on Aldgate and Bishopsgate: archers and gunners, horses dragging cannon along the dust-dry road.

Last night, heeding Cecily's calls for help, the Earl of Essex came to the city with five hundred men. He works now with Anthony to reinforce the defences. But when the gates come under attack, when fires are set at their bases and burning arrows shower into London's streets, they decide it's time to fight.

Essex, an old hand, has fought sieges before, in France with Cecily's husband. He knows when to sally forth and when to sit tight.

'A man defending a wall's worth five men attacking it,' he says. 'But if they break the gates they're in the streets and it's carnage.'

So he'll take a force through Bishopsgate, and Anthony, strapped into armour though he can scarcely bear weight on his leg, will lead five hundred out of the Tower's postern and flank the buggers trying to break Aldgate down.

'You can't,' says Elizabeth, her hands on Anthony's metalled shoulders, her eyes wild. 'You're wounded. You'll die!'

They're at the foot of the stairs that Anthony has pegged his awkward way down. Outside his men are mounted and ready.

'Come on, lad,' says Essex, pushing past him. 'No time for this.'

'Elizabeth, I must . . .' Anthony looks desperate over his sister's shoulder at Cecily.

Well, I don't know what you expect me to do, she thinks. She hasn't spoken to her daughter-in-law since the first morning of the attack, but now she shakes her head, steps forward, speaks gently.

'Elizabeth, you must let him go . . .'

'You'll leave me with that woman,' Elizabeth says, grasping at her brother. 'She'll hand me to the rebels as soon as look at me. She hates me. She hates us all.'

Anthony's cheeks flush scarlet. 'I'm sorry,' he mouths over her shoulder. Then takes his sister's wrists and draws her from him. 'Elizabeth, I think the King's Mother would do no such thing. And the rebels won't come here. I'll not let them. Let me go.'

There are tears on Elizabeth's face now, and Cecily steps forward, takes her hands from his and turns her about.

'Stop crying,' she says. 'Stop it.' A shake, enough to rattle her. 'Remember what's expected of you. Are you not the Queen?'

So Elizabeth gulps and wipes her eyes, and they step forward together, straight-backed and calm, as the men ride out. And when they're gone, Cecily holds out a hand to her, and says, 'Come inside now and wait with me.'

But Elizabeth only looks at it, turns on her heel and walks back into the Tower, to her son's nursery, where she turns the key in the lock.

All day the smell of burning in Cecily's nostrils, the endless bombardment shaking her bones, but Essex's boldness works and the battle for the city's gates is won. By nightfall the Bastard's host has fallen back beyond Southwark to St George's Fields and Anthony is safe within the Tower. They're braced for another attack but, next day, a force of fifteen hundred arrives, under Edward's standard.

'God keep you,' he writes. 'I send these men ahead and come at speed myself.'

The message to the Bastard is clear: the King comes, and the bridge is not so burned we can't spike your head upon it. He pulls back to Blackheath, then to Rochester, the men of Kent to their homes. And then, at last, comes Edward, cheered through the streets, flanked by his brothers and Will Hastings. He rides to London Bridge, its broken buildings, its blackened frame still reeking. He steps his horse on to it, turns about to address the crowd.

'We'll rebuild,' he shouts, and there, on the bank of the river, from which the barricades and cannon have not yet been cleared, he calls the mayor and London's aldermen, sets them on their knees and knights them, every one.

'Good Mayor Stockton,' he says, drawing the man to his feet. 'Thank you for my city.'

And the good man weeps and kisses his hand. And the people cheer, though weakly, and when they've thrown their hats in the air once, push them firmly on their heads again and turn for home. They're tired of war and fighting, and kings who come and go.

'Do you think that's it?' they say to one another.

'Don't know,' comes the answer. 'Is there any other fucker left to fight?'

40.

21 May 1471

Only one. But he's not exactly fighting. Mad Henry's still in the Tower, where Edward put him when he came back from Barnet. The poor fool had welcomed Edward's coming. 'I thank God for my cousin of York,' he said. 'I know myself safe in his keeping.'

But, perhaps not.

'I want him dead.' Edward's words fall heavy as rocks and no sound follows them. Cecily looks about the table at the wreckage of their dinner, the smeared plates and greasy linen, the carcass of a bird congealing in fat. There's Anthony at the end of the board, eyes on his gimped leg stretched out before him. Then George, nose in his wine cup, Will Hastings leaning back, turning the tip of his knife against the table as if to say, 'Just give me the word.' At her own side sits Richard, his lips a narrow line across a pale face, his steady eye on his brother. Next she looks to Edward, then his queen, who lays her hand on her husband's, and says beneath her breath, 'God, yes.'

Richard is first to speak. Cecily knew he would be.

'He's a sick man, Edward. Is he really such a threat?'

Elizabeth's eyes narrow. 'Thomas Neville was a threat,' she says. 'For mad Henry's sake he'd have murdered me in my bed. And skewered my infant son on a pike.'

Richard inclines his head, concedes. 'But Henry is, or was once, an anointed king.'

'So am I,' says Edward. 'Yet men don't turn squeamish at the thought of burying a blade in me.'

'God protects you,' Hastings smiles, grim. 'But I think He has no more use for mad Henry.'

'Yet there are men who do,' says Edward. 'Henry's useful to every upstart fool or traitor that wants to raise an army against me. I've fought for my crown twice. I've killed my dearest kin to keep it.' He's thinking of Warwick and John Neville, Cecily knows. 'I've no wish to be always looking over my shoulder and thinking, is some other stupid fuck going to have a go for Lancaster?'

Cecily folds her napkin, drawing its smooth linen between her hands. Once, long ago, her husband had had the chance to end the misery of Henry, and bungled it. She imagines all that might be different if he hadn't.

'It must be done,' she says.

Richard's eyes have not left his brother's face. 'But who would do it?'

Edward turns to face him, but doesn't meet his eye. 'I'm afraid it falls to you, Richard. Constable of England. It's your job to condemn traitors, I think.'

Cecily watches the blood drain from Richard's face; his fist upon the table, clench. She reaches and lays her hand upon it, feels the warm reminder of his father's bull's blood ruby press against her palm. It is such a thing to ask of someone.

He takes his hand away, nets it with the other before him on the table.

'What shall I do, Edward? Shall I try him before a court of his peers? I've little evidence to bring and, to my knowledge, he's never lifted a sword.'

'You've the evidence of all that's been done in his name.' Elizabeth is waspish. 'Isn't that enough?'

'Hush, Beth,' says Edward, and to Richard, 'I'm a king and his only peer. I find him guilty. And I want it done tonight. We ride in the morning and he must be dead before we go.'

'And what will we tell the world when it's done?'

'That when told of his son's defeat and death he expired of sheer displeasure and melancholy.'

Richard's grimace twists his face. 'No open deed then.' He

turns the ring on his finger, rubs his thumb across its stone. 'You'll need to order me, Edward. For my soul's sake.'

'I do. And if there's guilt in the deed, I take it.'

Cecily feels rather than sees Richard's one sharp nod, before he pulls back his chair and moves towards the door.

'Richard,' Edward calls him back. 'It must be by your own hand, mind.'

'Yes,' he answers. 'I'd rather assumed that.' The door is open. He hovers on its brink, then, without looking back into the room, asks, 'When it's done, Edward. Will you grant me what I asked?'

'I'd grant it anyway, to my loyal brother. With all my heart.'

Richard nods again. Once. And is gone.

'What's he asked for?' says George with a whine. 'What hasn't he already got?'

Edward knuckles his eyes with his fists. 'Nothing to trouble you, George.'

George isn't alone in wondering, so when Edward orders everyone away, Cecily stays and asks.

'He wants to marry Warwick's girl, Anne,' he tells her.

She had stood, but now she must sit again, and shake her head to take it in.

'So,' she says, rueful, 'what Warwick wanted comes out in the end. George for Isabel. Richard for Anne.'

'The irony has not escaped me.'

'I'd no idea he thought of her.'

'Nor I, till he broached it.'

'When?'

'Yesterday, on the road.'

Cecily is thinking hard. 'You've been dishonest, son. This will certainly trouble George.'

Edward grimaces. Isabel and Anne, as their mother reminded Cecily so long ago, are their parents' only heirs. Because Anne, newly widowed by Edouard's death, isn't yet of age, George has it all. If she marries again he might be made to share it. Well, he won't want that.

'Richard's very clear about what he wants.'

'Other than Anne?'

'He wants the north. All that came to Warwick through his father, your brother. Middleham, Sheriff Hutton, Barnard, Penrith, the rest of it. He says he'll hold the north for me. I can't think of anyone who'd do it better.'

'He doesn't need to marry to get that. You can attaint Warwick and grant it to him anyway, can't you?'

'I can, and I would. In an instant. But, you know Richard. He's such a stickler. He wants to do right by the girl. Says it's not her fault her father was a traitor.'

He's so like his father.

'Well, I dare say it's not.'

She's fourteen, Anne Neville. Been a wife, become a widow. Might have been a queen had things gone differently. Now she's just a dead traitor's daughter and George her keeper.

'Anyway,' says Edward. 'Richard will, he says . . . now, how exactly did he put it? "Put my proposal to her." He says, "She may, of course, say no."' Edward smiles, humourless, shakes his head.

'She's a fool if she does,' says Cecily. 'If she's not careful, George'll put her in a nunnery.'

Edward's face is serious again. 'We must be very careful not to let that happen. In any case, marriage or no marriage, I can't let George have all that Warwick had.'

'God, no.'

'So it's the north for Richard, however I can manage it.'

'Your challenge then. To find a settlement that'll satisfy them both.'

'It is no easy thing. To satisfy George.'

'But he must, I suppose, be rewarded.' She remembers that day on the water steps at Baynard's, his terms for returning to

Edward's side. Beyond restoration, he had said, there must also be reward. And she'd thought him dangerous then and a little mad. 'But he must also be curtailed.'

They're quiet now, for a while. Each thinking of what George might do. Of what Richard is doing even now at their behest. Beyond the window, it's grown full dark and the moon is rising, cool and indifferent, rippled in the glass.

'Well,' says Cecily, rising to close the shutters. 'It would be hard to deny Richard anything after what you've asked of him tonight.'

'I suppose.'

She has to ask. 'Why him?'

'Who else? I asked him to kill a king, Mother. That's not an idea I can put safely into any head but his.'

They'd imagined Richard would come back to tell them. He doesn't. Only sends a note by a servant with a single word. 'Done.'

So, she goes to him. Finds him alone in the room allotted him, bare and perfunctory, his armour on its stand a silver ghost. He looks deathly, has stripped to his shirt sleeves.

'I hope there's nothing more you want of me tonight, Mother. I ride with Edward at first light. Thomas Neville won't catch himself, you know.' He's fumbling for something in a bag half-packed, or unpacked.

'What are you looking for? Where's your squire?'

'I've sent him away. If I want to speak to anyone tonight it'll be a priest. But somehow, even that seems beyond me.'

'It was terrible, Richard, I know. But necessary.'

She looks at his long, slim hands working into the bag, the snipped finger, awkward still in its leather sheath. She wonders how he did it. A pillow over the head? A knife under the ribs?

'You know, your father died in that man's name.'

'But not at his order, Mother,' he says, suddenly sharp. 'Not by his hand.' He pushes the bag aside, without finding whatever he was looking for, leans against the wall and folds his arms about himself, speaks softer. 'Anyway. It's done. The proclamation will be ready for Edward's seal within the hour. Melancholy and displeasure. I've arranged for his body to be taken to St Paul's in the morning. A full honour guard. If Edward's not happy with any of that, he can change it.'

'You're meticulous.'

She edges towards his armour, floats a hand down the breastplate, can't help but test a buckle or two.

'Let it alone, Mother.'

She steps away, folds her thumb beneath her fingers, feels on them the slide of leather soap. Someone's done a good job.

'Edward told me you want to go north.'

He eases himself to sit on the narrow bed, nets his hands between his knees, giving up any hope of avoiding a conversation.

'I think. I hope, the wars are all but over. I want a home. I want a sphere of influence worthy of what I am. I want to do good work for my brother the King. But in my own lands.'

She sits beside him, looks at his pale profile, the fall of dark hair. 'You sound like your father.'

'Well,' he shrugs, 'there are worse things.'

'Many,' she agrees.

'I like the north.'

'You like Anne Neville, too, I hear.'

'In truth, I barely know her. She was a child when I was with Warwick. She seemed . . . intelligent.'

'Good Lord, Richard. Will you be the first man in England to marry a woman for her mind?'

'No. Well, not only for that.'

'For her inheritance then?'

He spreads his palms.

'Edward would give you the north without a marriage.'

'I don't want it as a gift. I want it in law. By inheritance. I want it to be hard for Edward to take it back.'

She's shocked. 'You think he would?'

'Mother, you know how he is. How he gives with one hand, takes away with the other. I love him, God knows, but it's true. Remember John Neville, thrown out of his earldom into a magpie's nest?'

Yes, she remembers John Neville. Dead with the sun in splendour backed against his heart. She puts her hand on the bed beside her son's. 'When you're back, then, we'll see what can be done.'

'If she'll have me.'

She lets her shoulder touch his. 'Who wouldn't have you?'

He grimaces, like a man who isn't sure he'd have himself.

Next morning, when her sons have ridden out with the dawn and mad Henry's sad procession has trailed its way to St Paul's, Cecily decides it's time to acquaint Marguerite with her loss. Henry's queen, now his widow, came to the city yesterday as part of Edward's train, bare-headed in an open cart, like the prize in a Roman triumph, spat upon and mocked. Now she sits alone high in the White Tower, a key turned upon her. A prisoner, at last.

She doesn't stand when Cecily enters, but lifts her chin, looks unsurprised, and says, 'I wondered how long it would be before you came.'

Cecily crosses the floor to the room's only other chair, draws it up to sit opposite Marguerite, smooths her sleeves, folds her hands in her lap. She has dressed very fine for this, with a tall henin whose veils, thin as a nun's prayer, lap her shoulders. Her neck is spanned by pearls her husband gave her when first they went to France. She thinks Marguerite will remember them.

'I've come,' she says, 'to tell you that your lord husband is dead.'

Marguerite says nothing, moves not at all.

'Well.' Cecily shrugs, the veils shimmer. 'I didn't expect that you would care.'

The ghost of a movement in Marguerite's hand, a dismissal. That soft, sibilant voice. 'We have both lost husbands, you and I.'

'It's not the same, I think.'

Marguerite's eyes narrow. They were wide once and bright, now their lids fold heavy about them and they are rimmed with red. She's forty-one years old, but her hair is streaked grey and deep-gouged lines draw the corners of her mouth down.

'If, as I suppose, it is your wish to grieve me, Lady Cecily, you should tell me of my son.'

There are so many things she could tell her about Edouard. How he died, the wounds he carried. George, who inflicted some of them, revelled in the telling. She could lay them all on his mother now. Flay her with them. But it seems, suddenly, pointless. So she says instead, 'He'll be decently buried in the abbey, at Tewkesbury. Quietly, but not without honour.'

Marguerite looks away then, closes her eyes, draws a gasping breath. There are times when a little kindness, the smallest morsel of mercy, is a torment. She would rather hear of Edouard in his blood. She doesn't want him clean and shroud-wrapped under stone, but heavy and broken in her arms. She wants to be seared to the core by the coldness of his flesh, to suck ravenous kisses from his breathless mouth, to gorge on grief.

Cecily watches as Marguerite tries to speak. It looks painful, as if her mouth is full of blades. 'What is it, Marguerite?'

'Your own son's throat was cut, of course,' she croaks. 'From ear to ear.' The tip of her finger traces the route across her neck. 'Your Edmund, I mean.' She steals herself to look up again, to measure the depth of the blow inflicted. 'I may not have seen my own son dead, Cecily, but I've seen yours.'

Cecily sits straight-backed, her high-plucked brow clear; she has known Edmund's loss long enough to face it unflinching. 'Yes,' she says and swallows hard. 'But I have other sons.'

She too can wound with words. Marguerite's tears, come at last, are scalding, her words torn and raw. 'I had only him. Only him and no other in all my life.'

Then Cecily is on her feet, reaching out an arm. Marguerite turns away as fingers come to rest upon her shoulder. 'Then be thankful, Marguerite,' she says. 'Had you others, we would kill them all.'

She steps away as Marguerite weeps. She walks about the room. It isn't grim. The walls are limed white, there is a narrow window, its sliver of glass casting pale green light across a clean flagged floor. A bed. Christ in agony above it. A fire, not lit. She waits for the shivering sobs to stop, then turns. Marguerite is collecting herself, straightening her spine, blinking as her hands pull wetness from her cheeks. Cecily sits opposite her again, folds her hands.

'Are you done, Marguerite?' she asks.

'Yes.' It's barely a whisper. 'Yes. I am done now.'

'Then we must decide what to do with you. You needn't stay here. I can find somewhere for you. Somewhere quiet. A woman or two to wait on you. A chaplain for your prayers. You'll be guarded but . . .' She sighs. 'You might find a little peace, Marguerite. Wouldn't you like a little peace?'

She doesn't answer.

41.

28 September to November 1471

Westminster

Cecily sends Marguerite to Ewelme in the quiet Oxfordshire hills, to Alice de la Pole, who was Marguerite's friend, who brought her, a girl of fifteen, from France and told her England would love her and that she'd be a happy queen with Henry. Well, what else could she have said?

'I hope she doesn't hold it against me,' Alice said when Cecily asked her to be Marguerite's keeper. 'Yes. Send her to me.'

And Cecily's sons ride out after Thomas Neville and catch him at Sandwich. He begs Edward's forgiveness, is given it and taken north in Richard's company. But when he makes a break and tries for France, Richard drags him back and lops his head. All this Cecily reads in letters from Yorkshire, where Edward has sent his youngest brother to make the royal presence felt in lands where the Nevilles have long held sway; to feel his way into lands Edward has promised will be his own.

When Richard writes, he asks a favour. 'If you're able, Mother, have an eye for Anne. But for God's sake, don't tell George I want her.'

Must I always look out for my sons' women? Cecily thinks. But at least the Queen's off her hands now, with Edward back safe in his city. Elizabeth's surrounding herself with her Woodville kin, showing off her son, and spurning her husband's family. Most especially she's spurning George, who makes himself big telling all who'll listen how he saved the kingdom for his brother. When he talks, Cecily sees Edward's fingers flex and wonders how long the peace between them will last.

George's wife, long-faced Isabel, is much about court with her husband. Cecily wonders if she's content with the marriage she itched for so badly, now that she's had to suffer exile and loss for it. Well, it looks like she's making the best of things, dressing very fine and smiling too much. No Anne with her, though it's no secret she's in Isabel's household, where George has demanded she be placed. With his thoughts on her inheritance, he wants her beyond other men's reach. So, one afternoon late in August, when Isabel is watching her husband lose to the King at the archery butts, Cecily comes to her side and says, 'I wonder why your sister doesn't come to court with you?'

Isabel looks nervous as another arrow lands off centre and her husband agitates and blames the fletching.

'She is, I think, doubtful of her welcome.'

'Now, why should that be?'

'Well. Her marriage of course. I mean, she was the wife of a very great traitor.'

Cecily lets herself laugh. 'But dear Isabel, so were you.'

When Isabel's face colours she lays a hand on her arm. 'But we're all friends now, surely. Come, let's ask my son.'

And she steers her towards the smiling King, who puts his bow tip to the ground and raises an eyebrow as Cecily approaches. 'Mother?'

'The Lady Isabel is concerned that her sister may not be welcome among us. I'm sure we can reassure her?'

Edward shifts the bow to arm's length and speaks so all will hear, 'The Lady Anne is my cousin. I'll always be glad to see her.' Then he looks down the line of men. 'George, bring our cousin to court.' Isabel makes her courtesy and Cecily smiles, first at Edward, then at George, whose face is thunderous.

*

Next evening, Anne comes. Cecily has never seen her before. Like her sister, she was kept much in the north as a child. She's small for her age and slender to the point of thinness, but her skin is good, her eyes a clear hazel, and her hair, drawn back tight beneath her cap, is a soft faded copper, like a coin left out in the sun. She wears yellow, and walks bravely, chin up, hands folded in her sleeves, Isabel beside her, George hovering behind. Edward, seeing her, invites her to dance and they make a decent fist of it, then he brings her to Cecily and sits her down.

'My mother will introduce you to everyone,' he says. 'And tell you all you need to know.'

She comes again in a fortnight. And then a fortnight again. She sits with Cecily and with her sister, says little unless spoken to. But when she does speak it isn't nonsense, and Cecily sees her watching everything and concludes Richard's probably right. She's sharp, this one. Anne watches George most of all with a bland expression that, Cecily guesses, masks distaste. On her third visit Cecily asks if she plays chess and yes, she does. So, since the day is fine for October, they take the game outside and, when Isabel sits down beside them, Cecily says, 'Really, my game does suffer when I'm watched.' So Isabel can do nothing but leave.

When Anne makes her first move, Cecily sees that her mouth has turned up at the corner.

'Your sister seems very careful of you.'

'More than is strictly necessary, I think.'

'You come see us so rarely. I wonder why?'

'Perhaps I'm not used to the ways of court.'

'Nonsense, you were brought up in the finest court in the north. Your father's. There can be nothing here that discomforts you.'

It's Anne's turn to move again. She scrutinizes the board harder than can be necessary so early in the game. She's thinking. Coming to a decision. Weighing up a risk.

'I come when given licence. I live in your son's household and must come and go as he chooses.'

'I imagine you don't like that.'

Anne has given up the pretence of the game. She looks away. Down towards the river where comes the sound of barking and laughter. Someone's chasing a dog. 'I don't.'

'Perhaps I can help?'

Anne turns and Cecily knows herself watched. Assessed. 'Would you speak to the King for me?'

'Perhaps.'

Anne looks away again and back. The dog is caught. 'My father is not attainted.'

'He's not.'

'So, the Duke of Clarence, George, says he holds all of my father's lands by inheritance. By right of my sister, his wife.'

'I suppose he does. Say that, I mean.'

'But surely, half should be mine.'

'Well. Had you a husband who could press your case.'

Her voice turns bitter. 'I have not.' She still holds a pawn in her hand, turns it in her lap. She's wearing yellow today. Cecily's sure she's seen this dress on her sister. Borrowed, then. Kept short.

'Forgive me, Anne. I notice you don't wear mourning.'

'I don't grieve.'

She is matter of fact, puts the piece back on the board. It's a move and Cecily responds to it. A knight edges forward.

'I see.'

'You won't press my case for me then, with the King?' Anne asks.

'I might. But a woman alone to hold such honour as you might command? And you're young, Anne. What you need is a husband who can stand against the Duke of Clarence.'

Anne screws her face against the impossibility of that.

'My son, Richard, you know, is unmarried.' The girl turns to her, startled. 'I only mention it. I think you know him?'

'He was in my father's household when I was a child. I sat by him at dinner a time or two. I was . . . shown to him. My father, you know . . .'

'Yes. I know. But what he wanted doesn't matter any more. What you want might.'

'Are you asking if I will marry your son?'

'I'm asking if you'd consider it. Were he to make an offer. Were the King to support it with a grant of your inheritance.'

The girl blinks. 'I didn't expect . . .'

'No. I imagine. You'd need to be patient, though. Richard won't return until the winter. Nothing can happen till then. So, don't answer now. Consider it. Tell me next time. On balance, I'd say, don't speak of this with your sister.'

'I keep my own counsel.'

'I imagine you do. Now, let's finish this game or people will wonder what we're about.'

The next time Anne comes to court a month has passed, but the girl looks a little more hopeful and says to Cecily as they pass each other in a corridor, 'Yes.'

42.

London

It's December before Richard comes back, ploughing south through heavy snow and bringing Christmas with him.

'I've laid the ground for you with Anne,' Cecily tells him when he comes to her at Baynard's. 'It's up to you now.'

'You do know,' he says, 'that it'll be a fight?' He looks worried.

To win George away from Warwick's side, Edward made him many promises including, it seems, the Warwick inheritance. George has chosen to understand that Edward meant all Warwick had, not just the lands that came to him through his wife which, as Isabel's husband, George could sensibly lay claim to, but the great northern inheritance too, that has been Neville forever and which Richard hungers for.

George has, so far, resisted all attempts at clarification and says, when pressed, 'It must all be mine. In reward for my service.'

'Anne seems ready for a fight,' says Cecily. 'She wants what's hers.'

'I mean, it will be a fight between George and me,' says Richard. 'And Edward drawn into it.'

'Well. It's been a quiet month or two. I suppose it's time someone started a fight with someone.'

He slumps to a chair. 'It's madness. Three brothers. Between us we could do something good with this country. Make it something for France to be afraid of again. But George . . .'

'Is a vain fool and an open door to trouble, I know.' He seems surprised by her candour. 'Richard, do you imagine being some-one's mother makes you blind to their faults?'

'No. I suppose not. Well, not you anyway. But now it's my wishes that will make George troublesome again, and where will it end this time?'

'Don't you be a fool too, Richard. Do you think the way to appease George is to let him have all he wants? He'll always want more. You shouldn't take Anne with anything less than the north and half the Beauchamp inheritance that was her mother's.'

'I think so too.'

'Good. So make that your starting point. But know what you'll settle for. And please. If you can achieve it without driving him into open rebellion, I'll be grateful.'

'Hmm. I'll do my best.'

'Anyway. Anne will come to the Christmas court. See if you still think she's worth it.'

Anne comes four times to court at Christmas. When Richard dances with her, George bristles. When he's seated beside her for the nativity feast, he writhes. When Richard gifts her, on twelfth night, a golden sun with diamond letters R and A, he looks set to kill. When Edward tells him next morning that Richard is asking for her hand, he says, point blank, no; that in law Anne is as good as his sister and he'll not give consent. And when Richard goes next day to George's London house, the servants say Anne is unwell and will see no one.

'Go again tomorrow,' Cecily advises. 'But meanwhile set men to watch. It's not beyond him to take her out of London.'

A week, and word is Anne still sickens so, at its end, Edward issues George with an order to give her up and Richard licence to take her.

'Go when George is away from home,' advises Cecily. 'And take men with you to search the house.'

He finds Anne in the kitchens, where her sister had her bundled as Richard's men arrived and the search of the house began.
He hears her cry of 'Richard!' from behind the door of the but-
tery, the key of which has been turned against her.

'Open this door or I'll have it broken down,' he commands,
and Isabel, sobbing now as his men ready their shoulders for the
work, orders it opened. Anne emerges smoothing her skirts,
shaking only a little and her eyes flashing anger.

'Are you hurt?' he asks.

'Not at all,' she answers, a lift to her chin.

'Good,' he nods. 'Then will you come with me, Anne, away
from this nonsense?'

He holds out a hand. She takes it. 'Most gladly.'

As Richard's men clear the way and he leads her out into the
air, Isabel hurries after. 'Sir,' she cries, 'my Lord your brother
commands my sister to remain here, for her own protection.'

'Anne goes where she wishes, is commanded by no one and
requires no protection,' he throws over his shoulder. 'And if your
Lord my brother thinks otherwise, he can take it up with me.'

He takes her through the snowy streets to the sanctuary of St
Martin's-Le-Grand and tells her she is her own woman now and
can decide her own fate. If she says no to him, he'll settle something upon her so that she might live free. If she says yes, he'll
make her his duchess and fight for what should be hers. It's not
the most romantic of proposals but she, very sensibly and with
grim determination, says yes.

And suddenly London's streets are full of men in George's livery
picking fights, and George is telling anyone who'll listen how he's
robbed, and Edward can't get a minute's peace for his brothers'
quarrelling, until Elizabeth, who is seven months gone with
another child and tetchy, says, 'For God's sake just settle it!'

So Edward calls them both to put their case before him, but
when they've bickered away days with testimony and lawyers,

they're no further forward. The best George will say is that Richard can have the girl, but not an inch of land. 'I rely on the law,' he says.

So Cecily sits George down and says, 'Let me explain the law to you, son. The lands you claim through your wife belong by law to her mother, who is, though you men choose to ignore it, not yet dead. So come to terms with Richard, or I'll recommend to your brother the King that he settle the lands on Lady Warwick, as is her right. Now, she's been under arrest since Tewkesbury and writes frequently from Beaulieu to assure me she'll do much to secure her freedom including, I imagine, signing most of those lands over to Richard at the King's request. Legal and clear. So, George, don't rely on the law, because if Edward wants to use the law to give Richard even more than he's asking for at your expense, he can. Rely instead on your king's mercy and forbearance which, I do assure you is, like my own, not boundless.'

To Richard she says, 'What will you settle for? What will Anne settle for? Because for God's sake, we need peace. And you, who are the most reasonable of all my sons, will surely give it to us.'

And Richard, who at times is driven to curse his own reasonableness, squares his jaw and says, 'I must have the north, clean and clear. And I find I must have Anne.'

So Edward gives him the north and all the lands that were the Earl of Oxford's too, and Anne is his full willingly, so, surely, at last, it's done.

'Is it ever done though,' Cecily says to Edward, 'when it comes to George?'

43.

June 1472

Greenwich

A summer wedding. Quiet, as the couple wish it to be. 'Only family,' says Richard. 'No fuss.'

'Anne might like a little fuss,' says Cecily.

'No. She wouldn't.' And it must be supposed, since Richard has visited Anne at St Martin's most every day since he took her there, that he should know.

But because Anne's family are mostly dead or captive, and because George won't come and forbids Isabel, the bride has not even a sisterly maid to attend her on the day, nor any mother but Cecily to stand at her side.

'You've more sense than to mind that, haven't you?' Cecily says as their barge rounds the river's curve and brings them to Greenwich.

Anne doesn't look as if she minds. She sits patiently in the stern looking forward over Cecily's shoulder, tiny in her pale green gown, soft as a sage leaf. She wears Richard's golden heart at her throat and her hair falls in a shine down her back. She looks certain of herself, like a person who is setting out towards a known destination on a clearly marked path.

'I should think I have,' she says, and a slight shudder runs through those narrow shoulders. 'My family were at my last wedding. It didn't make it a happy occasion.'

Cecily wonders just how unhappy it must have been if the family she prefers to have about her now is the one that killed her father and keeps her mother under lock and key. Yet she can't resist testing the ground.

'That marriage,' she says, 'might have made you a queen. Had things turned out differently.'

Anne's eyes narrow as she looks across the light-flecked water. 'I never for a moment believed that would happen. Nor wanted it. It was as if we were all caught in a madness.'

Now the shudder is very real and all the sunshine gone from her look, so that Cecily feels she must lean forward, touch her knee to call her back.

'Well, never mind it,' she says. 'Today we're sane and things will be better. And, in any case, we are family. Your grandfather, Salisbury, was my favourite brother.'

Anne, only four years old when that man died, likely doesn't remember him. But she puts her hand on Cecily's own and says, serious and intent, 'And you've been a good mother to me already. I'm grateful.'

Then suddenly she's smiling and lifting a finger to point. 'Look. There's Richard.'

Cecily turns her head and sure enough, as Greenwich's gleaming palace glides into view, her youngest son is standing on the water steps, waiting for his bride. He must see them coming, for he lifts a hand to wave.

'I'd rather be Richard's duchess,' says Anne, 'than Queen of all the World.'

It's a strange thing, Cecily thinks, that name, Richard, living so happily in Anne's mouth. When they come at last to the altar, and the girl makes her vows, she speaks it as if her lips were framed from birth for its vowels and consonants; for its rolling start and its cadent fall that, as Cecily remembers, will bring her tongue tip light against her teeth. Silently she lets her own mouth recall the movement of it; the many times she spoke it and saw her husband, her first Richard, turn and smile as her son does now at Anne; that wide, open smile that lit his face and was always, ever, only for her. It's as if the blade of loss lodged so long in her heart has been given a new edge, and she almost gasps at the pain of it. Then suddenly the marriage promises are made and Anne leans up to whisper something in Richard's ear that sets him laughing and brings all the room to life. Cecily shakes herself. It's so foolish, to be sentimental at weddings.

She imagines there'll be little sentiment at today's other wedding, when Margaret Beaufort takes Thomas Stanley as her new husband only eight months after she laid her old one to rest.

Henry Stafford lived half a year with the belly wound he got at Barnet, a butcher's mess, stubborn against healing. At last, the rot got in it and he died in a stench, blackened and bloated. Margaret nursed him through it all and wept for him after.

But though Margaret's grief for her husband is bitter, it can't equal her grief for her son who, though he lives and breathes still, seems more lost to her than ever. He's in Brittany with his uncle, Jasper Tudor. Prisoner and exile both.

Jasper came too late to aid Marguerite at Tewkesbury and, hearing of her defeat, fled to France, taking young Henry with him. Slippery bastard. Edward's spies could find no word of them and Louis only shrugged his Gallic shoulders and said, 'They are at the bottom of the sea, *n'est-ce pas*? I care not.'

'I swear I'll fight that fucker one of these days,' spat Edward.

'So you keep saying,' said his mother.

But they are not drowned. Summer storms drove them to the coast of Brittany and the arms of Duke Francis. So Edward wrote to his ally saying, 'Jasper Tudor is a threat to my realm. I'll send envoys to bring him and the boy back to England.'

'*Non, non, non, mon ami*,' Francis replied, all concern. 'For love, I will save you the labour and keep them here where they can cause no harm.'

'He'll sell them to Louis when it suits him,' Cecily sneered.

It was a late September morning, the dogs were being whipped up outside and Edward, inside, itched for the hunt. 'Let them rot in Brittany,' he said. 'I don't care.'

Exasperated, Cecily rounded on him. 'Am I the only one who ever thinks ahead? Henry Tudor's the only Lancastrian man left with a drop of royal blood in his veins.'

'Beaufort blood.' Edward, all dismissive. 'Bastard blood. What matter?'

Cecily took the news to Margaret at Woking. It was a week before her husband died, just as the rot was setting in. Margaret looked ill herself and little wonder.

'Then Henry's beyond our reach?' she said.

'For now, at least. I'm sorry.'

And she is. She knows young Henry could be Margaret's comfort and believes her to be his best chance. She'd keep him on a straight course. He could be Earl of Richmond one day, friend to the King. But every day in Jasper's company makes that less likely. Young men are shaped by the company they keep. He'll learn to hate the house of York and distrust it. He'll become a bitter exile, a malcontent. Never truly dangerous, perhaps Edward's right. But a burr beneath the saddle. A man with a grudge.

When Cecily saw Margaret again in December she looked weary. Not thirty yet, but the contentment of recent years had leached from her.

'What will you do now?' Cecily asked.

A deep sigh. 'I think I must marry again.'

Cecily could hardly have been more surprised. 'I didn't think marriage, in general, was to your taste.'

It's not. Margaret would rather face hellfire than have any man touch her. She's never forgotten the first time, with Henry's father, who said he would be gentle and wasn't, who started with stroking and touching and kissing till she shivered and grew wet, but ended with thrusting and bruising and holding her down, and by bringing pain even worse than the terrible labour that came after. She'd learned, later, that the terms of their marriage contract gave him no rights to her lands until their union was fruitful, and for that reason he'd taken her, twelve years old and one day married, to bed.

'No,' she says. 'But I must have a place at court, Cecily. Which only a man can give me. I must be present to make sure my case isn't forgotten.'

'Margaret, do you not trust me to make sure it's not?'

'It isn't that I don't. I just . . .'

Cecily concedes. 'No. I understand.' She knows – where the futures of their children are concerned – women are slow to trust.

And so today, as Richard marries Anne in hope, Margaret marries Thomas Stanley in grim determination. Like Margaret, Thomas is recently widowed and comes from old Lancastrian stock, but he's long been on the side of York. Cecily still doesn't trust him. Last year, when Warwick had looked like a winner, he supported him. Though he turned his coat back fast enough, once the tide turned.

A lapse, Edward called it. He's not the only man that's had one.

No, Cecily conceded, he isn't. But still. Anyway, he's Steward of the King's Household now, so for closeness to the court Margaret couldn't have chosen better. And they each have something the other wants. Position, land, influence. It's what most marriages are made for, not least Cecily's own. But then, she's been a widow twelve years now and has all the power and influence she could want. King's Mother. Sometimes though, after so many nights alone, she thinks she'd give it all up to return to those coin-bright days when she was young, with a full nursery and a swelling belly and a husband for whom she was, always, Queen of the World.

Dear God, such nonsense. She really must stop coming to weddings.

'Mother, aren't you going to wish the happy couple good night?'

And she looks up to see that everyone has risen from the table and Edward is ushering the whole company to the door, and a piper and drummer have appeared to help escort the newlyweds towards their bed, and Anne is laughing while Richard looks embarrassed and just a little drunk. And she goes out with them into corridors full of laughter and music and Edward's foolish ribaldry, till they come to a door, which Richard bars with his arm, and says with a smile but some firmness, 'No further than this, my friends. We wish you good night.'

And everyone groans and calls out, 'A kiss for the bride then!'

And Cecily watches while the youngest of her sons cups Anne's face and puts his lips to hers before drawing her inside, closing the door and leaving them all to wonder. Like the others she drifts off at last to her own bed. But the thought of it stays with her long into the night: Richard's tapering hand gentle against Anne's cheek. His father's ring, that snipped finger.

44.

August to December 1473

London

If Cecily was maudlin at Richard's wedding, it must have been Jacquetta's fault, for, in the days before, she'd travelled to Grafton to see her old friend laid to rest. Jacquetta hadn't weathered well since Warwick killed her husband and her son, since the world she thought safe teetered and spun. When she came out of sanctuary with Elizabeth last spring she was gaunt, by the time she died, cadaverous, but for a great swelling in her gut that racked her with pain so terrible it seemed she'd stepped into purgatory still breathing.

'Were her sins so terrible to deserve this?' Cecily asked her chaplain when last rites were done. 'God is less merciful than I. Whatever wrongs she did me, I absolve her of them.'

Elizabeth was with her mother at Westminster when she died, but didn't make the pilgrimage to Grafton for the funeral. Only six weeks from the birthing of another girl, she thought the journey too arduous. 'A three-day ride,' sniffed Cecily when Edward told her she wouldn't go. 'Jacquetta would have walked it barefoot for her.'

'Should I remind you,' Edward said, 'that you never actually liked Jacquetta?'

True enough. But when she looked about she found Jacquetta to be her oldest friend, born in the same year, met at sixteen. 'You're right,' she says. 'Even dead she annoys me. What business had she dying already? Look at me, I'm not old.'

Though sometimes she feels it. Fifty-eight this summer. She

has birthed twelve children; six of them still live. All of them are out in the world and her eldest King of England with, please God, the chance of a peaceful reign at last. So, in the year that's passed since Jacquetta's death and Richard's marriage, she's made some changes of her own. She divides her time now between Baynard's and Berkhamsted, the lordship of which Edward has gifted her because it has a comfortable castle, a pleasing town clustered in its skirts and is only thirty miles from London. It reminds her of Fotheringhay; she can stand on its walls and hear church bells and sheep.

Her friends visit her there. Her children sometimes. Edward comes, never Elizabeth. Never George, of course. Richard's in the north, but his diligent letters find her every week wherever she is, full of business and work well done. Her daughter Anne comes with her new husband. Since the Pope's dispensation released her from marriage to Henry Holland, and since Edward sent him to rot in the Tower, she's taken Thomas St Ledger to wed, for no other reason than she likes him. He's nothing much, just a good man in Edward's service. Cecily would normally disparage such a match but, since her daughter seems full of light in his presence, she welcomes him, and lets him kiss her hand.

And so she's content at Berkhamsted, and orders its business as she chooses. And whenever she feels the itch for politics, the need to be at the centre of things, she packs her bags and comes to London.

She's come now for family matters, for two of her sons' wives have been brought to bed with children. For George's Isabel, a daughter. For Edward's Elizabeth, a second son.

'He thrives,' Edward tells her when she arrives in his chambers. It's just past midday, there's a glass in his hand and he looks like he's been celebrating diligently since news came of the boy's arrival.

'Good,' she tells him. 'I'm glad.' And relieved. One son is barely enough.

'We've named him Richard, in honour of Elizabeth's father and mine. And my brother, I suppose. Do you think he'll be pleased?'

She smiles. 'Our family is most unimaginative with names. But it's good news. Two sons now, almost as close in age as you were with Edmund.'

Not that they'll see much of each other, these royal boys. The King's three-year-old heir is settling into his own domain as Prince of Wales. Elizabeth has been with him there spring through summer and gave birth to her new son in Shrewsbury. When she brings the baby back to London, she'll leave its brother at Ludlow, the centre of a princely court, tutored by his uncle Anthony to be a ruler and a prince.

To be a Woodville, Cecily thinks. She'd rather he was under other guardianship. The King's own family, not his wife's. Richard's best of all. But he's busy in the north and, besides, Elizabeth wouldn't stand for it. She keeps to her own kin, these days. Easy enough. There are so many of them they litter the corridors.

'So is your queen's mood any sweeter?' Cecily jibes, pouring for herself.

He won't rise to it, just holds out his glass. 'I'm told she's very well,' he says. 'They're both very well. She'll be back before September's out.'

'You'll be sorry. You'll have to give up your whores.'

'Does nothing escape your notice?' Edward's never been faithful, but lately he's given up discretion.

'I'm only at Berkhamsted, Edward. I can hear them panting from there.'

He laughs, leans back in his chair, stretches his legs before him and winks.

'Had your father faced me with such women, I'd have gelded him.'

'No doubt. Elizabeth doesn't mind. As long as she's the one with a crown on her head.'

'Lucky you. Now. Business.' She takes the glass from his hand and sets it down.

He looks after it, as if measuring the time till it can be picked up again. 'You mean George, I suppose. Are you planning to see him?'

'Aren't you? I thought you'd find common ground, celebrate your virility together.'

'I've sent gifts. The less I see him the more likely he is to stay alive.'

'That bad?'

He mimics pulling out his hair.

'This business with Oxford?'

The Earl of Oxford, who escaped Barnet with his life, found a welcoming billet with King Louis, and has made a nuisance of himself pirating English shipping ever since. In May, though, he landed with a force and is holed up in the craggy monastery at St Michael's Mount. From there he ventures into the Cornish countryside, raiding.

'So George offered to take an army into Cornwall and winkle Oxford out for me. When I told him I wouldn't trust him to take a dog to Cornwall you'd have thought him a nun and I'd called him a whore. All wounded pride and woe is me. And when I told him I'd send Richard instead . . .'

'I can imagine.'

'So, for the sake of peace, I stood Richard down and sent someone else.'

'Thank you.'

'Mother, why didn't you drown him at birth?'

She sighs. 'I sometimes wonder. You have him watched?'

'Of course. And his watchers tell me how he complains to anyone who'll listen about how I rob him, oppress him, thwart his authority. How I favour his brother at his expense.'

'It's rather he that's robbed Richard. And we let him get away with it. We're lucky Richard's so tolerant. George has had by far the better share of Warwick's lands.'

'Ah, well, Warwick's lands. That's all up in the air again. I wish I'd never let that bloody woman out of Beaulieu.'

He means Anne's mother, of course. In June, Edward gave in to Richard's pleading to have her released into his care. 'For Anne's comfort,' Richard said. 'She can do us no harm and Anne some good.'

'So, George hears of it and next day comes ranting that it's all a plan to grant Isabel's inheritance back to her mother, so she can give it all to Richard. "I'll be robbed again," says George. So, to answer your first question, no. It's best I don't see him.'

Cecily groans. 'I'll speak to him.'

'I suppose Edward's happy with his son?' George asks, sulky, when she emerges from Isabel's room. The baby is small and the mother exhausted. Pale and listless in her bed two weeks on from her delivery.

'As you are with your daughter, I imagine.'

'I'd have a son three years old now, if he hadn't died on a fucking ship because Edward wouldn't let us land at Calais.'

She holds back, for the moment, from reminding him that he put his wife on that ship and was in rebellion at the time. Instead, she lets him talk, laying his grievances at her feet. When he's done, she calmly refutes them one by one. 'Your share of the Warwick inheritance is ratified by Parliament. You have more titles, more land and more honours than your brother Richard. Of course you weren't trusted to deal with Oxford, you've kept evil company with him in the past. You're not oppressed, just watched, and with good reason.'

'What reason?' he asks.

'George,' she reminds him – and by God, it's time someone told him straight – 'because you've been a proven traitor.'

And he looks at her in wide-eyed disbelief, as if such a charge is unimaginable, unfathomable, unfair. As if he's wounded to the core by it.

'But,' he says, and seems in every way to believe it, 'my brother's kingdom would have been lost without me.'

And, truly, in this moment, she fears for him.

'George, without you, your brother's kingdom might never have been at risk.'

He shakes his head, no, no, no. 'I'm a good brother,' he insists. 'I'm a good son. You wrong me.'

There's sweat on his brow and he trembles. Then, to her shame, he weeps, so that she must sit him down and put his head to her shoulder and hush him, like a child, while her mind reels and her belly shrivels in disgust and she thinks, dear God, all his life, I've fought to keep this son alive.

'George,' she says. 'George. Listen to me.' She takes his head in her hands and looks into his swollen eyes, his face smeared with tears and snot. 'You are Duke of Clarence, Earl of Warwick and of Salisbury. You are Chamberlain of England. Your brother has given you honours no other man could equal. You have lands aplenty, a wife, and God has given you children. Can you not be content? Will you not just stop? Because, if you don't. If you don't. I don't know what will become of you.'

It seems he can't stop. Come winter, when Edward is away in Nottingham, George brings armed men into London's streets, pushing and shoving and saying he'll bring justice against his brother the Duke of Gloucester at his sword's edge.

Richard, when he hears of it, says, 'God knows, Mother, I want no violence, but if he comes against me, I will defend myself.'

'Edward,' she writes, 'George must be curbed.'

So, on his return, Edward calls him to his presence and says, 'George, you remain unhappy with the settlement I've ordered between you and your brother?'

'Warwick's lands are mine by right!' George screams in his face. 'All of them. Every inch. I'm robbed!'

And Edward, taking him easily by the throat and backing him

against a wall, says, 'It's for me to say what belongs to who. Push me and I'll take everything you have.'

'You won't.'

'Try me.'

'Back down, George,' Cecily warns him.

And because, really, he has no choice, he does.

A single concession is made to appease him. Warwick's wife, though hale and hearty, is declared legally dead, so there can be no question any more of her granting anything to anyone.

'So that's it, George,' says Edward. 'Settled.'

But no one really believes it is.

45.

July 1475 to July 1476

Barham Downs, Canterbury

He's been talking about it long enough. And what king, once secure in his own realm, doesn't want to go kick someone else out of theirs? So, with Lancaster now down and out and two sons thriving, Edward finally stops threatening to go to war with Louis and actually does it. Cecily rides to Canterbury to see the muster, for there has never been, nor will again be, such a spectacle in England. Thirteen thousand men pour on to Barham Downs with all their gear for war: their horses and harness, their cannon and shot, bows, blades, whetstones and polish, their cook pots, trivets, and tents. Lumbering on heavy carts come the siege engines and bombards that will break castle walls, the hooks and chains that will pull down their gates, the small boats and bridges that will get men over rivers, the shovels and axes that will dig them a trench, the horseshoes and boot leather that will keep them marching on this conquest of France.

'Is Louis shaking in his shoes?' Cecily asks Edward as she stands beside him in the clamour.

'Should be.'

It's the largest force England has ever sent against France, and Duke Charles swears Burgundy will equal it when they cross the Channel. For the past year, he and Edward have been re-drawing the map of Louis's kingdom: You'll have this and I'll have that when the old spider is dead.

'And you'll be King of France, Edward. And we'll grow fat on the spoils.'

He's a great one for promises, the Duke of Burgundy.

Cecily isn't so sure. While Edward's been dreaming of conquest, she's been counting the cost. He's in hock to the whole of England for this campaign. Glory's expensive.

'You'd better win,' she tells him. 'You'll need all the revenues of France to pay your debts.'

She chides herself. Of course he'll win, where's your faith? You've always said he could best anyone in a fight. But she wishes there was less flesh and more muscle on him. She wishes he'd spent more time in the tiltyard. He has new armour, because the old no longer fits. In truth, he's barely lifted a blade since Tewkesbury. But, she reminds herself, he still stands a head taller than any man on the field and shines like a god in the sun.

'Look,' says Edward raising an arm. 'Here's brother George.'

Well, at least all of this has given George someone else to be angry with. He hates the French with a passion these days, and boasts he'll break Louis's nose with a blow. After all, did not Louis wrong him just as much as Warwick did? He rides in beneath his banner, the black bull of Clarence, with a thousand men at his back. He leaps from his horse and embraces his brother as if bound to him, irrevocably, in love. Cecily wonders what promises he imagines Edward has made him this time, what portion of France he expects will be his.

In the late afternoon Richard comes with twice George's number.

'What's this then?' says Cecily, pointing at the great white boar that snarls from his standard. Every man in his company wears one on his sleeve and another, silvered, flashes ruby eyes from Richard's cap. 'My new blazon, Mother. Anne says the boar might not be the biggest beast in the field, but he's the most fierce. And he'll fight till his heart bursts.'

He looks to his king for approval, who claps his back and says, 'That's you, Richard. She's right.'

She'd forgotten how young Richard is. Just twenty-two. So far he's fought only for survival, dirty wars against his kin. Now he'll fight for glory against England's old enemy, a fight he thinks worthy of him at last. The eyes in his dust-coated face are alight.

Edward writes to Louis, 'Edward of England is coming, the white boar and black bull at his back. Surrender, or those noble beasts will hunt you through every part of France.'

Louis sends thanks for Edward's letter. 'And written with such style! I can hardly believe an Englishman penned it.'

Two days later, mounted on a cart tail so everyone can see, Cecily watches the army march out. Though it takes half a day to pass her by, she doesn't move until the rattle of the last baggage cart has given way to twilight and birdsong. She camps with her people on the empty field and, when sleep won't come, listens to night noises and wonders how long it will be until she sees her sons again. The conquest of France won't be done in a season. It might be years. Meanwhile, who rules in England?

The Queen didn't come to the muster, she's in Westminster with her sons. She had Edward bring their eldest from Ludlow and named head of state, Keeper of the Realm. Nothing wrong with that, in truth, Cecily admits. He's Edward's heir and Elizabeth's his mother. But while the boy keeps the realm, she keeps the boy, and the council, which rules in his name, is packed with her people. Men who go to conquer France don't always come home. He's four years old, Edward's boy. It'll be a dozen years before he comes of age. By then, whose man might he be?

The thought of it keeps Cecily wakeful, and her old bones cold.

But her worries prove needless. Edward's back before September's out, his war over without a cannon shot or a town taken. But he returns wealthy nonetheless. Old Louis, richer in coin than fighting men, offered him seventy-five thousand crowns just to go away. Fifty thousand a year if he never comes back. And Edward, who has never walked away from a fight, who has taken on all comers and won, shrugged his shoulders and said, 'All right then.'

He puts on a show for London, riding through the streets like a hero. But the soldiers who march behind him look sullen and the crowd perplexed.

'Have we won then?' they ask each other.

Doesn't look like it.

Cecily studies him at the homecoming feast, grinning too much and talking too loud, while Richard looks thunderous and George drinks, then she follows him to his private chambers and stares at his servants till they scurry out. She shuts the door on them, smooths her sleeves and watches him prowl. For the crowd he's been all bravado, for her he's all belligerence. 'What do you want now?' he growls.

'An explanation, Edward,' she says, looking up from the smoothing of her silks. 'I'm curious to know where the glory is in all this.'

'You said yourself, glory's expensive.'

'Indeed. While shame, it seems, comes with a stipend.'

He stops in his tracks then, looks at her as if she's offered him a blow in the street, and lets his fists curl.

'Oh, Edward, really?' a nod to their fleshy readiness. 'If you won't fight Louis you surely won't fight me.'

'Didn't have to fight,' he hisses. 'I took my father's lesson. You should be pleased.'

'Your father taught you to roll over for the French, did he?'

His fist becomes a pointing finger as he comes towards her, his voice a truculent growl. 'Only fight when you have to, you said. Always look ready to win. I was ready, Louis shat himself and . . .'

'Bought you off?' She stands her ground, scathing.

'Sued for peace.'

'Really? The way I heard it, Charles let you down and you didn't have the stomach for the fight.'

It's true. When Edward arrived in Calais, Charles wasn't there. Off fighting the Swiss instead. 'Make a start,' his message said.

'I'll join you later.' Though he never did. It was always next week, next month. Take Reims and I'll come to your crowning.

'I'll never trust that two-faced bastard again,' snarls Edward, turning away, shoulders hunching.

'Louis must have thought you had a good chance of winning even without Charles. Didn't you?'

He comes to the window now, slumps down in its seat, elbows to knees, eyes to his boots. She crosses the floor to sit beside him, waits for him to speak, to slow his breath, to wipe a meaty hand across his brow.

'Tell me, on your honour,' he says at last, 'did you truly think I could take France?'

She studies his profile as he waits for her response. The first lines are creasing the corners of his eyes, the first veins threading his cheek. He turned thirty-three this spring, handsome still, but you can't help but think the shine's gone off him. He looks older than he is.

He's asked for honesty and she'll give it. 'I thought you could take Normandy. Anjou, perhaps. The Aquitaine. Lands that were England's in your father's day. That would have been something.'

'Hmm.' He nods. 'And spend the rest of my life fighting to hold on to them? Wondering if Burgundy will keep my back or stick a knife in it? I don't want to end my days battling in France. I don't want to bleed my guts out of my arse in a French ditch like the fifth Henry. I want to rule England. I want my son of an age to rule when I die.'

'I see.' And she does, though thinks it not kingly.

'Is it so bad?' he wheedles. 'This deal with Louis leaves the Crown richer than it's ever been in my lifetime or yours. It binds his heir to marry my daughter when she's of age. Lizzie will be Queen of France. Her children will rule there. Is that so bad?'

She supposes not. 'If Louis can be trusted to keep his promises.'

A shrug. 'If he doesn't, I'll go back.'

No, she thinks, you won't. But what's the point of saying so?

She sighs. Well, at least he's here. What's left of him. She reaches a hand to the velvet of his sleeve. She doesn't want him dead in a ditch either, God knows. And not while his heir is a child under the Woodville thumb.

'Our more immediate problem is the men who loaned you money in hope of rich return,' she tells him. 'I don't suppose you can afford to pay them back?'

'I'm not that rich.'

'Or the soldiers who thought to get rich on plunder?'

'They've had their wages.'

'But no glory, Edward,' she chides. 'And a king who walked away from a fight.'

He hangs his head.

It's up to her, she sees, to be businesslike. 'Well then. We must convince them that, instead of being bought off, you've won a bloodless victory. And that that's the best kind.'

'Now that's a war of words, Mother. Your area. Advise me.' And now he looks truly miserable. 'And tell me how to win back Richard's love, for I fear I've lost it. Do you know, he was the only one among my nobles who wouldn't accept a pension from Louis?'

'Then he's angry, not fallen out of love. Disappointed.' She tilts her head. 'Is that what Louis calls it, the money he gives you? A pension?'

He nods.

'We'll call it a tribute, such as a vassal might pay a great king.'

He shrugs, truculent. 'Richard will call it a pension. As might be paid to any clapped-out old soldier.'

'Well, Richard's still young enough to be in love with honour. Be his hero again. Give him a quest.'

'A quest?'

'Yes. For him a quest, and for England a distraction, a message: the house of York is so formidable no enemy dare ever come against us. Even mighty France.'

'And how do we deliver this message?'

'Long ago you wanted to bring your father home from Ponte-fract. I said the time wasn't right, that it would expose our weakness. Well, now we'll make it a show of strength. Bring your father home to Fotheringhay and bury him like the king he was born to be. Your brother Edmund too. Tell the people we've righted every wrong ever perpetrated on England, and now we honour our dead. Show them your father, whose right to rule you've made good, and the brother who gave his life for your cause. Show them your sons, who'll rule forever when you've gone. And your daughter, whose children will rule France.'

He looks up, his mind racing to draw level with hers. 'Remind them they're lucky to have us?'

'Exactly.' She sighs. 'Bury your father, Edward. You wanted to do it once. Richard still does. Give him the work, and he'll love you for it.'

'Yes,' he says. 'All right. But I'm building a royal mausoleum at Windsor, surely there would be better. A place of kings?'

She hesitates. But no, she'll keep this promise to her husband at least. They raised the church at Fotheringhay together, a prayerful shelter, a stone bed for their long, shared sleep.

'No,' she says and gives no quarter. 'Fotheringhay.'

So, next summer, Richard rides at the head of the procession that guides his father home. The rot of a man nearly sixteen years dead in a gilded coffin, the carved image of him above it, hands clasped in prayer, painted eyes transfixed upon an angel that hovers England's crown above his head. Behind him, his valiant dead son. In every town and hamlet the crowds come out to cross themselves and gawp. And every night, in abbeys and churches, men of God wrap them in candlelight, wash them with prayer. Richard stands guard as the people come in wonder, to touch the catafalque, to make their salute, to gaze at the banners draped about the bier, the gilded arms of England and France.

When they come at last to Fotheringhay, Edward is waiting at the church door, his children about him, dressed as his father's image in the mourning robes of a king. He takes Richard in his arms, calls him brother, and weeps when he falls to his knees promising loyalty and love.

Cecily, of course, doesn't go. She once thought her husband would make her a queen, and no queen attends her husband's funeral, for the glory must all be his. But Richard tells her of it after, battering her heart with every detail.

'You've done well,' she tells him. 'You're a good son.'

She watches him bask in this unexpected praise, but then his face turns serious again. 'I was afraid,' he confesses. 'When it came to the making of my father's effigy, I had to instruct the sculptor, but in truth, I could barely remember his face. Edward said, "Have them model it on your own, you're so alike." Is that true, Mother? Am I like him?'

'Yes,' she says. And then, because you shouldn't puff a man up too much, 'Though he was taller.'

He was. And his back as straight as a lance, while Richard's twists more with every year. No one who doesn't know would notice it, but she feels it in the occasional roll of his shoulder and the way he'll sometimes angle himself to stand. She knows better than to ask if it pains him. He wouldn't tell her if it did. He keeps his body hard and his thoughts to himself. Like his father in that too. Yes, he's like him. Thank God he spends his days in the north; sometimes it hurts too much to look at him.

When Richard is gone she snuffs the candles, sits in the dark and lets memory take her back to the very spot where her husband now lies, before Fotheringhay's altar, where the light will fall upon him every morning as the choristers fill the air with song. To the right a little, so there'll be room for her beside him when the time comes. Five of her children lie about him, lost in the first year of their lives, and Edmund now, brought with his father from Pontefract, slaughtered the same day, forever seventeen.

No other child of hers will follow them there. They are royal now and will do better, even in death. Though she chides herself, this severance grieves her. How will I find them, she frets, on the day Christ wakes us, if their faces are not all about me? Her confessor tells her each soul goes to God alone, with only Christ as guide and keeper. 'You have care of them only while they live.' He means it as a comfort, but how can she lay her burden down if, in life, her care has failed?

It preys on her mind. This has been a season of grief. As the year turned, after Edward came home from France, his mausoleum at Windsor received its first sad guest. Her daughter Anne, her eldest, her first, was brought happily to bed with Thomas St Ledger's child.

'I will be like you and have a dozen children,' she told her mother, smiling through the first of the pains.

'Tell me that again when you're on your fifth,' said Cecily, smoothing oil of roses across her daughter's drum-tight belly.

But Anne only took her hand and stilled it in her own. 'I will welcome them all. I find, that . . .' and the discovery delights her enough to force a laughing blush. '. . . that I who wanted nothing of Henry Holland, want everything and all of Thomas St Ledger.'

Such foolishness is tolerated in women in childbed, so Cecily only smiled, drew Anne's hair together and bound it at her shoulder, ready for the work.

The child, a daughter, came and lived, a small red squaller with not a shred of hair. But Anne bled and bled till the bed beneath her turned crimson. When at last Cecily prised her fingers from Anne's dead grasp she went to tell St Ledger, who stared at her in horror till she looked down at her empty hands, fingertip to wrist, caked in her daughter's blood.

46.

July 1476 to June 1477

London

There is some respite from grief. Richard returned home from France to find himself father to a son, who arrived early but thrives. His letter to Cecily hums with the pleasure of it. His Anne has miscarried twice since her marriage and each loss seemed to weaken her.

'Now she's made well by doting,' he writes. 'She hardly has time for poor me, so taken is she with him. He's a fine, straight-limbed boy. We've named him Edward, for my brother the King.'

Though the parting is painful, she sends Annette to him saying, 'She'll be as tender of your son as she was of you. And I'm sure no other woman's prayers can bind a boy to life as hers can.' Annette writes back that she has never seen a child so doted upon by its father, nor a wife so happy to see it.

In October, Isabel gives George a Richard. She already gave him an Edward twenty months ago, who is walking and talking now though, since his coming, Isabel has done little but cough. After this babe, she coughs more, then coughs blood. She dies three days before Christmas. Her baby struggles on till New Year's Day then, unsure of earthly tenure, seeks certainty in Heaven.

'Bring them to Windsor,' says Edward, moved to pity. 'We will bury them with honour.'

'Yes, bring them home to us,' says Cecily, remembering her own children lost. 'Let them rest among their kin.'

But no. 'In my own lands,' George says. 'I'll not be robbed of them as you rob me of all else.'

So Isabel and her child are laid to rest in Tewkesbury, with George standing vigil through the night as if he fears men might meddle, or demons come to claim their souls.

The turning year brings another death, which gives less grief but more trouble. Charles of Burgundy, still fighting the Swiss, is cut down in the snow outside Nancy. His body, found days later naked and savaged, must be hacked with axes from the icy river into which it was thrown.

'It had thawed by the time it was returned to me,' Meg writes her mother. 'It was rotten and it stank.'

Cecily's daughter has no time for grief, even if inclined to it. By the month's end, Louis is pushing up against her borders. Since Meg has given her husband no child in near nine years of marriage, her stepdaughter Mary is heiress to the duchy and Louis says he'll marry her to his dauphin and take Burgundy without a fight. It's a rough kind of wooing, when the proposal is proffered at the edge of a blade.

'Edward,' Meg writes, 'I need an army to fight France, and a husband for Mary.' She suggests, of all people, their brother.

George, who would marry his dog for a duchy, says, 'Send me, I'll go!'

Edward says no to both. No to a marriage that would make George a power in Europe. No to an army set against his new friends the French. Richard, who has come south to press the point with him, complains to Cecily. 'Our sister sheltered us in exile and Edward does nothing for her! See where his damned alliance with France has brought us!'

'You don't think George should be Duke of Burgundy, do you?'

He shudders at the thought. 'But if Louis takes Burgundy, he'll come for us next, alliance or no.'

'And if George marries Burgundy he'll ally with France and they'll come for us together. But don't worry. Meg only offers the marriage to force another man's hand.'

'Whose?'

'Maximilian's.'

It's a name he didn't expect. 'Heir to Austria's Archduke?'

'And Holy Roman Emperor one day, yes. Close your mouth, Richard, you're not a fish. A better prospect than George, don't you think? Meg's no fool. So, let Max marry Mary and fight for Burgundy. Your brother's leaving the field clear.'

'We won't fight France?'

She shrugs. 'Best we don't.'

His mouth twists. 'Because Louis's our trusted ally?'

She smooths her sleeves, looks him in the eye. 'Yes.'

He throws up his hands. 'Pah! Because Louis bought my brother with a pension.'

'Tribute, Richard.'

The marriage is made. He's handsome, Maximilian of Austria, eighteen years old and as formidable on the battlefield as Edward once was. Mary of Burgundy is more than pleased, Meg has saved the duchy, and Edward can, without guile, tell Louis, 'I, of course, would have wished it otherwise but, there it is.'

George, though, who sees himself thwarted again, says, 'What about me? How am I to be recompensed?'

'I love my sister,' says Richard. 'But I wish she'd not given George another reason to feel aggrieved.'

Summer finds Cecily rattling from Berkhamsted to Westminster again. She begins the journey in anger, and the heat and dust of the road do nothing to quench it.

She finds Edward mid-morning and far from his best. Still in his rooms and, though freshly buffed and shining like the king he is, his eyes are puffy and his scent of mint and ambergris does nothing to cover the staleness of his breath.

'It gets harder as you get older, doesn't it? The drinking?'

'The recovery time's longer,' he grants, pinching the bridge of his nose between finger and thumb, grimacing.

'I hear you were at it with your stepson Thomas Grey last night.' She says the name as if it insults her mouth. 'Whoring too, I expect. He's younger than you, remember. You can't expect to keep up.'

He paddles among the wreckage of his breakfast for a cup, sloshes beer into it. 'You really do hear everything.'

'Well, I've heard that your brother George, my son, is arrested.'

He hesitates. Pours a second cup for her. 'I suppose I should have told you.'

She nods, slow. 'Yes. Instead it was left to servants to clack it into my ears.' She leaves the drink untouched.

'Then you'll also have heard how he speaks against me.'

'That you thwarted him in the Burgundian marriage, that you want him dead, you wrong him at every turn, you plan to poison him . . .'

'Yes,' he sits back. 'All that.'

'Standard fare from George, I'd say. Do you have to lock him up for it?'

He shrugs, truculent. 'No, not for that.'

She waits. When he's slow, she prompts him. 'Then this story I've heard about Ankarette Twynhoe is true?'

Edward spreads his hands. 'Charged, indicted and executed in the course of a day by a jury of George's own household men.'

The widowed waiting woman, who had served Isabel for years and nursed her through her final fatal childbed, had denied, with vehemence and horror, George's charge that she hastened with poison the death of the lady and her newborn. It had been a month before news of it reached Edward, dropped into his ear by Anthony, the Queen's brother, to whom Ankarette's uncle had clamoured for redress. It was his conviction that his niece had died for secrets she, at his own urging, had disclosed to Anthony Woodville about life in the Clarence household; of George's precipitate rages, his hatred of his brother, his vicious whisperings bordering on treason.

'She was a Woodville spy, then?' asks Cecily.

'No,' Edward explains carefully. 'She just gave information.'

'Tittle tattle,' she sneers. 'I expect Anthony licked it up like a dog. No one alive hates George more than your queen and her kin.'

'Can you blame them?'

She shrugs. Who could?

'Anyway,' he says, 'Anthony's honourable enough. And it doesn't alter the fact that George has subverted my laws. For that, and for other things, he is arrested.'

He pushes back from the table, busies himself with pouring again.

She puts out a hand to cover his cup. 'Other things?'

He sighs, puts down the jug and runs the heels of his hands up his face. 'All right. Those men hanged at Tyburn last month, Burdet and Stacy?'

She remembers, vaguely. 'For necromancy. Spells to help some sad wife rid herself of a troublesome husband? What's it to do with George?'

'Burdet is a man very well known to my brother. He's even worked for him in the past.'

'So?'

'They were guilty not only of sorcery but sedition, too. Though we've kept it quiet. Handing out pamphlets in London's streets that say I'm unfit to rule.'

'Well, that sounds like George, but . . .'

'So we had their homes searched . . .'

'I'm sure you did . . .'

'And found horoscopes predicting the day of my death. Mine, and my son's.' He raises an eyebrow. 'We won't make old bones, apparently. They confessed, under some duress I admit, that the horoscopes were drawn up at George's order.'

She closes her eyes. It's all so ridiculous.

'It's a short step, Mother, from predicting a man's death to bringing it about.'

'Oh, Edward it is very far . . .'

He holds up a hand to silence her. 'There were other papers. Papers they planned to publish, papers that accuse me of witch-craft, of murder . . .'

'All nonsense.'

'. . . of being a bastard . . .'

She disdains it with a sneer, 'Warwick's old lie.'

He leans to her, speaks very low. 'And of fathering bastards. Of being a very great philanderer.' His voice falls lower still. 'And, of another woman, before Elizabeth.'

They stare at each other. Cecily's mind is reeling backwards to Eleanor Talbot, dead these nine years, buried with the secret of Edward's priest-blessed promises at the Carmelite Friary in Nor-wich, to which she gave her vows.

'George can't possibly know of that.'

'Burdet's accomplice, Stacy, was an Oxford man. So was Robert Stillington.'

'As are a thousand other men!'

'There are others who know. Eleanor's sister, your own sister, Katherine.'

'Neither of them fool enough to speak of it to George. Nobody fool enough to speak of it at all. I've made sure of that.'

He sighs, buries his face in his hands. She reaches out and pulls them aside. 'Were any names mentioned in those papers? Anything other than speculation? Do they explicitly mention a marriage?'

He shakes his head. 'No. But they name my sons bastards and my marriage to Elizabeth unsound.'

'Then it's nothing more than Warwick's old charge, that Eliza-beth's mother brought about your marriage through witchcraft.'

He concedes, 'Yes. Probably. I suppose.'

Then a dark thought comes to her, and she's suddenly afraid. 'You won't kill your brother for this?'

'I want an end to his treasons. But, no,' he says, slow. 'Much as I'd sometimes like to, I won't kill my brother.'

He rises from his chair, walks away from her to the window and looks out. The silence is broken by the sound of women's laughter in the pleasance far below. She thinks she hears the Queen's peals among them.

'Edward.' She has to know. 'Does Elizabeth know about Eleanor?'

He turns back to her, leans his hands behind him on the sill. 'God, no.'

'Anthony?'

'No.'

She sits back, lets her racing heart slow. 'Then we're safe enough. Besides, it's all deniable.'

'Yes.' He shakes himself as he walks back to her, as if shrugging off a wet coat. 'Yes, of course it is.'

'You were such a fool, Edward,' she says rising to meet him.

'Yes,' he admits. 'I know.'

She lets herself lean against him, tired of being angry.

'So, what do we do about George?' It seems to matter to her still, the work of keeping her foolish son alive. That and the rent his death would leave in Edward's soul. 'Please don't kill him.'

He takes her hand into his no longer sword-callused grip. 'Of course not. Look,' he says, 'let's leave him where he is a while. Frighten him a bit. Let him see his actions have consequences. When he grows more reasonable, I'll let him out again. How's that?'

47.

Summer gives way to autumn and a bitter winter. Cecily has forgone the pleasures of Berkhamsted for Baynard's, swearing nothing will take her from London and the speedy traffic of news while George remains immured. But news is scant, and the terms of his imprisonment bar all visitors, even her. She saw the sense of it at first; let the shock of being alone bring him to his senses. But time feeds her uncertainty. Six months should be long enough for George to grow reasonable, or for Edward to find a way to make him so. But the King only says, 'Not yet, Mother,' and will not look her in the eye. While the Queen's smile tells her, 'My husband's brother is exactly where I would wish him to be.'

Cecily is stalwart, she is silent, she stands by Edward's side while Woodvilles preen. But Christmas is coming and enough is enough. So she sends a note that tells Edward she'll not come again to court until George is free.

Before the foolery of twelfth night, Edward brings himself to Baynard's. He says for a bit of peace; she suspects, though, to cajole her. But his temper's bad and his demeanour worse. Like a man in a mess looking for someone to get him out of it. Like a boy thwarted, used to getting his own way. He struts, he frets, looks bilious and won't eat her food. 'My court,' he tells her, 'is rife with rumours of division within our house. Your absence fuels it.'

'Our house is divided,' she tells him. 'My son is my son's prisoner. And since your queen's pleasure at it offends me, I've taken myself from her sight.'

He grimaces. 'Elizabeth is . . .'

'. . . keen to see your brother rot. And on that point you'd rather please her than me.'

He draws himself up, makes himself angry. 'She's my queen, Mother. And my wife.'

'Actually not,' she scoffs. 'Isn't that the problem?'

When the feasting time is over it's her youngest son who sits miserable by her hearth, his hands netted before him. He's come south for the first time in more than a year. 'Wasted a Christmas I could have spent with Anne,' he complains. Instead he's divided his time between Baynard's and the court, trying to make peace between his mother and his king.

'I've no love for George, God knows,' he admits to her. 'But Edward's anger against him now is greater than I've ever known it. Yet the cause seems no worse than it ever was.'

'Perhaps there's more cause than you know.'

'If there is, why won't he tell me? Why won't you?'

Cecily turns to him from the window, where she's been watching the merchants and traders struggling up Thames Street through the snow. His face, gazing into the fire, speaks little of his thoughts, but the repeated turning of his bull's blood ruby is eloquent of disquiet. He's spent a hard season, she can see, holding back border reivers from Melrose to Jedburgh in service of the King. There are new creases at the corners of his eyes. Got from staring across long moors into wind and sun, she imagines. But even with the Scots on his tail, he'd be happier there than here. Surely he'd earned a Christmas at home. She draws up a chair before him, lays a hand on his shirted arm beneath the bell-sleeved doublet. It's thin as wire, but the muscles are strong.

'I know no more than you.' Still keeping Edward's secrets, even from this son.

He shakes his head. 'Edward's always forgiven George, for every treason. I've resented it often enough.' He's thinking, she knows, of when George tried to keep Anne from him, of having to fetch her, frightened, from his kitchens. He grimaces, as if at a wound still raw, then he looks at her again, with eyes as dark and honest as his father's. 'But now he won't forgive, or explain himself, and when I press him on it, he rages.' She watches him take a breath, swallow hard. 'I believe,' he says, 'that the Queen stokes his anger.'

She nods slow. 'Well, she hasn't forgotten that it was at George's order, and Warwick's, that her father and brother were killed.'

'Eight years ago, Mother. An old tale, surely.'

'As fresh as this morning's snow for Elizabeth.'

His shrewd eyes pin hers. 'Does she want him dead?'

She looks away. Yes, she thinks, she wants him dead. She'd want it more if she knew the truth. 'I think she hates him and despises us,' she says. 'She trusts only her own people these days. Anyone else is suspect. George especially, but any of us, really. Even you.'

'Me?' The thought is ludicrous. 'How've I offended her? I'm never here.'

'By breathing? Her kin whisper that you rule like a king in the north. More powerful than Warwick ever was, they say.'

'And more loyal than a thousand Warwicks, thank God.' He crosses himself hastily and shrugs. 'I'm not worried. Edward knows what I am. But I fear for George.'

'Edward promises me he means only to frighten your brother. That he'll free him, once he grows reasonable.'

'Then I think you should go back to court, Mother. And remind him.'

But no time.

'Well, look what the river's washed to my door.'

The evening after Richard's visit, the lights of the King's barge appear on the river. Cecily sees them from her window and comes to greet him. On her threshold, she extends a hand for his kiss, pleased that he has broken first and come to her. But he only heaves the weight of his fur-lined cloak on to a chair and walks beyond her to the fire, leans his hands against its broad lintel and lets his head fall heavy between them.

He has brought the cold air with him and it settles along her spine. 'What is it?' She steps up, lays a hand against his shoulder. The face he turns to her is grey. 'What trouble now?'

'I must speak to you about George.'

Now all warmth is leached from the room, from her heart. 'He's not to be released?'

'No, Mother.' He swallows hard. 'He never can be.'

She strains words past the dryness of her throat. 'You'll tell me, I am sure, that there's good reason?'

He won't look at her, but turns, scrabbles for her hands and clasps them in his. 'Mother, he knows about Eleanor.'

Her breath tightens, hurts. 'All of it?'

'Yes,' he whispers. 'All of it.'

She pulls her hands free, turns to pace the room, and into her silence, he pours the sorry tale. A letter found among George's papers signed only by a priest, God's servant on earth, who says he is dying and can't bear to take his secret to the grave. He writes of a lady's deathbed ramblings; of a confession his vows won't allow him to repeat. It closes, 'I write to you as you are England's rightful heir and beg you to speak to Bishop Stillington, who is close in matters concerning the lady Eleanor Talbot. Ask him to reveal to you the King's secret that lies buried at Norwich.'

'And did he? Speak to Stillington?' She throws the question over her shoulder as she walks.

'Yes. Who denied everything, of course, other than that I'd tumbled her. But, well,' he hangs his head.

'Nothing conclusive then? Nothing we can't deny?'

'We could deny it, yes, burn the letter. But,' and it's as if the words are dragged from him with pincers, 'Elizabeth knows.'

'God, no. How?'

'Anthony . . .'

Her stomach is sick with dread, her mind racing ahead of his words. 'Anthony found the letter? You were idiot enough to have him search George's papers?'

He shakes his head. 'I never thought . . .'

'No, Edward, you never do!' She has reached the end of the room and turns on him where he stands, useless and hulking in the light of a fire that gives no heat. 'And now, for Elizabeth's sake, to keep this secret, you'll kill your brother?'

He spreads his hands. 'Mother, I think I must.' The words are wrung from him. 'I've wronged her . . . and our children. And I promised her . . .'

Her knees buckle beneath her, but she draws on rage to keep her upright. There is a rich vein of it. The air of the room battles her as she strides back to him, her lips drawn back from her teeth, her hand reaching. She hears him gasp as her fist closes on the softness between his legs.

'For this?' Her grip tightens. 'For this I am to lose a son? Because when you were a boy, stupid with lust, and Eleanor wouldn't let you prick her, you said, "Look, I'll make you my wife." And because you were stupid, stupid, stupid enough to swear it before a priest!'

She pushes him away and he staggers for a chair. She's pacing again, the breath ragged between her teeth, her stomach heaving. Elizabeth won't rest now till George is dead. She comes to the window, grinds her fists against its sill. Behind her she hears him say, 'You too made promises to Elizabeth, Mother. That her enemies would be your enemies.'

'My own son?' Her knuckles burn against rough stone. There's blood on them.

'And you know what George is.'

'Yes,' she shouts. 'A traitor, a mad man and a fool. But he's my son.' It takes the wind from her, the blow of her fist against her own breast. It reminds her where her heart is. Yes, she knows what George is, just as she knows herself. And she knows too that once, long ago, when faced with evil choice between two brothers, she sent her good son Edmund into danger, rather than risk Edward. It is a curse, she thinks now, that in the end, she always chooses him.

'Mother . . .' his voice behind her, trembling.

She turns to where he sits, his hands between his knees, his huge frame shaking. She walks the length of the room to reach him, pours wine and sets it down. He grasps for her hand but she keeps it from him.

'Drink,' she says. 'Steady yourself.' Then, when he's gulped and done, she asks, 'What will you do?'

'Bring him to trial.'

'On what charge?'

'Sedition. Burdet's papers.'

'Is that all you have?'

'And for planning rebellion.'

'You have evidence of that?'

'Enough.'

'And no doubt you'll stack a jury full of Woodvilles happy to condemn him.'

'Mother,' a sob escapes him. 'I'd hoped . . .' The heels of his hands grind against his eyes. 'I'd hoped you'd think of some other way.' His voice is desperate. 'Any other way . . .'

'That I'd fix it?' she sneers.

'Yes,' he says, choking.

She shakes her head, she'd thought it fixed sixteen years ago when Eleanor agreed not to press her claim, then nine years ago, when she was dead. She'd thought it a small thing, talked out of existence. She's as much to blame as Edward and as like to be damned. 'No. It's beyond fixing now.'

His head hangs in shame. 'Then you bid me kill my brother?'

She lifts his hand that lies open on the table and presses the heavy gold of its sovereign's ring against her brow. It sets a cold burn upon her, like a brand. 'I bid you live, Edward. And be a king.'

George has always favoured sweet wines. The smell of it twists her mouth, but it will serve. Its heaviness will mask any flavour. She bends her shoulder to the work, blending the green of copper verdigris with the dry, murderous, lime-white powder.

Edward had not denied her, in the end, one last visit. The sight of him had shocked her. George had been almost as beautiful as Edward once, and charming, when he chose to charm. Now he was white, haggard, his eyes glassy, already deathlike, and the smell of drink sour on him. It seemed, too, that the strain was telling on his mind. His voice was high, his words garbled.

She listened as he spat out his hatred of Edward. As he begged her to intercede on his behalf. She comforted him as best she could and, when he wept, took him in her arms and kissed his tarnished hair, stroked his face and hushed him when he spoke his fear of the axe. As the King's brother, he'll escape the quartering, but he knows as well as she that death doesn't always come with the first stroke. At last he cried himself to sleeping and she sat through long hours with his heaviness in her lap. When he was born, she remembers, she fought the very Devil to keep him living. Now she'll set the fight aside and give him to God.

The constable was silent as he escorted her from the room, as if shamed that a mother should see her son in such condition.

'Is he always drunk?' she asked him.

'The King says he's to have any comfort he asks for but company.' He shifts his feet. 'Mostly, he asks for wine.'

Two days have passed since that fearful scene and, in all that time, the sight of his terror-ridden face has hung before her eyes. I can do no more for you than this, George, she thinks as she seals the flagon. It is a mercy.

'Carry it with care.' Cecily hands the flagon to her steward. 'Take it to the Tower and give it to the constable. Into his hands only. Tell him it's a gift for my son, but that he's not to have it till the priest has been and gone. He mustn't drink till he's shriven.'

Edward will send Stillington to George tonight to hear his last confession. He begged to be excused the duty but really, who else could be sent?

She has told her women to stay away. Banished her servants till morning. She climbs the stairs to her chamber. They've left the candles alight. With bare fingertips she snuffs them, holding each flame tight until it dies. The singeing of her skin makes her eyes water, but the room is dark, there's no one to see but God, and she expects no compassion from Him. She pulls a heavy chair to the window and sits, looking out to where the moon rides the black river to the Tower, then down, at the golden rosary threaded in her hands. She rolls the first bead across burned fingers. It will be a long vigil.

Next morning, when the Tower guards come to wake him, they find the Duke of Clarence already cold and dead, his eyes staring. From the flagon, broken beside him, the wine has flowed, so that he lies in a pool of it, thick and dark, like blood.

48.

Eltham

Cecily wonders, sometimes, when Edward lost his appetite for war. He's spoken once or twice, always in his cups and late in the evening, of Towton, that long-ago Easter battle that confirmed him king. The sun had not yet risen when it began and was on its way to set before all was over.

'We fought through every daylight hour,' he told her. 'Blinded first by snow, then by blood. Sweating like pigs in our armour.'

When it was done at last, when he tore off his helm desperate for drink, for a breath of air that didn't stink of himself, the bitter cold had sheared his lungs like a blade. He'd fallen to his knees then, coughing and shaking, till Warwick pulled him to his feet and they propped each other upright, laughing in great gulping cries among the carnage of thirty thousand dead.

She'd tried to imagine it; that moment when winter air, thinned by exhaustion and elation, sent men reeling, drunk on their own greatness. How could anything match it?

'Did you ever imagine, in those days, that you could lose?' she asked him, curious.

'No,' he said, draining his cup. 'I never thought of losing when I fought beside Warwick.'

So perhaps that's why. Perhaps being forced to fight against Warwick instead of with him finished it for Edward. Or seeing his cousin's corpse on the flagstones of St Paul's made the airy idea of death corporeal.

Perhaps that's why he gave up the dream of France to live on a pension. And why, when suddenly this summer James of Scotland brought war to the northern borders, he first bellowed, 'I'll go up there and break the bugger's arse!' Then changed his mind and said, 'No, Richard, you do it.'

And Richard did. In a single campaign from May to October he won back Berwick and took the fight all the way to Edinburgh, where he made a truce at his sword edge and left the Scots shame-faced and licking their wounds. It only adds to his glory that he did it in such business-like fashion, within the funds allotted and barely a drop of blood shed. English blood anyway.

So this Christmas court is all for Richard, who stands now under the freshly gilded roof of Eltham Palace with the King's arm about his shoulder and his name a taste of glory on every man's tongue.

'Thank God for my brother,' Edward beams. 'He barely needs an army. He can take all of Scotland on his own.'

'Why stop at Scotland?' someone shouts, and Cecily turns to see who. It's Thomas Stanley, who captained Richard's siege at Berwick and is second only to him in the King's honour this Christmas day. Margaret Beaufort, tiny at her hulkish husband's side, catches Cecily's eye and raises her cup.

Later, when the feasting is done and the music strikes up, Cecily comes to Richard and offers him the honour of dancing with her, so he bows and leads her to the floor.

'You're a credit to our house,' she tells him. It's time she gave him praise. And he's not too old to blush at it.

'Oh, I do what I can.'

The dance turns them, away and back again. 'Anne isn't here with you?'

'Not one for court life.'

'She's well?'

He grimaces. 'She lost another, while I was in Scotland.'

'I'm sorry.'

His face is sad. 'I begin to think we'll have only the one. Well,' and the sadness lifts a little, 'he is a very great blessing.'

'And how is he?' she asks, because she knows nothing gives him more pleasure than speaking of his boy. And yes, there it is, that open smile.

'His Latin's bad. His riding master says he has a good seat. And he wanted very much to go to war with me in Scotland.'

'At barely six?' She smiles. 'It'll be a while yet before that happens.'

As the music falls and the dancers bow, his face turns wistful. 'Is it foolish to hope for a world where it needn't happen at all?'

She nudges his shoulder. 'Yes. Probably. Besides, he must equal his father.'

'Ah well,' he says. 'There is that.'

The dance master claps his hands and declares a saltarello with its leaping steps.

'Too much for me,' says Cecily and lets Richard steer her from the floor. But, instead of re-joining the crowds that line the hall, they drift into the corridors in search of quiet.

'Could you do it, do you think?' she asks as they walk.

'Do what?'

'Take Scotland on your own as your brother says?'

'Why bother?' says Richard. 'I've been fighting shadows half a year. The real enemy's France. I've always said it. Louis will pension England till he's strong enough to fight her. If he takes Burgundy, perhaps he will be. And at the moment he looks set to do just that.'

That's the trouble with Richard, he says things as they are.

This spring Meg's stepdaughter, Burgundy's young duchess, was thrown from her horse into an early grave. Now the dukedom belongs to her four-year-old orphan, and even Maximilian and Meg together are hard-pressed to hold it for him, with Louis battering hard at their door.

'If Burgundy falls,' Richard says, 'Brittany will fall with it. Then Louis will come for us.'

'Edward is giving some support to your sister, you know,' she chides.

Richard's unimpressed. 'Precious little. Not enough.'

'It's a delicate balance, Richard. Burgundy and France.'

'Hmm. I think Louis's pension tips the scales.'

This is a conversation Cecily doesn't want to have. It might incline her to agree with him. 'Well,' she says, taking her arm from his, 'shall we return to the hall?'

When they join the crowds Edward is dancing with his queen. He's only a little drunk, and his fine clothes – broad at the shoulder, fur-lined and glittering – make him seem almost the golden giant he ever was. Certainly, men still hang on his words, and he can still coax from embers that fiery dazzle that leaves women breathless. And yet it sometimes seems to Cecily that there's a caution in men's dealings with him now. As if behind their hands they whisper, 'There's the king who put his brother to death. A mad, treasonous brother, but still . . . Had him upended in a barrel of malmsey.' For that's the story that was put out; that Edward allowed his brother the choice of how to die and George chose to drown in drink.

Cecily shakes herself and decides it's time for bed.

Next morning, after St Stephen's mass, Edward leads men out after stag. That's too hard hunting for Cecily these days, but she prides herself that, even at sixty-seven, she can sit a horse for a day's ride and throw a merlin from her fist. Certainly she can keep up with Margaret Beaufort, not yet forty and looking even younger today, fresh-faced and happy for once. Of course, there's no denying young eyes see better. Margaret sends her hawk after prey Cecily has barely spotted. Her groom already has a brace of rabbits at his pommel when she taps Cecily's shoulder and points to where a hare has emerged incautious from the scrub. Cecily throws and her bird is on it, her man labouring through knee-high drifts to retrieve.

'My thanks. You see further than I these days, Margaret.'

'Oh, just used to looking ahead, I suppose.'

'Well, you've happy cause to do that now.'

The face Margaret turns to her is suddenly lit with hope. 'Yes,' she says. 'Pray God soon.'

It's been a long time coming, but it seems Margaret's boy Henry might find his way home at last. Not so much a boy now. A man of twenty-five, near a dozen years in exile and a head full of God knows what ideas. So, early this year, when Brittany agreed to give him up in exchange for men to fight the French, Cecily urged Edward to bring him home, and quickly. 'Best have him here, where we can keep an eye on him.'

So word's been sent to Henry Tudor that he can be Earl of Richmond and a parcel of land carved out from Margaret's estates to make a living for him.

'Come home,' his mother has written. 'Live as a lord in the favour of this king.'

'Come home,' Edward has urged. 'I'll welcome your fealty.'

'Perhaps in time for Easter,' says Cecily. 'Will you bring him to see me?' And when Margaret nods, and when expectation of such pleasure bursts her face with a smile, Cecily is surprised to find herself nothing but happy for it. She leans across the space between them, takes her friend's hand and squeezes. 'You've waited a long time, I know, for our promise to be kept. I'll be as glad as you when it's done.'

They ride on quietly a while then, until the cold begins to bite and Cecily looks up to find the sky streaked with coral and the low sun early on its ebb. She shivers and shakes herself, so that the hawk pulls against its jesses and lifts a shearing wing. 'Shall we head back?' she suggests. 'Find a good fire to warm us?' And, when Margaret nods, they rein in and turn for home.

49.

There's warmth and fire enough when they return to Eltham. A bonfire of anger and humiliation. They've barely crossed the threshold when a boar-badged boy, one of Richard's lads, steps into Cecily's path and says, 'My lord asks that you go quickly to the King's apartments. There's news . . .'

From the corner of her eye Cecily sees an empty-satchelled messenger skulking away, head down like a kicked dog. Not good news then.

She hears the shouting ten yards from the King's chamber door. Elizabeth, raw-throated with rage.

'What will my daughter be now then?' she cries. 'What prince in his right mind will marry the jilted daughter of King Louis's fool?'

'Open!' Cecily commands, and a shamefaced guard throws the door wide. Edward's face, turned to her, is more terrible than she's ever seen it. His anger she expected, but the shock that wrestles with it is new. As if the messenger had come with a battle axe and knocked him on his back. He turns to Elizabeth, who rails on, vicious with contempt.

'What a fool you are,' she spits. 'What a vain, half-wit fool my bed is cursed with.'

He raises an arm, and Cecily thinks for a moment he'll strike, but Richard slides between them, holding out his arms.

'Edward,' he says. 'Our mother is here.' To the Queen, 'Your Grace, should we not sit down and be calm?'

But calmness is beyond Elizabeth. 'Who will my daughter marry?' she demands, screeching.

From behind Richard's restraining arm Edward bares spittled

teeth and snarls, 'Oh, she'll learn from you how to get husbands. She need only show a man her cunt and say, "Only if . . ."'

'Sit down, Edward!' says Richard, pushing him towards a chair.

Elizabeth screams, bent double with fury, impotent tears streaming, then turns on her heel and thunders for the door. Passing Cecily, she shoulders her aside. 'You deal with it,' she snaps. 'Deal with this idiot son of yours since you had the breeding of him. Dear God, how I hate you all!'

In the aftermath of her going, Edward slumps into the chair, head bowed, hands flailing, his whole body shaking. Richard steps to his side, lays a hand on his shoulder; Edward scrabbles for it, grasping. The only sound now is his laboured breath, as if he's run twenty miles or fought Towton again in the snow.

'Would someone tell me what has so enraged the Queen?' asks Cecily, straightening her sleeves. 'I take it we have Louis to thank.'

'And Maximilian,' says Richard. 'I suppose.'

'Tell her, Richard.' Edward's voice is strained.

And out comes the news from Burgundy. Faced with a fight he can't win, Maximilian has capitulated, made a treaty with France and sealed it with the marriage of his two-year-old daughter to Louis's heir.

'And so you see,' Edward spreads his hands, 'Lizzie's betrothal is broken off, she will not be Queen of France and, for that, my wife is enraged.'

'Is it concluded?' Cecily asks Richard, looking to him over Edward's shaking head.

'Papers signed. Vows made,' he confirms. 'The child goes to France in the new year.'

'And I am confirmed as Louis's fool. Louis's dupe,' says Edward. 'You were right, Richard, I should never . . .'

'No, no, Edward. It's not as bad as it seems,' his brother urges. Though, of course, it is. There's more lost here than a marriage.

Edward takes back his hand, buries his eyes in it. 'Louis will invade.'

'Not likely,' says Richard. 'And not yet. This alliance is fragile. We'll speak to my sister.'

'What can she do?' Edward whines. 'Maximilian holds power in Burgundy and has no love for me.'

'Oh, Edward,' chides Cecily, 'have you yet to learn what women can do?'

Richard nods, shakes him. 'Mother's right, Edward. We'll speak to Meg. We may yet win Burgundy back.'

'Enough of this.' Cecily kneels before Edward, pulls his hands from his face and pushes his shoulders to upright him. 'What are you thinking? Maximilian hates the French and Louis has always been afraid to fight you.' He turns his eyes from her, shamed. 'Look at me!'

At last he lifts his grey-streaked head and the paunches of his cheeks take some colour.

'Get some muscle on you, Edward,' she says, shaking him. 'No one's ever beaten you in the field. Against any odds, you win. If Louis comes, you'll burn him.'

From Edward, she goes to Elizabeth, and finds her on her bed, Margaret clasping her hands. The anger has leached away, but her face is tear-wrecked.

'Margaret, I must speak with the Queen alone.' She turns to Elizabeth. 'If I may, Your Grace.'

Elizabeth nods, pulls herself to sitting. When Margaret has made her courtesy and left, Cecily sighs. It's her first time alone with Elizabeth since Fauconberg's Bastard came up the river and tried to blow them from the Tower; since Elizabeth accused her of breeding a family of villains, traitors and fools. Since George died, it's been hard even to look at her.

'I'm sorry,' says Cecily, daring to sit beside her. 'It's a setback.'

Elizabeth shakes her head at the understatement, brings long fingers to her brow. 'Yes. Yes, it is.'

'But he's overcome worse. So have you.'

'That was when I still believed in him,' her voice is bitter with loathing. 'When he wasn't fat and wasted. When he'd not made a whore of me. Or bastards of my children.'

For God's sake. Cecily lays a finger against Elizabeth's lips. 'Hush now. Yes, you've been wronged. But I've given a son's life to set that right. So don't speak of it.'

Elizabeth turns away. 'Only to you, who knows already. What a fool you've made of me, madam. You and your son between you.'

Such nonsense. 'We've made a queen of you, Elizabeth. It's what you wanted. And your daughter is still England's princess. We'll make another match for her. These are only the twists and turns, you know. The world totters. Save your tears for when it falls.'

She stands to leave, folds her hands within her sleeves. 'Now. I will call your women. You must put your queen's face on and appear at Edward's side tonight as if you care nothing for France. It's all about how things look, Elizabeth. You should know this by now.'

On the other side of the door a pale face waits.

'Margaret.'

The younger woman's voice trembles. 'This news. It means, I suppose, that my Henry won't be coming home?'

It's hard, but best tell it like it is. 'What do you think? Brittany, with Burgundy, will ally with France now.'

Tears spill on to Margaret's cheeks and her body seems to fold upon itself.

'You mustn't always weep, Margaret.'

Cecily walks away. She's tired of wailing women. But she goes no further than ten steps before she turns, comes back, puts an arm about Margaret's shoulders and draws their brows together. 'Don't give up. The world turns. There's always a way, Margaret. You only have to find it.'

50.

8 April 1483

Westminster

Edward almost died when he was born. The astrologers blamed a preponderance of fire in his chart, which threatened to consume him. He's learned to manage the fire since, to draw upon its power in support of his will. It's what kept him moving through the snow at Towton, drove his impossible march to Tewkesbury, made him the winner in every fight. Even now, in fat middle age, it draws women, lusty, to his bed. Cecily believes it's what men most love in him. In his heated presence they're reminded of their own virility, their power to take the world by the neck and shake it.

Now though, the fire shakes him.

He has burned in fever seven days since Easter. He'd been training hard since Christmas, losing flesh, gaining muscle, then spent Lent at Windsor, riding to the hunt or sparring at arms. He kept the Lenten rule, even laid off drink and sent his whores to sleep alone. His letters to Cecily joked of it.

'I'm like a fighting monk,' he told her. 'A saint with a sword.' Then one day, sporting on the river, he took bets he could swim its width. They dragged him out halfway, floundering, blue with cold, beyond shivering. And since then he's sickened.

Now, propped in his great bed in Westminster, he sweats and struggles and Cecily, stiff from a two-day journey on rutted roads, leans in to lay her cheek against his. He is a furnace, bellowed by hot breath. Her nose fills with the stench of sickness, her heart with cold, dark dread.

'Why was I not called earlier?'

She left Berkhamsted yesterday morning, barely an hour after William Hastings's letter arrived.

'Come now,' it urged her. 'His life is feared for. Our king, your son, my friend.' And then. 'Beware the Queen.'

Elizabeth stands stiff at the bed's tail, her eyes fixed on her husband, as if by looking away she might rob him of the breath he needs to keep himself alive and her a queen. 'We thought he would recover. We still hope. It's a chill.'

But when Cecily looks across the bed to where his physicians stand – the apothecary who has dosed him with liquorice and comfrey, the surgeon who has bled his choleric veins – their solemn faces say there's little more they can think of to do. Behind them, the priests of the King's chapel try prayer.

'He was despaired of two nights ago,' whispers Hastings at Cecily's side, and Elizabeth's face, turning on him, is venomous as he continues. 'And so I sent for you because the Queen would not.'

'You despair easily, Lord,' Elizabeth sneers. 'This king never loses a fight.'

'I know,' he cuts back. 'I've been beside him for most of them.'

Edward stirs in his bed, opens red-rimmed eyes and grinds out, 'Mother?'

'Yes.' She lowers herself to sit beside him, lays her hands on either side of his head, strokes thumbs across sweat-slick brows. 'I'm here, Edward.'

He agitates, raises his hand. She grasps it, limp and flailing.

'Get everyone out,' he says.

'Son . . .'

'Get them out.'

He splutters and coughs and the room begins to empty. Elizabeth, staring Hastings down, edges closer to the King's side until Edward says softly, 'Go, Elizabeth.' And then, no less kindly, 'Piss off, Will.' And reluctantly they leave.

Alone, Cecily watches his face. His eyes sag as if he will sleep again, but he draws a noisy breath and rallies. 'My son,' he says, 'is very young.'

Barely twelve. And a hundred and fifty miles away at Ludlow, in the keeping of the Queen's brother.

She tightens her hold on his hand. 'We'll see him grow,' she tells him. 'You and I.'

He grimaces, as if some terrible spasm of pain passes through him. 'I wanted to live and see him a man.'

'You will.'

'No.'

When he struggles to hold her gaze she turns away, squeezes sore eyes shut. She who has looked squarely at everything all her life can't bear to look at this. It's not the sickness that breaks her, nor the ravaged face, but his surrender. His giving in without a fight.

'Don't fail me now, Captain Mother,' he says.

'Why not? You're failing me.' The sobbing breath that rises in her chest will surely choke her. She pushes it out, forbids another.

'Yes,' he sighs. 'Failed you and failed my son. I've let the Queen have too much rule of him.' His lips draw back, a failing grimace. 'I've been a very great fool,' his voice falters, his red eyes tear, 'for that woman.'

'A fool, indeed.'

'Love, though.'

'You're a fool still.'

'Yes.' A gasping breath. 'Mother, Elizabeth is afraid.'

'I know.'

'And hated. Her family too.'

She nods and says again that she knows. Of course she knows. The whole world waits to pull the Woodvilles down. She knows it and so does Elizabeth who, since Warwick, has trusted no one, scorned all but her own kin.

'And she, in turn, hates,' she tells him.

'Yes. Will Hastings mostly. But not only. They'll fight. There'll be war. My son the centre of it. And France . . .'

God yes, France. Louis will take the neck of England like a wolf.

'I made them swear an oath to work together. Hastings and Elizabeth. For my son's sake.'

She nods. 'Good.'

'They'll break it.'

She sobs, 'Yes.'

He grasps her hand. 'It must be Richard. No ruling council, no shared power. Richard alone, regent and protector till my boy grows.'

Richard who is in the north, keeping the King's peace, minding his own business. Too far away to know his brother's dying. Throw him into this hornets' nest and he, who no one has any good reason to hate, will be hated by all.

'Then you must set it down,' she tells him.

So she calls for his lawyers, who come and write his stuttering words. 'This is my will,' he concludes. 'Make copies. I will sign.'

An hour later, she coaxes him from sleep and puts a quill in his hand. She has called back Hastings and the Queen, and his Chancellor Archbishop Rotherham, to bear witness. Edward the King, he scrawls three times. A copy for the Queen, for the council.

'And one for you, Mother. Keep it close.'

'I will But you must fight, Edward.'

He nods and sleeps. As evening draws on he struggles and cries out, fearful against the dark.

'Light more candles,' orders Cecily. More and more until the room is ablaze. In their soft light, he sweats less, his face pales and he no longer trembles. She dares to hope, but the doctors say no, it is the fading, and point to the bluish tinge of his lips.

They call for his confessor, who sends them away and speaks with the King alone. When they are called back, he is sleeping again. Elizabeth brings his children, all who are at Westminster; from jilted Elizabeth, a woman of seventeen, to baby Bridget, still in her nurse's arms. The second of his sons, the one who matters less, pushes against his mother's skirts and cranes his neck to see. They are each given their place beside the bed, where their frightened faces hang in shadow.

Sometime after midnight the sound of his own breath wakes him and he starts, eyes wide and terror-filled. He calls out for Elizabeth, who steps away, her hands across her mouth. So instead, Cecily leans forward to grasp his flailing hand. He mumbles about sins innumerable, of gluttony and faithless whoring, arrogance and pride. Of Towton's dead buried facing west so they'll never see Christ's coming. Of Warwick betrayed, who was the brother of his heart. Of George. Tremors run through him at that, and it seems he chokes on air.

'No, no,' says Cecily, desperate. 'Not that. Lay that last to my account.'

Then, 'Elizabeth,' he whispers. And says no more, but only breathes a rasping breath on and on. She hears the bell toll the second hour then the third. His mouth has fallen open and his lips draw a circle about a void.

'Edward,' she calls as his breath fades. 'Edward.' But there is suddenly no more sound, other than the children sobbing and a priest committing her son's soul to the communion of saints. She looks up. The candles are on their ends now, sunrise still far off, and her fingers, grasping his, ache. The door behind her is open, Elizabeth already gone, Hastings and the councillors hurrying after. They go to rearrange the world, she thinks, and clenches her muscles to rise and follow, to keep her promise. But the candles swirl about her, her heart thuds through her bones and she can't find her feet. She senses hands reaching out but, before they have her, she falls into a darkness that feels like death.

51.

Baynard's

Cecily wakes in her own bed, her eyes crusted with old tears and the smell of herself thick in her nostrils. She wants to sleep again, or to lie in that stillness on the edge of sleep where the mind knows nothing and is quiet. But it's too late. Thoughts are stirring, and the dull thud of her heart, the pressing ache in her bladder, are proof she lives despite all wishing. The sounds from the river tell her she's at Baynard's. From the red beyond her eyelids she knows it's day, and from the deep cold in her bones she knows that Edward is dead, the blood-warming fire of him quenched forever. She feels her lashes tug stickily apart, licks dry lips with a ravaged tongue and squints. Someone is sitting beside her. She screws her eyes, and when she opens them again, there's Margaret Beaufort in darkest mourning, her small hands clasped in her lap.

'Why are you here?' she asks. 'Who let you in?'

'I'm sorry. The Queen bade me bring you home. I ingratiated myself with your people. So much so, they've let me come again and sit by you.'

'You've been and come again?' She's confused.

'Gone three days and come again. I'm sorry. I know you wouldn't wish to be seen like this. But I've been afraid for you.'

'My son is dead.'

It's always hardest, the first time you say it, and she feels her heart shear and clang, a broken thing beneath her breastbone. Edward dead, three days. Three days cold and dead, while her own body, the stench and stink and hateful bludgeoning pulse of it, lives on and uselessly on. She wants to cry out but can't speak above a whisper. Her throat is coated and vile. She remembers being made to drink something, cold metal against her lip, a gagging cough. Three days.

Beside her Margaret is speaking. She wishes she would stop, but no. 'Yes, Edward is dead. I'm sorry.' And now her voice is urgent, hushed. 'But you've another son. You must write to Richard about what's been set down in Edward's will.'

She can't find it in herself to care. 'Richard's to be Protector. The council will write and tell him. Will have, already.'

Margaret shifts in her seat. 'Three days, Cecily, and they haven't yet. Nor will they if the Queen can help it.' Her voice is low, fearful. 'You must warn him. The Queen opposes his appointment. And that's a short step from opposing his life.'

She can make no sense of it. Her mind is stupid, fogged and slow. 'My son is dead, Margaret,' she complains, then feels fingers at her shoulder digging bruisingly and deep. Margaret's lips are against her ear, her voice in her head saying, 'I speak of Richard, Cecily, your living son. You must get up and fight for him.'

There are hands on her. The lifting pain pulls her up, she feels her feet scrabbling for purchase as pillows are pushed behind her and all the time, Margaret's voice. 'The Queen wants her son under her own family's protection. And they say they can rule England well enough without your son the Duke of Gloucester.'

'The Queen says that?' She has found her voice.

'It's been said in my presence. Her son, Thomas Grey, says it.'

'Dear God.' She pulls forward, forces her legs to move, swings them from the bed. Her head spins and she reaches for Margaret to steady her. 'Is she mad?'

'A very dangerous madness.' Margaret talks fast now, as if she wants only to give her message and be gone. 'There's fighting already among the council and in the streets. Hastings's people and the Queen's mostly, but every man looks to himself. The

Queen says an army must be sent to bring our new king safe from Ludlow and he must be crowned the moment he arrives. Hastings says he'll take himself to Calais if she tries any such thing. You know he's Captain there. He could raise a force.'

'I know very well what Will Hastings can do,' says Cecily, her mind racing now.

'There'll be war, Cecily, unless you prevent it. Now, I must go, and you must write your son.'

The room is quiet when Margaret's gone, but for her own sawing breath. To push herself to standing is a torment, the journey to the door an endless struggle, but her voice when she calls out sends servants scurrying. 'Fetch a messenger,' she orders. 'Fetch my secretary, paper, ink!'

'Get yourself to London, Richard,' she writes. 'But fetch our new king first. You must come to the city at his side.'

'I've had the same advice from Will Hastings,' he writes back. 'Though more forthright. He says, "Take possession of the King," as if a king is a thing a man can own or command.'

Cecily is kept waiting a week for an audience with the Queen, who is too busy, too grief-stricken, or cannot speak of the future on the days of her lord's funeral.

'She speaks with others, well enough,' Cecily snarls. 'She speaks to the lords and the council. She makes a date for her son's crowning and sends a company of two thousand to armour him home.'

Then at last, when Edward is entombed, and the great days of his mourning are done, Elizabeth admits Cecily to her company, though does not bid her welcome. Instead she holds a paper at arm's length, between finger and thumb as if it carries a contagion. 'A letter from your son Richard, Duke of Gloucester,' she says.

'He's written also to me,' Cecily tells her. 'Of his grief for his brother. Of the great duty he owes to your son, the King.'

'I think he means to rule my son rather than be ruled by him.'

Elizabeth is at her queenly best, stately in the royal blue of mourning. But her eyes are tight, her cheeks sharp and a blue vein pulses at her throat.

'I think he means to do no more than your husband's will. Edward named Richard England's Protector, and your son's.'

'At your urging,' Elizabeth snarls. 'On his deathbed. In his sickness and under duress. Did you dictate the words for him?'

'Ask his lawyers, who had them from his mouth.'

Elizabeth sneers and turns to her eldest son, who has hovered behind her all this time. 'Tell her, Thomas.'

And Thomas Grey, who has uttered barely a word in Cecily's presence in all the years she's known him, finds his tongue at last. 'His lawyers. Our lawyers, now, tell us the will does not stand. It expresses only the old King's wishes, which may be overturned by the council for the safety of the new King, and his realm.'

'Ah,' says Cecily, taking time to straighten her sleeves though her fingers are numb. 'I too have lawyers. They'd agree with you. Edward's word was law, only while he lived. But there is a point in question: is the safety of the King, or his realm, threatened by Richard?'

Elizabeth comes close, draws her lips from her teeth and hisses. 'I would trust no son of yours with anything of mine.'

'Why, because George wronged you?'

'Oh,' she speaks as if a great pain assailed her. 'If it had been only George!'

The Queen's breath is shallow and rapid. She turns away, stiff and jilted, stumbles, her body folding till she almost falls and Thomas Grey steps forward saying, 'Mother . . .' But she gasps, shakes him off and straightens as Cecily watches.

'Why not send your over-protective son away and let us speak together as women who understand the world?' says Cecily.

'No, Mother,' says Thomas, making to step between them.

But Elizabeth turns and with a hand imperious but shaky,

waves him away. 'Go a while, Thomas. Stop your hovering.' And he moves to the door, nervous like a cat.

When it closes behind him Cecily sighs. 'You're afraid. I don't blame you. In the past you've had every cause for fear, God knows. But not now. Richard has never wronged you. Nor have I.'

Elizabeth pulls back to her height, begins to circle Cecily on shaky steps. 'You despise me.'

'That hardly matters,' says Cecily, standing still while Elizabeth totters.

'You never wanted my marriage.'

'Yet I've given a great deal to defend it.'

'Richard blames me for George's death.'

'I don't think so. He harbours no illusions about George.'

'He rules like a king in the north, they say. He craves power.'

'Who says? Honestly, Elizabeth, I think Richard craves nothing more than a quiet life.' She shakes out her hands, clasps them before her. 'Is this the full list of your complaints?'

Elizabeth's lip trembles, her clasped fingers whiten. 'Edward made a sham of my marriage, bastards of my children . . .'

Cecily holds up a hand. 'I have told you, forget that. Never speak of it.'

'How can I forget, when you yourself might make it known?' she hisses.

'Dear God, Elizabeth, why would I?'

'To destroy me.' Her eyes narrow, her face draws close. 'It was you, after all, who named Marguerite's child a bastard and used it to bring her down.'

Now Cecily returns her stare, her eyes steady. 'Well, yes, I did that. But you see, Elizabeth, Marguerite was not my son's wife. And her boy was not my grandson.'

She waits while Elizabeth's glare falters, while her head shakes and judders, unsteady as her thoughts. She feels old suddenly and very tired. She's not spent so much time on her feet since she followed Edward's funeral hearse from Westminster to Windsor. Her legs ache and a grey mist hovers at the edges of her eyes.

'Elizabeth,' she says. 'Can we sit down?'

Elizabeth nods once and, tentatively, they lower themselves into chairs. Cecily sighs, stretches a crick from her neck. 'Is this your fear? That we would put down your son?'

Elizabeth doesn't speak at first, but tears start in her eyes, then, 'George would have.'

'I'm not George. Nor is Richard.'

Elizabeth lowers her eyes. 'But does he know?'

Cecily's answer is certain and clear. 'No. And he wants only what you and I want. A smooth transition of power from Edward to Edward's son. Believe me, he's your best chance of making that happen.'

'Before you meddled with Edward's will my husband was content for his son to grow up in my family's protection.'

'I think he didn't foresee this turn of events. Foresight, I regret, was not his gift.'

'And yet I don't see . . .'

'. . . Why things can't carry on that way?

'Yes.'

'Because the nobles of this realm will never allow such power to rest in Woodville hands. You might think it wrong. You might think it unjust. Perhaps it is. But it's the truth.'

'That's why you had Edward name Richard?'

'No. That's why Edward named Richard. Oppose his will on this and you risk a civil war that could open the door to a French invasion. And the trouble with war, Elizabeth, is neither you nor I can guarantee who'll win.'

'Will Hastings already has soldiers in the streets.'

'To be fair, so have you.'

'He calls out for Richard.'

'He upholds your husband's will, so I suppose he would.' How to put an end to this? 'Elizabeth, I will humble myself, if I must.'

She comes stiffly to her knees, takes the Queen's hands in her own and sets her brow against them. 'You have enemies, Elizabeth, I know. Richard is not among them. Make him your friend and you'll be King's Mother, honoured, respected, safe. I will rejoice to see you so.'

Elizabeth stares down at her, first squeezes her hands then, all uncertain, pulls her own away as if burned. 'I don't know . . .'

'Elizabeth,' she sits back on her haunches, 'I have never betrayed you.'

Cecily takes the road home, not the river. She wants to judge the mood in the city. From her carriage she watches men go about their business with their heads down and their mouths shut. Muscled guards in noble livery strut or linger, hands on sword hilts, fingers itchy. Many wear Will Hastings's badge: the man-faced lion with a scorpion's tail; a smile and a sting.

She calls him to her and he comes.

'I'm disappointed, Will,' she tells him. 'You promised Edward you'd make peace with the Queen and her kin.'

He shrugs. 'They make no peace with me.'

'I was relying on you to be better than them.'

'They'll put a knife in my back as soon as look at me.'

'Tush! Are you afraid?'

'No. Because Richard of Gloucester will come and put them down.'

'Don't bank on it,' she tells him.

Her bed is wide and empty. She stretches her limbs into the coldness of the linen, resisting the urge to curl about herself or to nurture any warmth within her blood. It is a heretic thought, but she feels certain now that Hell is an ocean of ice, not fire, and she must learn to swim in its depths, for she feels so very far from Heaven and, with Edward's sun burned out, no power remains on earth to bring heat to heart or flesh. She listens to the bell toll every hour and hopes she has done enough to hold a peace till Richard comes. She hopes and hopes. She's tired of talking and even her tongue seems frozen at its root. She lies awake all night then sleeps till mid-morning. Misses matins, terce and a mass. Her chaplain chides her for idleness and sloth.

'I've lost my son,' she reminds him, bitterly.

'Who has left you his own son to take his place,' he tells her. 'By God's mercy you'll find all you've lost in him.'

Will I though? she wonders. She barely knows her grandson, he's been so long in Ludlow with his Woodville kin. Perhaps she'll find nothing in him but Elizabeth; her petulance and prejudice, her insecurity and fear.

She waits for word from Richard. It's slow to come, but when it does it sends her racing again to Westminster. Too late. The palace is in uproar, the Queen already gone; fled into sanctuary with her children, her servants and her jewels. Chancellor Rotherham stands among the chaos with Richard's letter in his hand bearing news that mirrors her own: the Queen's brother, Anthony Woodville, and Sir Richard Grey, her son, are arrested and sent north. The charge is a treasonous rising against the Lord Protector. An attempt upon his life.

'I have now, for safety's sake,' Richard writes, 'taken possession of the King.'

52.

Westminster

'Possession,' says Cecily. 'A little inflammatory, don't you think?'

Richard, standing beside her in Westminster's great hall, rolls his shoulders, right then left, and says tight-voiced, 'I only meant I have him safe.'

'I see.'

'Mother, I . . .'

'Hush. Not here.' She directs his gaze forward again to where men approach the dais on which the boy king sits, then watches the nervous tic that taunts his eye until he rubs it. She doesn't imagine he's had much sleep. Not easy sleep, anyway.

He's brought Edward's son to London on the very day Elizabeth had decreed for his crowning. That event, he has told the council, is delayed for now, until it can be arranged with proper circumstance, due reverence and no rush. He rode into the city at the King's side and, behind him, four wagons piled with arms; swords and pikes and sharp-bladed lances, salets and gambesons all bearing Woodville badges. Confiscated, he says, from men who came to meet him looking for a fight.

Now he's brought the uncrowned king to his high chair in Westminster Hall and called all lords, secular and holy, to swear fealty to him. Cecily watches, reading faces, guessing allegiances; Woodville or York, the Queen's kin or her own? This divided world that Edward's life stitched together, splintering and splitting now he's gone.

Richard was first to give his oath. On his knees and in that earnest voice of his. He swore not only to serve his king, but to honour and protect the King's Mother, 'If she will only come out from her unnecessary sanctuary and acknowledge the will of her late Lord, my brother.'

Men rolled their eyes and leaned on one another's arms. 'Let her stay where she is, for Christ's sake. Let's have a man in charge who knows what he's doing,'

Now, together, she and Richard watch the line of men make their pledges and, when all are done, Richard leads her to the King, who stands as she approaches. He's sprouted in the five years since she saw him last and is almost Richard's equal for height. But she sees no promise of his father's breadth in him, and his hair is as light as his mother's. There's something bloodless about his pale-lashed eyes, but their look is piercing enough and falls on her with suspicion. She sinks into her deepest obeisance and waits for him to raise her up.

He does not.

'My father,' he says, in a voice that's on that awkward break twixt boy and man, 'once told me yours was the sharpest mind in England. That you are the greatest champion of our house.'

'I'm gladly your champion, my lord.'

'Then perhaps you'll champion me to your son here, so that my uncle Anthony and my half-brother can be returned to my side.'

'They're lucky I didn't execute them on the road,' Richard tells her.

It's evening. The young King is safely lodged in the Tower's royal chambers with such company of his own as can be trusted, and servants of Richard's who will keep a watchful eye. Richard has come to Baynard's to explain himself to his mother. Though his voice is even as it ever is, there are smudges of blue beneath his eyes, his mouth is a thin line of worry and the ruby on his finger turns and turns. The sight of him is a cold hand against Cecily's heart. He's so like his father. And so, like him, beset.

'Tell me what happened,' she says.

So he explains how he'd arranged to meet the King's party at Northampton, how it had all been agreed by letter with the Queen's brother, Anthony.

'We'd determined to come to London together, present a united front; the King's uncles from both his families bringing him to his crowning.'

But when Richard arrived at Northampton, at sunset on the appointed day, he found the King's party had pushed on ten miles or more to Stony Stratford and only Anthony himself remained to meet him.

'I've always found Anthony a reasonable man,' says Richard. 'Pompous like his father. But reasonable. He said they'd been worried there wouldn't be room at Northampton to accommodate both our companies.' Richard sneers, 'As if Northampton doesn't have a castle. As if it isn't spring and men can't sleep under the sky if they have to.'

Anthony said they'd ride together to meet the King next morning, but seemed jittery and out of sorts, so while he slept, Richard sent out men to scout the road they'd take. They came back to report an ambush lying ready; men wearing Woodville badges, bearing Woodville arms and answering to the youngest of the Queen's Grey sons.

'I'd only six hundred in my company,' says Richard. 'There were two thousand in the King's, and five hundred more come with Richard Grey. All waiting for me in the road.'

Elizabeth must have sent him after our meeting, Cecily realizes. Mouth and belly twist into a snarl. What a fool that woman is, to dare try and take the last of my sons from me.

'So I took another route to Stony Stratford and . . .' Richard stops the ring's turning, clenches the hand that wears it into a fist and wraps the other about it. 'Mother, can you tell me why the Queen makes war on me when I have never in my life wronged her?'

What to say?

'Because your brothers wronged her, I suppose. You inherit their fault and her mistrust.'

'How did Edward wrong her? Except by bedding any woman still in possession of her teeth.'

She waves the question away, her knowledge of the answer, and only says, 'She wants to control her future. That means controlling the King. You stand in the way of that. Isn't that what Will Hastings told you when he wrote?'

'Yes, but,' he screws his face, 'I'm careful of his word in this. He has no love for the Woodvilles and God knows, they hate him. The Queen calls him Edward's pander.'

'Sure they shared enough whores,' Cecily accedes.

'Now he plays for my favour. You saw him today, laughing and backslapping, talking me up.'

'You're Protector of England, Richard. Every man will play for your favour now.'

'Except those who want to put a knife in my back.'

'Well, yes.'

'Hastings wants to be to me what he was to Edward.'

'And what's that?'

'A fixer. A right-hand man. A bosom friend. In my confidence and my reward.'

'Why shouldn't he be?'

'No reason. Except I don't much like him.'

She can see why he wouldn't. Easy with his words, Will. Easy with his morals. Light with the truth, when it suits him. A chancer.

'Your brother loved him.'

'And I loved my brother. None better. But I didn't always like him either.'

And at that, his eyes fill, as if his own words have turned a knife on him. 'I'm sorry,' he says. 'He was like a god to me when I was young, and I know all that he was to you. But what a hornets' nest he's left us, Mother.' He puts his head in his hands, runs them hard through his hair. 'What an unholy mess.'

And then he wants to speak of his brother's dying, of what he's heard and what he's imagined and what he feels could hardly, possibly be true. And when she talks of it he weeps in earnest, so she sits beside him and places her hand on his back, where the hidden twist of unnatural bone mirrors what she knows of her own heart. I had four sons, she thinks, and am left with only this. And he's a good son. But now her own tears scald her face and she knows herself to be a bad woman, for if God would only grant it she would go to Him on her knees and beg to trade all of this one's years for a single day under the heat of Edward's sun.

He's up early next morning, but she's earlier still and waiting. She's spent the night in prayer, taking it back, repenting and recanting, for she knows how fickle God can be; how he can take you at your word when least you mean it, when your thoughts are grief-shadowed and your mind upturned.

'I'd never trade him,' she has pledged. 'I'm glad of him. I'll fight for him. I'll fight that foolish queen if I have to.' She'll take on God, if it comes to it. What else has she ever done than fight for her children?

He looks a little better. She asks him if he's eaten and when he says no, sits him down and puts food in front of him.

'What will you do?' she asks.

He'll meet with the council. He'll ask them to confirm his protectorship. He'll set a new date for the coronation, a date that will be kept. He'll offer the Queen his pardon and protection. He'll explain to her his honest intentions and reunite her with her son.

'And I'll try to convince my nephew I'm not the Devil,' he says with a grimace. 'I think I made a little progress with that, on the road. But the job won't be finished while I'm at odds with his mother.'

'I'll help with that if I can. I'll visit him this morning. And I'll try to talk to the Queen. Though I'm not sure she'll listen.'

'I'd be grateful.'

'And Will Hastings?'

'I'll tell him to get his soldiers off the streets. And that I love him for Edward's sake and value his support. I'll confirm him in every position my brother granted. He'll lose nothing with me.'

Then a servant arrives to say that the Duke of Buckingham has come looking for the Duke of Gloucester and Richard rises and says he must go.

'I saw him with you at Westminster yesterday, Harry Buckingham. He travelled with you?'

'I called him to meet me on the road. He's family, isn't he?'

Indeed he is. Her sister Anne's grandson. She died two years ago but he didn't come to her funeral. He's a year or two younger than Richard himself. Married to one of the Queen's sisters. Not happily. One of the marriages Cecily made for policy when he was a boy with a rich inheritance and Edward newly burdened with a wife poor in everything except relations.

'The Woodvilles don't much like him,' Cecily warns him.

'The Woodvilles don't much like anyone.'

'Your brother didn't trust him.'

'Or was that the Queen?'

Fair point. Hard to say. Though his grandmother called him feckless.

Richard's at the door by now. 'Anyway, as I say, he's family. I want the support of my family. God knows I've little enough of it left.'

'Richard!' He's almost gone, but she calls him back. 'Don't go about the city unguarded.'

'I won't.'

She suddenly fears him leaving, follows him to the door. 'Will Anne come, your wife?'

He shakes his head. 'I'd not risk her on the road I came.' He means any road, thinks Cecily, that might lead towards danger or away from the home she loves. She has smiled at it at times, the extravagant tenderness of his care for her. Last year, and at great expense, he tore down the wall of his castle on the Tees to make an oriel, for no better reason than that Anne fancied the view it would give of the river rippling seaward, and the morning light by which she would sit with her ladies and read.

'She'll come when things are more settled.' He looks embarrassed. 'Till then I must only miss her.'

'Then Richard, don't stay alone at Crosby Place. Until Anne comes, stay here with me. I'd be glad of the company.'

'And I'd be glad of your counsel. Yes, I will. Thank you.'

And he goes away looking pleased and grateful and she remains, feeling shamed and sad.

53.

4 May to 26 June 1483

Baynard's

It becomes a pattern. Richard leaves early, returns late. Harry Buckingham usually calls for him, or Richard's off to meet him, or he's the last man he's seen. The council approves Richard as Protector and he has everything to do. He meets daily with the council, makes new arrangements for the coronation, strengthens coastal defences to guard against the French. He appoints new men to mind his business in the north.

'Because my life will be always tied to the court now,' he tells Cecily with resignation and regret.

He spends hours of every day with the young King, explaining the decisions he takes on his behalf, seeking approval, finding only surly acquiescence.

'I don't rule you,' he insists. 'I serve you.' But he confides in Cecily that every day the boy asks only of his mother and his kin.

There's not much to tell him. Elizabeth keeps to sanctuary and will accept no visits from Cecily.

The city is quieter. At least by day. But at night, when men have been drinking, there are scuffles in the streets. One of Hastings's people is found dead in a gutter and witnesses swear they saw men in Woodville colours loitering at the scene. But the witnesses are Hastings's men too, so who's to say? Two of Buckingham's servants are beaten, one so badly his brain is addled. His fellow says their assailants ran towards Lord Hastings's home, but Will's not the only man with a house on that street.

And if Buckingham's men have grown cocky, who can blame

them? Their lord is a great man these days and, some say, cocky himself. Richard's given him dominion over all of Wales, which Harry named as his heart's desire and just reward. Men mutter he rises too high, too fast. Not least Hastings, who's had no reward at all except to lose nothing. But it's enough, don't you think: Chamberlain of England, Captain of Calais, Master of the Mint?

As June comes in Anne arrives and Cecily has never seen a man so happy as Richard to be reunited with his wife. She herself, though, is shocked at the sight of her. Anne is thin to the point of wasting and spends two days in bed recovering from the journey.

'She'll soon be well again,' says Richard. 'Now summer's here.'

He moves with Anne to his town house of Crosby Place and now it's her he returns to in the evenings. Cecily misses him, so most days she winds her way up Bishopsgate to find out from her daughter-in-law, if not from her son, what goes on. She is met one day, a warm day in the middle of June, in the entrance hall by Anne, who is thinner than ever, wide-eyed and trembling.

'Thank God you're here,' she says, taking Cecily's arm. 'Richard's taken William Hastings's head.'

And she draws her to a room where Richard sits stiff-backed, white-lipped and shaking more than his wife, who goes now to her knees before him, and whose hands he grasps like a man drowning. Behind him Harry Buckingham hovers, his head uncovered and an eye lividly bruised.

'What have you done, Richard?' Cecily demands.

'Justice,' he says, teeth bare and spit-flecked. 'He attempted Harry's life last night. He cuts at the heart of my power.' His fingers twitch. 'My right arm.'

'And more,' says Buckingham. 'He was in league with Louis . . .'

Richard interrupts him. 'It seems if I wouldn't destroy the Woodvilles for him, he'd turn even to the French to get the job done. Show her, Harry.'

And Buckingham hands her a list of Hastings's treacheries which, he says, calm and cold, was presented to the council this

325

morning and is even now being posted on the doors of London's churches.

'We've had him under watch some time,' Richard says. 'Last night was only the latest of his crimes.'

She scans the document. A lawyer's hand, but Richard's words; his earnest phrasing, careful indices, scrupulous accounting. On such and such a date Lord Hastings did write this and that to King Louis. On this day he spoke against the Queen, met with these men, said these words. The list is long and entries in it pre-date Edward's death. In this month he perverted justice to this man's detriment. In this he interfered with the workings of the mint. The last is added hastily and in a fresh hand. Last night, Thursday, 12 June, he did set men upon the Duke of Buckingham. A treasonous strike at the Protector's power.

'All of this, and envy,' says Richard. 'He was the same with Edward. He couldn't bear that any other man come first with me.'

No, thinks Cecily. I suppose he never could. She's not forgotten who stirred up the mob against Henry Beaufort, who made sure of Warwick's death at Barnet. For all his charm and chancing, Hastings was always a knife in the dark.

'Who else of mine would he have taken, Mother? How long before he came for me?' His mouth curls, bitter and resentful.

Anne looks up at Cecily from her place at Richard's feet as Buckingham speaks again. 'Bishops Morton and Rotherham are imprisoned too,' he says. 'They were part of the Queen's plot to kill Richard on the road . . .'

'And were plotting with her even now to come at me again,' Richard says.

'But she's in sanctuary,' Cecily answers, her mind racing to unravel treachery.

'No one pays any mind to churchmen coming and going at the abbey,' says Buckingham. 'They've been in and out of there like rats.'

'Oh, dear God.' Cecily's hand comes to her mouth. At the sight of it, Richard hangs his head.

'What am I to do, Mother? I can't bring my brother's son to his throne, or keep the peace in England, if I'm dead.'

She knows, of course, what he must do. She's known since that first morning when she went to see Edward's son at the Tower. When he looked at her with undisguised suspicion and said, 'By my father's order I've lived as a prince under my family's protection. I see no reason why as king I must live under yours.' She'd shown him his father's will and his eyes had narrowed. 'Written in your presence I'm told. At your direction.'

The boy is twelve years old and all his mother's. He'll be a man soon enough. Already there's a whisper of hair on his chin. How long till he claims his majority? How long can it be kept from him? Three years? Less? And if his mind can't be changed by then, Richard's a dead man. If he even lives that long, thinks Cecily. A protector's life skates upon a knife edge when men scrabble for control of a king.

That night, at prayer, she binds her rosary about her fist and fixes her eyes on the dead Christ, limp and bone-broke in his mother's arms. She renews the pledge she made in panic scant days ago: to fight all comers for Richard.

'But you're bound by other promises,' God and conscience remind her. 'You swore Elizabeth's enemies would be your enemies. That you'd see Edward's son on his throne.'

'Then my promises run counter. Which should I keep?'

But God is silent then. There's never any use going to Him for straight answers. She's complained of it to her confessor a thousand times. He only ever smiles and says, 'Has He not given you head and heart to make right choices?'

So I'll do as I've always done, she determines. And find God's will in my own.

The Christ's hair is as dark as Richard's and blood drips like rubies from his hands.

Crosby Place is dark and quiet when she returns. She rouses the doorman, who confirms her son's not yet abed.

'I've sent everyone away,' Anne says, summoned to meet her in the dimness of the hall. 'He must have a minute's peace, don't you think?' Then she colours, embarrassed. 'But I'm glad you're here, of course.'

You're probably not, thinks Cecily, following her through the shadows into the inner spaces of their home. And I'm not sure it's peace I bring him.

'How is he?' she asks.

'Exhausted,' says Anne. 'Grieving.'

'Not for Hastings, surely?'

'For his brother, who he says is now more lost to him than ever. All these days he's prayed for Edward's ghost to come with a word for him. Now he says he fears it, for what would Edward speak of but recrimination for the death of his friend?'

'There are no ghosts, Anne. And Hastings was a traitor.'

'So I've told him,' she says. And her voice, though thin and weary, is a voice a man will listen to. Cecily pats her hand, and nods.

Richard rises to greet her as Anne closes the door with a hush. The room is hot and, though it's summer, there's a fire burning, which is as well for there's no other light to see by. Still in his dark mourning, Richard's face is stark and white.

Cecily leads him back to his chair, draws up another and sits by him. 'Are you a pauper for candles, Richard? And for air?'

'I'm sorry,' he says. 'I can't seem to be warm.' And his eyes flit to Anne, who takes up a taper from the fire and carries it about the room opening pools of light.

'You can't regret Will Hastings, Richard. He's not the first man whose death you've ordered.'

'Christ, no.'

'And I dare say there'll be others.'

'Yes,' he says. 'Anthony Woodville and Richard Grey for a start.' And though she'd not thought it possible, he blanches further still and rubs his hand across his face. 'This kingdom is riven with faction. I see no way through it. I think my brother has left me a curse.'

As his hand falls she catches it in hers, feeling in her grasp the stub of his snipped finger, the rub of his ruby ring. 'What if I can show you a way through it, Richard?'

He looks up at her and her mouth turns dry. Her heart trips in her breast.

'Mad Henry was a curse to two protectors,' she tells him. 'Humphrey of Gloucester when he was a child, your own father when madness made him a child again. Both died at the hands of others who wanted to control the King.'

He hangs his head. This much he knows full well.

'I urged your father to free himself of it by taking the throne.'

His head jerks up again, his eyes hard and dark. 'Well, there's no chance of that for me.'

'Isn't there?' Her tripping heart turns painful, but she presses on. 'What if I told you your brother's sons are bastards?'

The chair tumbles. He's on his feet, staggering back from her, his face a mask of horror and disbelief.

She daren't stop now. She gets up, follows him across the room leaving Anne on her knees, bewildered and staring.

'He married Elizabeth in secret, Richard, you know that.'

'Yes,' he cries. 'But he did marry her.' He looks at her as if she, no less than the words she speaks, is monstrous.

'But she wasn't the first, Richard.'

He shakes his head, begins to walk, as if he wants nothing more than a distance between him and all she is saying, but she follows, relentless, as she must.

'Three years before Elizabeth,' she tells him, 'he made the same vows with Eleanor Talbot, old Shrewsbury's daughter.'

He turns and stares at her, as if he thinks her mad or devil-sent. 'If it's true, how do you know of it?'

'I had it from her own lips. And from his. And from the priest who joined their hands and signed the cross over them.'

'No,' he says, backing away from her.

She pursues him again. 'Come on, Richard. Is it so unbelievable? You know what he was for women. And for promises.'

As he stumbles Anne comes to his side, soft-footed, low-voiced but urgent. 'Sit down, Richard,' she urges. 'Before you fall.' And she leads him by the hand, sits him by the fire and pushes the hair back from his face; its unruly waves and kinks.

Cecily follows and sits beside him again. His dark eyes won't look at her.

'When did you know?' he asks.

'Soon after it was done. You'll ask now why I kept it secret. Well, what was I to do? These weren't solemn vows spoken in a church. They were drunken promises stumbled over to get her into bed, the priest barely more sober than he was. You might say, as I did then, that this was no marriage. Just the foolishness of a boy too drunk and lust-addled to know sense, and God will turn a blind eye to it. It suited me to think so then. I wanted better for him.' She shrugs. 'Now, given the times, you might instead say this: that your brother was married in the sight of God, his sons are bastards and you are England's rightful king.'

He opens his mouth, closes it again, shakes his head as if to empty it of hornets and asks, 'But Eleanor Talbot's dead, surely?'

'Since the year Meg went into Burgundy, yes. Buried with the Carmelites in Norwich.'

Anne's voice is level. 'But she was alive when Edward married Elizabeth. That's what matters, yes?' She looks at Cecily, seeking confirmation. 'It makes that marriage void?'

'It makes it void. Yes.'

'Richard,' Anne gasps, laying her hands tender against his cheeks.

He takes them by the wrists and pushes them away. 'No,' he says. 'No, no, no.'

'Richard,' Cecily's voice is steel now, 'England needs a steady hand. A man to rule her, not a boy. You wanted a way out of this mess and here it is. Protectors are at the mercy of factions. Kings put factions down.'

'But my brother's sons.'

The pain in her breast is worse now. Almost, she can't breathe. 'Elizabeth Woodville's bastards,' she corrects. 'They must learn to bow. We will make the lesson gentle.'

'I can't do it.' He turns from mother to wife as if searching for salvation. 'Anne?'

Anne reaches for his face again, pulls him close and sets her brow against his. 'What will happen if you don't? They'll kill you. The Woodvilles will, or someone else. Then what of me, Richard? Our son? When they're finished with you, they'll come for us.'

The choked cry that comes from him is like a death.

Cecily sits back now, lets her head fall forward and her eyes close. She thinks she couldn't drag another word out of herself. But it's all right. Anne will do the talking now. She listens as she tells him it's their only chance. That he'll be a good king. That he'll rule the country as he's ruled the north, with justice and fair dealing.

'But will it stand in law?' he asks, desperate. 'Will it stand before God?'

Cecily rouses herself. 'Call in your lawyers, Richard. Call in your churchmen. Ask them. Ask Robert Stillington, he was the priest that married them. Ask Eleanor's kin. Come on, Richard. You're halfway to a lawyer yourself. Build a case.'

In the days that come he does so. He wears men out with questions, and the answer is always the same: there were promises. There was a priest. And witnesses enough to Eleanor's testimony long before she died. Mouths that have been shut are opened and their words are written down.

Two Sundays later, on the day Edward's son was to have been crowned, he is instead named bastard, and sermons across the city take Solomon for their text: bastard slips shall take no root, nor shall the ungodly thrive.

'What now?' men say.

'God must decide,' says Richard.

And when Anne looks to her, desperate, Cecily says, 'We'll give Him a nudge, shall we?'

So Buckingham is sent to put the case to the lords and the city, evidence laid out on the table, witnesses called to answer.

At Baynard's, Richard waits, his wife quiet beside him, his mother pacing. 'They'll come,' she says.

And they do. Just as twenty-two years ago they came for Edward. They come in delegation to the courtyard of his mother's home and send up their petition, begging him to be their king.

On the balcony above, Cecily lays her hand on her son's shoulder and says, 'Go down now, Richard, and tell them yes.'

And she watches him go, as if a tether draws him, down the stairs and into their midst.

'Behold your king!' Buckingham shouts, his voice a booming bludgeon at Richard's back.

'Will you have me then?' says Richard, his own voice quiet in the lull that follows.

'Yes,' whispers Cecily against her teeth.

And all the crowd cries 'Aye!'

54.

London

Cecily keeps away from Richard's coronation. She's too tired, she tells him. 'Too tired and too ill and besides, you don't need me.'

It's true. Sometimes her heart stabs and races, so that she must press a hand beneath her breast and sit before she falls. Or its unsteady beat wakes her in the night, juddering in her bones. Perhaps death is coming. She is two years from seventy, so it could be no surprise. Or it's the ghosts she told Anne she doesn't believe in, rattling their grievances at her door.

She doesn't spend the day idly though. She goes to the Tower and sits with Edward's boys. The youngest came out of sanctuary in June. Richard gave Elizabeth an ultimatum: 'I won't crown one son without the presence of the other.' A moot point now since he'll crown neither. But they couldn't let the boy stay where he was.

She speaks to them of the journey they'll take to the north 'It's good country,' she tells them. 'Fine hawking. Your uncle the King is much loved there.'

The youngest seems keen enough after weeks among his mother's skirts, but his brother only looks at her with red-rimmed eyes before turning his face to the wall. He weeps for his uncle Anthony and half-brother Richard Grey. Well. Only a fool would have let those traitors live, and Richard isn't that.

They'll go soon and secretly. The north is far away, and in its broad expanses, two boys can grow unnoticed among men who owe their living to Richard and know how to keep their mouths shut. It's been explained to them. They'll have time to reflect. To adjust. To feel the fast-turning world grow steady under their feet. In good time they'll be given offices appropriate to their station; their station as the Lords Bastard, the old King's natural sons.

'If you're amenable, it will be a good life,' Cecily tells them. 'I pray you'll be so.'

For now, it's best the world forgets them a while, and Woodville plotters be left wondering where they are. Even Cecily won't know exactly. She's told Richard not to tell her. She wants no solid image of them. No temptation to ride to their side.

Later, Margaret, who carried the new Queen's train to the abbey, comes to Baynard's to tell Cecily how lustily the lords of England had cried out 'Aye!' for Richard. Cecily wants to ask who didn't cry out. Which men stood quiet, sucked their teeth and need to be watched. But she thinks Margaret won't tell her. Her own husband, after all, might be among them.

Margaret says Anne seemed a little tired by the ceremony, that her head bowed under the weight of her crown. But that at the feast after, she danced light-footed enough beside her husband.

'She must be missing her son, I suppose.' Anne came alone to join her husband in London, leaving her son in the quiet of Middleham's castle.

'She'll see him soon enough.'

'Then she's fortunate. I've no such hope for my own.'

Dear God, thinks Cecily. Does she imagine I've time to think of Henry Tudor now?

It's time she did, though. Louis surely will.

Margaret persists. 'Richard says Louis petitions Brittany for Henry to be sent to France. He thinks Duke Francis won't do it. But won't let him come to England either.'

'Well, when you're threatened by a man like Louis as Francis is, you don't give up the one thing you have that he wants.'

Margaret's head dips. 'So you see, I'm without hope, and Richard will do nothing.'

'*Can* do nothing. For now. You must wait, Margaret. Be patient.'

She expects tears then, but Margaret's face hardens to granite. 'I've been patient twelve years, Cecily. Twelve long years.'

At the door, when they've drily kissed one another's cheeks, Margaret bites her lip, stays close and asks, 'What now for Edward's sons?'

It's the question the whole kingdom asks and to which no answer is given.

'Safe in their uncle's keeping, Margaret. What else would you imagine?'

'I'll not rule as Edward did, Mother. From Windsor or Westminster and forget the rest. The court will be wherever I am, and I'll be about the country where people can see me. Where they can bring me their grievances and get justice at my hand.'

'Is that wise?' she asks. 'The nobles of England like their king to stay home and out of their business.'

England isn't used to an active king.

But he's gone nonetheless by month's end, Anne riding pale but determined at his side. And since the city is left to John Howard's charge, newly made Duke of Norfolk at Richard's hand, and because it would be intolerable to spend a day more of summer in the city's stink, she returns to Berkhamsted. She hopes its quiet turn of days, its rhythmic hours of prayer, might slow her heart. Even if God won't speak to her, she'll put herself in His company a while.

She leaves word for Elizabeth, who is only Dame Grey now and will not see her. 'When you're ready to bring your daughters out of sanctuary, send word to me and I'll come. I would see them comfortable, Elizabeth. And you.'

But there's no answer.

August is hot, so she's glad to sit in the shade and read

Richard's letters. From Reading he writes that he's granted Hastings's widow her lands and custody of her son. 'Why should she suffer for her husband's sins?'

From Tewkesbury he recalls his part in his brother's victory there. In Oxford and Cambridge he debates with scholars. In every town he accepts rich gifts in kind, but rejects those in coin.

'I tell them to keep their purses closed,' he says. 'I'd rather their hearts than their money.'

'Though you probably need the money, Richard,' Cecily chides.

His own heart, she knows, draws him north. In Pontefract he's met by his son and writes he's never seen Anne happier. They travel together to York – 'my northern capital', he calls it, 'my heart's home' – where, in the Archbishop's palace, his boy is made Prince of Wales.

'You'd have been proud to see it, Mother. He stood straight as a rod and spoke clearly the whole ceremony. And the people cheered him to the roof.'

He says he'll create a college of a hundred priests there, an engine of prayer for England and his house.

Come September, she begins to think those prayers might be needed. As the weather turns sultry, he writes of rumours and uncertainty, of discontent in southern counties.

'But I've sent Buckingham there, so expect to hear soon that all's well.'

A week later he writes again. 'I've sent Anne and Edward home to Middleham, I'm coming south. I don't know yet what the trouble is, but the Woodvilles are deep in it. And Bishop Morton.'

But Morton's in Buckingham's custody in Brecon, so she wonders how that can be.

'Would you like me back in London?' she asks him.

But he tells her, no. 'Stay where you are, it'll come to nothing.'

Come October, as the weather turns wet, Richard's riding hard and mustering men. There's a watch set on the south coast and the Duke of Norfolk has blockaded the Thames against rebels from Kent. And now, again, Cecily's heart is racing and if she wanted to go to London she'd be hard-pressed to get there for, dear God, it's never rained like this. The rivers are up and the roads themselves turned to rivers, so that messengers appear half-drowned or not at all, and she barely knows what's going on until, in a torrent, some poor mud-caked fool slides from a near-dead horse to the cobbles of her courtyard with a letter, damp and curling but written in Richard's hand. It tells her that his cousin Harry Buckingham, 'That most untrue creature living', is captured in treason, and men are sent to arrest Margaret Beaufort who, with Brittany's blessing, has invited her son Henry Tudor to invade.

She can read in his words the cracking of his heart. 'And between them,' he writes, 'they've told the world that I murdered my brother's sons and sit, a usurper, on their throne.'

She has berated Richard for ever trusting Harry Buckingham, but must turn a lashing tongue upon herself when it comes to Margaret. She's told others so many times: always look for treachery where you least expect it. Your most dangerous enemies aren't those who skulk in dark corners, but those who greet you with a smile in the morning and keep company with you under God's good sun. I've been the world's greatest fool for thinking Margaret Beaufort harmless, she tells herself. And who should know better than I what a mother will risk for her son?

'Well, Margaret. It was the weather defeated you,' she says, sitting across a table from Henry Tudor's mother in the small room where she's been brought to await judgement. 'And weather's God-given, so you know your cause is damned.'

The Severn broke its banks, so Buckingham couldn't bring his army across it. His men deserted him and went home out of the wet.

'I'm told an old friend handed him to Richard for the reward on his head. A funny old world, eh, Margaret, when you can't trust to friendship. He grovelled for mercy, apparently. But Richard knows justice. His head's off in Salisbury marketplace.'

She watches Margaret swallow hard, leans towards her. 'And did you know? Tight-pursed Duke Francis gave your boy only seven ships and sent him off in a storm. Not much, is it? I'm told five of them are on the seabed. Not your son's, sadly.' And now, as if confiding, 'Though we almost had him, off Plymouth . . .'

Margaret, who's sat silent till now and blank-faced, opens her mouth on a single choking breath.

'. . . if we had,' Cecily continues, 'I'd have brought you his bollocks in a bag.'

Margaret blinks, slow, recovers herself. 'I'm very sure.' She lowers her head. 'If you know where he is now, will you tell me? I'm not above begging.'

Cecily would like to tell her he fled and foundered, but even now, can't quite find it in her. And, besides, it isn't true.

'Come ashore at Normandy, we think. But we're wise to him now. And wise to you. Margaret,' it's painful to say it, 'I'd never have believed it of you.'

She watches as Margaret closes her narrow shoulders about herself. She looks as small as a child. 'Perhaps you should have,' she says and brings up her fists against the ache in her head. 'I've always said I'd do anything. Anything. To bring my son home.'

Cecily rises, walks about the table, leans down to speak close in Margaret's ear. 'Even kill mine?'

Behind the shelter of her arms, Margaret sobs.

'Don't dare cry, Margaret.'

Margaret's fists lower, her fingers uncurl and meet in supplication, a guard against her lips.

'Yes. Damned though I would be. For my son, I'd kill anyone. With my bare hands.' She lifts those hands to Cecily, and raises her eyes, which are dry, wide open and clear. 'As I think you would, for yours.'

And Cecily must walk away from her now, or strangle the

breath out of her, for it's true. Did she herself not kill George for Edward? And did she not put down Edward's sons to keep Richard safe?

'You do know,' she says from the room's end, 'just to be sure. That Edward's boys are not dead.'

'Oh, Cecily, yes. You could destroy nothing of his. Nor could Richard. But it's an easy thing to convince men of. Very easy to convince Elizabeth.'

'I can imagine. So, in return for her support to destroy Richard, you promised to marry your Henry to her daughter and make a queen of her.'

'And so restore Elizabeth's family.' She pauses. 'If not her sons.'

'Them you'd have killed yourself, I imagine?'

Margaret blinks, slow and steady. 'Inevitably, I suppose.'

'It's a desperate course.'

'I'm a desperate woman.'

'And what did you promise Buckingham?'

'He was very easy to flatter,' she says, laying her hands palm up on the table. 'He thought he was making himself king. And that all he had to do to win my support was create a role in England for Henry. Earl of Richmond would do. I was humble. I asked nothing more.'

'And you'd have killed him too, after?'

'Yes.'

'This is a very full confession.'

She shrugs. 'You'd find it all out anyway. Think of me as a chess player. Explaining my moves now the game is over.'

'You've never beaten me at chess.'

A single bark of bitter laughter that turns into a sob. 'Yes,' she says. 'I know. Though I've studied your game for years.'

55.

March to April 1484

Westminster Sanctuary

'Elizabeth.'

Cecily doesn't bow and Elizabeth, plain Dame Grey, no longer queen, gives no other return to her greeting than a slight and imperious inclination of her head. There can be no doubt that ten months in sanctuary have aged her. How could they not? Her hair is now more white than silver, the lines about her eyes etched into an expression of suspicion and mistrust. But she's as slender as ever, and the skin stretched over the fine bones of her cheeks is near translucent in the low morning sun that glitters the abbot's physic garden. The blue-grey fur of her hood, cut from the winter backs of northern squirrels, is soft and bright as hoar frost.

They stand on God's ground where no man holds sway. From here Elizabeth could turn on her heel and return to the cramped rooms of the abbot's lodging where her five daughters wait. Or she could summon them, and walk with Cecily through the gate in the wall that leads to the world. Richard has promised them protection if they leave sanctuary. He has sworn it to the lords and the council. A not ungenerous pension for Elizabeth, a home of her choice away from the court, good marriages for her daughters when the time's right to make them. A pardon for past treasons. A wiping of the slate.

It's too cold to sit, so they walk the narrow paths between the garden's beds. Bare soil is speared by hopeful shoots, the grass beyond nodding with snowdrops, yellowed with aconite. Elizabeth walks steadily, as if without thought of direction.

'You must know this garden well, by now,' Cecily says.

'Every inch. I've walked it every day for near a year. Except those days when I was too afraid to venture outside for fear your son's men would come and drag me out by my hair.'

'And yet, they never did, did they?'

'Where are my royal sons?'

It would be, of course, the first question.

'Not dead, despite what Margaret told you.'

'Then I may see them?'

'Best you don't. But I can show you this.'

She takes from the purse at her waist a paper and watches as Elizabeth unfolds it and reads. She knows that Elizabeth will find there a report of her sons' progress. Carefully curated, of course, to give no clear idea of their location or the identity of their keepers. It will tell her Edward's Latin is good, though his French better. That his brother Richard excels at archery and was gifted a fine bow at Christmas. That in November, on his thirteenth birthday, Edward joined the hunt and brought down his first hind. That they are in good health, though Edward lost two teeth to rot in the autumn. Inside the letter is another, smaller slip on which each boy has signed his name. Edward in a steady cursive script. Richard with a careless smudging hand.

'These prove nothing,' says Elizabeth, holding her boys' names up close to her eyes. 'They could be forged.'

'Yes, they could. You'll have to trust us for that.'

'Trust you?' Elizabeth sneers. 'You said you'd see my son crowned.'

'That was before you tried to kill mine.'

Elizabeth folds both papers, puts them in her sleeve. They've come to the end of a path and so turn again, walking back towards the abbey's looming towers.

'Why does it matter to you?' asks Elizabeth. 'Whether I stay here or leave.'

'I think rather it must matter to you. Is this where you want to end your days?' She squints into the sun. Why must everything always be such an effort with this woman?

'Face facts, Elizabeth. Last month Parliament confirmed in every way Richard's title and your children's bastardy. Margaret's plots and scheming are over. Buckingham's dead. No saviour is coming to free you. You're being offered a way out. If I were you, I'd take it.'

'If you were me, you'd have some plan. Some connivance. You always do.'

'Not this time, Elizabeth.'

'You do nothing that doesn't serve you. Why do you want me out?'

'I'll be honest with you, as I've always been. Margaret's lies have damaged Richard. There are men, still, who call him murderer.'

'All he need do to prove himself otherwise is to show my sons, alive.'

Cecily sighs. That's true enough. She's urged him to it a dozen times. But he says he won't expose them to such a circus, nor make a spectacle of them in men's eyes. 'Haven't we done them enough harm, between us?' he says. 'They're settled where they are. I've set their course and won't be moved from it.'

He can be as stubborn as ever his father was. And as wrong-headed.

'Richard won't do it. A kindness, though you'll not see it that way.'

'If I leave here, you might well imprison me.'

'We might. But not likely. Take Margaret for your example of our conduct. A woman might burn for treason such as hers and yet she lives. Why would we treat you less kindly?'

'She isn't free, though.'

'A mild enough captivity. Margaret's husband is her gaoler. Her confinement is his duty for which he answers to the King.'

In truth, Cecily's not sure how kind it is, though Richard meant it so. Margaret no longer has property, possessions, liberty or hope. Her servants and her household are taken from her. She wept when she was told how it would be. Not, Cecily thinks, from relief. Such a woman as Margaret might prefer to have burned than to live so denuded in the power of a man.

'In your eyes, madam,' says Elizabeth, 'I'm no less guilty than she.'

'That's true.'

'Though what you offer me is rather better.'

Cecily halts and Elizabeth can do nothing but turn and face her. 'It would be hard to burn a woman who was once a queen. And Richard, God love him, is more merciful than I. So, you'll go free. But don't be mistaken, you'll be watched. You may appoint your own servants, within reason, but you'd be foolish not to assume at least one of them will be ours. But you'll not be confined, and your daughters will have marriages and be welcome at court.' She points. 'You want them to have a life, don't you? All you have to do is gather them up and walk through that gate.' She folds her hands in her sleeves. 'Our best offer, Elizabeth.'

And so Elizabeth comes out and Richard greets her in Westminster Hall, calls her sister and kisses her cheeks.

Days later, he's on the road again. As if he can't bear to be in the city, to be anything but on the move, as if he'll slip from the knife edge he walks on if he stands still a moment to look about. He lives in expectation of fresh invasion. Henry Tudor's back in Brittany, his uncle Jasper with him.

Henry has sworn a holy oath to try again. When it suits Duke Francis or the French well enough to back him, he will. He says he'll put down the usurper Richard, he'll avenge the murder of Edward's sons. He'll marry their sister and create a royal house to stand forever – York and Lancaster united as one. His will be the last great war, he says. He barely stops short of calling it holy.

Cecily can't help but remember that first Christmas after

Edward was crowned, when in a fit of kindness she let Margaret spend the season with her gap-toothed skinny-limbed son. I had him within my arm's reach, she thinks. I should have taken him out and drowned him. I should have put him in a barrel and rolled him down a hill.

To take England Henry will need more than the seven ships Brittany gave him last time. But the French look ready to help. The spider Louis is dead. Scuttled off within half a year of Edward, leaving a child heir, just the same. The boy's sister rules as regent, styles herself 'Madame'. But there are men – 'Always, there are men,' complains Cecily – who jostle and push for power. It serves Madame well, when the mood is on her, to pour vitriol on an Englishman who has stolen a boy's throne. 'We will not stand for such things,' she says. 'In England or in France.'

Richard spends Easter at Burton, marks the anniversary of his brother's death at Nottingham. He'll stay there a while, in the heart of the country. A good place to watch and wait. He writes Cecily that he distracts himself by re-writing the laws of England. Juries will be regulated and impartial, a man's goods not seized till he's proved guilty of a crime. A new court of requests will give legal advice to anyone, whether they've money to pay for it or not.

'The noble and the rich have owned the law too long,' he writes.

'Yes,' Cecily chides. 'They like it that way. And you depend on rich men and nobles.'

He seems, for a while, happier. Anne is with him. He writes of warmer weather, good hunting and close friends. 'We think of sending for Edward to join us here from Middleham,' he writes. 'You'll approve, I'm sure. Taking my son riding in the forest will keep me from the law.'

But before Cecily can applaud this idea it's too late either for Richard to send or Edward to come. Death brings the boy from Middleham to his Heavenly Father, and his eight-year-old limbs lie shroud-wrapped and still.

'They say it was sudden,' Richard's letter confides. 'Woke complaining of belly ache and wouldn't eat his breakfast, by suppertime they'd given him last rites. They say he cried out all day for his mother and, at the end, for me. I would have ridden through fire.'

But two messengers had come within three hours. The first said, 'Come quickly.' The second met them at the gate and said, 'Too late.'

'Anne is mad with grief,' Richard writes.

Cecily sits heavily down, clutching at the dry bed of her own old womb. She's lost count of how many children Anne's miscarried. 'Sometimes I think I should keep from her,' Richard once confided. 'Since it's the cause of such sorrow and loss. But I think that would grieve us both more.'

Well, there's cause enough now for grieving. A childless king, a queen bereft, invasion threatened and a kingdom staggering, unsteady on its feet.

'Why could Margaret Beaufort's son not die?' she challenges her confessor. 'Why must he be so lusty and so strong while this boy, so needed and so loved, is taken?'

He gives her penance for vicious thoughts. Hail Marys and Our Fathers she's not sorry enough to say. But in all of her churches she orders masses, choirs to sing a soul to Heaven, the lighting of candles to guide its starry flight. She keeps an all-night vigil before the boy is buried, but God keeps His silent distance. Only the ghosts of her own dead sons crowd at her back: grey-eyed Edmund on the tail of his father's battle, George with his vicious teeth stained red with wine, Edward's kissing mouth a gaping darkness, hollow and empty as his crown.

56.

Westminster

Twelve years ago, Anne wore green to her wedding. Pale patterned velvet soft as a sage leaf's dusty underbelly. It reminded Cecily then of verdancy, of dawn grass under a dewy shimmer. She wears it now for the Christmas feast, and it conjures only an image of rot, a bloom of decay on gone-over fruit. There can be no question that, within her velvets, Anne is dying.

Richard leads his wife slowly through Westminster's crowded hall, her arm threaded tight through his. Though she stops here or there to greet friends with a word, there is only relief in her eyes when she reaches her place at high table, and when Richard eases her into her chair, her skeletal fingers scrabble at its arms.

It's for this reason that Cecily has braved the weather to come to Westminster for the season. Richard's letter blew into Berkhamsted on a cold December wind. 'Please come,' it begged. 'God help us, we must put on a show.'

As she travelled, rain turned to snow, so that she arrived chilled and ill-tempered, but a good fire and a sound night's sleep and she was herself again. How can it be that her old bones go rattling on, while those of a woman not yet thirty look set to crumble to dust?

'I'm well enough,' is all Anne will say. But Cecily watches as she fingers each course set before her, turns away titbits offered on the tip of Richard's knife. Only, she sucks on a little marchpane when the sweets come. Craving sugar, Cecily supposes, the forgiving break of it on her tongue.

When the music strikes, Cecily, sitting at Richard's other side, hears him whisper, 'You're certain?'

And Anne urgently replies, 'Yes, yes.'

It's expected that King and Queen will open the dancing, and Anne seems determined to do all that's expected. Though her steps are slow, they are steady, and only at the turns does she falter, leaning in. The tune is mercifully short, and here comes Richard leading her back, his face pale, his mouth a brittle line of worry. Then, as they reach the dais, Anne turns to her husband, a hand against his breast and urges, 'Dance now with your niece.'

He falters a moment, then nods, and when he has her seated again, walks slowly back to the floor, holds out a determined hand and says, 'Will the lady Elizabeth dance with me?'

And Edward's eldest steps boldly forward as the players lift their instruments and couples take their places in a sigh of silk.

Anne leans across Richard's empty place, her eyes unnaturally bright, her cheeks high with fever, and breathes beneath the music, 'Isn't she like her father?'

And, Cecily concedes, she is. Her bright smile, her sure steps, as if the floor and all the turning world were hers, so that Richard seems almost diminished by her, smaller and more slight as the turns of the dance lead him ever further down the spangled hall.

'But her gown, Anne,' Cecily says. For Lizzie is wearing Anne's same green velvet, shot with silver to mark a difference.

'It becomes her better than I,' says Anne, rueful. 'My gift. To show the world we cherish her. That she's ours, not Henry Tudor's.'

But Cecily can only think that, all unwitting, Anne has shown the world an image of death and life, and of Richard caught between them in a dance.

'I'm told the King of Portugal's sister is short of a husband,' Anne confides when Cecily visits her rooms next morning. She's still in her bed, her head overlarge against the pillow, her body barely a stir beneath the coverlet. 'I've mentioned her already to Richard. Devout as well as beautiful, apparently, and with a serious turn of mind. She should suit him.'

'You're all business,' says Cecily.

'It's as well, don't you think? I did my best last night, but I don't expect I fooled anyone. With every breath I wound him. People say he killed his brother's sons and is punished for it by the death of his own. With a sickly wife, he looks more guilty still. Besides,' and here her voice comes close to breaking, 'he needs another son and I can't give him one. Best let the Portuguese lady try.'

She coughs, and the linen square she presses to her mouth comes away tinged pink and the spit that sheens her teeth is flecked with blood.

Recovering, she adds, 'Portugal also has a cousin in need of a wife. The Duke of Beja. He'll do well for Lizzie.'

'Well. Certainly it would be good to have the girl quickly married.'

'Yes.' Anne's smile is a twisted, painful grimace. 'If I'm quick about my dying Richard can broker both marriages together.'

Cecily's eyes fill with tears, her throat with choking shame. This morning she went early to Anne's physician and asked, 'It's the consumption, isn't it? How long might she last?' and was relieved when he answered, not long.

'Anne,' she says swallowing hard, 'doesn't it hurt to speak so?'

Anne makes no answer, but her hand scrabbles among the sheets to find Cecily's, and its bony grip is desperate and tight.

Anne struggles on through January, but come February can't rise from her bed and her physicians bar Richard from her chambers.

'The contagion,' they mutter, averting their eyes.

And his counsellors say, more forcefully, 'You'd be a fool to risk it.'

He defies them, sits all day by Anne's side and will not shift. Come evening, desperate, they beg Cecily to come and coax him. She arrives just as the light is fading and candles are being lit against the dark. Anne greets her, tries a smile and says, 'Lady, will you take my husband away and feed him, you see he's thin as water.'

'Come now, Richard,' Cecily urges, but he'll neither look at nor heed her, only he thins his mouth and shakes his head, and clasps Anne's wasted hands more tightly within his. But when Anne says, 'Richard, I'm tired now,' and Cecily urges, 'If she's to live, she must rest,' he nods at last and pulls himself to his feet. When he leans down to kiss her, Anne finds strength to turn her face from him, and cries out, 'Richard, no. The danger!' So that he must satisfy himself with kisses to her fingers, desperate and hungry, while tears score his cheeks and Anne sobs.

Cecily guides him to the door. He comes slow, as if with every step he drags the world's reluctant weight behind him and, at any moment, may resolve to sever himself from it and turn back, content to draw an early death from the poison of his wife's embrace.

'So, she is lost to me already,' he tells Cecily, as the room's door closes soft behind them and they face the shadow-filled corridor that leads back to the duties of a king. 'Lost the day our son died, I think, and my love not enough to bind her to life.'

Cecily takes his arm and walks with him, and at length he speaks again. 'You've buried a husband and nine children, Mother. How do you bear it?' She only shakes her head. For the moment she can't speak, for she sees the pain of those many losses forged into a single blade and set against Anne's failing heart. Anne had only one child, a single treasure irreplaceable and lost. It's beyond bearing. She turns now to her own singular son, lays her hands against his face and kisses his brow. When she finds her words again, they are a surprise to them both. 'Because I still have you, Richard. And while you live, your father cannot die.'

Cecily sits with Anne most mornings. She believes herself leathery enough to be immune to sickness, but at the doctors' urging keeps to the far side of the room and breathes through a nosegay of gillyflower and tansy. She writes to Annette, 'Come south and pray for your mistress.'

But the old nurse sends word that such a journey is beyond her now, and besides, she's lost all faith in prayer since she shrouded Richard's son for his burying.

Letters are sent to Portugal, and Lizzie, when told of them, nods and asks for a tutor to coach her in the language. '*Eu não quero Henrique Tudor*,' she learns to say. 'I don't want Henry Tudor at all. Give me instead the Duque de Beja. Give me Portugal and the sun.'

March comes and Richard sends Anne primroses every day, tiny bunches tied with white cord. Cecily lays them on the pillow beside her and says, 'Richard tells me you've always loved them. That you wait for their flowering every spring.'

Anne's beyond talking now, but she turns her head to see them, cracked lips drawing away from yellowed teeth loose in her gums. On the sixteenth day he sends them, she doesn't turn. Her face has fallen open as if the hinge of its jaw is gone, and her breath quakes and rattles among its broken pieces. She made confession days ago, so when the priest comes at noon and marks the cross on her breast and brow there's nothing more to be done.

Cecily prays for the rattle to stop now. This death is too awful and is taking too long. Then suddenly, from beyond the walls, comes the sound of scurrying feet, of nervous voices and dogs whining and people crying out, 'The light, the light!' And when Cecily hurries to unshutter the window she sees the bright day turning dark and the sun eclipsed, smudged from the sky as if God has set his thumb to strike it out. When she turns again, the room is quiet and Anne is gone.

They bury her at Westminster and already, among the congregation, in the corridors of the court, in taverns and on street corners, rumour spreads like a fresh contagion: Richard poisoned his barren wife to be rid of her. He wants another, fertile queen. His lecherous thoughts turn to his niece, Elizabeth. 'Remember how he danced with her at Christmas?' people whisper. 'How her dress mocked the dying Queen? He murdered her brothers, the monster, and now he'll have her.'

He is distraught. 'Pay no heed,' Cecily tells him. 'Get the girl into Portugal and the gossip will die down soon enough.'

She knows it won't, though. These lies come from across the Channel, from Henry Tudor's court in exile, now cosseted in Paris by the new French king.

'If I hear of such things coming from your tongue,' Cecily writes Margaret, 'I swear I'll come and tear it out.'

Richard defies her and his council. He issues a proclamation to be read in every city, and goes himself before London's mayor and council to swear that it has never entered his mind to make such a marriage with his niece, and that his heart is as heavy for the death of his wife as ever man's could be. When it's done he comes to Baynard's and stands at Cecily's door insensate, so that she must draw him in, strip his chilled body of its clothes, put him to bed and call a physician to bleed him of his melancholy humour.

Next morning, when he's pale as death but on his feet again, she urges him once more. 'This can't go on,' she says. 'Get Lizzie married into Portugal and show the world your brother's living sons.'

He only shakes his head and says that he will speak again to Portugal. 'But I will not have my nephews hounded and harassed.'

'Yet you are hounded and harassed yourself,' she reminds him.

She goes back to Berkhamsted and leaves him to it. He's talking to Brittany and Burgundy, trying to wean them away from their alliance with France. He's speaking to the King of Portugal, whose sister is slow to make up her mind. He sends Lizzie north, to stifle the gossip. From there she sends him notes, increasingly frantic. 'Give me the Duke of Beja,' she writes. 'Give me comfort and my heart's desire.'

57.

May 1485

Berkhamsted

By the time Cecily sees her son again, May's in. He comes to her in Berkhamsted, where the orchards are thick with blossom and the carp hang lazy in their pools. But there's no pleasure in such signs of summer, they only mean the fighting season's here again. Richard's on his way to Nottingham, that still point at England's heart where he'll muster men and wait to see from which direction trouble comes. There can be little doubt. In the French court they've taken to calling Henry Tudor King of England.

'A little pre-emptive,' says Cecily.

'Their Parliament has granted him funds for an invasion,' says Richard. 'He has a fleet in preparation at Harfleur.'

She's coaxed him out into the sunshine of her garden. He looks like he's spent too many hours indoors, dark-eyed and pasty-faced. And since he arrived last night he's commandeered her hall and been cooped up there with his officers and the men of his household. They look as harassed as he looks despondent, bothering over endless documents, reports and commissions, troop details and requisitions, the movement of arms and men. They'd looked up at her almost with relief when she strode in among them at the end of the afternoon and asked, 'Richard, have you come here for my company or to use up my ink?'

Now he walks beside her, at the slow pace she sets, his eyes on the path before him, his hands still busy, turning his father's ring about that snipped finger.

'So, he'll come then,' she says. 'Henry Tudor.'

'Yes.' He shrugs, an awkward roll of his shoulder that seems painful. 'Let him. I'm as ready as I can be and would as soon have it over.'

She nods. They've come to the end of the path, where an oak tree stands with a bench set beneath it that looks out across the garden thick with roses towards the sun-drenched walls of the keep. She brings him to sit beside her. There is a rill of water playing, the hum of bees.

He lifts his head at last to look about him. 'It is lovely here,' he says. 'I can see why you like it.'

She teases. 'I thought you preferred the north's rugged moors to our tame southern gardens.'

'Ah, well. I've been cooped up in Westminster half a year. An hour among your roses must do me for a holiday.'

Hands on thighs, he stretches his back to rest his head against the old tree's trunk, his eyes closed against the brightness. But it seems he stretches to ease an ache rather than to bask in sunlight. He grimaces and lets out a noisy breath, before he shakes himself, lets his hands fall between his knees and returns to studying the ground. She's afraid for him. He doesn't look like a man ready for a fight. He must be coaxed.

'You must look forward, Richard. Perhaps you can go north again when this is done.'

'Perhaps. It's hard to imagine.' His fingers find his ruby and set it on a turn. 'You never went back to Fotheringhay, did you? After Father.'

'No. I didn't.'

'I think it's the same.'

'Then make me a promise.' She takes his hand and chafes it. 'If the north can't comfort you, visit me here a year from now. Henry Tudor will be dead and forgotten and you'll have a new wife on your arm. Perhaps even a child in her belly.'

She'd hoped to cheer him, but his face falls and a hard line scores deep between his brows, as if a new wife and the getting of a son is nothing more than the next hard task he'll be set to.

'I wonder what a new wife would make of me.' He signals with a hand across his shoulder to his back. 'Of this. Anne never seemed to mind it.'

'No sensible woman would.'

'Oh, I think you know that's not true. Perhaps she'll say, "He must truly be a homicide and a tyrant, look how God has marked him."'

'You're neither of those things.'

He grimaces and his voice is flat. 'Am I not?'

She decides to be harsh, to shake him out of this. 'Why?' she challenges. 'Have you killed your brother's sons as people say?'

He's quiet a moment, then, 'Perhaps I have. Between us both, Mother, you and I, perhaps we have.' The ring on his finger is turning again. 'Or made their lives impossible, it's much the same.'

'I've never heard you talk nonsense before. I thought you were my clever son.'

'If Henry Tudor wins, what do you think he'll do to them? To marry Lizzie he must declare her legitimate. He can't do that without making them legitimate too, and with a better claim to England's throne than his own. He'll kill them and say the tyrant did it.'

'If he can find them. You've got them hidden, haven't you? Besides,' she takes his shoulders, turns him to face her, 'he won't win.'

'And if he doesn't, what's for them then? A whole life hidden away? We've told ourselves they'll accept what's been done to them. What if they don't? There'll always be someone to whisper in their ear that I've wronged them. Will I have to fight them in the end?'

She shakes him. 'If it comes to it.' But the thought is terrible.

'Oh, Mother.' He rolls his head, all sadness, and his hands are gentle at her wrists as he pushes them away. 'Do you think I could?'

'Richard, God has given you the throne. You must . . .'

'No, Mother.' He raises a hand, fine-boned and emphatic. 'I took it, remember? You told me at the time it was a choice.'

'I say you chose right.'

'I know. And so I convinced myself. And church and state said yes to it. But God has taken my wife and my son, so I'm no longer sure what He thinks.' He looks away and back again. 'Perhaps Henry Tudor will tell me.'

She's frightened into anger now. 'Oh, is that what you think, Richard? When will you learn? A strong man shapes God's will, he doesn't submit to it. Your brother won every battle because he never gave God the option to be on anyone's side but his.'

Two days later, when she bids him farewell at the gate, he does as he's never done. He takes her hands in his and kisses them, holds them against his heart and says, 'I'm sorry I'm not Edward.'

She pulls her hands free, wraps them in the hair either side of his face, pulls so it will hurt a little, leans in and says, 'You're Richard. You're my son. And nothing less to me than he was. It's my most grievous sin if I made you think so.' And it's true, though she's learned it late.

It's very quiet when he's gone. So she takes herself to the room he slept in, sits on the bed already stripped and tries to conjure the feel and scent and sound of him. On the desk beneath the window sits his father's ring upon a slip of paper, written in his own hand. 'Mother,' it says, 'I think it's time this came back to you.' And signed, 'Richard, your son.'

58.

24 August 1485

A rider clatters into Berkhamsted at evening, as a late slant of sun through Cecily's casement turns the golden beads of her rosary to fire. It only takes a moment for his feet to hit the cobbles, for a groom to grab his bridle, for her steward to rush from the keep and catch his arm before he falls. And in that moment, her heart cracks, for the face that casts desperately about him, and the voice that cries, 'I must see the King's Mother,' belong not to some common messenger, but to Francis Lovell, who is Richard's chancellor, his friend since the old days with Warwick. They belong to a man who has seen the end of things. A desperate man. A man on the run.

Five days past, Richard wrote that he was leaving Nottingham, riding south and west to face Henry Tudor, who had landed in Wales with a rag-tag army of traitors and French mercenaries.

'Give me your prayers, Mother,' his letter said, 'as I give you mine. God will judge if they're worth anything.'

He meant: God will judge us.

And in those five days she has lost herself in prayer. She has kept the hours. She has fumbled the words of the Ave and Pater Noster in her hands until the sense of them has gone from her and every rub of bead against her thumb has become a single word: Richard. But now, as footsteps come rapid on the stair, she draws herself to her feet and lets the golden string pool from her fingers to the table, tangled and senseless and done. Her knuckles ache, pain sears her knees, and the old familiar pull of grief threatens to take her down. But she grasps for a chairback, checks herself and recovers. The door is opening behind her as she squares her shoulders and turns.

She has seen this man a hundred times, walking with Richard, handing him a paper, their heads bent together over some point of business. He has a good face, steady and calm. It's as raw as beef now, flayed by the sun and scoured by the wind of fast riding, his eyes red from the road's grit or weeping.

'Come, Lord Lovell,' she says, her hands clasped in her sleeves to still them. 'Whatever you have to tell me, I will hear.'

'Richard . . .' he says as he come towards her, and then he's gulping back a cry, his bruised hand to his brow, his knees set to buckle. Her steward pushes a chair under him as he half sits, half falls. Seeing it done, she signals the man away.

'We will manage,' she says. 'Lord Lovell and I.'

When the door is closed again she pours wine, marvelling that her hand can be so steady while her heart shakes loose within her frame. She passes the cup to Francis, watches as he gulps, gasps and draws a dusty sleeve across his mouth.

'I think you're here to tell me that my son Richard is dead.'

He nods, the empty cup cradled in his hand, his mouth a bitter twist. 'Yes.'

She sits now because she must. Because her head feels broken, open to the air, and the breath of her body pouring from it. Because it is one thing to live in dread of an inevitable, fearful something, another to hear a living voice confirm it.

'I'm sorry,' he says. 'Richard told me, if I lived and he didn't, I should come, if I could, to tell you. That you should hear it first from a friend.'

She wants to say, but I barely know you. And how did you survive when he did not? Why didn't you cast your body between the blade and him? But she knows how chance in battle leaves one man standing and takes his neighbour, how in the press of fighting, men are wrestled far apart.

Richard, she thinks, would say it differently. He would say, if God has marked a man for death no shield can save him.

So she only asks how, and when.

The armies met two days ago outside Leicester, he tells her. And Richard died in the bloody thick of it, fighting on foot, unhorsed and betrayed. He stretches out a hand, shaking. 'Within an arm's reach of Tudor. A sword's length.' His fist closes, draws back to his breast. 'I saw him go down, but couldn't reach him. Then there was a horse without a rider. So I took it, and I fled.'

She nods, yes. Men will flee. 'Who betrayed him?'

He almost spits the name. 'The Stanleys.'

Now her fingers clench till bone grinds on bone. 'Thomas Stanley?'

Margaret Beaufort's husband and gaoler. Margaret Beaufort, who she let live.

He nods. 'Yes. And his brother, William. Though ordered, they didn't ride with us or come to the muster, but on the morning of battle there they were . . .'

'. . . lined up beside Tudor.'

His face twists with disgust. 'No. Hovering on our flanks. Hedging their bets.'

'And what,' she asks, 'brought them in against us in the end?'

He shakes his head. 'We bettered Tudor for numbers, but it was clear from the start the Stanleys held the balance. Norfolk, with our vanguard, was taking a beating. Richard called for reserves, but they didn't come. Then one of the scouts pointed and we saw Tudor himself with just a handful, sliding off west to where the Stanleys' army stood. As if he doubted them as much as we did, as if he went to chide them and be sure. And Richard said, "There's our target." ' He runs shaking hands through filthy hair. 'It was madness.'

So Richard had seen a chance and taken it, leading his two hundred household knights at a gallop up the battlefield's broiling flank to strike at his enemy's heart. He got within an arm's reach. A sword's length. A prayer. He'd brought down Tudor's standard bearer, so that the dragon of Cadwallader lay snarling in the mud. He'd brought his shoulder back for just one more blow and then . . .

'It was madness,' Francis says again, his voice breaking. 'But we came so close.'

Her head fills with the sound of it; the ground-shattering rush of the Stanleys' three thousand, the crash of contact, the screaming of horses under a barrage of blows. Her breast is shattered by the spear thrust that burst his destrier's heart and brought him down. And behind her eyes, blind to all else, she sees him rise from the wreckage, Richard, the last of her sons, bright in his armour, dark in his doubt, asking God with his body if he has the right to live and rule.

She falls, lost beneath the battering of a hundred blows, until she feels the shaking arms of Francis Lovell pulling her upright, back into life. This time he pours for her, and she takes the cup and drinks. The wine is red, thick and warm, and coats her tongue with the copper taste of blood.

They gave Francis a bed in the north tower, in a hidden room, for he's a hunted man, and through the short sleepless night she thinks of him there.

'What will you do now?' she asked before they parted.

'I must get abroad.' But she saw how his eyes slid from her and wonders now what he's about. What other commission Richard has given him that he keeps hidden?

So next morning, early, when he's up with the dawn and ready for the saddle, she's there before him, waiting in the courtyard. 'There'll be a watch for you on every port.'

'I know.' He looks about him, as if he expects a hand on his shoulder even here, even now.

She lifts his hand and puts a purse of money in it. 'Can you get as far as Colchester, do you think?'

'I hope so.'

'Then go to the abbey. I'm known there. They'll give you sanctuary if you tell them I'm good for the debt.'

'Thank you.'

He unbuckles his saddlebag, tucks the purse deep inside.

'You can wait out the time there. At least you'll be closer to the coast.'

'Yes.'

She's silent while the bag is latched again, while his horse, a fresh one from her own stable, shuffles its feet. Then she has to ask. 'You go to Edward's sons?'

He won't say it, but he leans against the horse's neck and nods.

'Will you tell me where they are?'

His hands, still shaky, busy themselves with a stirrup leather. 'Richard said best you don't know.'

'Why?'

'Because Tudor's men will ask you. He wanted you to be able to swear ignorance and not perjure yourself.'

'Did he not know how many perjured oaths I've sworn?'

He's done with the leathers and rests his brow against the saddle's pommel. 'I'm sorry.'

'Are they beyond Tudor's reach?'

He shrugs. 'For now.'

'Well. He has put them beyond mine at least.'

His face twists as if her voice is a blade and cuts him.

She hadn't meant to hurt and so concedes, 'Perhaps it's for the best. I am, it turns out, not a nurturing mother.'

He seems not to hear. 'Tudor will marry your granddaughter. You'll be kin to the Queen. I hope it will be enough to keep you safe.'

'It hardly matters.'

'It mattered to Richard.'

If he doesn't go now, he'll see her weeping and she couldn't bear it. 'You should ride.'

He nods, heaves himself into the saddle and gathers the reins in his hands. 'I hope I haven't endangered you further, coming here.'

'I'll deny ever seeing you. I will say: Francis who?'

'Thank you.' Then he turns his restless horse in a circle, sets his spurs against its flanks and is gone.

59.

24 August to 10 September 1485

She has acquired the habit, in these weeks, of waiting upon God, so with Francis Lovell gone, she puts herself in His presence, listening only to the depth of His silence and throwing into it no challenge or plea. There is nothing He could grant that would bring her comfort, so no need of words. Dead men, after all, don't walk back into the world.

The people of her household go about, of course, and the news they bring back finds its way to her. That Tudor has dated his reign from the day before the battle, so that all who fought for Richard can be condemned as traitors. That he scours the country in search of Edward's sons. That he comes soon to London to be enthroned, but has had already a godless crowning, when Thomas Stanley recovered Richard's coronet from the field and placed it, bloodstained and battered, on his head. She hears that Richard's body was brought naked over a horse to Leicester and left two days in its blood beneath the market cross. She imagines how men would have come out of their houses to stare at it, how they'd have pointed to its twisted spine and spat.

She needs no imagination to predict what use Margaret Beaufort will make of it.

'See how his sins are revealed in him,' she'll say. 'Give thanks for my saviour son, who has put down a God-marked monster. A tyrant. A murderer. A curse.'

It will help people forget that all they know of Henry Tudor is that his father was nothing but a commoner's get on a widowed queen and that his mother's family was barred by bastardy from the Crown. And the voices that would speak for Richard will be silenced. And men like Francis Lovell, who knew him well, will keep their mouths shut, or run.

'Crook-backed Richard usurped his nephew's throne,' Margaret will say. She will have it written down and sent about. 'He made him and his brother bastards and killed them in their sleep. Now my Henry will right those wrongs by making their sister his queen, and her sons will inherit the crown the tyrant stole.'

And the people of England, who just want a bit of peace, and the nobles of England that disliked Richard's clean-sweeping laws, will say, 'Well then, haven't we had a lucky escape.'

Yes. Cecily knows exactly how it will be done. Didn't Margaret tell her last time they met? 'I've been studying your game for years.'

She's ready when the summons comes. A request to attend the King's Mother, at Westminster. Not an order. Though the escort sent to fetch her is well-bladed and she's told none of her own people need come.

It's mid-September but warm still, and the fields she passes through are busy, the last of the harvest coming in and the ground made ready for the plough. Spring lambs are being weaned for the autumn market and their mothers' plaintive calling echoes across the turning earth. The world that stopped for her on the battlefield at Bosworth spins relentlessly on and on.

When she is led through the corridors of Westminster she sees few faces she recognizes. Those she does, turn carefully away. She is brought to the rooms that were Elizabeth's, that are singled out for the use of queens. They pass beyond the audience chamber to a private room, withdrawn and quiet. The door is opened for her and there, by a window, Margaret stands very still, while the women who wait on her, and a secretary who has been scribbling at a desk, rise slowly and bow.

Cecily knows well enough what's expected. She steps forward, falls into a deep obeisance and says, 'Lady.'

And then Margaret comes to her, orders the room emptied of all others, lays a hand on her shoulder and says, 'Will you sit?'

They are silent till settled, then Margaret speaks again. 'It seemed right to greet you here. I'll vacate these rooms, of course, when your granddaughter marries my son. Though I'll stay close at all times as her guide. She'll be in need of guidance, no doubt. In the meantime, until she's married, she'll be in my care and so, today, I stand in her place.' She lifts a hand as though the conclusion is obvious. She is, beyond question now, England's first lady. The King's Mother.

'Is she here?' asks Cecily. 'My granddaughter?'

'Men have been sent to fetch her. We expect her any day.'

'And her mother?'

'Brought from her home some days ago. We were most eager to bring her into our care.'

'I'm sure you were.'

Margaret feigns a sad look. 'I'm afraid she won't see you. She believes your son murdered hers. I'm sure you'll understand that, in this new world, it's best she continues to believe that. She'll grieve, of course, but it will make her more comfortable as Queen's Mother.'

'And more conformable to you, I imagine.'

'We hope so.'

'Whereas you and I both know her sons are still very much alive.'

Margaret's eyes, focused hard on her now, have lost none of their sharpness. 'I imagine, if I ask you where they are, you won't tell me.'

'No,' Cecily says, emphatic. 'Because I know what you intend towards them. But in truth I can't,' she confides, 'because I don't know. It was Richard's best kept secret. He would entrust it no more to me than to you.'

Margaret's eyes flicker as Cecily watches her. 'Of course, you may be lying.'

'I may, absolutely. So what will you do, Margaret? Starve me till I talk? Call me traitor and threaten to burn me? I've seen a woman burn. It would have frightened me once. Not now.'

Margaret looks away and, for a moment, the face that has been so smooth and firm falls a little, as if she has taken a small pain. 'I would do neither of those things to you.'

'Why not?' Cecily says, allowing her voice to sharpen. 'You've done far worse.'

Margaret nods her head, sighs a little, clasps her hands, still small as a child's, then looks up as if resolved on something. 'I suppose I have. I will answer to God for it, but not to you. I told you once I would do anything to bring my son safely home.'

'You did.'

'And you told me, when my hope was at its lowest ebb, that there is always a way. That I had only to find it.'

She remembers. So even this end rests with her. 'Oh, Margaret.'

And suddenly those small hands reach out and take hers, tightly. 'If there had been any other way.'

And suddenly it's too much. There is such a pain within her breast. She feels the bones of her face twist and a single cry escapes before she can bite it back. Then Margaret is on her knees before her, her thin lips close and pleading.

'Please don't weep, Cecily,' she says. 'I can bear anything but that I have brought you to weeping.'

So she seals her eyes and slows her breath until she is numb again, and when she has recovered speech she says, 'I will not weep.' Because, after all, if there is any woman alive who understands what a mother will do for the safety of her sons, surely it is she? 'Though I will never forgive you.'

'I know.'

'I will go to my grave cursing you.'

'I know. Of course. But will you let it be?'

And because she has no more sons to fight for, because she's old and tired and sees nothing else that can be done, because

Edward's daughter will at least be Queen and her sons rule when Henry Tudor lies mouldering, and because in the end, surely, it's a woman's work to salvage something, Cecily nods her head and says, 'I will.'

When they've sat a while, when they are quiet and composed and their breath has become even, Margaret says, 'Let me tell you how it will be. You will live untouched. Your estates, your wealth, you'll keep them. You'll be honoured at court whenever you choose to come.'

'I'll be watched.'

'You would expect that.'

'I should have watched you better.'

'Yes,' a softening of the voice, an acceptance, a nod. 'You should.'

'I'll give you a word of advice.'

Margaret cocks her head, waiting.

'Don't trust the Stanleys.'

Margaret smiles, tight. 'Yes. Your advice is always good. I know what my husband is and what use I put him to. For the moment, he's the King's stepfather. So.'

'And now I'll tell you something true. You'll never know a minute's peace. You'll be wondering, always, where Edward's sons are and when they'll come against your boy. And when you die, there'll be no rest either, because no sin can be absolved unless you renounce the fruits of it. And you'll never give up Henry, or the crown you've bought for him with treachery and lies.'

'No. I must learn to live with that.'

Cecily looks at her, at the pinched resolute face of a woman that has waited so long, fought so hard and dares even her own damnation. 'Well,' she says, 'in that too you must take your lesson from me.'

The thin lips almost smile. 'Yes. Always, and in all things.'

Margaret comes to her feet, smooths her skirts, reaches a hand to help Cecily rise.

'Will you come and meet my son? I've spoken of you to him. He will accept your obeisance. It is expected that you will give it.'

So Cecily rises, and follows her through the corridors of the court, between the mass of courtiers scurrying for their place in this new world, past the line of petitioners waiting for their moment with this new king. They come at last to the great hall where Edward once held audience, where he greeted men with a loose-limbed smile and her, always, with a kiss, and there, in his place on the dais, sits Henry Tudor, thin as wire, spare of feature, leaning earnestly to listen to a man before him on his knees. He looks up at their arrival, eyes darting, sees first his mother, at which his face settles, then her. In the time it takes her to walk the length of the hall he has risen, stepped forward and inclined his head.

She dares a moment to examine him. He has his mother's thin lips, but his ditch-water hair and pale eyes, small and hooded, can have come only from his Welsh father. They are the last eyes, she thinks, to have seen Richard living. She imagines them, white-rimmed, wide with terror as her son's fierce axe swung down. And she gives herself what God did not: that extra breath, that flawless stretching moment in which the blade would fall and smash. And with that happy sight before her, Henry Tudor drenched in his blood, she bends the knee.

THE END

Historical Note

Cecily Neville

Cecily lived for ten years after Richard's death at the Battle of Bosworth. She died at her home in Berkhamsted on 31 May 1495 at the age of eighty. She outlived all but two of her twelve children: her daughters Meg and Elizabeth, by then dowager duchesses of Burgundy and Suffolk respectively. Of the ten who predeceased her, five died in infancy, two in battle, one in childbirth, one of illness and one by execution, or just possibly, a mercy killing. Either way, drink was involved.

Henry VII consistently safeguarded Cecily's landholdings and sources of income. They occasionally shared servants and transacted business directly, as did Cecily with her granddaughter the Queen and Margaret Beaufort. She rarely left Berkhamsted in this time, maintaining a rigorous daily routine that balanced religious observation with the management of her extensive business affairs. At her death she bequeathed prayer books to Margaret, including a breviary bound in cloth of gold. She left a fine psalter to her granddaughter the Queen and to King Henry a gift of money – a rich but impersonal bequest.

Henry conceded to her wish to be buried at Fotheringhay alongside her husband, Richard Duke of York. Her tomb, having been badly damaged during the reformation, was rebuilt by order of her great-great-granddaughter, Elizabeth I, in 1573. When her body was exhumed she was found to have a finely penned papal pardon fastened about her neck with red ribbon. It seems she felt she had sins still standing against her account that would require settlement at Heaven's gate.

In this final stage of her life, she styled herself as the Lady Cecily, Grandmother of the Queen.

Margaret Beaufort

Margaret died at Westminster aged sixty-six on 29 June 1509, two months after attending her son Henry's deathbed at Richmond and five days after witnessing the coronation of her grandson, Henry VIII, which she helped organize. She was interred in the royal Lady Chapel at Westminster Abbey, close by her son and his queen.

After Henry gained the throne in 1485, she adopted the title created by Cecily, the King's Mother, and seems to have modelled her conduct in this role on that of her predecessor. Like Cecily's to her own sons, Margaret's devotion to Henry's cause was absolute and her involvement in his affairs wide-ranging. They conferred on matters of policy, business and finance, she accompanied him on royal progresses and assisted in great state occasions, including the marriages of both her grandsons, Arthur and Henry, to Catherine of Aragon in 1501 and 1509 respectively. Like Cecily, she was an astute manager of her own business affairs. Henry re-granted her all of the lands she had held prior to her attainder and more, and she administered them with rigour and skill.

Certainly, Henry came before all men in Margaret's account, including her husbands. At Henry's first Parliament she was declared *femme sole*, an extraordinary move that gave her the power to act independently of Thomas Stanley in every regard. She later backed this up with an oath of chastity. It seems certain that her most personally fulfilling marriage had been with Cecily's nephew, Henry Stafford, but it was Edmund Tudor that she referred to and reverenced in her later years. Despite the brevity and likely brutality of the marriage, he took precedence as the progenitor of her only child. It seems she judged the value of everyone and everything in her life in relation to her son, who she addressed in letters as, 'My dearest and only desired joy in this world.'

Despite her greatness and the achievement of her heart's desire, it seems she remained haunted by fear for the future and a need for divine forgiveness. Bishop John Fisher, her confessor and spiritual guide, recorded the shedding of penitential tears accompanied by a deep sense of foreboding, even at moments of personal and dynastic triumph. Her religious observation was strict to the point of being punitive. Even in old age and ill health she fasted regularly, wore a hair shirt and spent hours on her knees despite painful arthritis.

Elizabeth Woodville

In Henry VII's first Parliament, the invalidity of Elizabeth's marriage was overturned and her children legitimized, an essential prerequisite for the marriage of her daughter to the new King, which took place the following January (1486). She was also granted her full dower. She attended the christening of, and stood as godmother to, her daughter's first child, Prince Arthur, born in September 1486. However, this would be the last ceremonial event Elizabeth would attend. In February 1487 Henry stripped her of all her lands and she retired to Bermondsey Abbey, possibly at the King's insistence. At the same time, her son Thomas Grey was arrested and sent to the Tower.

It seems likely that Elizabeth and her son had become embroiled in what became known as the Lambert Simnel Affair, a rebellion led by Francis Lovell to regain the throne ostensibly for Edward Earl of Warwick, the son of George Duke of Clarence. However, there is evidence to suggest that Simnel was, in fact, the eldest son of Edward IV, smuggled abroad by Richard III in his final days.

It also seems that Elizabeth was unhappy with the new regime's treatment of her daughter as queen, believing that she was oppressed within the marriage. Certainly her daughter was not crowned until November 1487, and it was Margaret Beaufort who accompanied her in procession and sat at her right hand. Elizabeth, already at Bermondsey, did not attend.

Elizabeth remained in Bermondsey until her death on 8 June 1492 aged fifty-five. Her will asked that what small personal possessions she had be used to pay her debts. She had nothing to leave to her daughters but her blessings. She was buried without ceremony at Windsor two days later. A memorial service held two days after that was attended only by her son Thomas Grey and some Woodville family members. Her daughter the Queen did not attend, being in confinement with her second child. King, nobility and churchmen were conspicuous by their absence. She was at least granted her wish to be buried beside her husband. But it is fair to say she died in poverty and was laid to rest in modest fashion.

During her life, Elizabeth mourned the deaths of all five of her brothers, all but one of her seven sisters, and two of her daughters, as well as her youngest son by Sir John Grey. She also suffered the disappearance of her sons by Edward IV. It seems likely that Elizabeth went to her grave with no certainty about the fate of her two royal sons.

Marguerite of Anjou

Marguerite did not long enjoy the peaceful retreat Cecily had arranged for her after the defeat of her cause at Tewkesbury in 1471. As part of Edward IV's Treaty of Picquigny with France in 1475, she was ransomed by Louis XI for 50,000 crowns. She was obliged to surrender all of her English claims before departing for her home country. It seems Louis didn't act out of charity or honour: on her return, and after the death of her father, he demanded she sign over to him her family patrimony of Anjou.

Marguerite remained as Louis's pensioner until her death at Château de Dampierre near Saumur on 25 August 1482 at the age of fifty-two, a year before the downfall of the dynasty she so defiantly opposed. On her death Louis, presumably because she had little else to leave him, demanded her dogs. She was buried in the cathedral at Angers, but her tomb was destroyed during the French revolution and her body cannot now be found.

The Princes in the Tower

This is not the place to discuss the uncertain fate of Edward IV's sons, known to history as the Princes in the Tower. Suffice it to say, there is no conclusive evidence that they were murdered by Richard III or died during his lifetime, while a growing body of compelling evidence indicates they survived well beyond 1485 and returned to threaten Henry VII's throne. This new evidence offers scholars an exciting opportunity to re-examine this crucial episode and reach new conclusions. I hope they will embrace it.

Acknowledgements

Writing this novel, and seeing it published, is the realization of an ambition I've held close for forty years or more. People tell me I should be proud of having held firm for so long, for being dogged and determined and seeing it through. Well, yes, I am proud, of course, and very happy. But I'm also extremely grateful to all the people who have encouraged (and endured) my lifelong obsession with the Wars of the Roses and the women who – in so many ways – determined their course.

My thanks, first and always, go to my partner, Caroline. She has not only encouraged me to follow my dream, she has walked ahead of me every day, clearing obstacles from my path. Thanks too to my families – the Garthwaites and the Bennetts – not only for supporting the endeavour, but for celebrating the achievement with such glorious abandon.

The same must also be said of my longstanding friends, who are simply family of another kind. So, very special and heartfelt thanks to Pamela Petro, Susan Aslan, Amanda Barry, Suzanne Howe and Peter and Rosemary Diamond. Most particularly, thank you to Lisa Betteridge, my dear friend and sister-of-my-heart for thirty-six years, who championed this book (and me) with such loving enthusiasm for so long, and died between completion and print. She walked this road with me almost to its end. She lives on in my heart, and in the legacy she left us: her husband Mike and her children, Ella, Louis and Evie.

Thanks also to my writer friends and fellow authors, who understand better than any the sheer work of writing, and who keep my nose firmly fixed to the grindstone. So, to Ellen Lavelle, Penny Sandle-Keynes, A. K. Blakemore, Joanne Burn, Costanza

Casati, Imogen Hermes Gowar, Liz Hyder, Naomi Kelsey, Tim Leach, Victoria MacKenzie, Sarah Moss, Mike Parker, Kate Sawyer, Sara Sheridan and A. J. West, a very special thank you. Let's always be there for each other, both for the graft and for whatever glory might come of it. Gratitude laced with admiration goes to the many historians who have advised (and challenged) me along the way – most particularly, Matt Lewis, Joanna Laynesmith and Nicola Tallis. And fond thanks to the curators and custodians of three very special Wars of the Roses locations who made me so welcome: Dr Matthew Payne of Westminster Abbey; Julie Biddlecombe-Brown of Raby Castle, Cecily's childhood home; and Claire Watson-Armstrong of Bamburgh Castle. Your love of character and place is so compelling. Impossible also not to mention Dominic Smee, who shared so candidly his experience of scoliosis and of pitting his body against the challenges of horsemanship and fighting that Richard III faced in life.

Thanks, too, to other creative souls who, to my utter delight, have taken my fifteenth-century women to heart: to Amber Anderson, Kate Phillips and Rosie Day of Just John Films, and to Ella Hickson, maker-of-dreams.

Thanks, of course, to my wonderful agent, Imogen Pelham – a steadying influence at all times – and her colleagues at Marjacq Scripts, Leah Middleton, Catherine Pellegrino and Diana Beaumont. Also, of course, huge gratitude to everyone at Penguin Viking, most obviously my enthusiastic editor Rosa Schierenberg, who seems to have relished the deep dive into medieval womanhood I've taken her on! Huge appreciation too to Viking's Kayla Fuller and Laura Dermody for marketing and publicity support, and to the entire sales team for pounding the streets – actual and metaphorical – for *The King's Mother*! And applause to Emma Pidsley for a simply stunning cover design – that's going to be a *very* hard act to follow!

Finally, I offer a special shout out for the booksellers – both individuals and shops – who have supported me since the publication of my first novel, *Cecily*, back in 2021. You are too many to name individually, but be assured you have a place of honour in my affections. You've been one of the unexpected joys of publication. As friends, advocates and allies you've been welcoming, generous and fun. Despite Covid, the cost of living crisis and all the other challenges you face at the front line of the book business, you remain indefatigable and do so much for us all. Thank you. And to every reader who has taken the time to be in touch, to ask questions, to comment or to praise – my heartfelt appreciation. As authors we write in the hope of creating connections with readers; of sparking fresh insights, engaging emotions and, ultimately, of giving reading pleasure. So it's particularly gratifying to hear voices coming back. I will never tire of it.

Table 1: The Houses of York, Lancaster, Neville & Beaufort in 1461

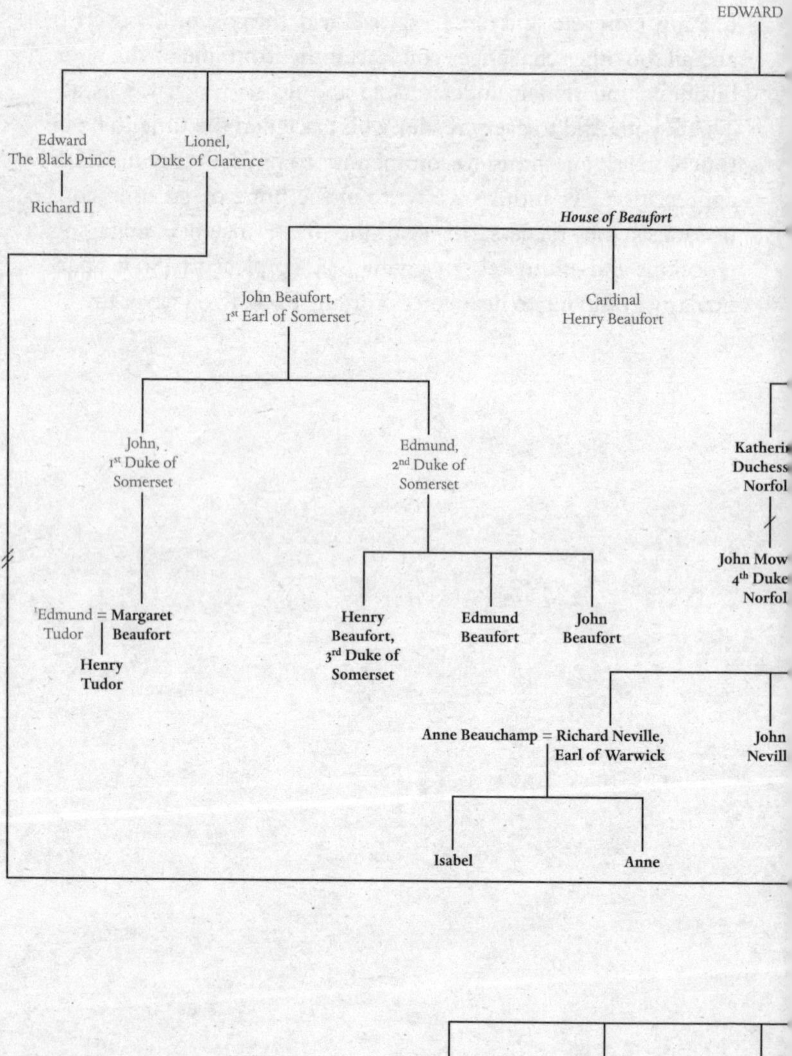

EDWARD

Edward
The Black Prince

Lionel,
Duke of Clarence

Richard II

House of Beaufort

John Beaufort,
1ˢᵗ Earl of Somerset

Cardinal
Henry Beaufort

John,
1ˢᵗ Duke of
Somerset

Edmund,
2ⁿᵈ Duke of
Somerset

Katheri
Duchess
Norfol

John Mow
4ᵗʰ Duke
Norfol

Edmund = **Margaret**
Tudor   **Beaufort**

Henry
Tudor

Henry
Beaufort,
3ʳᵈ Duke of
Somerset

Edmund
Beaufort

John
Beaufort

Anne Beauchamp = Richard Neville,
Earl of Warwick

John
Nevill

Isabel

Anne

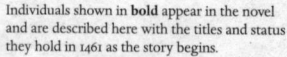

Anne,
Duchess of Exeter

Edward IV

Edmund
Earl of Rutl

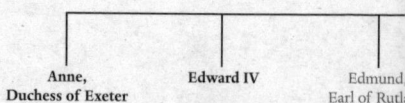

Individuals shown in **bold** appear in the novel
and are described here with the titles and status
they hold in 1461 as the story begins.

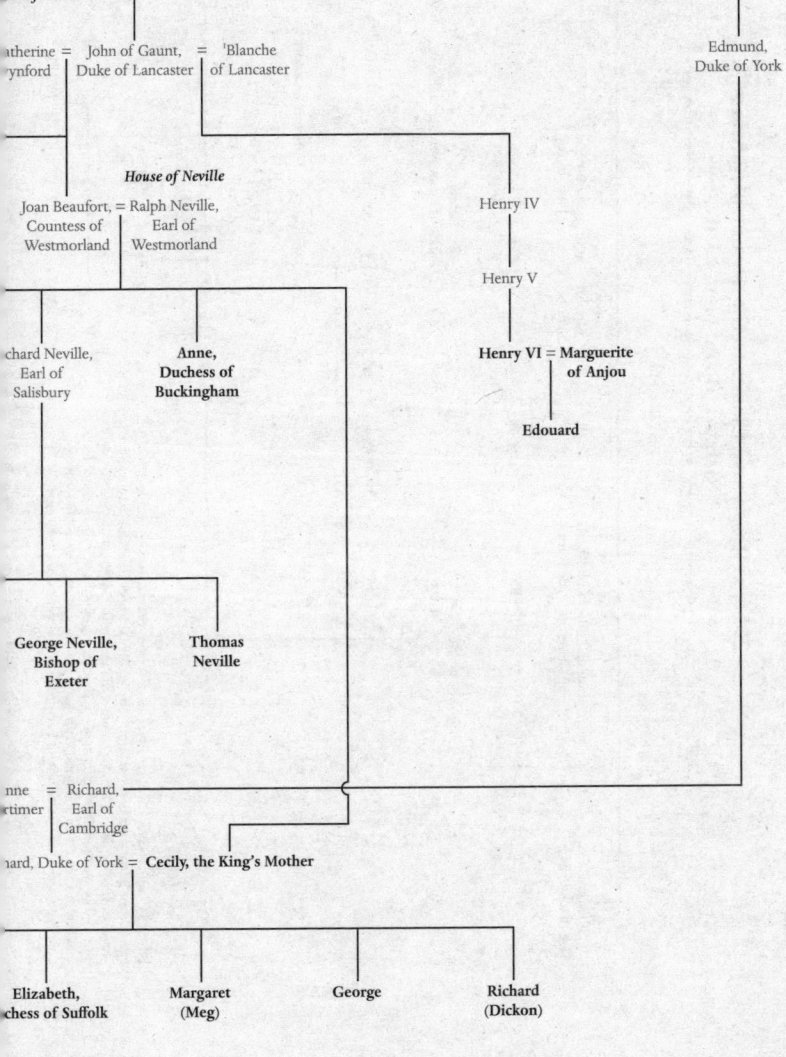

House of Lancaster **House of York**

Catherine = John of Gaunt, = Blanche
Swynford   Duke of Lancaster   of Lancaster

Edmund,
Duke of York

House of Neville

Joan Beaufort, = Ralph Neville,
Countess of   Earl of
Westmorland   Westmorland

Henry IV

Henry V

Richard Neville,   **Anne,**
Earl of   **Duchess of**
Salisbury   **Buckingham**

Henry VI = Marguerite
            of Anjou

Edouard

George Neville,   Thomas
Bishop of   Neville
Exeter

Anne = Richard,
Mortimer   Earl of
         Cambridge

Richard, Duke of York = **Cecily, the King's Mother**

Elizabeth,   Margaret   George   Richard
Duchess of Suffolk   (Meg)   (Dickon)

Table 2: Respective Claims to the Throne of Edward IV, Richard III and Henry VII

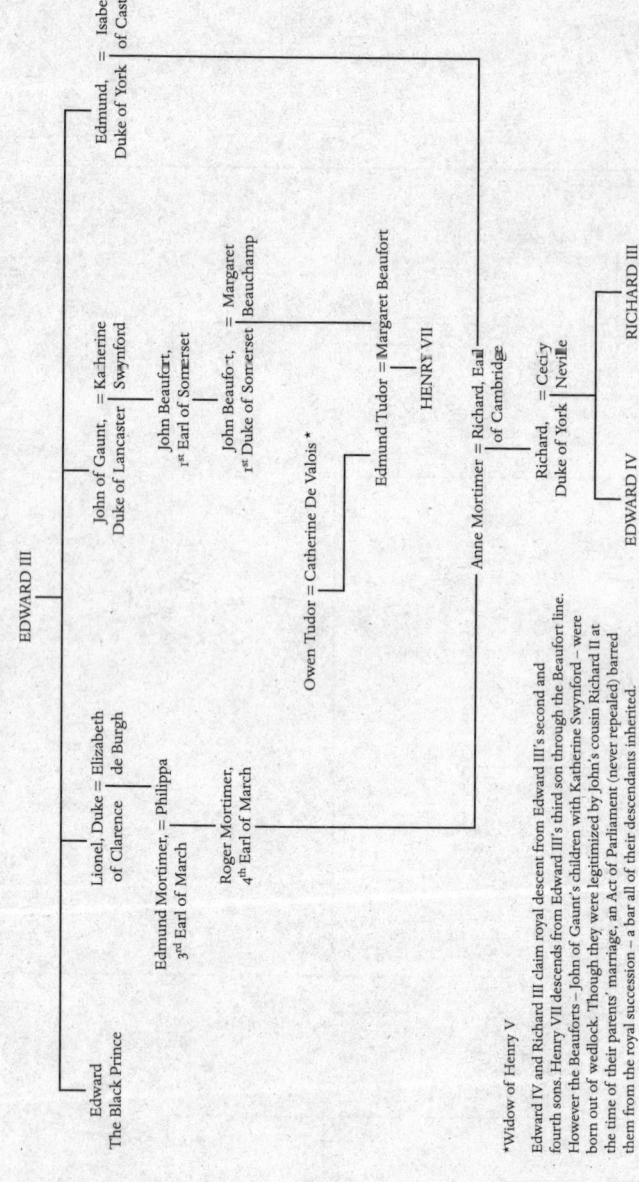

EDWARD III

- Edward The Black Prince
- Lionel, Duke of Clarence = Elizabeth de Burgh
  - Edmund Mortimer, 3rd Earl of March = Philippa
    - Roger Mortimer, 4th Earl of March
      - Anne Mortimer = Richard, Earl of Cambridge
        - Richard, Duke of York = Cecily Neville
          - EDWARD IV
          - RICHARD III
- John of Gaunt, Duke of Lancaster = Katherine Swynford
  - John Beaufort, 1st Earl of Somerset
    - John Beaufort, 1st Duke of Somerset = Margaret Beauchamp
      - Margaret Beaufort
  - Owen Tudor = Catherine De Valois *
    - Edmund Tudor = Margaret Beaufort
      - HENRY VII
- Edmund, Duke of York = Isabel of Castile

*Widow of Henry V

Edward IV and Richard III claim royal descent from Edward III's second and fourth sons. Henry VII descends from Edward III's third son through the Beaufort line. However the Beauforts – John of Gaunt's children with Katherine Swynford – were born out of wedlock. Though they were legitimized by John's cousin Richard II at the time of their parents' marriage, an Act of Parliament (never repealed) barred them from the royal succession – a bar all of their descendants inherited.